One Million Euro

Rorie Smith

TAN TAN BOOKS

Cover photo by Lahnet of Fotolia
Produced by simonthescribe
Published by Tan Tan Books, Freathy, Cornwall.
tantanbooks.co.uk

ISBN-13: 978-0-9929503-2-3

simonthescribe

For Jeanne

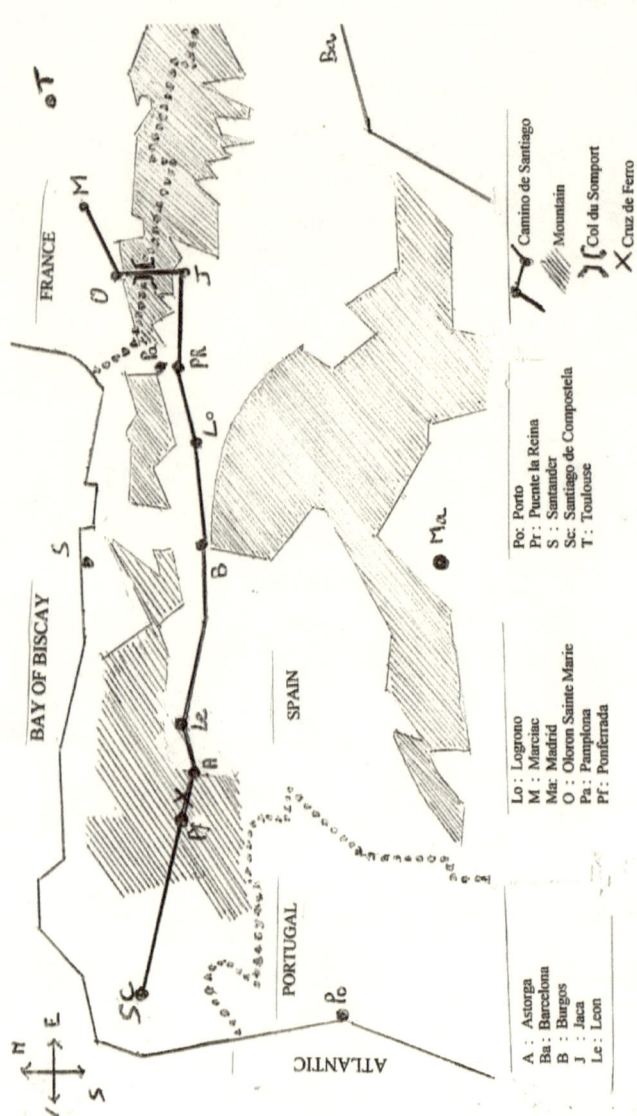

Scale 1:5,000,000

A : Astorga
Ba : Barcelona
B : Burgos
J : Jaca
Le : Leon

Lo : Logrono
M : Marciac
Ma : Madrid
O : Oloron Sainte Marie
Pa : Pamplona
Pf : Ponferrada

Po: Porto
P : Puente la Reina
S : Santander
Sc: Santiago de Compostela
T : Toulouse

Camino de Santiago
Mountain
Col du Somport
Cruz de Ferro

1

OSCAR Bebbington robbed the bank in Zaragoza and got away one with One Million Euro. It should have been otherwise.

The night before the robbery, staying at a hotel in the foothills of the Pyrenees, a man in the bar had asked him if he could drive.

Venezia, who had been listening intently to the story, picked up her glass.

"And?"

Oscar leaned across the table. His face was suddenly intense.

"I told him if there was a better driver north of Madrid I would like to meet him. I've done all the courses, even the advanced police ones."

Venezia put the glass down again. Her voice was sharp.

"So who was he then?"

Oscar's voice was equally taut as he replied:

"He was El Lobo, the Wolf, the most notorious bank robber in all of Spain. During his career he has shot dead two policemen. He said if I could drive as well as that he would have a job for me the following day."

After that we sat back speechless. Oscar had told us he was recently retired from a career in the soft drinks trade.

Finally Venezia began to laugh.

Then old Jack Phillpotts, who was sitting alongside Venezia at the table, added in a low voice:

"But the police are going to be hot on your tail if you've robbed a bank Oscar."

"No it's OK Jack, I disguised myself."

Then he put on a pair of sun glasses raised his collar and pushed his arms out forward as if driving a car. This meant nothing to the younger pilgrims in our group but it made Jack sit back and smile.

"Oh yes I have got that straightaway." He was pleased to have the connection with someone of his own generation. "You are pretending to be Stirling Moss the racing driver."

2

When we had recovered from the shock of hearing all this news we finished up our lunch and had coffee and then stood blinking in the bright autumn sunlight outside.

"We had better get a move on," Jack said finally as he tightened the girth of our two donkeys. "There is still a long distance to go before nightfall."

So with that we began our descent down the steep rough path from the Col du Somport. Jack and Venezia took the lead and soon we reached the remains of the old refuge at Santa Cristina.

All pilgrims know this place. Only the outline of the walls are left now but in the Middle Ages it was one of the great refuges.

At any one time there might have been several hundred pilgrims here, resting up and recovering from the climb up the Pyrenees before pushing on further West.

Then we continued our descent until we could see below us in the distance, at the foot of the pass, the outline of the town of Jaca. Then beyond that, pointing in the direction of Navarre and then ever West, the valley of the Rio Aragon came into view.

Some time after that we stopped our little caravan at the abandoned international railway station at Canfranc Estacion. This is another marker point for pilgrims on their journey.

According to the information we read it had been built in 1928 as part of a railway traverse of the mountains but now it lay abandoned. We noted the seized up railway wagons and the tracks with grass growing out of them. Then we stood on the platform looking up through the cracks in the roof at the sky.

"Well, I have seen some queer things in my time." Jack Phillpotts shook his head as we left. "But whoever would have thought of that. A station as big as Temple Meads in Bristol left to rot in the middle of nowhere."

After that we walked on in silence, deep in our thoughts, enjoying the autumnal afternoon sun. But then as we crossed a wooden bridge over a rushing torrent of green icy melt water, the question that had been on all our minds was finally enunciated by Jack. He addressed himself to Oscar.

"If your share of the spoil was One Million Euro there must have been a hell of a lot of money in that bank vault. El Lobo must have got away with a king's ransom."

For a long moment Oscar did not reply to this question. We continued our descent and all we could hear was the sound of our own breathing and the striking of the donkey's feet on the path. After a while we began to think we had offended him and that he was not going to reply at all.

Denis and Echo were at the front leading our two donkeys. Wilson was behind them. But then finally he did give us this response:

"El Lobo told me I had to wait at a certain corner and keep a watch in my mirror. We went through it in great detail. If he approached at walking pace everything was fine but if he was running it meant he was being chased and I was to drive like the wind."

We slowed our pace so that we could all hear him clearly.

"When I spotted him in the mirror he was going flat out. So I pushed the door open quickly and he jumped in, he was in a state and he threw the bag with the money on the back seat and I took off with a squeal of tyres."

Venezia laughed and turned toward Oscar.

"Well it is no doubt certainly a contrast to where we are now up in the silence of the mountains with a just couple of donkeys. It sounds to us like you are directing the action in a film."

"You are right there Venezia," Oscar replied. "I was driving to my limit. There were twists and turns and a stretch of one way street that we took in the wrong direction. Then when we finally stopped he grabbed the bag from the back seat and jumped out and ran off. Then I drove on another half mile and parked up. After that I thought I had better make myself scarce so I hopped back over the border to France."

It was left to Echo to ask, as was his habit, the pertinent question.

"I am guessing there was more than one bag on the back seat Oscar?"

"Yes, there were two," Oscar replied looking around at the pilgrims.

"And they were almost identical. One contained the One Million Euro, the other contained my pilgrim clothes. And unfortunately, in a moment of confusion, El Lobo picked up the wrong one."

There was a silence when we heard this. Venezia put her hand on the back of one of the donkeys. Then Jack Phillpotts turned to Oscar.

"Well you have really put us in the cart there old chum." He spoke loud enough so that everyone could hear. "Now we will have both the Guardia Civil and El Lobo chasing after us. It is odds on the robber will be looking for his money back."

3

Ten minutes later we were still thinking about this news, and what it meant for our little band, when Jack further pronounced:

"The sun is starting to dip down pilgrims. If we do not find a place to pitch our tents soon are going to end up sleeping the night in Jaca."

With that information to hand we sent Wilson ahead as our scout and he reported back a short while later that he had found a good flat spot with grass for our donkeys and easy access to the torrent which flowed down the mountain beside us.

So we stopped and lifted the panniers and the saddles off the backs of T and B, our two donkeys, and Jack led them to the water by their harnesses.

When they had finished drinking Jack tethered them, saying he would come out to re adjust the tethers before we slept so they would have enough to eat through the night.

While he was doing this Oscar and Denis erected the tents while Wilson collected wood for the fire.

Jack had been correct in his assertion. By the time the tents were up and a good strong fire was burning the early autumn night had fallen and a cold wind had settled in and we could look up to see first Venus and then the other stars up above watching us.

Venezia along with Echo prepared dinner, putting a griddle over the fire and laying out strips of beef. Wilson opened bottles of wine and cut thick chunks of bread and we fashioned rough seats out of our baggage and sat down in anticipation of our dinner.

Then as we waited, and the wine circulated, a dispute broke out between Jack Phillpotts and Wilson.

"The beginning of a narrative is always difficult," Jack pronounced as he adjusted the griddle over the fire. "So to help our readers I think we should each stand up and introduce ourselves."

"No Pilgrim Jack you are wrong there," Wilson replied firmly. (It was well known that he had aspirations to be a writer himself). "We have already introduced a lot of material and we are still only a few pages in. If we are not careful we are going to cause confusion."

In the end, after further discussion, a compromise was reached and each of the pilgrims agreed to stand up and give a brief two line summary of themselves.

Echo stood up first. His voice was rich and strong as, in the manner of a game show contestant, he announced loudly:

"Hi, I'm Echo. Six foot two. Black as your hat and all the way from the Democratic Republic of the Congo."

He was followed on to his feet by Venezia.

"Hi, I'm the jolie Quebecoise as mentioned on the back cover. Five foot nothing in my stockinged feet. I have a difficult choice to make between Echo and Denis."

Wilson got reluctantly to his feet after that.

"Wilson. Socialist, climber. Originally from the North, exiled to Dreary Devon. Currently an unemployed article writer."

He was followed by Oscar.

"Oscar. You know me already. Meek and mild, except when bank robbing. Salesman. Ginger hair, receding."

Next it was Denis.

"I'm Denis Dennis the half Belgian dentist. Tall and spindly. Too hesitant by half."

Last up was old Jack Phillpotts himself.

"Jack Phillpotts, at your service. Landlord of the Bastard's Baby on the Barbican in Plymouth. Anyone can find a better run pub or a better drawn pint in the county of Devon I'll say he's a liar."

After that Venezia shouted "grub's up" and there was no more talking until we had finished.

(For readers interested in statistics: Our journey had begun to the east of Marciac in south west France ten days ago and we had now walked one hundred and thirty miles - this included the crossing of the Pyrenees via the Col du Somport. Our estimate was that we had a further five hundred and twenty miles to go before we reached Santiago de Compostela in Galicia).

(A note about names: The route we walked in France is called the Chemin d'Arles. However the generic name for all the pilgrim routes in Spain is the Camino de Santiago. The particular portion of the route we were on now is known as the Camino Aragones).

4

When we woke the following morning it was to see the valley below us covered in a sea of mist. After we had marvelled briefly at this new vision we loaded up our two donkeys and made our way down onto the valley floor. We skirted the town of Jaca, still wreathed in the fine mist, and then turned sharp West following the Rio Aragon until we approached the village of Santa Cilia de Jaca.

There we noted two other backpacks, denoting other pilgrims, propped up outside a bar. So always pleased to meet other travellers and smelling the coffee from within, we hitched up the donkeys to a rail and entered, glad to be out of the clammy mist and in front of a warming wood fire.

The two other pilgrims came over to join us straightaway. The first of them was a tall raw boned Scot with a rough manner and a low gravel voice. The other man was older and American. We talked casually for a while, discussing the state of the footpath and mentioning other pilgrims we had met en route. Then Venezia turned to Oscar and said in a quiet aside:

"The older one, the American, with his beard and his slow way of talking is a perfect match for the long dead poet Walt Whitman whose picture adorned the edition of Leaves of Grass that we studied in High School."

While the two of them considered this revelation the conversation continued on in a general manner until we had finished our coffee. Then Jack Phillpotts looked out of the window.

"It is time to move on pilgrims and bugger this weather." He shook his head gravely. "If not we might as well pitch our tents for the day right now."

We then turned to our two new friends and extended an invitation to them to walk with us, which they both said they were glad to accept.

As we walked, following the open valley floor, the river to our right, we studied our new companions.

The American was tall, broad, fleshy faced and bearded, only the back stooping slightly giving away any age. He had a slouch hat on his head and an old fashioned shirt with a draw string at the front.

Venezia was walking alongside Oscar.

"When we studied his poetry," she said quietly, "We were told that the sentiments he expressed in Leaves of Grass were both universal and timeless."

But Oscar was of a more sceptical nature.

"Well now Pilgrim Venezia, can you back up that assertion?"

So the pair of them dropped back and Venezia briefly gave him these lines from the first edition of his epic poem Leaves of Grass.

> *Walt Whitman, an American, one of the roughs, a kosmos,*
> *Disorderly fleshy and sensual ....*
> *Eating drinking and breeding,*
> *No sentimentalist ....*
> *No stander above men and women or apart*
> *From them ....*
> *No more modest than immodest.*
> *Whoever degrades another degrades me ... and whatever is*
> *done or said returns at last to me,*
> *And whatever I do or say I also return.*
> *I speak the word primeval....*
> *I give the sign of democracy;*
> *By God! I will accept nothing which all cannot have their*
> *counterpart of on the same terms.*

This went some way to satisfying Oscar and then the other pilgrims that our new companion was indeed 'a man of substance.'

Our efforts to interpret the role of our Scottish friend were less successful. It was Echo was expressed our doubts.

"He certainly has that rough look of a Dundee man. It is a look that is often attributed to the weather and the poor food of that city. But I am still not convinced."

Jack Phillpotts, who was also a fan and therefore knew the history, also declared himself unsure.

"If he is the real business it will be the making of our pilgrimage. But he is a man of such authority and stature that he is often imitated."

It was agreed after a short discussion that Echo would put a series of discreet questions to him. So when the moment was right he approached him as indirectly and obliquely as he could:

"There was a certain incident on the touchline of a certain football ground where the police had to intervene after a referee's decision was …"

By the time our voyage was concluded we had all become 'fans' of the Great Man but to begin with we had to become familiar with his 'little ways.'

We would always watch with alarm as his face reddened and his cheeks puffed out. It would be an exaggeration to say that his eyes popped but certainly his visage for that moment did gain an extra dimension.

Then came the sudden close proximity of the face, followed by the hot breath and the violent finger stabbing movement.

Then in the way that thunder follows lightning a mouthful of the most terrible abuse, delivered in that familiar arrhythmic patois, would roar out.

In this case, in answer to Echo's half voiced query, it came out as:

"If yous bloody windae lickers (Trans: mentally handicapped people) dunna ken who a'hm, a'hm naw showin' you ma birth certificate or ma marriage lines."

Then he turned on us savagely and continued:

"And if yous dunna wanna believe it yous can bloody drown yerselves in the River Tay and nobody'l bother to fish y'out."

He glared at us all again. But then as suddenly as it had begun the explosion terminated and the reddened visage slowly receded back into itself.

This was the first time we had been exposed to this sort of disaffection, our group being normally close knit and harmonious. As we continued walking we could not help but feel a degree of fear for the future of our little band with the arrival in our midst of such an explosive personage.

It wasn't until midday, after Walt had brought us to a village tavern to eat, that we began to reason to ourselves that there should be room for all sorts on the Camino de Santiago. With that our spirits slowly began to rise again.

Then in the afternoon our little caravan fell back into its comfortable rhythm. The sun warmed us and a gentle breeze kissed our cheeks and we began to think that we had over reacted. We started to consider instead the good fortune that had brought two such Eminent Persons to walk with us.

Soon the path widened so we were able to walk two or three abreast and it became easier to converse.

We recounted to Walt the story of how Oscar had driven the getaway car for a bank robbery and how he had come by One Million Euro and how as a result both the police and El Lobo were certainly looking for us.

Walt shook his head in disbelief when we had finished.

"On one pilgrimage I was in a boat when it overturned. We were crossing a certain river and three pilgrims were drowned. But this is certainly a first. A pilgrim robbing a bank? It's unbelievable."

The reaction from our Scottish Footballing Friend gave us further confirmation as to his identity.

"None ah ma players wud rob a bank." He looked around fiercely. "They'd no be interested. They've all got more money than yous lot'll see in a dozen lifetimes."

But then all thoughts of robbing banks and being chased by the police were put to one side when we were forced to halt by a difficulty common to all pilgrim groups. Jack was suffering a recurrence of problems with his feet.

(Pilgrims always read guidebooks before they set out. Most of the advice offered there can be safely discarded. The only warning that should be heeded is Look After Your Feet. There will be more on this later in the narrative).

On this occasion, relinquishing the reins of the donkeys, Jack lowered himself slowly to the ground and Denis and Wilson helped him remove one of his boots.

"Thanks boys." His face was a grimace. "This is a bugger and no mistake, but if I do not get it sorted out I will not be able to walk another mile."

In ten minutes when the new blister had been identified and treated and dressed by Venezia, Jack got up on his feet again and hobbled around until he was comfortable and shortly after that we were on our way again.

5

That night Walt led us to pitch camp in a wood two miles to the East of where the Rio Aragon flows under the bridge at Puente la Reina de Jaca. There pilgrims passing over the years have erected a thousand small stone cairns or bornes stretching a hundred yards deep either side of the path and a mile in either direction.

As the light fell and the darkness grew, mist enveloped us and water began to drip down on us from the trees. This gave the camp a gloomy and chilling air.

But as we ate Walt explained that while this place was exceptional, with its multitude of bornes, all along our Pilgrim route we would find individual bornes or cairns where pilgrims had added stones.

"Then there is the crossing into Galicia," he told us. "It is at the summit of Mount Irago, weeks to the West of us yet. There a giant iron cross, the Cruz de Ferro, stands. At its base it is heaped with stones that pilgrims have brought from their homelands."

When we had finished eating and Echo and Venezia had cleared up the plates and the last of the wine had been poured out Jack Phillpotts, with a nudge from Oscar, finally rose to his feet and coughed and formally began the address he had been considering all afternoon:

"Walt," he said. "We have been travelling together as a small band since we began our journey in France. And now you have joined us and we are pleased to welcome you both and to show you the hospitality which is legendary in our home town of Plymouth. Venezia has also made us aware of your reputation as a poet and we hope that you will favour us during the course of this journey with a reading from your verses."

He coughed and paused here for a second and we looked up at him quickly hoping that he had not lost his nerve. But then he gathered himself together to continue.

"However at the same time we are puzzled as to why we have been singled out for the particular honour of your presence. Some of us have even said we can manage quite well by ourselves. So if you could offer us an explanation, I am sure we would all, including the readers of this narrative, be most grateful."

Then he sat down feeling slightly awkward as if he could have expressed himself better, but Venezia leaned forward and touched him on the arm to reassure him that he had put our case well.

Then Walt rose to his feet to reply. The tone of his American voice was long and languorous and complimented his open slow moving face. There was warmth about him that drew us to him. He considered for a long moment before speaking.

"Every book needs a hero," he told us finally. "And that will be the function of our friend here Sir Roy Babadouche. He will ensure that our narrative is read widely. He is well known as a football manager, but he is also a leader of men, a quality much to be praised."

Oscar who was not a fan of the Glorious Game looked uncomfortable when he heard this reasoning. By contrast Echo and Jack Phillpotts, who were fans, nodded sagely.

Then Walt changed direction.

"So you ask, why do you need a guide at all, especially when you have been managing so well by yourselves up until now?"

Sitting around our flickering camp fire, listening to the water dripping from the leaves around us, we waited for the answer to this question. This is how it came:

"I first made this pilgrimage many years ago with a certain Aimery Picaud, a Frenchman." He looked at us. "Some of you may have heard of him, he wrote an account of our travels. We came over the Somport, on the path you've just followed, in the middle of the winter in the snow and had to stay a month at the refuge at Santa Cristina to recover before we could go on. I was a hypothermic case and they thought Aimery would lose all his toes."

Walt stopped, as if recalling the journey, then looked around at our little forest camp.

"So you could say perhaps that I have the experience."

We sat silent for a moment. Then Venezia got to her feet.

"Walt have you been chosen to lead groups on pilgrimage to Santiago de Compostela because in your poems you show such humanity and richness of vision?"

Walt laughed heartily at that.

"Oh no Venezia. It is not my intention to turn this journey into a poetry seminar. I was cured of that fault many years ago. I will tell you that story. It was after we had endured a stinking hot day crossing the Meseta. In the evening a young pilgrim told me to my face that if he heard one more line of my 'insufferably boring' work known as Leaves of Grass he would personally take the book and stuff it page by page down my wide open gullet."

Walt laughed again. It was a sound we grew to love over the weeks ahead.

"It was a lesson leaned. Readings will be spare and spaced apart. I go at your head as plain Walt Whitman and nothing more."

And with that he stopped and looked around and said he hoped he had given a satisfactory answer to the question that Jack had asked and that we would discuss the matter further as we walked.

That night in out tents we listened to the sounds of the night in this strange wood and wondered what the future, on this our pilgrimage, would bring. The following morning we were not at all surprised when Denis said that when he had got up in the middle of the night he had seen the faint outline of encampments of pilgrims past. He told us that he had seen their fires and heard the low murmurings of their voices.

(At this point readers have a choice. They can wait until the conclusion of this narrative or they can turn and read the epilogue now).

6

But during that night we leave our unlikely pilgrims lightly sleeping under the dripping trees and divert back to the start of our journey in France.

We had suffered the agonies all pilgrims suffer at the beginning. Our feet had become sore and blistered and the muscles in our legs had ached. But as we progressed slowly, crossing the low rolling hills of the Gers where the autumn colours were fine and delicate and then on through the wooded dips and slopes of the Bearn, we changed. We learned to cook over an open fire, we learned to pitch and pack up our tents and we found a suppleness and strength in our feet and our legs. Near Pau we saw the sun rise blood red into the morning sky for the first time.

Then the weather changed and autumn gales began to blow hard. Roadside poplars were bent double and for days our progress slowed as we were head down under grey and rain drenched skies.

Then one day, sheltering in a wooden barn, leaning against bales of hay and agricultural implements, waiting for the wind to drop and the deluge to slacken, we started for the first time to tell our stories.

"I am going to pick on you to start," said Jack Phillpotts gruffly, pointing at Denis.

Denis was the most hesitant member of our group. He was tall and spindly and with a pale open face and a shock of untidy brown hair. He would have preferred to let another pilgrim go first. But he could see that Jack was adamant. So after a moment's pause he stood up and took a deep breath and this is how he began:

"I am Denis Dennis from a family of dentists so I could hardly do anything else but be a damn dentist. Mother is Belgian (this caused a sharp reaction from Echo, who being from the Congo hated all things Belgian) and practises in Ostend. Father, English, wooden as an upright chair, decamps to Canterbury. For the moment that's all you need to know about family."

Then he paused and took a deep breath before saying:

"She was a thing."

We looked at him.

"I mean the boat. A power boat. She went through the water like a shark. I'd bought a half share with another dentist. You want a thrill mate, you buy a power boat. Nothing like it."

He was about to continue when Echo suddenly interrupted.

"Sounds like you came into the dentistry game at the right time Pilgrim Denis."

The angry note in Echo's voice made Denis turn quickly. His normally meek and acquiescent visage became suddenly harder and stronger.

His voice was sharp as he replied:

"There was an opportunity to make money and I took it what and what was wrong with that? Maybe you and Pilgrim Wilson and the rest of your socialist friends should encourage that sort of thing rather than sneer at it."

"But did not your conscience trouble you?" Echo was leaning back. He was enjoying the contest. There was a little smile on his lips now. Denis had swallowed the bait and did not realise how he was being played.

"My conscience?" Suddenly the years were being rolled back and we were seeing a Denis we had not seen before. His voice gained in volume and strength.

"Do you know what are you talking about Echo?"

He had turned to him face on.

"I had spent ten years putting right the teeth of ungrateful people who did not take care of themselves. You have no idea what it was like. The mess people left. The way they bounced cheques and broke appointments. I can assure you Echo that if you have spent ten years dealing with those sorts of people you would not have asked that question."

But Echo had no intention of leaving the dispute there.

"I don't agree Denis. The actions of people like you leaving the NHS to go private and specialise in cosmetic surgery left a lot of people unable to find an NHS dentist."

Denis raised his hand abruptly and angrily when he heard this.

"I have told you before Echo. If there were not enough NHS dentists that was not our business. The government should have opened up more dental training programmes or heaven forbid paid us all properly or even got more dentists from abroad."

"From abroad?" Echo hit back sharply. "From Africa perhaps? Leaving the teeth of my poor people to rot in the midday sun?" Venezia intervened here and turned to look admiringly at Echo.

"You are certainly very well informed on that period of the opening up the dental profession in the UK to market forces Echo my dear."

Echo bowed slightly forward as he received this compliment.

"In the Congo we are not as poorly educated as people in the West like to believe Venezia. We do have regular access to books and journals from abroad."

It was at this point Jack Phillpotts interrupted gruffly to close the argument.

"Gentleman please. This is not a book about the optimal way to fund a dental service. We have heard all those arguments before. They are a side issue."

He turned to Denis.

"Denis continue with your story, please."

Denis paused for a moment to regain control of himself. The rain was still beating down on the tin roof. Then he continued on quickly, deliberately ignoring Echo.

"We took the boat out of Plymouth Sound and rounded Rame Head and anchored in Whitsand Bay. You all know it. It was an August day. The hottest of the year. We could have been in the Caribbean. There was a light breeze rocking us, we could see the sea bed below clear as anything. The girls watched us as we dived in. I remember the sensation very well. Slicing down through the water, fingers touching the rippling sand. Then we were up again lungs bursting and shouting out, the girls cheering and applauding. When they had towelled us down, they were both blondes and handsome, we drank champagne and ate lobster with our fingers. Then we paired off and descended below deck until it was time to go home."

He stopped and looked around at Echo and Wilson to get our reaction to this tale of excess. Wilson was grim faced and Echo was deliberately looking out of the door of the barn checking on the weather. He continued.

"It is the next day, a Monday. I have entered my surgery, about to recount to my staff and to my patients my wonderful weekend. But then I sit down at my desk to slit open an envelope and read that my world of speedboats and girls and money has come to a sharp and terrible end."

Echo turned back quickly to look at him.

It was just at this point, as we eagerly awaited the denouement, that Jack looked up and noted that the rain had stopped and that the wind was abating.

"That is a good moment to stop," he pronounced as he got slowly to his feet. "A cliff hanging moment. We certainly need to get on now if we are going to make any progress today."

So with that we shouldered our packs and emerged from the shelter of the barn and shook ourselves awake and carried on, deprived of the end of Denis's story for the moment.

For the next while we were head down against the Autumn winds, but then one day suddenly the weather cleared, the sky turned to a pale eggshell blue and for the first time we could see clearly ahead of us the snow capped peaks of the Pyrenees, the gateway over the mountains to the south and Spain.

In Oloron Sainte Marie, we met up with Oscar for the first time and purchased our two donkeys, T and B, from a local farmer. This greatly eased our passage as we climbed slowly up toward the snow line. Jack Phillpotts, the least fit of us, was especially pleased that the donkeys could relieve him of the weight of his backpack.

Night fell as we approached the Col du Somport. We were lucky to find a barn where we could shelter. In a corner was a bale of hay for the donkeys. We also discovered a pile of cut logs and Denis and Wilson soon had a good fire going at the front of the barn.

Then we went outside to stand in the snow and stare up at the mountain peaks pale in the moonlight ahead of us. After that we turned to look down into the valley at the faint points of light in the villages below. Then we all give thanks for where we were, even those of us not believing in a God.

In the morning we woke stiff and cold, to discover that a fresh fall of overnight snow had covered the path up through the Vallee Desbieys, slowing our pace. We arrived finally at mid morning at the Col du Somport in brilliant sunshine and stood looking down into the valley below, feeling at last the hot breath of Spain on our cheeks.

7

Dawn was breaking as we stepped out of that gloomy and misty wood and crossed the Rio Aragon to enter Puente la Reina de Jaca. As we ate churros and drank coffee at a stand up roadside bar Roy, his face ruddy under a thick woollen hat, turned to Wilson.

"Wha's the story wi' the donkeys then?"

We were looking out of the window at where they were tied up to a rail.

"Well," Wilson said placing a churro into his mouth. His bespectacled faced was pinched by the early morning cold. "They are T and B, Thatcher and Blair, mere and fils. We have placed a red dot behind Thatcher's right ear and a blue dot behind Blair's left ear so that we can tell them apart."

"It is a joke." Jack Phillpotts turned toward Roy, his face stern. "We have two socialists with us. Card carrying, the pair of them." He nodded to Wilson and Echo. "They are trying to make a political statement."

"Aw right," said Roy a thin smile tightening around the corners of his mouth. "A couple ah comedians eh?"

We had ceded the leadership of our little group to Walt without question. We had recalled what Venezia had said to Oscar, that he was a figure of great historical importance. And so, in whatever form it was he had come to us, we felt honoured by his presence.

But with Roy we were not so sure. As we set off again Venezia turned to Echo:

"Echo. You call me the jolie Quebecoise. But I don't know anything about the Glorious Game or about Roy and his achievements. If you could give us an outline. I am sure that will make me appreciate him more."

For a long moment Echo considered this request. Our bearing was near enough due West, the river to our right, the cold and clammy mist still swirling around our legs. When Roy moved up ahead to talk to Walt, who was at the head of our little caravan, he was able to begin. He kept his voice low and his delivery had a measured (if deliberately exaggerated) gravitas.

"Sir Roy Babadouche has just handed over to his deputy after twenty years with one of our great London football clubs. There, in a glittering career, he piled trophy on trophy. Now he is fast growing into the role of elder statesman. He is becoming an international ambassador of goodwill, in demand by both Prime Ministers and Presidents. It is said if he were to run for office in the United Kingdom, for which ever party, he would be elected by a landslide. There are even those who say he should be Prime Minister."

Jack looked sceptical. He was aware of Echo's 'theatrical' reputation and his tendency to exaggerate and embroider and he thought was on the wrong track. He was sure that Roy's only political act, aside from voting Socialist at elections, which would have been the norm for his background, was a short period as a trade union representative on the dockside in Dundee.

Echo, sensing that he had failed in his initial attempt to describe how 'Barnstorming Babadouche' took the country by storm every winter, furrowed his brow and tried again.

"Roy Babadouche was raised in terrible poverty in the slums of Dundee. It was only his legendary ability with a football that saved him from a life of drink and degradation."

Again Jack looked startled when he heard this. Echo was certainly playing fast and loose with the facts. He knew that Roy had been raised in a close knit and loving family in a solid working class quarter of Dundee. He also knew that if he had not succeeded at football, a job for life had been reserved for him in the docks.

But Echo, feeling that he was on the right track now, was continuing confidently with his story.

"His club was known worldwide and Sir Roy had success without parallel. But this success never went to his head. He was always pitch side on match day Saturdays, giving advice to players and officials alike. And he was always a man of the people. He could sink a pint of Guinness with a group of working men as well as he could sip a glass of champagne with the star of the latest Hollywood film. He drove his Bentley through the West End of London but he never forgot the Ford Consul in which he began his married life all those years ago in Dundee."

Echo paused here and looked around our little pilgrim group. He wanted to see how the latest version of the life of our newest member was being received. Then he went on :

"There is an assumption, (an assumption that would prove to be correct, Walt confirmed later) that Our Hero will soon be elevated to the House of Lords where his words of wisdom, as Lord Babadouche of Dundee Docks, will be listened to with great interest and appreciation by his fellow peers."

After we had listened to this encomium we turned to look at this gigantic sporting hero who had come to walk among us this cold and clammy morning. We noted his red bully beef face and his wide sportsman's frame, we noted the chunky ring on his pinkie, and we saw his limpid valved heart pumping firmly and strongly as he strode eagerly forward.

How was it then that we did not eagerly embrace this Sporting Leviathan, this Great Hero? Why is it that do we not immediately clasp this Great Scotsman to our bosoms?'

It was Denis who gave us our answer.

"It is because he is used to living with footballers who are sleek and speedy as greyhounds and who are as rich as Arabian millionaires. It is difficult for him to adjust to life among ordinary pilgrims."

With this explanation in mind we looked once again at Our Great Hero. His woollen hat was pulled down over his head and his shoulders were hunched forward to keep out the clammy cold. His mouth and head were close up to Walt's ear as he talked, disclosing some private information.

Finally to break the silence and because we had noted that Roy and Walt had now turned toward us to see what was happening, Jack thwacked poor Blair on his rump with a stick and said out loud:

"We are pilgrims so we pass the time telling stories."

"That's right," Oscar added, glad to be off the topic of Roy and his Great Achievements for a moment. "In the Middle Ages the movement, on foot and horseback across Europe toward Santiago de Compostela, was the greatest flow of humanity the modern world had seen."

Walt nodded in agreement.

"The legend is that the bones of Saint James are in a silver casket in the Cathedral. People followed the four paths that led to Santiago, crossing mountain, plain and river. They wore cockleshell badges as emblems to show they were pilgrims. Many of them had never left their home villages before and they were astonished at their own achievement."

"But we are very modern pilgrims," interrupted Venezia, her voice suddenly sharp. "Because none of us believes in God."

"But we have another reason for making the journey." It was Wilson speaking now. "We have decided that in the modern world we go on pilgrimage to regain our humanity."

"Wha's tha' ?" Roy asked roughly. He had dropped back from his position at the front of the caravan next to Walt. "If you's naw believin' in God I dunna see the point in goin' on a pilgrimage. Yous might as well stay home and save yer'selves the bother."

At a later point in our pilgrimage we came greatly to admire Roy but at this moment our sentiments were in the negative.

Oscar dropped back and muttered to Jack: "If we are going to have to put up with Biffo the Dundee Mule all the way to Santiago, I am going to pack it in right now."

"Pilgrim Oscar think of it another way," Echo answered him. "He will be our Noble Savage. He will guide us in his innocence and naivety."

Oscar gave a snort at this.

"Innocence! Old Muttonhead more like. I don't know what is to become of us. We were doing well enough before."

We walked in silence after that. It was left to the first rays of sunlight, as they began to penetrate the mist and warm the day, to dissipate our anger and frustration. Then soon after that we were able to discard our jackets and sweaters which was a further lift to our mood. Then finally the mist cleared and we were able to look around. The Rio Aragon was to our right. On the opposite bank, perched on a series of rocky bluffs, were a number of austere looking stone villages.

It was then that Walt, sensing our unhappiness with Roy, turned to Echo.

"So what is your part in this great adventure Pilgrim Echo?" His voice was as rich and languid as ever. "We all tell our stories on pilgrimage and we are certainly keen to hear what brought you from Africa to England."

8

Of all the characters in this narrative the personage of Echo is the most difficult to get down correctly. He should be the easiest. He is loud, he is direct, he speaks his mind. He is well informed - to the extent that we began to refer to him as our African Autodidact. But at the same time his manner can switch quickly from theatrical and extrovert to downcast and angry. The best way to describe him is to say that he is like a pot on a stove that is always threatening to bubble over. The difficulty is to gauge exactly which aspect of his personality is about to spill over at any one time.

(As to his name there are two theories. The first is that when he arrived in England his English was so bad that he was forced to repeat everything he said. The second possibility, which we considered the more likely, was that behind every story he told there was always the 'echo' of another tale).

But this morning, as he had done before, he caught us on the hop when in response to Walt's question he shouted out suddenly, in the manner of a mad fairground barker:

"Nigger! Yid! Paki! Wog! Asylum!"

The obscene words rang back to our ears from the bluffs opposite and birds rose in the sky startled as we stared at him our mouths open - even our two poor donkeys.

He looked round at us with a smile on his face.

He was our Theatrical Pilgrim, our Congolese showman and he had done what he intended, which was to gain our attention.

It was only Roy who took exception. Like all Great Sportsman his Competitive Spirit came into play and his lip curled and his face hardened.

"The first and last am I." Echo was grinning broadly. His voice was rich and confident. He was fully aware of the impact he was making. "A Congolese gentleman seeking asylum in a wise and ancient land."

He gave a bow and a flourish of the hand. We could see Roy beginning to thrust out his chest dangerously.

"I refer of course to the fair port city of Plymouth, amidst the rolling hills of Devonshire. Where a Congolese gentleman knows all will be well, and all manner of things will be well, provided his head is not smashed in on a Saturday night by a fired up Janner (trans: native of Plymouth). This Janner, by the way, will in turn threaten to beat, skin, burgle and bugger you before stealing the sixpence out of your hat to run off laughing."

We smiled here (with the exception of Roy whose visage, in the grand manner, had now turned to the consistency of the granite of Aberdeen) at both the intricacy of the language and the quality of the visual imagery Echo displayed. And he certainly knew our city alright.

But now he changed his tone. Pointing a finger he lectured us angrily:

"People Like You in well proportioned double storey homes, with central heating and Hot Running Maids, cannot comprehend the terrible life of an asylum seeker forced to live like a Rabid Dog on the Rotten and Leprous Streets of this old port city."

Roy adjusted the bright blue baseball cap that he had placed on his head to shade his eyes from the sun and stared hard at Echo. We feared that if Echo continued like this it would not be long before Roy began to advance toward him.

Then Walt looked up at the sun and calculated, even though it was not high, that it had reached its zenith for an autumn day.

But Echo was not through with his performance yet. He still had further to go. He lowered the tone of his voice. It was now sad and mournful.

"Now here is poor Echo sitting on a bench on Royal Parade in front of the Guildhall. There is snow on the ground and he has holes in his shoes. He hasn't eaten in two days or washed in three, even the Rabid Dogs detour around him, yelping with fear. He has a thin blanket wrapped around his shoulders and he is shivering with cold."

He let his words pause . Then suddenly he smiled.

"But then, at his darkest moment, when his thoughts have turned once again to the injustices perpetrated on the Congolese people by their brutal Belgian masters, the effects of which are still being felt today, a fellow Congolese immigre approaches and taps him on the shoulder to say: 'There's a job going if you want it, old boys network and all that.' "

At this point Walt, sensing a breakpoint in this strange story, cut in quickly:

"Much as we all admire the inventive and theatrical qualities of Pilgrim Echo the sun is not going to get any higher today so if we are going to stop and eat now is the time. And we all need to rest our feet, especially Pilgrim Jack."

This was a message that was received with relief, even by Roy. The path had led us temporarily up onto higher ground so now we were some distance from the river. We stopped at a suitable spot and Jack took off his boots and then with his trousers rolled up and with the pleasant sensation of having his naked feet splayed in the soft grass, he supervised the unloading of our donkeys and then set them free to graze. After that we assembled the bread and sausage and fruit we had bought in Puente la Reina de Jaca and set about our picnic.

As we ate, and took our break from the story Echo was telling, we looked down to where the river was starting to swell out behind a large dam, the Embalse de Yesa. After that we turned back to see the Pyrenees behind us, already growing faint under the blue afternoon sky. We could still make out the line of the snow crest.

Then from the panniers Echo and Venezia, who were always our faithful and trusty cooks, produced a small gas stove on which they brewed us good strong coffee. Then we spent half an hour lolling on the grass looking out over the river until finally Jack got to his feet and reached for his boots once more.

"Time to get a move on Pilgrims." His voice was gruff, as always, when making this pronouncement. "If not we might as well just give up and pitch our camp here for the night."

We watched as he went over to where the donkeys were grazing. Then we all followed his action, raising ourselves reluctantly to our feet. After that we loaded up our donkeys once more and then we were ready to go.

After a few minutes Walt invited Echo to continue telling us his story. We were all, with the exception of Roy who had been walking ahead of us talking quietly to Walt, eager to hear how it would ' pan out.'

Roy had also, we noted, exchanged his blue baseball cap for a red one. Later we learned that this was his way of indicating that he was in a foul mood and did not want to be disturbed. We called it his Storm Warning.

But Echo, aware that he still had the majority of his audience, was eager to continue. He strode out joyfully and his voice was loud and clear.

"My new job is with the Cornwall Trustee and Savings Bank. I am an overnight cleaner. I pick up the used condoms and pasty wrappers from underneath the tables in the offices. After a year when I have gone through enough of their waste and read enough of their files I enter the office one morning in a suit and amaze my superiors with my knowledge of their industry."

He had been galloping through his story and paused for a second to take a breath. Then he continued.

"When the moment is right I play the Race Card. I tell my masters that when the hordes of immigrants from the old Belgian Congo and the rest of Black Africa invade the UK and arrive in Cornwall they will need somewhere to do their banking. So my offer is this: I will be their conduit, their pipeline, their way into the Cornwall Trustee and Savings Bank! At this the bankers nod heavily and sagely, reporting to themselves, 'that man shows good forward thinking.' So that is how I am hired as a financial adviser."

Venezia passed him a water bottle as we walked and Echo took a break from his unlikely tale and took a long swig. After that and for the rest of the afternoon he amused us with tales of his life at the Cornwall Trustee and Savings Bank.

But when the sun dipped behind a bank of cloud we began once again to feel the warmth seeping from our bones. We stopped and replaced the jackets and sweaters we had discarded in the morning. Oscar had put on a thick hand quilted jacket that had been lovingly created for him back home by his wife Sheila. The colours of the patchwork quilt, the squares of dark orange, the greens and russet browns, blended perfectly with the paysage through which we were travelling.

Soon the light began to change. The river had lost its earlier sparkle and turned a steely grey. At this point Wilson, who was as always our scout, went on ahead soon finding a sheltered spot back from the river where we could pass the night. Even though we were in the valley of the Rio Aragon with hills on either side we were still high up on the plateau that would lead eventually to the great plain of the Meseta. This meant that the nights were cold.

Wilson collected our fire wood and Oscar and Denis busied themselves with the tents. Jack along with Roy, who had removed his red baseball cap and who was now acting as his reluctant assistant, saw to our donkeys. They unloaded them, stowed away the panniers and then made sure they had access to water and sufficient grass. Venezia and Echo were our two excellent cooks. When we had our camp set up we could see that behind us were the lights of a small village which Walt named as Martes. On the opposite bank of the river we could see pin points of light from the austere stone villages that we had noted during the day.

When we had finished eating and the night had properly fallen, so that an observer of our site would have seen only our fire and the outline of our faces and the glowing ends of cigarettes, Walt turned again to Echo.

"You had better tell us how that story ends up Echo. The readers will have to know how you got from working in a bank to running that dining place. But just don't go on all night about it."

Echo looked around at the faces of the other pilgrims around the camp fire. Judging that he would have to go quickly to keep our attention this is how he began:

"A fine summer's morning, two years later and I am sitting in my office, reading the Wall Street Journal and contemplating a move to America, when my secretary pops her head around the door.

" 'Sir, there is a Chinese gentleman to see you,' she announces. ' Fine so show him in,' I reply. Dr Han, or the Dancing Doctor as we called him in the end, was from Singapore and had opened an acupuncture clinic in Plymouth but he had spent so much time chasing the local girls in the night clubs that he had neglected his business and now needed a loan.

"So I sit him down and gently ask, 'And what collateral do you have Sir?' to which he replies, 'Only the Emperor of Peking Chinese takeaway that I bought on a whim.' So I take a deep breath and say in turn, 'Bugger the Cornwall Trustee and Savings Bank I will buy it off you.' "

(It was an incontrovertible fact, we all knew, that Echo was the owner of the said takeaway on Ebrington Street in Plymouth and that it was an establishment with an excellent reputation in the neighbourhood).

There was a pause here while another bottle of wine was opened and it was passed around and fresh cigarettes were lit.

We were all enjoying the story now. Only Roy was unhappy. In a rough and rather unpleasant aside to Walt, which fortunately was not picked up by the rest of the group, but that is certainly typical of a certain type of sportsman who cannot bear the presences of other Competitive Males, he muttered :

"A'hm naw listening to Echo anymore Walt. He's a cocky bugger. If we wus in Dundee the neds(trans: local criminals) ahd gi'im a good kickin' by now."

But our Theatrical Pilgrim, ignorant of the animosity that was building, was continuing in full flow.

"How Poor Echo cursed his impetuosity at his impulsive purchase!

"The paint was peeling off the front and the windows were broken. How, if he had been able, he would have turned the clock back and returned the whole thing, toute suite, to the Dancing Doctor!"

He looked at us eyes large and round and full of laughter.

"Not to mention the difficulty of pushing open the door as the space behind it is full of unopened post including court summons and threats from the usual loan sharks."

Jack Phillpotts, who himself banked at the Cornwall Trustee and Savings Bank, looked glum at this news. He had the same dread all businessmen have of the morning post with its wave of demands and threats and summonses. But Echo was continuing.

"I used Cornwall Trustee and Savings Bank notepaper to inform all the creditors that Dr Han had fled the country for his native Singapore. I wrote that if they persisted with their usurious demands I would put the word out and the boys would come round with the tyre irons and smash in their knees. They were a tough old bank even then. After that I called in the rest of the Congolese community and we scrubbed and cleaned taking off layers of dirt until we were back to bedrock. The whole place gleamed and glistened like a new pin."

Wilson started to laugh and shake his head at this point.

"You were certainly different Echo. I am sure there has never been another restaurant or takeaway like it before."

Echo responded with his own big bass bubbling laugh.

"You are right there Wilson. I am sure there was no one else like me. A charcoal black Congolese, tall as a jungle tree, cooking Chinese grub wearing a conical rice grower's hat. It is the one I wear here. That was my trademark. The Dancing Doctor had worn it for a Christmas party and then discarded it. I found it when I was cleaning up. I also had tee shirts made up with my face on them wearing the hat and underneath the legend The Emperor Of Peking Rules in Plymouth, Innit?"

The fire was starting to die down now and the wine was near enough finished and we were starting to yawn. We had enjoyed Echo's story but we were beginning to think of our beds.

"Finish it up Echo," said Walt. "We are all half asleep."

Echo nodded.

"Right oh Walt. The postscript is very short. It happened a month after I had bought the Emperor of Peking and as we were preparing for our opening. I went into Waterstones bookshop on New George Street in Plymouth and said to the girl behind the counter, who I took to be Chinese, because to us they all look alike, that I had bought a Chinese take away and that I needed a cook book to provide me with instruction.

"So she said 'Certainly Sir,' and led me to the cook book section and took down a book with a lot of squiggly writing. Then she said, 'This is the cook book my mother swears by.' So I replied, 'That will do me then,' and bought the book and started to cook from it, not realising of course that she was Japanese and not Chinese and that what I was cooking was Japanese food and not Chinese food."

"So what on earth did you tell the customers?" It was Oscar, who had never even visited Plymouth, and so did not know the Emperor of Peking Chinese takeaway, who asked the question.

"We said it was a new type of cuisine taken from a special area of the China that not many people visited," Echo replied. At this we all laughed and even Roy managed a weak smile.

Then with the story concluded and feeling our eyes beginning to close, we had been walking all day and were tired, we finished up the last of the wine and were soon in our sleeping bags in our tents, leaving only the stars of the cold night to watch over our little encampment.

9

Our routine in the morning was the reverse of the evening. Oscar and Denis, with Wilson to help, dismantled our camp. Venezia and Echo provided our breakfast and Jack busied himself with our two donkeys. By the time we had reached the city of Pamplona, Roy had been appointed his official assistant. Or as Oscar cruelly put it, "The great Sir Roy Babadouche has become Jack Phillpott's understrapper."

Loading up our donkeys in the morning was a task that had to be done carefully. If the heavy panniers were not correctly balanced they would slip to one side. If this happened it caused a considerable delay as everything had to be unloaded and the packing started again. In the evening Jack always made sure his donkeys had access to grass and water.

Most of the time on the road our life fell into a pleasantly familiar pattern. We walked through the day, stopping for breaks and for lunch and then erected our camp once again in the evening. We were concerned with the state of the footpath, the state of our feet, the state of the sky above us and the distance to our next stopping point.

When our spirits were high all these details were a pleasure, a series of rituals almost, that took us through our day. But the converse was also true. On a day when the sky was grey or the rain was falling then these patterns could seem deadly boring and monotonous.

But this morning fortune shone on us. After we had packed up and were making our way once more along the river valley the sky above was clear and blue and the sun on our backs was pleasantly warm.

At midday we came to the ruined castle at Ruesta where there is a refuge for pilgrims. There we drank beers with the hospitalero (trans: the manager of a refuge, usually acting and unpaid, normally a former pilgrim) a small stout Swede. He told us that a number of the villages along the river valley, including Ruesta, had now been abandoned. After centuries of habitation they had been overtaken by the need to create the new reservoir.

In the afternoon we began the long climb up the forestry path that would lead us out of the valley, moving up through the trees until we could smell fresh pine once again. As we stopped to catch our breath we looked down to the pale blue and turquoise waters of the lake below and to the Rio Aragon which flowed fast and cold into it. It made us sad to think that the villages we could see perched austerely on the bluffs above the river on the opposite bank had now seen their last of life.

We stopped to drink from our water bottles and to allow Jack and Roy to realign the panniers on poor Blair's back. Walt adjusted his slouch hat and bent forward.

"I must be getting old." He turned toward us. "I am sure the hike up was never as steep before." Then when he had recovered his breath he began to address himself to Venezia.

"Echo has given us an excellent start with his story. Venezia my dear will you now give us an account of your early life in the beautiful Province of Quebec?"

"Well thank you Walt," Venezia replied graciously giving a slight blow. "How kind of you to flatter my homeland."

(Like Echo and indeed all the other pilgrims Venezia was a complex mixture. In stature she was small and lithe and graceful. Her hair was cut short and her features were dark and rather Latin. The overall impression was balletic. She was also our optimistic pilgrim, full of light and sunshine. But at the same time Echo, who along with Denis was deeply in love with her, had composed a little ditty that showed another side to her personage. He would recite it slyly when she was not about.

The sun has got her hat on
She's coming out to play –
With salami slicing cut throat razor
To chop you all way!)

Before beginning her story Venezia waited until we had once again begun our slow progress up the forest path. Jack and Denis were leading our two donkeys. Roy was walking just behind them. Finally this is how she began. Her voice was strong and the register was light and clear.

"Once upon a time in Quebec there was a little girl who wore thick glasses and had crooked teeth. And because she was so ugly she had no friends and her only companions were the characters she discovered in the books she read."

On receipt of this information we all registered our surprise, including Roy. This was a description that did not square in anyway with the beauty who stood before us now. It was left to Echo to voice the only possible explanation:

"But then of course this ugly duckling grows up and turns into a beautiful swan."

Then he slipped his arm around her, a move always felt by Denis as a shard entering his fragile heart.

"Oh Echo dear," Venezia turned and smiled sweetly at him before brushing away his arm. "Oh charmant. Oh thank you."

The sun was beginning to dip and once again we could feel the warmth slipping out of the day.

"So what is it you were you reading then with your crooked teeth and your thick glasses," Wilson asked finally. Like all of us he knew that Venezia possessed strong imaginative powers. He had also heard Oscar, in a colourful phrase, describe Venezia as taking her life from the Book of Imagination.

"Oh, Jack London," Venezia replied finally, looking hard at Wilson. "And Jules Verne, and Rider Haggard, and Mark Twain. By the time I was sixteen I had been everywhere from Alaska to Africa, to outer space and the bottom of the sea. I lived for adventure. I was a regular tomboy."

Venezia would have continued but at that moment we arrived at the top of the ridge and emerged out of the forest. We stopped for a moment there to catch our breath. It had been a climb up that had taken us several hours.

This was also an important point on our pilgrimage. It was the moment when we gave a last backward glance and adieu to the Rio Aragon and the faint line of the Pyrenees in the distance behind us. After that we turned to the West and looked ahead of us down to the open fields of Navarre. We could see tractors ploughing the dark autumn earth. We continued on for a short while and then set up camp for the night in the lee of a deserted barn.

When we had our tents up and our donkeys had been led to a small stream where they could drink we once again turned our attention to the vexing and serious problem of Jack's feet and for the moment the story that Venezia had been telling us was put to one side. Jack was sitting on the ground by the entrance to his tent. He was complaining to Venezia and Oscar.

"If I do not get some proper repairs done to my feet soon I am sure I am going to be done for. I am never going to make it to the next town, wherever that is, never mind Pamplona or the end of our journey."

At this Oscar helped the poor man off with his boots and then Venezia peeled off his socks to reveal that the toes on the right side of his foot were chafed and bleeding. The damage to his left foot was less extensive, although an examination did show another good size blister developing on his heel.

Denis fetched water and Venezia cleaned the wound with a cotton pad and covered it with plaster. When we had done the best we could to patch him up it was left to Walt to offer his advice on the case.

"Some times the old ways are the best. I wear these rough old sandals which never give me a moment's bother. When we arrive in Pamplona, Pilgrim Jack, I am going to accompany you to a shoe shop and purchase footwear that will not cripple you."

(And that is exactly what we did. Denis and Oscar bought lighter pair of shoes as well. Thus we learned that our own personal experience, and Walt's sage advice, was worth more than all the recommendations in the guide books that pilgrims read before departing).

An hour later when we had finished eating Jack got up to alter the tether on the donkeys. When he returned and wood had been added to the fire so that it crackled up into the night Wilson said he would like to ask Oscar a specific question about the robbery in Zaragoza.

"Well, what is it," said Oscar abruptly. He did not like other pilgrims interfering in what he considered 'his' robbery. "I have already given you the details."

He stared hard at Wilson. Even though he had taken part in a robbery he still regarded himself as a ' proper' member of society and viewed Wilson and Echo's political views with great suspicion.

"It's the notes," Wilson responded. He was not put off by Oscar's tone. "We need to know if they are new or used. It will make a great difference to our plans, as to what we can do with the money."

Oscar was about to reply, as would have been his right, ' It is my money and so I will decide what we do with it,' but he changed his mind and instead went into his tent and came out again a moment later with the bag containing the One Million Euro.

He placed it on the ground by the fire and opened up the top and we all leaned forward. It was then that we saw to our disappointment that the notes were in clear plastic packets and so were obviously new and easily traceable.

But then to our relief Oscar lifted off a layer of the plastic packets to expose beneath a layer of older notes. A selection of these were then passed to Denis who, with the experience he had gained in prison, examined them by the light of the fire.

"They are certainly old and from different periods," he pronounced following an examination. "The serial numbers are not consecutive which is a good sign."

After that Oscar put the money back in the bag and returned it to the tent and Venezia and Echo got up to wash the dishes in the little stream. A few minutes later Walt finished the last of the wine in his mug and stood up slowly.

"Pilgrims. I bid you all good night." He was swaying slightly. "I am even falling asleep as I speak." And with that he turned and walked slowly and slightly unsteadily toward his tent.

We all walked long and hard during the day and thus we all, Walt included, felt entitled to a 'decent feed' and a 'good drink' when we stopped in the evenings.

However as a result of his early and slightly unsteady departure Walt missed out on the ' fun' that was shortly to follow.

We were sitting round the fire idly talking among ourselves. We were finishing the last of the wine when Echo, moving a foot to get comfortable, accidentally kicked an ember which briefly flared in front of Roy. This made Roy rear up and all the tension that had been building up unbearably inside him was suddenly, like a volcano, released.

"Yer wee African numpty." His voice was a dangerous snarl. We noted his iron hard visage and realised immediately that a crisis was upon us.

Then the tone of his voice dropped so it was like rough gravel. He brushed down his trousers angrily.

"Yous flick ash on a man in a pub in Dundee yous get yer heed stove in African boy."

At this accusation Echo put aside his mug and rose to his feet menacingly.

"You talk like that to a boy from the Congo," he said slowly, "they going to take your face off with a machete and stick it on a pole man."

Then Roy also rose to his feet and the next moment to our horror the pair of them were facing off, fists up in the manner of two bare knuckle prize fighters.

Venezia, her usually confident features registering sudden alarm, jumped to her feet too, but Oscar pulled her back. His voice was sharp.

"Leave them be Venezia. It has been on the cards. They are two dogs ready to fight."

They circled dangerously in the moonlight, these two ancient Leviathans.

But in the end, thank God, only one hard punch was landed. Echo caught Roy a glancing blow to his cheek just under his right eye. Roy staggered back under the weight of the punch.

It was at that moment that Jack, he was a publican so he knew how to handle these matters, stepped in between the two protagonists and pushed them abruptly apart.

"If you had scrapped like that in my pub," he told them both sternly as he backed them away from each other, "I would have banned you both for life."

After that Venezia took Echo to one side while Jack calmed down Roy. However our efforts to get them to shake hands failed and when we went to our tents our fears about the 'suitability' of Roy to be a pilgrim weighed heavily upon us. In the end we all slept badly that night worrying for the future of our journey together.

10

In the morning when we emerged from our tents it was to find below us a sea of white clouds stretching far out to the West. Normally this idyllic paysage would have set us up with a feeling of great optimism for the day ahead. But when we saw that Roy's right eye had swollen up with the blow that Echo had inflicted and that this damage could not be hidden from Walt, our hearts were full of fear for the future.

Breakfast was eaten in silence and then we packed up our camp and set off, descending via a slippery stone path into the mist, the donkeys picking their way carefully, until we came to the village of Undues de Lerda. There we discovered a bar where we spent an hour warming ourselves before a welcoming wood fire.

As we had anticipated Walt was harsh in his criticism of Echo. His voice was sharp and angry.

"Roy will almost certainly go home. Goddamit, learn to keep you damn temper under control Echo. It's a damn disgrace."

He looked around the bar. He was bristling with fury.

"You've ruined months of work. If I had my way I'd pack you onto the first train out of here."

He paused for a second and then renewed his attack.

"Damn it Echo, can't you see that someone like Roy Babadouche is the face of modern Britain?"

At this we all turned to look at Roy, his right eye swollen and half closed. Then Venezia, unable to keep a face straight any longer, began to laugh.

A moment later Echo and even Roy joined in and then Walt himself gave a grim smile. He shook his head.

"If old Aimery Picaud had been here he would have made a fine enough story out of it. It would have been meat and drink to him."

After that the terrible tension which had been present in our little group began to relax itself. Roy and Echo shook hands and slowly we began to talk of other things. We hoped that we could salvage something from this disaster and that the damage to our pilgrimage could be repaired.

Then we left the bar and continued our descent down the stony path. A short while after that the sun finally dispersed the mist and we were able to see ahead of us the track that would take us to the small town of Sanguesa. The bright morning light, as well as lifting our spirits, also gave the fields of dried up grass and stubble a golden air. Toward midday a heat haze developed and we adjusted our hats against the brightness of the sun.

And so that was how, after the adventures of the night before, our little caravan swayed slowly along, the day warm, the path now soft and dusty beneath our feet.

(Would a casual observer, watching us as we walked along, descending along that rough cart track toward the town of Sanguesa have thought us any different from other pilgrim groups? At the front of our little group Jack and Echo were leading our two donkeys Thatcher and Blair, who were laden with the panniers containing our equipment. The rest of us followed behind. Venezia, punishing Echo for his fight with Roy had temporarily transferred her affections to Denis. Behind them Walt was recounting some detail of his life to Oscar and Roy. Our dress perhaps was more eccentric than other pilgrims. Echo wore a red tee shirt with the logo for his takeaway on the front. On his head to shade him from the sun he wore the wide conical rice growers hat left behind by the Dancing Doctor. Venezia also wore a wide brimmed straw hat. In the brim she had placed a red poppy which she had picked from the roadside. Wilson wore a black tee shirt, dark glasses and on his head a rimless black fedora. The other pilgrims said this ensemble gave him a sinister air. Roy had his blue baseball cap and Walt his wide brimmed slouch hat. In Pamplona Jack bought himself a good strong pilgrim's staff to help him on his walk and two of our number, Venezia and Denis, bought small cockleshells, the pilgrim's symbol, which they wore about their necks).

That afternoon when the sun was starting to dip down we passed through the small town of Sanguesa. Then we crossed the Rio Aragon once more before climbing over rough ground to reach the tree line on the opposite bank where there was shelter for camping.

After we had set up our camp and our dinner had been eaten we lit up cigarettes and Roy opened another bottle of wine. Then Denis, not wanting the wounds of yesterday to be re opened, turned to Walt to ask:

"Can you give us some of your poems Walt? And can you tell us about the time when you were a young man in America and what you did there?"

When Walt heard this request he turned to Denis and after a moment's thought he replied:

"As to my life, well I experienced the Civil War, worked in New Orleans as a newspaper editor and saw President Lincoln on a number of occasions. As to my verses I limit myself. But as you ask I will give you these few lines.

This is what he declaimed for us:

Trippers and askers surround me,
People I meet, the effect upon me of my early life or the ward and city I live in, or the nation,
The latest dates, discoveries, inventions, societies, authors old and new,
My dinner, dress, associates, looks, compliments, dues,
The real or fancied indifference of some man or woman I love,
The sickness of one of my folks or of myself, or ill-doing or loss or lack of money, or depressions or exaltations,
Battles, the horrors of fratricidal war, the fever of doubtful news, the fitful events;
These come to me days and nights and go from me again,
But they are not the Me myself.
Apart from the pulling and hauling stands what I am,
Stands amused, complacent, compassionating, idle, unitary,

Looks down, is erect, or bends an arm on an impalpable
certain rest,
Looking with side-curved head curious what will come
next,
Both in and out of the game and watching and wondering
at it.
Backward I see in my own days where I sweated through
fog with linguists and contenders,
I have no mockings or arguments, I witness and wait.

When he had finished and we had mulled over the words and the sentiments expressed in them, Jack Phillpotts turned toward Walt.

"If the other pilgrims do not object I would like to recount an experience that I have been reminded of by the words of your poem."

Walt looked around our little group, our faces flickering from the light of the fire, and seeing that we were all agreed, even Roy, he nodded his assent.

Those who did not like Jack Phillpotts called him a curmudgeon, but his pub regulars defended him. They called him a fountain of good common sense and a defender of old fashioned virtues.

He kept the Bastard's Baby, on the Barbican in Plymouth, in the traditional manner. There was always a fire in the grate in winter. The chairs were precarious and uncomfortable so most people stood or leant against the bar. Under protest his long suffering wife Marjorie had finally been allowed to serve food, as long as the menu was plain and the dishes English. His beer was excellent.

Jack was also the oldest and least fit of our pilgrim band. He wore an old fashioned open neck shirt and grey flannel trousers held up by a thick leather belt. On his feet, and the cause of most of his troubles, were his old army boots.

This was the story then that he told us that night around our fire. It was a story that surprised us because it showed up his personage in a light to which we were not accustomed.

(It should also be stated before he starts that One Million Euro is not a narrative about Plymouth, nor even of the county of Devon or of England. This is one of the few deviations, that concerns Plymouth, that we will allow).

Jack's accent betrayed, quite proudly, that he was a son of our city. This how he began.

"When the story of Plymouth for our times is told there'll be one person, in my view, who'll be placed at head of the chronicle. And that person, in my opinion, is a certain Mr Robert Lenkiewicz."

"Ah yes, a good painter," Walt nodded. "But dead these ten years now."

"That is right," Jack replied. "His studio was just along from the Bastard's Baby. You will think him a most unlikely man for me to nominate. You would have expected me to nominate a successful businessman, perhaps someone like Dan McCauley, who at one time has had beneficial stewardship of all three of our local football clubs. But Robert was alright. People came to talk to him. He understood people and he understood himself. I could see him in the poem you read."

Jack had been right of course. Robert Lenkiewicz was tall and broad with long flowing hair and there is no doubt he stood above everyone else living in Plymouth at that time.

Jack stopped to consider for a moment. Then he chuckled.

"I'll tell you this. He came into the pub one lunchtime, hair down to his waist and in his painters smock. 'Jack,' he said, looking around. 'This place is a disgrace. I am going to paint you a mural.' Just like that. And so he did. All along the side wall. It took him six weeks. In the end we were all in it. Me, Marjorie, the staff, a dozen of the regulars. Marjorie was very flattered I can tell you. I said to him afterwards Marjorie hasn't looked like that for a few years now Robert old son, you are working on memory there."

Jack eyed us.

"In her younger days Marjorie had a bit of a reputation and everyone knew about Robert. A different girl on his arm every week. But that was a long time ago now. I didn't have to pay him for the mural or anything like that. He just did it for the pleasure. All we had to do was give him a drink and a sandwich when he came in at lunchtime."

Jack stopped for a second and again we all remembered Robert Lenkiewicz and his paintings. He had breathed life into the Barbican. Some people said he was a modern day Rembrandt. Jack was continuing:

"When it was done we had an art critic down from London to see it. They never liked him up there. He never got his due. Not enough space men and pickled sheep. They said he was too simple but Robert saw through them all. The critic was a short arsed little bastard if ever I saw one. I can see him now going up to the mural and examining it.

" ' Landlord,' he says grandly when he returns to the bar." Jack was imitating his accent. " 'If my three year old infant daughter had been blinded at birth she could paint better than that.' "

Jack hunched up his shoulders and stared at us.

"They are all like that up there, it's bloody typical, that's why I never go near the place. But I can tell you pilgrims that fellow was out of my pub door quicker than a London cabbie can double charge a poor Devon boy."

We all laughed at this. Everyone knew and loved Robert Lenkiewicz and his colourful paintings. Roy passed around the bottle of wine. Finally it was Wilson who spoke.

"You are right there Jack," he said. "I have studied your mural on many occasions when I have been drinking beer in your pub and have appreciated it very much. Robert's work was always full of humanity and compassion. What I am against in painting, as in life, is fraud and hypocrisy and if you will allow me I will tell you a story that will illustrate this point."

Wilson as has been noted was tall and thin. He was a committed socialist and he had an intense air about him. His hair was close cropped to his head and he wore round spectacles through which his green eyes glistened.

But we were surprised on this occasion both by his views on art and by the animated manner in which he recounted his story to us. This is how he began as we sat round the fire that night:

"On the day in question I was on my way down to the Bastard's Baby when I decided to enter the Mayflower Gallery where a number of the Lenkiewicz paintings still hang. I agree with Jack. He is an important painter who has left a considerable body of work. His depictions of the urban poor in Plymouth are masterful.

"But while I am in the gallery studying these figures, I recommend particularly a picture entitled The Bishop, I became side tracked by a series of strange modernist paintings by an artist called L. Frost.

"But when I saw the price tag, well that gave me a jolt. So I looked at the attendant and asked him - why would anyone pay £14,000 for this?"

We observed Wilson for a moment over the flickering flame of our fire and then tried to imagine him in that gallery attempting to keep what we might call his ' Socialist Cool' with the attendant as they discussed such an inflated price figure. He was continuing:

"I can describe that painting to you now. It was about three foot long and two foot deep, the canvas a uniform satin blue with a single white line, vertical top to bottom, six inches from the left hand edge. Nothing else. I studied it closely to see if there was a message hidden or coded, but there was nothing that I could see. It was simply as stated, a satin blue canvas with white vertical stripe. So then I asked the attendant once again - why would anyone pay £14,000 for a canvas obviously inspired by a footballer's shirt or a kitchen tea towel?"

Wilson looked round at us over the flickering firelight.

"I can see the attendant is shocked by my question. But then he takes a deep breath and explains patiently that L. Frost, the grandson of the more famous Cornish artist T. Frost, has put the paint on layer by layer, even drying it coat by coat with a ladies hair dryer, and it is that which gives the canvas such a rich finish.

"So I turned to the attendant and told him that give or take the hair dryer he had described near enough how a garage worker sprays a car. His reply to this was that such paintings were considered a good investment and that last week a farmer had come in and bought two without hesitation."

Wilson paused as Roy passed round a wine bottle and our mugs were refilled.

"So then I said I have a friend called Turk who runs a garage and who drinks at the Bastard's Baby, Jack Phillpotts pub on the Barbican. He could produce paintings like that for you on an industrial scale and you could have a fine old racket going ripping off the local citizenry.

"At this the attendant takes a step back and looks horrified and shouts out in a high falsetto voice, 'No, No, No, Sir, I think not Sir, No Sir.'

We all laughed at this, imagining the attendant in the presence of our Socialist Hero. Then he was continuing:

"So I stare straight back into his ugly corrupt face and say why not, everyone gets rich, no one gets hurt, that's the way it works.

"He comes back at me then, sharp as a knife, and says because the name of your friend is not L. Frost and he is not the grandson of the well known Cornish artist T. Frost.

"Precisely I say and go out slamming the door of the gallery behind me."

At the conclusion of this story there was a silence and all we could hear was the fire crackling. We were all in sympathy with Wilson. (It was Echo who explained later that all revolutionaries and communists are at heart romantics and conservatives).

We had also drunk a considerable amount of wine by that time and sleep was starting to creep up on us so we were not fully alert to the trap that Echo then skilfully (and deliberately) laid.

"Well in that case," he said casually to Wilson, "If you do not like what you describe as the fraudulence of modern art I presume then you are inspired by the more 'traditional' realism of someone such as Jack Vettriano?"

This was a stone dropped into the pond impishly and provocatively, as Echo knew full well that Roy was a collector of the works of Jack Vettriano. But Wilson was ignorant of this fact.

"Well Echo there are limits to anyone's tolerance," Wilson replied strongly. "Robert Lenkiewicz is a fine artist with insight, courage and character. By contrast Jack Vettriano is tin eared and derivative and lacking in skill and integrity."

Hearing this Roy began slowly to stir from his fireside slumber. He had appreciated Wilson's story. He disliked the modern abstract paintings bought for him by his investment manager and had instructed his wife Mary to place them in the loft. But his collection of Vettrianos were displayed with pride in the living and dining rooms of their well furnished house in Godalming in Surrey.

When finally he opened his mouth to speak his Dundee accent had dropped once more to a deep and dangerous growl.

"Ah dunna ken what yous lot are blatherin' on about. Vettriano does ma family very nicely thank yer."

We could all see that Roy was beginning to ' boil up' again but Echo didn't have the sense to stop. He admitted later that it was a fault. But as he said, in Africa if you have a man on the ground you do not let him up to hit you again.

"I agree with you there Pilgrim Wilson," he replied, deliberately ignoring Roy's intervention. He had given his voice a deliberate faux innocence. "Jack Vettriano is a cheap paint by numbers operator whose paintings are bought by deeply ignorant people for whom art is indistinguishable from interior decoration."

At this Roy's terrible rage which he had been holding in ever since the fight did once again 'boil over.' He got to his feet, gloweringly tall (and handsome) in the glimmering light of the fire.

"I already said ta Walt tha' yous an African eejit," he growled at Echo in his rich gravelly Dundee accent, stabbing a finger towards his face. He was spitting out the words now. "Any player behaved like that in ma team I'd ah sold him on straightaway."

We all gasped at this but for the moment Roy was beyond caring. His fierce eye roved around our little group.

"You's all a crowd ah bloody dossers with ya daft wee pilgrimage. If I saw yous on the street at home I'm telling ya, I'd walk straight by, I wouldna give you the time of day." Then he turned to Walt. "What the hell you go' me into with this crowd ah eejits eh Walt?"

And with that, and without waiting for a reply, he turned on his heel and stalked off to his tent.

11

Early the following morning, with a hasty breakfast eaten and with the sky grey and rain threatening, Oscar and Venezia approached Walt who was standing outside his tent surveying our route ahead.

"We are fair minded people Walt," Oscar began, pulling the colourful quilted coat made by his wife Sheila around him to keep out the damp morning cold. "But we feel that Roy, with his background as a football manager, does not fit in with this pilgrimage we are attempting to make."

Walt looked serious as Oscar continued.

"We are concerned that his presence in the story may alienate readers. We think you could have chosen someone more suitable."

"Oscar is right," added Venezia. "We have all talked about it. We are all with him."

Oscar took up the attack again.

"Our readers will find it difficult to accept that in a story of people going on pilgrimage to Santiago de Compostela there can be a place for a football manager. They will say while you are at it why don't you bring in a clown and a talking dog and make a proper circus of the whole thing?"

A cold wind suddenly got up bringing the first spats of rain and Venezia thrust her hands into deep into the pockets of her jacket. Behind us we could hear the voices of Echo and Denis and Jack communicating as they pulled down the tents. Roy was tending to the donkeys at the far side of the camp and so could not hear our conversation.

After Oscar had finished Walt paused for a moment and then drew himself up to his full height and faced his interrogator. He had turned his visage so that it had become for a moment stern and wrathful.

"Oscar Bebbington you stand condemned." His voice was loud and angry. "You are a vendor of cheap sugared drinks. Young people's teeth are rotten because of you. Any civilised society would have given you a jail sentence rather than a pension."

Then he changed the direction of his attack.

"And do you think the name of Oscar Bebbington is going to sell any books? Will any reader search out your story? No, of course not. We will be remaindered and pulped before we have begun. What any book needs is a hero."

But Oscar was not a man who was easily intimidated. After all he had nerve enough to drive the getaway car for a bank robbery. His voice took on a sharp edge as he leaned forward.

"No, you are there wrong Walt. Roy Babadouche is a foul mouthed ring master and a waster who would be more at home at a bare knuckle fight in a Dundee pub on a Saturday night than he ever would at a civilized dinner table."

Jack and Denis and Echo stopped work taking down the tents when they heard this. Even Walt was shocked by the exaggeration and unfairness of this attack. Fortunately (for us all) Roy was still out of earshot and so could not hear what was being said.

"And the rabble who follow him." Nothing was going to stop Oscar's flow now. "They bay like dogs. Talk about bread and circuses."

At this point Walt held up his hand abruptly.

"You stop right there Oscar Bebbington before you go too far."

We could see that Walt had reached the limits of his tolerance.

"Football is the metaphor for our time. It is brutal and greedy, but at the same time it is glorious, dramatic, gladiatorial and explosive. It is the wildest tiger a man can ride."

Then he lowered the tone of his voice.

"They love him. He is their hero, their inspiration. He is the reason they get out of bed in the morning."

"Piffle," replied Oscar disgustedly. "He is a bruiser and a bully."

Now exasperated Walt turned toward Venezia and then over to where Jack and Denis and Echo were still working. We could see their breath in the cold morning air.

"I ask you all. Who will lead you to safety in desperate times?" He raised his hands. "Who is there who has that character and courage? A television celebrity? A politician? A film star?"

We heard the exasperation in his voice.

"None of them. Of course not. They are cowards to a man when it comes to a fight. It takes a peculiar man to do that job and I can tell you for certain that one of those ' peculiar men' is with us today."

Then as if he had had enough of the argument and wanted to close it off he added abruptly:

"Our heroes, our Gods. They give us our mythology, our narrative." He tapped the side of his head. "Without them we could not survive."

But this was finally a step too far for Oscar.

"Mythology!" His voice was furious. "Good God man what are you saying! Do you plan to turn Roy into one of those heroes? Are you going to make him the Odysseus of our time?"

He turned to the other pilgrims who were now all gathered around. Then he shook his head in amazement at what he had heard.

It was left to Venezia to put her hand on Oscar's arm to calm him. Then she turned back to Walt.

"But have you considered our women readers Walt? There are not many will want to read a book with a football manager at its heart."

"Not so," Walt replied. He was folding up the map he had been looking at. His voice was calmer now. "Roy polls well with the ladies. They consider his wit and force of character to be admirable characteristics."

"But what about our overseas readers?" asked Denis, who had now joined the conversation. "How many of those will be aware of the achievements of Roy?"

Walt put away the map.

"You would be surprised Denis at how far his fame has spread around this old globe. Go to a village in the Urals, a town in Outer Mongolia, you will be surprised, they know him everywhere."

It was at that point that Jack Phillpotts joined us. The exertion of getting the baggage ready for the donkeys had left him slightly breathless. Echo was just behind him. Jack was just about to enter the debate (on Roy's side) when he was forestalled by this announcement from Walt:

"Anyway if all goes to plan you will shortly be shown an example of Roy Babadouche's courage."

It was Echo who responded to this. His face had a knowing smile. "OK I see the plan now! Our heroic figure is soon to emerge!"

We were about to interrogate Walt further on this when we saw Roy coming toward us leading Thatcher and Blair and that was the end of the debate for the moment.

12

We had bought our waterproof capes from Gould's, the well known army surplus store on Ebrington Street, Plymouth, not far from the Emperor of Peking, and these had served us well when we had been buffeted by the storms in France in the foothills of the Pyrenees. Now we put them on once again as a thin cold rain began to fall.

To our left was the landmark mountain called Monreal. Walt explained that the following day we would round its flank, and that our route would briefly take a more southerly direction.

It was after we had been walking for an hour, our heads down, the rain on our capes pushing us deep into our thoughts, that we saw ahead of us on the path a pilgrim, his pack by his side, an umbrella over his head. In his hand he held a placard which read:

DISSAPOINTED IN LOVE.

PLEASE GIVE GENEROUSLY.

To see a pilgrim begging as he or she makes his or her way to Santiago is an unusual sight.

Later on in our journey we did meet a German outside the cathedral in Leon with his arm outstretched asking for money but pilgrims are normally more discreet.

A pilgrim ' down on his luck' might announce in a refuge that he is trying to make the pilgrimage from Belgium or Holland without money. His predicament will be recognised and he will almost certainly be treated to a meal. However if he approaches the same group at breakfast the following morning he may be turned away.

That is not to say we did not see genuine beggars on our route to Santiago. There are the destitute in all the cities, they pose on their knees with placards around their necks which tell heart rending stories of poverty and suffering, some of which are true and some of which are made up.

But this young man, he was square and solid in shape and had a dark beard that was neatly trimmed, did not seem to be suffering. There were no holes in his clothes and his boots looked sound, so we halted our little caravan to ask him about his sign.

The story he told us, we eventually invited him to join us at a bar that we found open in a small village, was that he had been studying economics at the Sorbonne in Paris when he had fallen in love with a beautiful girl.

The tone of his voice was as winsome as his story.

"Her hair was long and dark and her visage was shapely and sweet as an almond. The first time I saw her I knew I would dedicate my life to her."

"So yous fancied the wee girl then," said Roy gruffly. He had taken a dislike straightaway to this fancy Frenchman (with his exaggerated accent) who wore his heart so easily on his sleeve.

The Frenchman looked back uncertainly at Roy. His damaged cheek plus days outside living under canvas had roughened his visage. The Frenchman's eye then went uncertainly around the rest of the group. Then with a shake of his head he drew breath and continued.

"We were on the same course."

He took a sip of his coffee and tasted a sugared roll and glanced quickly at Roy again.

"But she was also like this."

He turned his head from side to side in imitation of someone impetuous and headstrong.

"She was planning to leave the course. She had fallen in with a new crowd, anarchists. They followed the teachings of Bakunin."

When he saw that this name registered only with Echo he gave a sigh. We began to think he was as impetuous and coquettish as his girlfriend. He took another sip of coffee and continued his story.

"They turned her head. She said the economics course we were both studying was a prop for a corrupt system. She wanted me to drop out and join her on the streets. She started to attend meetings and one day I saw her on the news on the television, she was addressing a crowd through a loud hailer."

This Frenchman certainly knew how to play to his audience. Echo and Denis were captivated by his tale. Venezia, sensing she would end up siding with the girlfriend, was withholding judgement. Wilson was also against, disapproving of all beggars. Jack and Oscar were puzzled but prepared to listen. It was only the hackles of our Great Scottish Football Manager that rose in immediate protest.

The Frenchman was continuing with his tale.

"It came to a head one evening. She said she would only stay with me if I left the course and joined her and the other protesters."

"Well I hope you didna' Frenchman," growled Roy, his rough Dundee voice spitting out the words. This man was the antithesis of the footballers he worked with every day. "You'd surely more sense than ta go chasin' after some wee hussy showing her tail feathers."

The Frenchman looked nervously again at Roy's battered features before continuing quickly on.

"I cut my lectures for a week. I went with her to meetings. They were passionate, they were romantic. They would blow up banks, they would follow the path of Baader Meinhof in Germany."

He turned to Venezia now.

"Then I woke up one night to find she had gone out. I had already begun to suspect she was having an affair with the leader of the group."

Roy leaned forward once more over the wooden table around which we were all sitting. His voice was rough and low.

"Did yous turn the trollop out then Frenchman? How much more were yous goin' to take?"

But the Frenchman had now turned toward Venezia. He was appealing to her dark Latin eyes. He spoke painfully, his voice rising .

"The next day there was an argument. She screamed terrible insults. It was mad, crazy, it went on for hours. In the end she ran out."

He paused at this crescendo hoping once more for Venezia's support. But Venezia was for the other side. Her visage was glacial. We remembered the little ditty that Echo had composed about her.

"Poor girl," she said finally. "Her heart must have been broken. She couldn't bear to see you again."

Rebuffed the Frenchman turned to Wilson in the hope that a fellow socialist might offer comfort.

"I was sure I would die of a broken heart."

But Wilson declined to respond. We knew his strict view on beggars. Better to let them starve so the state would wake up (eventually) to its responsibilities.

It was left to Oscar to finally offer our response. "So that is why you're on pilgrimage, to get over it all."

"Monsieur," the Frenchman turned toward him. "I come from a good Catholic family in Brittany. We have a tradition of pilgrimage."

Oscar looked sceptical.

"But you still want the rest of us to pay for it."

"Well, not quite Sir," the Frenchman replied slowly and drew his pack toward him.

"I discovered after she left that even anarchists need money to live. A small co operative business producing tee shirts and other articles of clothing had been set up. My girl had stored much of the stock in the apartment. And when she departed that fateful evening she left it all behind."

Denis's normally hesitant face lit up. "Oh so that is how you are paying your way to Santiago. You are selling the tee shirts!"

"Precisely Monsieur. Precisely."

We watched as he opened the top of his rucksack.

"But I hope you will not be disappointed. They have been very popular. I am down to my last few."

In the end we discovered that his stock of tee shirts and assorted underwear was more varied than we had anticipated. Walt was particularly pleased with a tee shirt with WRITE A POEM, SAVE THE WORLD written on the front and Denis blushed when he was handed a tee shirt with the logo SHE LOVES YOU.

Wilson, Echo and Jack bought good quality socks and Oscar took two large red spotted handkerchiefs.

Then the Frenchman put his hand into his bag for the last time. Then he looked at Roy with a certain hesitation.

"Monsieur I hope this will not cause offen ..."

His voice tailed away and we watched nervously as he drew out a combination set of tartan vest and underpants neatly monogrammed over the front with the inscription WELCOME TO BONNY DUNDEE and handed them to The Great Football Manager.

We waited for the terrible vent of rage to explode over us but instead to our surprise, and showing yet another side to his remarkable character, the gift was received with an engaging lop sided grin.

"Tartan combinations!" His voice was suddenly rich and full of humour. "Much ta be appreciated by ma beautiful wife Mary a'hm sure! I thank ye for that Frenchman. I'll certainly wear them next time ah'm at the match."

And with that surprising conclusion, a few minutes later, with handshakes all round, we took our leave from this enterprising young Frenchman. He said he would stay in the bar until the rain had stopped. Our plan was to continue on toward the small village of Monreal.

Over the weeks as we walked we heard other stories from pilgrims who had encountered him. He told a group of Germans he was a French Foreign Legion veteran and later informed an Italian pilgrim and his wife that he was hoping to recover from a terminal illness.

But we were not begrudging. He had told his story well and we had been happy to pay the small amount that he asked for his tee shirts and underwear.

13

That afternoon as we descended toward Monreal the rain continued to fall and the small amount of light and warmth that was left in the day was slowly extinguished by the towering mountain to our left. Talk ceased as we trudged miserably on under our capes. Even the two donkeys being led by Wilson and Oscar looked sodden and unhappy. The amusement we had gained from our encounter with the Frenchman was long gone.

We had been like this for a couple of hours when Denis began to shiver uncontrollably. Venezia shouted for the caravan to stop and we rubbed his hands and arms roughly in an attempt to restore circulation. The rain had got inside his cape and the layers of clothing that he wore had also become sodden, right through to the skin. So with Jack also announcing that his feet had begun to chafe and bleed again Walt said he knew of a tavern in Monreal where we could stay the night and dry out.

There are many forms of lodgings for pilgrims on the Camino de Santiago, from the humble refuge to the five star Parador, and they are all listed in the various guides that the pilgrims use. Walt said he would not have chosen the tavern we stayed in that night, he would have preferred to continue further on, but on this occasion we were left without choice.

The landlord helped Jack and Roy stable the donkeys in a shed at the back of the tavern. Then we got Dennis upstairs and out of his wet clothes and into a bed and Venezia sat beside him until his body temperature began to rise again and he stopped shivering.

The landlord, who was a thin miserly man, had told us that he was short of space and that we would all have to sleep in the one room. This had just the two beds in it, so we gave one to Venezia and the other to Denis, the rest of us making do with rough mattresses on the floor. Echo made sure he slept on the mattress next to Venezia's bed.

Then Walt talked to the landlord and it was arranged that a big fire would be built in the corner chimney downstairs where we could dry our clothes and soup and bread and wine would be provided for our supper.

Once we had filled ourselves up on this simple repast and the fire and the wine had warmed us, our spirits began to rise again. We were about to suggest that either Wilson or Jack begin their tales when Walt looked around and said the sparseness of this tavern reminded him of the places he had visited with his old friend Aimery Picaud and that if we would permit it, he would like to tell us of a certain incident that had taken place some years ago in a tavern in the town of Estella which was not many days walk from here.

So when we had all gladly assented Walt took a draught of wine from his mug and cleared his throat.

"Dear old Aimery Picaud! He was a monk, but he was no saint. He could start an argument over nothing."

He shook his head and laughed as he recalled.

"He was a little terrier, always worrying away. He was ugly too. His face was thin and his nose was too long. But once he decided on a course of action there was no stopping him."

He was stopped by a fit of coughing from Denis. Venezia placed her arm around his shoulders and drew him nearer to the fire. He was a young man and should have been able to withstand the rigours of the camino more easily. But as we would soon realise the terrible things that had happened to him had weakened him both in spirit and in body. Walt waited until we had settled again and then continued.

"Aimery said he had a commission, from Callixtus II, the Pope himself, if you can believe that, to write the first pilgrim's guide to the camino. In the end he called it the Codex Calixtinus. So everywhere we went he was scribbling down all the things we saw. I helped him as well, providing my impressions as we walked along."

He stopped again as Roy passed around the wine bottle.

"I've forgotten the exact year, but it was a long time ago. You can look it up on your computers if you want. It was certainly 12th Century. There weren't many who had walked the Camino before us. Later when people got to hear of the legend, largely because of what Aimery had written, they came pouring through in their millions. I always thought I should have got a credit for it as well."

We paused again as Wilson stepped forward to add wood to the fire in the corner chimney and the flames jumped up. We could see Walt's face flickering in the fire as he remembered his friend.

"Aimery had a tongue on him as sharp as a razor and he could use the most unpriest like language you ever heard if the mood took him. At the same time he was a scholar who knew his Bible and his church history better than anyone I ever met before or after."

Walt paused for a moment to reflect. Then he shook his head.

"Some of the things he wrote about the places we passed through, well, you can take it from me, we could never go back there again. Certainly not around here in Navarre or the Basque country. No Sir. Not if you wanted to emerge with your hide still intact to your frame." Walt looked around. "Aimery was a Frenchman, you've got to remember that. And even in those days they thought they were a cut above everyone else."

Dennis began to cough again and Venezia told Echo to ask the landlord for a blanket to go round his shoulders. When Echo returned and a pale looking Denis had been bundled up in the blanket Walt was able to continue:

"I had to tell him to take out some of his descriptions of the people we met. He could skewer anyone he wanted on the end of his pen. The problem was that he didn't know when to stop. The guides they write these days, they pussyfoot around trying to be nice, but he said what he thought. We were the first of the pilgrims. Millions of people followed us."

We stopped to think of this scribe of so long ago whose influence continued to this day.

"There's the tavern in Estella. We'll pass by it shortly. We were dog tired, we'd walked miles. We'd made friends with the landlord and he'd been serving us a good drop of wine. But when Aimery took against someone, especially when he was drinking, there was no stopping him. This time he'd latched on to a group drinking at the other end of the room. He had worked out that they were Basques and he'd begun to needle them." Walt laughed. "I can hear his high pitched voice even now. He was talking loud enough so they could hear, he made sure of that. He started off by saying that their women were so ugly they turned the milk sour. When they ignored that he said he'd prefer to hump a bullock than spend the night with a Basque woman. Well that was enough. The next thing the tables were turned over and punches were being exchanged."

As we absorbed this story Walt pulled back his hair and we saw the thin line of a scar running along his hairline.

"That's what I got for my troubles. One of them caught me with a table leg." He laughed again. "But you can say what you like about Aimery Picaud, there were people who wouldn't give him the time of day and said he got what he deserved, but he was no coward. We were outnumbered but he fought like a damned tiger. He got a broken nose and a bloody face but he didn't finish until we were in the snow with the door firmly slammed in our faces."

At the conclusion of this story we sat silently drinking our wine and looking into the fire and listening to Denis's occasional coughs. Finally Venezia leaned forward.

"Do you ever see him now Walt?"

Walt put his mug of wine to his lips.

"Now and again. Like the rest of them he's always around."

"Are we very different from those pilgrims of old Walt?" Now it was Denis asking the question.

Walt considered this for a moment and then replied:

"They were more serious people. God was important to them. They were certainly poorer, they suffered from chronic diseases. But they knew their world in the same way that you know yours. The differences between you aren't that great. You don't have to look down on them or pity them. Their lives may have been shorter than yours but they knew how to laugh, they could enjoy themselves."

We gazed into the fire again watching the flames and thinking about all those people who had come before us on this path.

14

During the night the rain cleared away and as we loaded up Thatcher and Blair outside the tavern the following morning the sky was clear and blue. We were later starting than usual, we had stayed up until the early hours drinking wine and talking, so the day was well advanced when finally we set off.

Walt was grumbling that we had been scalped by the landlord. Denis had regained the colour in his face and was no longer coughing. Venezia had once again patched up Jack's feet so that he was comfortable and Oscar, as if to celebrate the re emergence of the sun, had reversed the jacket which his wife Sheila had made for him. The patchwork on the inside was composed of wonderfully light shades of yellows and blues and greens. Venezia put on her sun hat and picked a fresh red poppy to go in the brim. Whenever we saw her do this, we took it as an omen that a good day lay ahead of us.

From Monreal the camino follows the flank of the mountain, curving slowly to the south. There are two landmarks for pilgrims to note. The first, directly below the path, is the irrigation channel called the Canal de Navarra and the second to the North is the great white mass of the Volkswagen factory in the industrial zone of Pamplona.

The path continues to follow the flank of the mountain until it comes to the village of Tiebas. After that it descends past tilled earth fields and the last of the dying summer grass until it reaches Puente la Reina. It is at this point that the Camino Aragones joins the Camino Frances, which is the main pilgrim road to Santiago. (The generic title Camino de Santiago covers all the Pilgrim routes).

That evening we camped two miles to the West of Puente la Reina. Walt told us that because the town was a junction point on the camino it was always full of pilgrims and as result the tavern owners charged high prices. Echo and Venezia cooked up spaghetti for dinner and afterwards, because the night was mild, we were able to linger over the fire.

In the morning we crossed the bridge over the Rio Arga to enter the town. From there we diverted North, on a route that Walt knew, leaving the donkeys with a farmer near Zizur Mayor so that we could finally enter the great city of Pamplona.

Pilgrims soon discover that there is a pattern to entering great Spanish cities on foot.

A final crest is summited and the happy pilgrims gaze down on the city in the plain below them. For that brief moment they feel like explorers viewing an ancient and undiscovered world for the first time.

Full of enthusiasm the pilgrims continue on quickly - only to find this vision of incipient paradise cruelly snatched away as the path dips down once more.

It may be many hours later before the pilgrims, by then irritable and in poor humour, finally arrive at the ' business end' of the city, also known as the municipal tip, also known as the unofficial kingdom of the gypsies and their dogs and their flocks of extremely smelly goats.

Walking on tarmac now, pilgrims pass through the industrial zone. This is in turn followed by an outer ring of residential apartment blocks.

(Spaniards prefer collective living. They find the English and the French, with their taste for individual houses and private gardens, to be rather sad. They do everything as a group or a family. It is certainly rare to meet a Spanish pilgrim walking alone).

(This whole process of entry and exit into big cities is a controversial topic among pilgrims and will be discussed more fully later in this narrative. Essentially there is a sharp divide between the more ascetic of pilgrims who prefer to traverse the country only by rural routes and in pastoral bliss and others who say that the industrial zones and the highways and all the rest of it are simply what the Camino is today, and that in future it will certainly alter again).

After the apartment buildings there are the offices, modern streets and shops, and then finally, through an ancient gate or across a bridge pilgrims will enter the old city, the historic heart - the whole process to be activated in reverse for leaving the city the following day.

So that was the way, following the footprints of the many thousands of pilgrims who had gone before us, we entered the great city of Pamplona, the afternoon sun gently warming us, a tune in our hearts and only the lightest of packs on our backs, the bulk of our kit having been left with the donkeys at Zizur Mayor.

"I always stay at the same place when I am here," Walt said as he led us up the Calle san Gregorio. He stopped and tapped on the door of a dilapidated three storey lodging house.

When there was no reply he tapped again harder and we heard footsteps shuffling toward the door which opened a crack. A shrunken elderly face peered out.

"Oh, it's you," the woman opened the door.

"Yes, it's me Mama," he replied cheerily.

"I was wondering what had happened to you." Her face was gloomy. She did not seem particularly pleased to see Walt. "Your normal room's free but don't expect it at the old price. Everything's gone up. It's terrible now. No one can afford to live."

She stopped to look again at Walt as if suddenly not sure she had got the right person.

"Well who have you got with you this time?"

She peered past Walt as we filed into the dingy hallway.

"My God what a crew. Sometimes I wonder where you find them Walt, I really do."

"Yes Mama."

Walt turned and winked at us.

We followed the old lady up the stairs noting the way her stockings were slipping down her legs beneath her apron. She was a big woman and heavy. She carried a large bunch of keys in her right hand which gave her a lop sided effect.

Earlier Walt had told us that she was the richest widow on the Calle san Gregorio but that she didn't believe in banks and kept all her money under the mattress of her bed.

The rooms were old fashioned and the beds creaked when we lay down. The paper was peeling off the walls and the water for the basin was supplied by a jug from the bathroom.

"This room's naw been touched in fifty years," Roy grumbled and we all nodded in agreement.

An hour later with the dust of the road washed out of our hair and in our ' town' clothes, Oscar had tied one of the red spotted handkerchiefs he had been given by the Frenchman around his neck in the manner of a boy scout and Venezia had put on a long turquoise coloured skirt, Walt took us downstairs and out onto the narrow street again. Then turning to our left we continued on to the Plaza del Castillo where stands the Cafe Iruna.

When we had sat down and Walt had summoned the waiter to bring us glasses of beer we took in the extraordinary and luxurious decor.

We noted chandeliers, enormous mirrors and windows ten foot tall. There were also exotic wall tapestries and a bar that must have been fifty feet in length. To our right there was a raised gallery, where we could imagine, almost, a Bishop preaching his sermon. Roy measured out the dimensions as against the size of a football pitch.

As we drank our beers the regular patrons of the cafe came up to Walt and shook his hand and kissed him on the cheek and enquired of his health.

"I always bring pilgrims here," he explained. "We stay at Mama's and then we come on here. I know everyone in Pamplona."

But a moment later this pleasant scene was interrupted when Echo suddenly pursed his lips and tapped the side of his head knowingly with his finger.

"It has been eluding me ever since we came in but I have it now." He was smiling broadly. "This is where the characters in Ernest Hemingway's 1926 novel The Sun Also Rises caroused and cavorted! This is the place. The hot sunshine. The glory of the bullfight. The decadence of the lost generation. This is it. The Cafe Iruna. Well, well, I never thought I would visit here."

He turned and looked around.

"I will bet a pound to a penny that we will find a reference to the novel somewhere in the cafe here, and perhaps even a bust of the great author himself."

When he heard these (deliberately) provocative words Walt's whole visage turned down. His voice became sour. He turned on Echo.

"If I had a dollar for every bar that second rate writer is supposed to have drunk in I would not have to scrape a living take groups like you on pilgrimage."

He stared at Echo angrily.

"And I'll thank you for remembering that you are with me now Echo, not with Mr God Almighty Ernest Hemingway also known as The Author Who Can't Write A Word Unless He's Got A Bottle Of Whiskey Inside His Overblown Gut."

And with that he placed his beer glass angrily back on the table and stood up and we all followed him, exiting quickly from the wonderful Cafe Iruna.

(From this we learned that for all his ' universality' Walt was still prey to the ordinary human failings - in this case jealousy of another writer's success).

From the Plaza del Castillo Walt led us down a series of darkened back streets until we came to a small restaurant with a red lantern hanging outside. The owner, a small Chinese man wearing glasses, was standing in the doorway. When he saw Walt he greeted him like an old friend and we went inside.

When we had sat down Walt turned to Echo.

"You should remember Pilgrim Echo this is a Basque city. It has a long history. People bring me information as to what is going on in the nationalist movement. You would do well to remember that. Pamplona is not just a city that celebrates bullfighting and second rate writers like Ernest Hemingway."

After that and with the topic of 'other writers' closed to Walt's satisfaction the waiters brought us more bottles of beer. Then heaped plates of chicken and pork and rice arrived and we fell on them like hungry wolves.

Readers may find it strange that pilgrims should eat at a Chinese restaurant rather than tasting traditional Spanish fare but Walt said that on occasion we needed an alternative to the plain diet of the road, at a price that our pockets could afford, and this particular establishment had never let him down.

We had just taken the first sharp edge off our hunger and were settling back to enjoy our repast when Wilson put down his fork.

"With the permission of pilgrims," he said, "I would like to relate a little story that takes us back to the start of our journey."

At this we all looked at our Socialist Friend and then Walt nodded his assent and so, a few minutes later, under the dim lights of a back street Chinese restaurant in the great Spanish city of Pamplona this was the strange tale he recounted.

(And recounted in such an unusual way that we felt somehow that we had not, as yet, judged him correctly).

"If I may I will take you back some weeks," he began. "I am in Jack's pub, the Bastard's Baby, and I am swapping pints and talking to Turk who, as you know, is a character in Plymouth who runs a garage. I am telling him of my unhappiness with my present work situation, which is as a daily article writer with a newspaper, and he is telling me that the only thing to do with a dead end job is to pack it in.

"So the next morning, taking his advice, I enter, as usual, this newspaper office where I am employed as said daily article writer and request an interview with the Great and Obese Editor.

"When I am standing before his desk I say: 'Sir, if there is a God in heaven he will certainly strike you down dead for all the lies, subterfuges and malfeasances undertaken and perpetrated to flog editions of your dirty little scandalous sheet, so I quit.'

"After that I make my way down the stairs and out into the street and breathe in once again the fresh air and sunlight. My only regret is not having made my little speech months before."

Wilson paused here and we pushed back our plates, our appetites sated and lit cigarettes. (It was the days when you could still smoke in restaurants). Then he was continuing.

"That evening I was back in the Bastard's Baby relating to Turk the blow I had struck for all working men when Jack leaned over the bar."

Wilson turned to Jack.

"What was it you said Jack?"

"That there was a fellow asking for you. He was sitting in the corner. He'd been there a good hour at least. Funny chap. Never said a word. White hair and sharp blue eyes. Might have been a sailor."

Wilson nodded.

"That's right. So I went over and sat down next to him and said, 'What can I do for you friend?'

"But I could see that he was waiting for something. So I ordered him a pint of Guinness and when he had sampled it he replied:

' Leave the pub and turn to your right and continue along the Barbican in the direction of the Hoe and you will see on the wall a golden cockleshell underneath which you will find a package, addressed to yourself.'

"So I did as instructed and discovered that the package was in an envelope of the deepest yellow and that my name was written on it in thick red flowing letters. Inside it contained a guide, directions, everything I needed to know about the pilgrimage on the Camino de Santiago. I have told you. I had just quit my job. I took it as an omen."

(The cockleshell is the pilgrims symbol. And the plaque underneath that cockleshell on the Barbican harbour wall states that in the Middle Ages pilgrims embarked ship from Plymouth to northern Spain en route for Santiago. They would have arrived in La Coruna and walked the shorter route, known as the Camino Ingles, to Santiago).

(The rise in popularity of the Camino de Santiago is a modern phenomenon. In the Middle Ages the pilgrimage was the greatest mass movement of the era. Millions of people made the difficult journey. But then the tide withdrew, the pilgrimage dropped out of fashion and the path fell into disuse. But it has revived itself again now).

Wilson leaned forward over the dimly lit table to continue his story.

"The next day I went down to Echo's takeaway, the Emperor of Peking. I knew you all because you drank at the Bastard's Baby. I recounted what had happened, and that I had studied the material contained in the package, and that I was setting off."

Venezia took up the tale.

"When we heard Wilson's story Echo said that he was going to close up the takeaway so we could set off as well."

Echo pushed his plate to one side.

"I may have been running a Chinese takeaway in old English seaport (full of the ghosts of old English sea dogs) but at heart I was still that simple Congolese boy. And when the spirit calls you like that, when you hear such a story told, you have to go, you have no choice."

"I don't know about the spirit," said Jack. "But the next night when Wilson came into the pub and told me that he was setting off with the rest of you I thought, well why not, I am sure I have earned a break as well."

"And let me guess Jack." Oscar turned to him. "Marjorie said, 'Yes why don't you go with them dear, we can all manage well enough here.' "

"You're right there," said Jack with a smile. "Her exact words were, 'I am sure the fresh air and the exercise will do you good dear.' She even helped me up into the attic to get down the bloody old army boots."

15

Pilgrims sleep early and the tapas bars of the Calle san Gregorio were only beginning to waken for the evening when we climbed the stairs of our lodging house. We had removed our shoes and were in our stockinged feet so as not to wake Mama (who also slept early). We heard the snores as we went past her room. Our thin mattresses when we lay down on them felt to us as if they had been filled with the finest duck feathers. Then minutes later, replete with good Spanish beer and good Chinese grub, we were away in the land of nod.

In Mama's kitchen the following morning the only conclusion we could reach, after we had considered all the other options, was that El Lobo had picked us up during the course of the evening, possibly in the Cafe Iruna, and then followed us back to our lodgings.

As we had custody of the One Million Euro for which El Lobo was searching we did not alert the police to the break in, preferring to conduct our own investigation. We quickly found a ground floor window that had been forced. After that we made the assumption that when he had entered he had opened the front door and left it on the latch so that he could make a quick escape.

We were all crowded into the kitchen. Mama was doling out great bowls of coffee and there were bags of thick churros that she had ordered in. Walt said he had not seen her so lively in years.

"I was sure I had dreamed it all," said Oscar as he put a churro into his mouth.

"I know what you mean," said Denis. "I was half asleep too. Thank God Roy was alert at least."

We all looked at Roy who was sitting proudly at the head of the table, head held high, looking now like the real hero that he was. We wondered, to our shame, how we could have doubted him before.

Poor El Lobo. We almost felt sorry for the unfortunate robber. He could not have known in which room Oscar, who always kept the money from the robbery close to his person, was sleeping. So the only option he had was to try all the doors in turn.

By the foulest of luck, for him at least, the first door he tried was Mama's. And of course if you are the richest widow on the Calle san Gregorio, with your fortune under your mattress, you always sleep with one eye open, alert to every floorboard that creaks and to every door that opens and closes.

For the third time Mama told us the story of what had transpired. Her hands were on her hips and her voice was powerful. She had a bit of a swagger to her now. She began to declaim.

"When he opened the door and I saw his face I was sure he was the devil himself. So I roared out, 'You are not having me or my money.' But he kept on coming so I lifted up the stick I keep by the side of my bed and caught him a hell of a whack to the side of his head."

She picked up the stick, which was now lying on the table in front of her, and raised it savagely above her head.

"What did he do then Mama?" Denis called out.

"He fled of course, the yellow tailed devil. Fled like the coward he always is."

Walt told us later that she had been a rabble rouser when she was young but that she had married a bullfighter from Cordoba who had beaten her up and crushed her spirit.

After that we turned once again to Roy who was, like the rest of us, enjoying his churros and coffee. Venezia looked at him admiringly.

"But weren't you frightened Roy dear? He might have had a gun."

We looked again at the tall brawny Scotsman seated rugged and handsome before us. Again we thought how we had underestimated and misunderstood him!

He was sitting at the head of the table. His features were composed and solemn. Once we had quietened he began to address us:

"Where I grew up in Dundee when the richest widow in the street shouts out in the middle ah the night there's only thing goin' on. Some wee stoat (trans: scoundrel, scallywag, petty thief) has his hand under her mattress and's trying to remove her bawbees (trans: valuables, jewellery or money)."

He looked slowly around our little group searching out, with his steely Football Manager's eye, anyone foolish enough to dispute this construction he had placed on events. Then he continued:

"So I'm up, quick as a flash. Straightaway focused. Pullin' on ma drawers, ready for action."

Again he stopped to look around and again we all were silent, admiring both the speed with which he had moved and the arrhythmic intonation of his Scottish patois. Mama, still rejuvenated and resplendent, leaned over to top up his coffee cup.

But now he was into his stride with his story and his words were beginning to flow.

"So I'm comin' into the corridor just as El Lobo's steppin' out ah the old woman's room. He's got the air ah a ratty man (trans: tramp who sleeps on the street). Hair down over his ears and big sharp teeth stickin' out. Got a whiff on him you wouldna believe. Then he sees me and he rears up but he knows he's cornered. So he does the only thing he can, he launches himself toward me tryin' to knock me out ah the game. But Roy Babadouche has been around a long time and knows a thing or too, so I waits till he's in close then I pulls ma ring finger clean down the side of his cheek as hard as I can and the wee stoat's straight down on the floor squealin' his head off, pumping blood, his hands over his cheek like I've cut his throat."

At this point all our eyes went to the heavy chunky ring that Roy wore on his pinky.

"And do yer know what the wee stoat did then?" He was staring fiercely around the table.

None of us could reply to this question as we were still trying to absorb this brutal information we had been given. Mama's eyes were wide open with admiration and envy for this strong bold man with his strange accent. She was certain he could have been as great a bull fighter as her husband.

"He only grabs out and catches ma foot and sinks his bloody teeth into ma ankle doesn't he?"

He lifted up his leg and rolled down his sock and we could see the thin line of the bite mark. He shook his head in disgust.

"I always tell ma players. Never give a sucker an even break. Oh dearie me. I had the wee stoat down on the ground, what ever was I thinking. I should have known he'd pull a trick like that, the wee bugger."

He looked round angrily.

"I'm hoppin' around on one leg trying to get ma balance back but he's up and gone, a slippery bugger, slippery as a Highland eel, down the stairs, through the door and away to fuck knows where."

He stopped there and we wondered for a moment if the story had come to an inconclusive end. It was Venezia who broke the silence.

"But what's really great." She had pitched her voice in a register that was deliberately sweet and pure. "Is the way you did not give up the chase Roy, even though you had been bitten on the ankle."

She looked directly at him, eyes wide with admiration. She compared him to her own Echo, who to his embarrassment had slept through the whole adventure.

"Yous certainly right there Venezia," Roy replied, seduced by her flattery. "Ah never gives up. I chased the wee bugger half way down the street dodgin' the people coming out of the clubs and the bars."

"Yelling out stop thief, stop thief," said Venezia, again admiringly.

"So I did," Roy replied. He looked around the room again daring anyone to challenge him.

Then Venezia let the register of her voice slip a note. "But in that case why didn't you catch him Roy dear?"

"Bloody hell hen!" Roy exploded. "Gi' us a bloody break! Ah dunna ken the layout of the streets in this town do ah? Dundee or London I'd have had him straight off but this is Spain. I could see him in front o' me, staggering all over the road, the blood pouring from his heed. He was a goner, anyone could see that, ah only needed a few more paces and I would have nabbed him but then the slippery bugger was away down a side street and into a crowd outside a club. Ah couldn't get through and he was off and away to his wee hidey hole."

He stopped and looked around angrily.

It was then that Echo made was later referred to as a 'sly and ill considered' intervention. Keeping his voice low he slowly placed a copy of the morning paper on to the table.

"But among the throng of night club revellers who witnessed the chase there were also photographers on the look out for local celebrities."

Roy glared at him.

The photograph took up half the front page. Roy was spread out, clad only in his tartan combinations, hair flowing, knobbly knees pumping, running hard. The headline above the picture read (in Spanish) THE GUV'NR GIVES CHASE – OCH AYE!

But Echo had mistimed his attempt at humour. The rest of us had analysed the situation correctly. Behind his back Oscar may have referred to him as Old Muttonhead and even Biffo the Dundee Mule, and we may all have considered at one time that Our Noble Savage was a suitable appellation. But we had now learned that Roy Babadouche was in fact a man of great courage and integrity - which were of course the reasons for his being knighted by the Queen.

So it was from this point in our journey that we welcomed Pilgrim Roy fully and unreservedly into our little group.

16

When Wilson, who has aspirations to be a writer himself, had finished reading the opening pages of this narrative he said that in his opinion not sufficient mention had been made of the fact there were other pilgrims walking this road as well.

"We don't have road to ourselves," he said. "We're not the only ones. There are hundreds more."

This omission is acknowledged by the writer, but by way of defence it is stated that it is not possible, due to limitations of space, to describe every pilgrim met on the way. However during the course of the narrative it is anticipated that a representative selection of the types of pilgrim encountered will be given.

The writer also states that because this group was led by a certain Walt Whitman, who had walked the path many times before and who had in places created his own route, and because this group generally camped out rather than staying in refuges, fewer pilgrims were met than might have been expected.

Because of these extenuating circumstances Wilson's complaint is considered to be an exaggeration.

For the record, from Marciac on the Chemin d'Arles in southern France, via the Camino Aragones and until we reached the junction with the Camino Frances at Puente la Reina, we encountered no more than twenty other pilgrims.

Again, and for the record, one of those was a middle aged man with short white hair who told us that when he had been walking through the Romanian countryside he had encountered a troupe of gypsies leading a bear.

"They had attached a rope to a collar around its neck and it was very tame," he told us. "I was even able to stroke its nose."

A second pilgrim, a younger woman, told us of the night she had spent in a hotel high in the Western Rhodope mountains in Bulgaria.

"I was woken out of a deep sleep by the sound of a man's voice singing," she said. "I sensed it was coming from high up in the mountains. It was so rich and deep but at the same time it was very melancholic. But when I described it to the owner of the hotel in the morning he said that he had heard nothing at all."

In the city of Pamplona we saw a number of other pilgrims, but being busy with our own affairs we did not talk to any of them. In the morning before we left we visited shoe shops and selected a light pair for Jack. We also had our credencials or pilgrim's passports stamped. (These credencials are presented on arrival at Santiago and are proof that the pilgrimage has been made).

17

From Zizur Mayor, where we picked up our donkeys once more, the path gently ascends the flank of the Alto del Perdon. When we reached the crest we noted the strange metal statues that have been erected there, in heroic mode, representing us pilgrims as we continue West on our endless struggle.

Here we stopped, the strong wind in our faces and Venezia lined us up by the metal statues.

"We must have a photograph," she said brightly. "It will be a record of our progress to look back on in the future."

Just then two German pilgrims, a man and his wife, came up the path behind us. This was our first encounter with Hang Dog Heinz and his Charming Wife. We encountered them many times again on our pilgrimage and learned something of their story. But for now, on this windswept crest with rain threatening, we were happy to ask them to be our camera operators, pressing the button, so that we could all be in the shot.

We lined up with Roy in the centre. His actions had been so heroic in Pamplona that he deserved the Captain's Position. To the left of him we put Walt and to the right Echo. Next to Echo went Venezia and next to her stood Denis. On the other flank alongside Walt were Oscar and Wilson. On the end of the line was Jack. Next to him were our two beloved donkeys Thatcher and Blair.

Looking at the photograph now it is easy to be disappointed that it is not more colourful. But that day the wind was up, the sky was dark, rain was imminent and we had on our thick coats and waterproofs. So it was something of an impromptu picture.

However Roy is smiling broadly and Echo has his arm around Venezia. But Wilson has been caught with his eyes half closed and Jack is looking down at his donkeys. There are two splashes of colour. The first is Oscar's multi coloured coat with its vivid greens and browns and occasional flashes of orange. The second is a red scarf that Venezia has wrapped around her neck.

What would someone think who saw this picture but did not know us? Would he or she discern our strengths and our weaknesses, our foibles and failures, our moments of happiness and despair? Would they know that Roy was heroic? Would they appreciate Venezia's beauty? Would the great sense of adventure that we all felt be somehow communicated? Or would the picture be simply put down and another picked up without comment? In the end only time will tell on that.

In a valley people feel constrained. But from a pass or a ridge with an open horizon and sky ahead, their spirits rise.

So when our photograph had been taken we looked back a last time over the city of Pamplona which we had been sorry to leave so quickly.

(Behind us now was also the Col du Somport and the Pyrenees and the valley of the Rio Aragon. Our path was always West.)

Then with the glorious wet autumn wind on our faces we began our descent down over the rough ground that would take us toward Estella.

(Those who go lower down by the road report observing the first vineyards since crossing the French border, indicating the approach to the wine growing region of Rioja with its capital Logrono).

Our descent was more difficult via a series of ' gulches' and gullies with steep inclines. This made it hard going for our two donkeys and led after a while to an abrupt exchange of words between Jack and Walt.

"I don't know why we didn't go by the road," Jack complained sharply as Thatcher lost her footing for a second time and slipped to one side. "My donkeys can't take much more of this."

"You have to let them go at their own pace," Walt replied crossly. "In the old days we never had a problem. You have to learn to lead them properly."

Further conversation was curtailed when Blair's pannier slipped abruptly to the right and we had to stop while Roy and Jack, both now in bad humour and blaming Walt, redistributed the weight and then tightened up the girth again. The wind had dropped but had been replaced by a thin rain. We paused briefly to eat the bread and fruit and chocolate we had brought with us.

"How much more is there of this?" asked Denis glumly as we ate. Our exhilaration of the morning had gone. The rain and the rough going had sapped our morale.

"To the city of Logrono about three days," Walt replied from under his cape. " I am taking us north of Puente la Reina. It is a   route I know. Then it is West. Estella, Los Arcos, Viana. As to this rough terrain, another couple of hours should see us through."

As we finished up our lunch and got ready to move on again Walt made an attempt to lift our mood.

"Pilgrims never fear. Logrono is an elegant city with beautiful ladies who dress in the richest fur coats. You can see them on a crisp winter's evening as they stroll past the brightly lit stores. You will enjoy it there. I always eat and drink well in Logrono."

But Echo, living up to his title of the African Autodidact and in 'impish' mood, perhaps because of the rain and the roughness of the path, gave us a contrary view.

"Actually Walt, Logrono Cono is a good old Spanish term of abuse. And it fairly indicates how the people of that fair city are viewed by other citizens of Spain."

After that we trudged on, tired now and simply concentrating on leading our donkeys and keeping our feet.

Half an hour later when the rain had reduced sufficiently we were able to push back the hoods of our capes once again. It was always a relief to be able to get rid of that clammy suffocating feeling those hoods gave us.

It was felt, by all members of our group, that the attacks by Oscar on Roy, especially in the light of what had transpired in Pamplona, had been hostile and unfair. So when Venezia began a critical interrogation of Oscar we felt that he was only ' getting what he deserved.'

"Your wife Sheila must love you very much to create such a splendid multi coloured jacket," she began. "But we have never heard you talk about her. Have you left her at home or what?"

"No," Howard replied sharply. "She just left."

"What do you mean she just left." Venezia's voice sounded surprised.

"What I said," replied Howard firmly. He kept on walking. "She just left. Vamoosed. Cleared off. Just like that."

After that we walked on in silence pondering this strange information. Then when we came to a space where the path opened out Venezia stopped and confronted him face to face.

"Are you telling us she walked out on you with out any warning at all?"

"Yes," Oscar replied. He was staring straight back at Venezia now. "That is exactly what I mean. It was a great shock. One day she was there and the next day she was gone, taking with her only a small suitcase."

All the members of our little caravan had stopped now. We were all gathered around Oscar.

"How long ago did this happen Oscar?" It was Jack putting the question now.

"Two years ago."

"Did she have a reason?"

"Not that I know of. I thought she was happy. There is no doubt it is a great mystery."

"What about your boys?"

"They are mystified too. They have had no contact either."

Even Roy was looking puzzled now. He opened his mouth to ask a question but Venezia had taken up the interrogation once again.

"Well did you notify the police?"

"Yes, of course, when I became worried. They said that if I did not tell them what I had done with her they would dig up the garden, but they never did. They said in the end they could find no evidence of any wrong doing, and that it was one of those things, that she was an adult and that if she wanted to leave that was her business."

We wanted to interrogate Oscar further, especially on the question of whether he had taken out any life insurance policies before his wife disappeared, but when we saw the closed look on his face and the way his lips were pursed we desisted. We also did not ask Oscar how he came to be on pilgrimage - though our suspicion was that it might actually be a ' pilgrimage of convenience.'

(However it should be stated clearly at this point that there is absolutely no evidence that Oscar was responsible for the disappearance of his wife Sheila. It was only the meanest supposition on our part. And again our judgement was certainly affected by the way Oscar had treated Roy).

After lunch we continued our slow descent, the two donkeys slipping and sliding on the muddy and uneven path. We had many things on our minds as we walked.

We considered again the heroic actions of Pilgrim Roy in Pamplona, but we worried also that we might have enraged El Lobo even more. We were aware that he could be lying in wait for us anywhere along the path. The story that Oscar had told us was also running through our minds.

At about four o'clock the landscape opened out to rough pasture where flocks of sheep and goats were being watched over by shepherds. The rain finally ceased, the wind dropped and the clouds parted and we were treated at last to some late afternoon sunshine.

This cheered our mood which had become discouraged by the rain and the difficulty of the descent and the strangeness of Oscar's story. As we advanced our pace, coming at last to a more open stretch which gave us a view over open country to the South, we could see fields of dark earth being tilled by tractors.

We stopped briefly so that Jack could adjust Thatcher's panniers. If the weight is not equally distributed, the whole ensemble can slip to one side. It was as Jack was working and as Roy was re tightening the girth that we saw in the distance coming toward us three pilgrims.

As they approached we could see that they were three women. As they drew near we greeted them. Two of the women, who were older, told us they were German, from Berlin. The third woman was from Macedonia.

The older of the German women told us:

"After our stay in Santiago we could not find the courage to board the plane so instead we are returning on foot and we are much happier for our decision."

They then told us the good news that about two miles ahead there was an old farmhouse that had been converted into a country refuge.

"It's not busy at all," the German woman said. "In fact you may be the only guests. It is actually run by Hans Klugman and his wife Lottie. Hans is well known in Germany as a musician."

With this information received and therefore not having to think of erecting tents and cooking over an open fire, and free from worry about being ambushed by El Lobo, we were more than happy to pause for a moment in the warm late afternoon sunshine to talk to these friendly pilgrims.

We arranged ourselves on the ground and Echo passed around slabs of chocolate. Then the Macedonian woman said that if we were not in a hurry she had a story she would like to tell us. Walt replied on our behalf that we were always happy to listen to a pilgrim who had a story to tell.

So this is the story that the woman, who called herself Elena and who had a round dark face and whose age we calculated at about thirty, told us:

"I will tell you first of all that I am from a small village in the hills of Macedonia, a little to the south of Skopje."

She paused, her eyes half closed, as if for a moment she was remembering this place. Then her eyes flicked open again.

"So, of course, I am married, my husband's name is Nikola and we have three children whose names are Petar, Marija and Violeta and whose ages in descending order are ten, six and four."

This information she disclosed quickly, as if laying out the undisputed facts of a case. Then she altered her position, stretching out a leg, as if she had become suddenly uncomfortable.

"Nikola, who I love very much, is a shepherd and he works with his father tending a flock of goats and sheep in the hills. Every evening I take Violeta our youngest, who is his favourite, to the edge of the garden to meet them as they come down."

She stopped once again. We could she was remembering those pastoral days. At the same time we noted that one of the German women, who we calculated must have heard this story before, had risen to her feet and was giving Thatcher a lump of sugar from the palm of her hand. Elena was continuing.

"Then one day in the town they open up a factory and to my surprise my husband gives up his life as a shepherd to work there. He says he is doing it for me and the children. So we can have a better life. Buy our own house, buy a car and so on."

She moved her position again, stretching a leg and looked at the other German woman who was still sitting next to her. We noted the scowl on her face.

"It's not right for him. I told him. I said you are a country man. You should be outside. Your face is growing pale from being in the factory. But not a bit of it. When a man gets an obsession."

She stopped and sniffed and looked around as if defying any one of us to question her story. The second German woman had risen to her feet now and was stretching her legs.

"Before we had the most beautiful life you could imagine. Now it is being ruined. Our poor family is coming apart. The children never see their father."

She paused and we leaned forward sensing that she was coming to an important part of her story. She lowered her voice.

"Then one night I have an amazing dream. I am on pilgrimage. I am dressed in brightly coloured clothes and I am walking, crossing mountains and rivers. The dream comes back the following night and then the night after until I am dreaming it almost every night. We begin to discuss it. And suddenly it starts to become more detailed. I can see myself kneeling before Saint James in Santiago de Compostela and he is answering my prayers.

"So I said to Nikola I am being called. There is a reason for this. You have your job in the factory. My parents can look after the children. None of you will miss me for a while. This is important. You are not going to refuse me."

She moved her position again as if trying to get comfortable. The German woman had resumed her place on the ground.

"Places are found for me to stay. Even companions to walk with. We have many connections with Spain. There are cousins who live in Bilbao."

There was a brief pause then before Venezia leaned forward impatiently and asked the question that was on all our minds.

"Well has St James delivered the miracle for which you hoped? Are good family relations restored?"

Elena paused before answering this question. Finally she said:

"I did as my dream indicated. I knelt in the cathedral. I asked for the intervention of Saint James. And now I have my two new companions here."

She indicated the two German women who were now both sitting one on either side of her.

"I have made many other friends as well."

She paused again. Then she said:

"My husband will pick me up in Bilbao in the car that he has bought with the money he has earned working in the factory. He is bringing the children with him."

She looked around our little group. We could see that her eyes were sharp.

"And so we will have to wait and see won't we?"

After a few minutes more of idle chat, when we exchanged information on the route and other pilgrim ' gossip,' we watched the three of them disappear into the distance until all that remained of Elena and her companions and the strange story she had told us was a small ball of dust on the horizon.

Then Venezia looked thoughtful.

"I hope that Elena has done enough to bring her husband to his senses and make him more attentive to her in the future."

Oscar was sceptical. "I doubt it. That is the sort of story you could read in any woman's magazine."

Roy and Echo nodded in agreement.

"I think they were up to something," Echo then said. "If we have our wits about us we will check our pockets and the panniers to see that nothing is missing."

This we did - finding to our disappointment that a considerable sum of money and a good quality pocket knife had gone.

The moral to that story is that while most pilgrims are honest, open and decent, there are rotten apples too. Pilgrims not paying attention to their security may find themselves counting the cost.

18

An hour later with the sun dipping toward the Western horizon and a tiredness creeping over us we turned down a track to a stone farmhouse surrounded by trees. As we approached we could hear music coming from the house.

Echo stopped and listened. Then he laughed.

"Well pilgrims here is a test. I suppose you will recognise the music as the Ride of the Valkyries from Wagner's Ring Cycle. But I always here it as the theme from the film Apocalypse Now which is based on Joseph Conrad's novel Heart of Darkness. And that is a book which documented the terrible cruelties of Belgian colonial rule in my beloved Congo."

When we reached the house a few moments later the music, which had been coming from a loudspeaker attached to an outside wall, was clicked off and a small man with an angry face and red hair emerged from a door and eyed us up warily.

"The menu is house choice if you want to eat." His voice was as sharp as his visage. "Normally I ask for a reservation. Seven thirty. No later. Gentlemen. Ladies. Please."

Then he took a handkerchief from his pocket and blew his nose loudly before turning on his heel and going back inside closing the door sharply behind him.

A moment later it opened again and a thin woman with a pale face and long hair emerged to show us where we could sleep and to indicate to Jack the field at the back where he could leave Thatcher and poor Blair.

We were eventually lodged in a bunk house that was clean enough. Walt looked around and pronounced himself satisfied.

"This does not really count as a refuge as we have it to ourselves," Walt told us as he looked around. "Refuges are usually full up with other pilgrims and stink like hell."

After that we sorted out our beds and then watched as Jack sat himself down on his bunk and removed his new shoes and socks to see how his feet had fared since leaving Pamplona.

"Well that is an improvement anyway," he said after he had concluded his examination. "It looks like you were right there Walt. Those old army boots were no good. The skin has not broken open again and I have been much easier today."

Then he stood up and stretched.

"I may be cured but I must watch out for my donkeys. They are hardy little fellows but I don't want them going lame like me."

He looked at Walt, who set our distance for the day.

"Don't push them too hard Walt. If they crack up we are done for."

(It was now the received wisdom among our little pilgrim band that Jack put the welfare of his two donkeys above the welfare of his fellow pilgrims. He was now training up Roy to be his assistant).

When we were ready we went out onto a terrace. There we sat at two plastic tables that had been pushed together. The yard at the back of the house contained two car bodies without wheels and a child's toy tractor. Suddenly the speaker clicked on again and we found ourselves privileged to listen to a selection of popular operatic arias as the sun set.

There were many things for us to contemplate and discuss as we sat there that evening on the terrace. While El Lobo and the danger he represented was still a concern, the music to which we were now listening reminded us of the power and presence of the great artists.

"It comes back to our previous debate," Wilson said. "We were discussing Robert Lenkiewicz. True artists have the power to touch us all. That is the test. The fraud will always leave you cold."

At half past seven the thin woman with the pale face emerged from the kitchen carrying a tray.

"There has been a delay," Her voice was as thin as her form. "An unaccountable delay."

She put down the tray on which we could see there were packets of biscuits and a good wedge of strong goat's cheese. "I hope you will enjoy this. The cheese is from our own flock."

When she had gone we tucked into the cheese and did enjoy it, but when we looked around the yard we could see no evidence of any animals.

Ten minutes later a naked light above us was switched on and the woman appeared again, this time accompanied by a small boy. She removed the tray with the remnants of the cheese and biscuits and replaced with it a selection of salads which once again we devoured hungrily.

Ten minutes after that, in the same manner, bottles of red wine were placed on the table followed by plates of rice and a good strong Indian curry.

"That is the ticket," said Jack as we ate hungrily. "I have been waiting for that all day."

Roy was also enthusiastic. "I couldna' find a better curry in Dundee on a Saturday night. It's rippin' ma throat out."

When we had finished we lounged back satisfied. Then as we drank the last of the wine and lit up cigarettes we realised to our amusement that we had eaten our excellent meal in exact reverse order.

We were contemplating this fact when the man with the red hair and the angry face came out from the kitchen.

Wiping his hands on his apron he said:

"Following the recipe book. Never made it before. Hope the delay did not ruin the enjoyment of the meal."

It was Jack who replied sincerely on our behalf: "We are all getting used to this foreign food now. There is something to it. If half the restaurants of England could do as good a job as you have done tonight we would be starting to get somewhere."

After that Roy poured our host a glass of wine and he sat down to join us.

We made our introductions learning as we had expected that our host was Hans Klugman and that it was his wife Lottie who had served us.

"A musician really. Last position conducting a symphony orchestra. Given it all up to move here with Lottie and young son Hans (Jr). Running this small pilgrim refuge now."

As we talked Lottie brought us more wine. It was Wilson who finally enunciated the thought that was running through all our minds.

"It is our intention to create a written narrative of this journey we are undertaking," he explained to Hans. "There is also a consideration that we may turn it into a film in which case we will need accompanying music."

Hans was already leaning forward and nodding his head enthusiastically. His angry visage of earlier in the evening, which we now put down to the stress of unexpected guests and trying out a new dish, had disappeared.

"Of course, of course," he replied. "Good idea. A film. You want music for a film. Yes indeed I will get to work on it straightaway."

Then he looked around suddenly anxious.

"Will tomorrow morning be alright? I can work through the night. It will be most exciting. I have not had a commission since we left Bremen a year ago."

After that he quizzed us as to our journey thus far, making notes on a piece of paper, and asking us how we saw the rest of the pilgrimage unfolding. We gave him an account of our adventures - although we did not mention, for obvious reasons, El Lobo and the bank robbery in Zaragoza.

After we had talked for an hour and finished another bottle of wine Hans laid down his pen and sat back and said he knew exactly what was wanted and that if we would excuse him he would start work immediately.

A little while later, after Jack Phillpotts had seen to his donkeys, making sure they had sufficient water and sufficient pasture, we finally went to our beds. We were confident that in Jack's words Hans would do a ' good job' for us.

In the morning when we rose the sky was already bright. When we were seated at the table on the terrace Lottie brought us steaming hot coffee and plates piled high with bread and butter and jam. As we were tucking in we heard the loud speakers click and then to our delight our ears were assailed by an intricate, playful and boisterous mix of melodies and songs.

For a moment we stopped eating and shut our eyes. Our host had interwoven a dozen different themes to create a single continual sense of movement. Denis later referred to it is an 'astonished' movement. We knew straightaway that it was music that would inspire us. We also knew that as music to a film it would carry any cinema audience with us as we made our way over the rich Spanish countryside.

When it was finished there was a crackling and then our host's voice came over the speaker.

"Hope that is alright. Had some problems with a couple of the sequences."

Then a couple of minutes later he appeared and we all shook his hand.

He looked happy and slightly embarrassed to receive our thanks. When we discussed a payment for his work he was firm in his refusal.

"A great pleasure. Arranging again. Only ask that when the narrative is completed credit be given to Hans Klugman of Bremen, musician, conductor, arranger and refuge owner."

And this of course we are happy to do.

(For the record Echo was able to identify: Mamani Keita, Kedide from her album Yelema; Orchestra Baobab, Pape Ndiaye; Happy Days are Here Again, Ben Selvin and the Crooners; La Mer by Charles Trenet; A waltz from Rigoletto played in quick time by an unknown pianist; Driss El Maloumi on the oud; Sing Hosanna - Give Me Oil in My Lamp by an unknown choir; Buena Vista Social Club, Chan Chan. The selection was bookended by tunes from the Galician folk ensemble Luar Na Lubre. There were other tunes, that even Echo, with all his learning, could not identify straightaway. The whole was presented as a continuous swooping swirling loop). (Readers can find links to this music at tantanbooks.co.uk).

Half an hour later Jack had brought our two donkeys into the yard and with Roy was loading them up when Lottie came out carrying a collecting tin. On the side of it was written in faded hand written letters Please Help The Lepers of the Belgian Congo.

As she passed the tin around Lottie explained:

"My father worked for many years as a doctor with the lepers of the Belgian Congo and said they were people in great need so I try to support them as best I can."

As can be imagined this affected Echo very much and he put a good sum into the tin.

(Wilson was the only pilgrim who declined to contribute. He reiterated his principle, quite sternly, that to give to beggars only allowed governments to evade their responsibilities to the poor).

Then Echo explained to Lottie his origins and his attachment to his native country of the Congo. Then the two of them then embraced and we could see that there were tears in both their eyes.

Then Walt took details of the leper colony, where it was and so on - we all knew what he was thinking - and after that we thanked our hosts and under bright clear skies we set off once more on our Westward journey.

19

Two hours later we passed the southern edge of the town of Estella where we stopped to buy essential supplies from a small store. As we stood outside the store enjoying the sunshine Walt was reflective.

"I have been thinking about our friend Hans Klugman and the music he has given us," he said slowly. "If were to be given my time over again I would prefer to be a musician rather than a writer. The music Hans has given us speaks directly to our souls. Words are always capable of misinterpretation."

When we moved on again Walt and Venezia took the lead with Jack and Oscar dropping back with our two donkeys.

As we walked we were struck by the way the sun, now casting strange pale shadows, was making Venezia's slim form merge with the grass and the trees and the bushes.

Oscar had already said that in his opinion Venezia took her life from the Book of Imagination. And certainly there was something 'ethereal' about her. By comparison the rest of us were very leaden footed.

It was left to Echo to supply, as always, a contrary view.

He told us privately: "Actually pilgrims in the takeaway you always have to be on your toes with Venezia. She is a regular demon. Any supplier failing to deliver is dismissed on the spot and no customer leaves without paying."

Then when we stopped for lunch and were lounging back on the rough grass, enjoying the warmth of the midday sun, happy to put off the moment when we would have to get on our feet again, Oscar, holding a mug full of coffee in his hand, turned to Venezia.

"You interrogated me severely yesterday as to my personal life. And before that you told us a story about how you were such an ugly duckling when you were young which frankly none of us believed. So now I am going to turn the tables." He looked at her. "We think there is an air of mystery and insubstantiality about you. We think you should disclose more about your background."

We were lolling in the sunshine. Echo was wearing his conical rice growers hat, Jack had removed his boots and socks to air his feet and Walt was working a new feather into the brim of his hat.

Because of this relaxed atmosphere Venezia, in high good humour, and sitting cross legged on the grass in front of us, a smile on her sweet lips, decided to tell us a rather ' teasing' story.

"Well Pilgrims," she began after we had settled down. "The story of my early life in which you are all apparently so interested can be encapsulated in seven simple words. My Father Was A Five Star General."

We stopped what we were doing and looked at her in mild surprise. Then we thought of her ability to cook over an open fire and erect a tent.

Denis leaned forward.

"You do mean in the army don't you Venezia?"

Venezia laughed.

"Well he certainly did not work in a haberdashery store did he Denis dear?"

Another day such a crisply delivered retort would have left Denis feeling foolish but this sunny day the normal ' cut and sting' of Venezia's tongue was absent. We were all in good humour and the joke was enjoyed.

It was Oscar who took up the questioning.

"I suppose that would have been a difficult upbringing for you then Venezia?"

"You could certainly say that Oscar. We lived in the far North of the Province of Quebec. The Good Old General and His Lady Wife taught me to sit up straight at table and not to answer back. Aside from that it was hell on earth. When I was sixteen years old I ran away to Mexico City."

She looked around gauging our reaction, then she said:

"I will not keep the suspense going for you boys any longer so I will tell you that I got a job in a night club as an exotic dancer."

At this astonishing information Jack Phillpotts opened his mouth and then shut it again without speaking. Roy removed his baseball cap and scratched his head and muttered something to himself in his low Scots patois. Even Walt looked staggered.

It was Wilson who first recovered his power of speech to comment, in correct Socialist Manner:

"That sounds to me like a classic case of Sexual Exploitation."

At this Venezia laughed delightfully.

"Oh Wilson, you are an idiot." She slapped her hand against her thigh. "I was having the time of my life. I was the headline act at The Lively Cat in Mexico City. I was Liza Minnelli in Cabaret. I slept all day and rich businessmen brought me champagne all night."

Her voice now took on the prim tones of a schoolmistress.

"I am now going to give you one guess each as to why I was dismissed from my job as the headline act at The Lively Cat in Mexico City."

We were all puzzled by this question and the strange turn this story was taking. It was Jack who finally took up the challenge.

"Alright I will have a go if that is the game we are playing. I will say the club was raided by the police."

"No Jack, not that."

After that we all guessed one by one and we all failed. Even a bewildered Roy joined in.

"Because you'd no paid yer council tax hen?"

We all laughed at this.

Then Venezia said teasingly.

"I will give you a clue. A false accusation was made."

But we were still unable to come up with the answer. This allowed Venezia, a moment later, to spring the trap she had carefully prepared. She leaned toward us a smile on her lips.

"One of our most important customers, a Mexico City businessman complained to the manager that I had one breast larger than the other. That is why I had to go. If it got out that The Lively Cat employed lob sided dancers the business would have been ruined."

Venezia looked around in triumph. She had stunned her male audience into silence. None of us knew which way to look. We had questions to ask but were too embarrassed to put them. Then Walt started to laugh.

"Very funny Venezia. A story well told. You should go into the theatre, become an actress. Because of course this is all made up to tease us gullible men. I happen to know that you are the respectable daughter of two Montreal school teachers and that you have never given your family a moment's trouble in your life."

At this Venezia got up from her position on the grass.

"Well I ain't saying no more." She exaggerated her Quebecoise accent. "I reckon I said enough already."

And with that she left us puzzled and 'gullible' men and went over to where Thatcher and Blair were grazing peacefully. Then she turned and imitated the call that Jack so often gave us.

"If we don't get these damn animals loaded up and get on our way we might as well pitch camp for the night right now."

20

The sky remained bright for the rest of the afternoon, and as the path had also flattened out, Walt led us forward at a good pace in the direction of our next destination, the city of Logrono. As we walked we mused over the story Venezia had told us and chuckled to ourselves at being so easily taken in.

But by early evening with the sky still clear the temperature began to drop and a decision was made to halt and pitch camp early. (We were nearby the town of Los Arcos). This would allow time for Oscar and Denis to help Wilson gather additional wood for our fire.

Soon we had our tents up, Jack was tending to the donkeys and as usual Venezia and Echo were preparing dinner. We had bought strips of lamb in Estella and soon they were grilling over the bright flames, the fat sizzling and bursting. The wood that Wilson, with the help of Oscar and Denis, had chopped and dragged back to the camp was piled up next to our fire ready to keep us warm through the evening.

We loved those clear cold nights when all the stars were bright above us. Walt drilled us in the basics. He ensured we could pick out the Pole Star and thus identify direction North. He also showed us where to find the main constellations and the planets.

But we also become keen watchers of the planes as they flew over us. (Pilgrims can become obsessive over small detail. In fact it could be argued that the whole journey, the whole pilgrimage itself, is one large obsession).

Our interest had begun when we had passed close to the airport at Pau in southern France. We had stopped to watch the heavy planes struggling, like awkward penguins, to get into the air.

After Pau we had begun to follow the vapour trails. When the day was clear we could make out the delicate silver bodies of the planes. To us they were shaped like winged bullets. For planes flying East to West we named the North American cities where we calculated they might land. In the end we could even pick out the air corridors where the planes turned (there is one over northern Portugal) to enter a different air space. Finally at the conclusion of our journey we passed by the airport at Santiago de Compostela and watched the planes landing.

Walt said we were drawn to the planes because we were at the opposite end of the scale from them.

"Their view is futuristic and cartographic," he said. "By contrast you are backward looking and myopic."

That night as we ate the lamb Venezia and Echo had prepared for us, feeling the rich texture of the meat and the fat in our mouths, we looked up to the night sky in anticipation. We were not disappointed. We counted a dozen planes, identifiable at night only by their flashing lights, passing over our field of vision.

"How strange it is," Venezia said, "That when we awake in the morning and emerge from our tents half frozen with cold the people above us now will have landed in Chicago or in my home town of Montreal."

Denis nodded and added:

"And it is certainly strange that as they pass over us now the passengers are, like us, also eating their dinner."

Would any of them have looked out of their plane window to reflect that a group of poor pilgrims were huddled around a fire below them in the manner of stone age primitives? Probably not.

When we had finished our dinner Roy opened another bottle of wine and passed it round so that we could refill our mugs. Then we had a sudden fear that he was going to revert to type when he began to complain about the cold.

"It's bloody baltic (trans: cold) out here." He shivered and pulled his thick coat around him. "Ten below easy. It's cold enough ta freeze the baws off a Highland Queen."

We all laughed at this but Roy shook his head.

"Naw, naw, ah dunna know about all this. Ah reckon ah'm turning inta some sort a mincy heid (trans: weak minded person). If ah had any sense ah'd be home right now tucked up beside ma beautiful wife Mary."

We now loved and appreciated Roy for his quick wit and his courage, but at the same we were no longer in awe, as we had been, of his standing as a man of International and Stellar Proportions. (The same could be said of our attitude to Walt). Venezia in particular had Roy's measure.

She faced him sternly now and said in her faux serious voice:

"You know full well why you are here Roy Babadouche, Sir. It is because you are Our Great Leader. Without your heroic efforts we would be completely lost."

Then she leaned forward and muzzled her face cheekily into his chin.

"And if you don't stop your complaining I am going to call you a Fausse Couche which is rude Quebecois French for someone who is the ugly one, the runt of the litter."

Roy looked puzzled at this. For a moment the situation was delicately balanced. Then he laughed and the moment of tension was defused.

21

Little by little as we advanced West toward Santiago de Compostela we were telling the stories of our lives and tonight it was the turn of Wilson.

"We know nothing about your background." Jack turned to him. "Only that you come from Northern socialist stock and that at one time you were a card carrying member. We also know that it is your ambition to be a writer of note one day.

Venezia gave us an indication of her personality this afternoon. It is your turn now."

Wilson thought a long time before replying to this request. We watched the flames flickering up from the fire as we waited. With his close cropped hair and his round glasses, through which his green eyes glistened, Wilson had an intense air.

Finally this is how he began:

"Well pilgrims you know already that I am an out of work article writer, an admirer of the work of Robert Lenkiewicz and a despiser of modern abstract painters. I consider that they have no soul. I also happen to consider that societies that are based on equality are better than societies based on inequality."

He turned to look at us. His base position now outlined he could continue.

"But as to the background of my youth I would like to tell you that when I was sixteen I was a daredevil motorbike rider in a circus in Blackpool. But that came to the attention of the authorities so I was sent down to Plymouth in Devon to live with my uncle and his family who were steeple jacks. They had my politics. We were all socialists. But they were workers as well. And when they weren't working they were climbing."

After we had absorbed this brief and rapid summary of Wilson's career to date we watched as he stopped and stared at us again over the fire.

"So if you are going to pin a label onto me I would prefer actually that it read both climber and socialist."

At this Echo leaned forward. It was a typical interruption from the African Autodidact.

"Pilgrim Wilson, if you are planning to make a career out of writing mountaineering novels it is going to be short and sweet."

We all turned to stare at him.

"The field is restricted. If you exclude technical details of particular climbs, there are only three types of mountaineering story. There is the ascent of the summit story, the surviving death after being hit by a catastrophe story, and the rescuing a stricken companion story. That's it. Everything else is a variation.

This 'impish' provocation could have derailed Wilson's story before it had begun. But (sensibly) Wilson ignored it. Instead he responded simply:

"Well Pilgrim Echo, why don't we let our readers decide on that when the story is done? I think they will find that what I have to relate is original enough."

And with that he turned away from Echo and under the stars that night began his tale.

"The story I am going to relate to you begins one blustery October morning ten years ago." He looked around. "I can tell you for a fact comrades that steeplejacks won't go up when the wind is blowing hard. Like everyone else they want to see another day."

Denis added wood to the fire and the flames jumped up. Wilson continued:

"Because we couldn't work I had decided to walk into the city centre of Plymouth to put in the post to a climbing magazine photographs and an article describing an ascent we had made recently of a razor sharp ridge near Chamonix. I had turned the corner to go up to the Post Office on Old Town Street when I came to a sudden stop by a building near the Civic Centre."

Venezia pushed her hand nervously through her hair.

"So what was it you saw Wilson?"

Wilson paused. We could see once again his sharp ascetic eyes behind his glasses assessing us. Finally he said:

"What I saw was a woman, aged about twenty five, full figure, long flowing hair, perched on a narrow balcony ten floors up. Yelling her head off she was threatening to jump."

Venezia, realising what was to come, put her hand to her mouth.

"But the police, the fire brigade. You could have been killed. The story could have taken a terrible turn."

"No," Wilson replied. "It was the police and the fire brigade that were the difficulty. Everything they were doing was spooking her. The only chance was to come up from below."

Now it was Oscar's turn to interrupt. He leaned across the fire toward Wilson.

"Are you telling us you were ready to risk your life for someone you had never met?"

Wilson turned on him quickly.

"But you risked everything to drive the getaway car for El Lobo."

"That's right. But I needed to see if I was still alive."

Wilson nodded his head and leant forward and addressed us all.

"You get a moment when you are tested. Turn it down and you'll be the lesser man for the remainder of your life. I had free climbed cliffs over the sea. I knew I could do it."

His face was angular and serious. Venezia was looking at him with admiration. She was getting further confirmation that there was indeed a romantic and adventurous side to his nature.

Wilson took a deep breath. As he spoke the light of the stars and the moon lit up our little camp.

"What I am going to describe to you is a vertical straight up one mistake and you're dead free climb. It was done barefoot with no ropes. The climbing face was rough cement and pebble dash with sharp block edges for hand and feet holds."

Venezia curled her arms around her upraised knees and stared at Wilson. The rest of us, Echo even, were also listening carefully as Wilson began.

"I went up over the first two blocks too quickly and in a state of acute anxiety. But then I slowed down, regulated my breathing and discovered a rhythm. Serious climbing is about technique, concentration and rhythm. It is always leg to opposite arm, pull up, pause, repeat."

"You make it sound easy," Jack said. Wilson laughed.

"No, Jack. The concrete block edges were cutting into my feet and my fingers were struggling to grip. The wind was rising and starting to tug at me. At one point I looked down, which is the worst thing you can do. I saw the fire brigade and the police and the crowd on the ground below and had a moment of sickening vertigo and nearly fell."

We were all desperate to question Wilson as to whether he saw his life flashing before him as he made his crazy climb. We also wanted to ask if there had been something in the visage or manner of the girl that had tempted him onto this life threatening adventure and also whether as he climbed, hanging from the side of the building like a human spider, he had a vision of said damsel's visage before him to encourage him. But he was deep into his story and we could not interrupt. His voice was tense.

"On a free climb the push up with the leg is always the most dangerous moment. There is only that vertical upward motion holding you on. For a second you are actually balanced in mid air. The slightest hesitation, or simply lacking the necessary leg strength, and unforgiving gravity will destroy you."

We waited anxiously as Wilson drew breath. Then he continued:

"I am becoming aware of the decreasing suppleness of my feet and hands. Their power to grip on to the feet and hand holds is draining away."

He stopped again, looking down, touching the tips of those fingers together.

"The wind is increasing in strength the higher I get. This is becoming a serious problem. It is threatening to pull me away from the wall. All I can do is flatten face, body, legs as close to the dirty concrete as I can. Along with fingers and feet they complete an almost sexual bond."

We are all leaning forward now, following closely, even Walt, even Roy. Wilson takes a deep breath.

"I'm coming up below the balcony now. Despite the cold the sweat is running down my face. Then I see that the penny pinching builders have changed to a different type of block. The ledges and cracks are shallower. I remember thinking to myself well, that's it, it's all over, now I am done for, because I can't hold on long just using finger tips and toes."

"In other words Wilson," it was Oscar speaking. "You were hanging off the rock hard concrete like a desperate and wounded bird!"

"Correct, Oscar. The strength is now draining rapidly from my fingers and feet. The cutting pain of the concrete ledges has been replaced by a quick growing numbness. I estimate that the time left to move up from this block to the iron strut work below the balcony can be counted down in seconds."

We stared at Wilson across the fire. His face was white and drained. He was reliving the climb as he told the story.

"I had to surmount the metal strut work of the balcony which was directly above me. With the first grab I failed and for a moment I was falling back into space, but then I heaved up desperately with exhausted legs one more time and hooked a hand around the iron work. From there I scrabbled up over the front of the balcony ripping my feet to bloody shreds to confront the blank and incredulous face of this beautiful woman in distress I had come to rescue."

Wilson stopped and looked around. At this stage we still had our doubts as to the veracity of what we had heard. But it was then that Denis said:

"God, Wilson was that you?" We turned to stare at him. "There were TV pictures. It was on the news. I was in Plymouth working as a dentist then. You were the talk of the town. I had no idea."

We paused for a moment absorbing this unexpected information. Then Venezia reacted positively.

"Oh Wilson that is a wonderful story!" She held him by the arm. "But whatever happened to the girl? Was she an angel in disguise who danced ballet on the tips of her toes? And you married in a castle! I am sure you have beautiful blonde headed children!"

At this Wilson sighed and shook his head sadly.

"No Venezia. For months she did worship me, dressed me in silks, bathed my feet. She called me adorable names - Prince, Lionheart, King. We were on the television, people voted for us in competitions."

"Oh God," said Walt interrupting. He sounded fed up. "Do get on with it. They are waiting for the wedding."

"Family only," Wilson replied in a low voice. "A church in the country. Traditional. Very English."

"And afterwards?"

It was Venezia asking. There was a note of doubt in her voice.

Wilson laughed bitterly. "A party in London paid for by a television company. High kicks, high jinks, broken bottles. Police and ambulances called at three."

"How long did the marriage last Wilson?" Venezia now sensed the worst.

"Two years, three months six days, before collapsing in acrimony, regret and exhaustion."

"And the climbing, Wilson dear?"

Wilson paused. Then he leaned forward. "They said if I could do that, I could do anything. I was offered a place on an Everest team three times."

"But the offers not accepted?"

"No. I was in love. I was obsessed. I would have been a liability, no good to anyone."

"And following the acrimonious divorce?"

"The plan was to return to work, scaffolding. But then someone said you have written for climbing magazines, if you want there is a job as an article writer for the newspaper. So that's what I did, putting all that crazy stuff behind me."

We sat for a long while in silence after Wilson had finished his story. The fire was dying and we could feel the cold of the night starting to creep in on us. How the tales of our pilgrim band surprised! Then we smoked a final cigarette and finished what was left of the drink before going out into the dark to relieve ourselves. Then Jack checked that the tethers were correct and that his donkeys had enough grass to last them for the night and we turned in.

22

As we slept that night we dreamed that the ghosts of pilgrims past were all around us.

Oscar and Echo watched them by the light of our camp fire. Venezia dreamed she saw them on the footpath. It was Jack whose dream was the most vivid.

He dreamed he was with them as the great cathedrals of Spain were being built. He heard the blocks being dragged into place and saw the architects and masons standing over, calculating, designing, drawing out their plans and then looking up imagining the spires that would burst into space when the buildings were finished.

Then we all dreamed we were with Walt. He had woken from a half slumber in front of the camp fire. We heard him say in his soft American voice: 'They're only curious, don't be afraid, they won't harm you'.

23

The following morning was bright, clear and cold. Jack was up first to see to his donkeys followed by Echo and Venezia who were able to coax a flame out of the embers of our fire. They added fresh sticks and soon there was heat enough to brew up our coffee. After that they handed round slices of bread and jam.

We ate standing up so that we could move around and keep warm. We were bundled up in thick jackets and had our hats pulled down to stop the morning cold nipping at us.

We loved the evening when we could pitch a tent and get a fire going and take our ease, but the morning was different. It was always a struggle to leave our warm sleeping bags and to emerge from our tents.

As we dismantled our camp we all had our jobs. Oscar and Denis took down our tents while Jack and Roy were responsible for loading up our donkeys. The clothes we chose to wear reflected both the state of the weather and our mood.

Oscar was wrapped as usual in the quilted patchwork jacket his wife Sheila had created for him. Venezia had enveloped herself in a rich blue sweater that belonged to Echo. Jack's trousers hung more loosely than ever due to the weight he had lost. And as we walked we were encouraged, as we always were now, by the wonderful music prepared for us by Hans Klugman. In the mornings it was always the sweet bird like voice of Mamani Keita that led us on.

Several hours later, with the sun discovering an unexpected warmth for this autumn day, we approached the town of Viana with a ' good sweat on.' Jackets and sweaters had long been discarded and we were in shirt sleeves and tee shirts. Echo was wearing his famous conical rice growers hat.

(Roy was wearing a bright blue baseball cap with the logo of his football club on the front. We had now learned that he chose a particular cap to indicate his mood. He had a selection of blue caps and the newer the cap, the better his mood. On the occasion he changed to wearing a red cap, which bore the logo of an opposing football club, he was in effect a raising a Storm Warming: The Great Man is in foul temper and not to be disturbed).

Walt then led us into the main square of Viana where there were a group of pilgrims gathered round the fountain drinking and washing their faces. Among them there were a number of pilgrims we recognised from previous encounters on the road. We greeted each other warmly as pilgrims do.

Then in a minute our eyes were diverted to the delicious cold water emerging from the pump. Walt was the first to strip his shirt open to the waist and plunge his head and half his torso under the water.

He emerged a moment later to shake himself dry like a big old shaggy dog. The local citizens stopped to stare as he shouted out looking at us:

"Oh, that's good lads. That is what I have been waiting for all morning."

We all followed him then dipping our heads under the cold water, enjoying the relief from the hot sun and the dust of the road. Then we settled down on the benches by the fountain to eat a meal of bread and ham.

As we ate, there were other pilgrims around us too, including a large Russian man with a thick beard, Walt said:

"Pilgrims, if you will allow, I will tell you a story I first heard some years ago. I am reminded of it now, having had that excellent dip under the fountain."

(The writer is aware of the danger of including too many anecdotes and diversions into the story, they can detract from the power of the main narrative, but when Walt tells a story, we should listen).

"A pilgrim finds himself in the capital of a small Balkan country," Walt began. "It is a warm summer's day with a light air and he is at a cafe in a square, taking his ease. In the middle of the square he can see there is a fountain with four silver jets. As he watches he notices how nearly everyone who crosses the square stops at the fountain to drink or wash their hands or splash water on their faces. Then he sees that people sitting at tables in his cafe are also asking the waiter to bring them glasses of water from the fountain.

"The pilgrim tells the waiter, when he comes to his table, that he is a pilgrim on his way to Santiago de Compostela. He explains that for a pilgrim, who is outside under the hot sun all day, discovering a fountain in a village square is an important moment.

"The waiter nods his head and replies that the water from the fountain is known to be beneficial to health and that it is why people always stop there.

"So the pilgrim sits there for a further half hour. Then he asks the waiter to bring him a glass from the fountain so that he can taste it. As he drinks he watches how the life of the square seems to revolve around the fountain. Business men in dark suits pause to drink and look around. Young men stand to the side of the fountain and smoke cigarettes. Girls chat in groups. He watches a woman take her baby and hold its giggling face to the water.

"He is thinking how sociable and friendly and wise the people of this town are when he notices a disturbance outside the bank which is to his right.

"Then suddenly a man bursts out of the door of the bank running as fast as he can. He runs first in the direction of the cafe where the pilgrim is sitting but then changes direction to go past the fountain. Under his arm is a bag. The pilgrim remembers him as young, with his hair cut short.

"As he is running across the square a second man appears, a security guard in a uniform with a rifle in his hand. The pilgrim says it all happened so quickly. The security guard yells out a warning but when the robber keeps on running he raises his rifle and fires a shot. The young man stumbles on a few paces before he collapses into the fountain smashing his head against the stone base as he falls.

"The pilgrim says the final tableau is grim. Bundles of the colourful bank notes slide out of the bag into the water mixing with the blood of the young man which is seeping from his wounds into the fountain.

"After that the pilgrim gets up and leaves the square quickly, so he never discovered what happened next, whether the young man recovered or died from his wounds."

At the conclusion of this story, which showed the importance of water and fountains and pumps to thirsty pilgrims (and by chance showed yet another pilgrim witnessing a bank robbery) the large Russian man surveyed our two donkeys and then looked at us suspiciously.

"You aren't the people everyone is talking about are you?" His accent was as thick and coarse as his visage. "They say there's a group led by a black man and travelling with a couple of donkeys. Well if that's you, you'd better watch it. There's some crazy guy waiting up ahead for you in Logrono. Planning to lay an ambush. Everyone's talking about it."

With this information the pleasant mood that had lasted during lunch quickly dissipated. We loaded up our donkeys and hurried on over the rough ground fearful about what we would find ahead of us.

Two hours later we were standing with our donkeys on the ridge from where we could look down on the city of Logrono.

We surveyed the city, watching the buildings glittering in the late afternoon sun. The mood of pilgrims can change quickly. Our pleasure at bathing under the pump in Viana was long gone. Right now our morale was as low as it had ever been. How we had been anticipating the delights of civilization! Soft beds, hot water, rich food! And now because of the wretched El Lobo, they were about to be snatched from us.

We were divided as to what course of action we should take. Jack advised caution.

"We got away with it in Pamplona," he said grimly. "We were lucky. But if the Russian is right and El Lobo is in Logrono it could be deadly. Remember we have One Million Euro of his money. It is a pity but I vote we give this place a miss."

Venezia put the opposite argument.

"The chances of being discovered are small." She linked arms with Denis, forming an alliance. "That's what we think anyway. Logrono is a big city."

Oscar shook his head in disagreement. "You're wrong Venezia. You're forgetting that I know this man. He is thorough. He will have calculated our arrival time and he will have the entrances to the city covered."

Roy also advised caution. "That fella is no the full coupon," he said sagely. "He could be waitin' for us wi' shooters."

In the end Denis volunteered to make a discreet reconnaissance of the city and report back. There was some reluctance to this proposition at first, we were concerned for his safety, but he insisted and by a show of hands we did all give our agreement. So that is how a few minutes later he descended the ridge. Then shortly after that as the path turned into a stand of trees, he was lost to our sight.

24

While we waited for Denis to return we busied ourselves as best we could with routine 'housekeeping' tasks.

Jack checked the feet of his donkeys and then using a thick brush began to comb their coats. Oscar and Denis unloaded one of the tents and rolling it out began to mend a hole where the material had rubbed and worn through. Echo and Venezia checked our supplies. If we descended down into Logrono we would be able to replenish from stores there but if we forced to circumvent the town, as was most likely, we would have to economise. Roy and Walt pored over maps plotting alternative routes around the city.

It was two hours later when the day was almost done and in spite of putting on our warm jackets we were beginning to shiver with cold, that Venezia, who had gone to the edge of the crest to check, shouted out:

"Here he is! It's Pilgrim Denis. He's coming back!"

And a few moments later Denis was back amongst us and we were all glad to see him. However the news that he brought was not good.

"El Lobo is certainly in the town. He has approached all the tavern owners and the shop keepers and told them to look out for a group of pilgrims with two mules being led by a black man."

Jack asked for more details and Denis looked serious.

"They say he has taken to carrying a pistol in his belt and is threatening mayhem if an attempt is made to capture him."

Then to our surprise, our situation was serious, he began to laugh.

"It is well known that pilgrims exaggerate their tales but still you have to hear this. First one group of pilgrims in a bar told me that El Lobo had begun to dress like a woman and that he was even wearing make up to evade detection by the police. Then two pilgrims in a cafe on the other side of the city told me his appearance had begun to change in another way. They said his jaw was extending and his teeth were becoming more prominent. In other words he is beginning to take on the physical characteristics of his name!"

At first we laughed when we heard all these stories but then when we realised their significance, that we certainly could not risk entry into Logrono now, we felt more discouraged than ever. We shook our heads sadly as we looked down to the city below. Under the darkening sky the first lights of evening were beginning to twinkle.

We were a subdued group who set up camp that night. Jack said to keep our fire low so that we could not be observed from the city. However once we had our tents up we did our best to return to our normal routine.

When we had eaten Wilson reminded us that we had still not learned of the fate that had befallen Denis after he had opened the letter at his dental surgery.

(It was the story he had begun to tell us when we were sheltering from the rain in the barn in France before we crossed the Pyrenees).

Denis's face went pale as he listened to Wilson's request.

"I have been dreading this moment," he replied slowly. Then he looked round at us. "But I suppose I have to face it sometime."

After a long pause this is the story he recounted to us.

"That Monday morning after the weekend with the girls on the boat I went into my dental surgery. And it was then that I opened a letter which informed me that I was to be prosecuted for defrauding the National Health Service."

He stopped and looked round at us. We could see the terrible shame and embarrassment on his face.

"It was not a great sum. I was going to repay it, at the time I was running an expensive lifestyle. But I am not asking for your sympathy. I had behaved like a fool and I had it coming to me."

At that moment, hearing all that pain in his voice we would have taken our humble friend Denis in our collective arms and embraced him and told him, despite everything, that we still considered him the most open and honest of our pilgrim band. (Venezia especially, who was becoming irritated by Echo, would have been quite welcoming). But before we could offer this reaction Denis had hurried on. His voice was shaking and fearful. The confidence of the afternoon had disappeared.

"In a year the business was gone, the girls were gone, the sports car, the speed boat, the flat were all gone and I was in the dock, bankrupt, before the Crown Court."

He paused, his hands shaking, his face pale, recalling the terrible court room ordeal.

"The female prosecuting barrister. She delighted in attacking me. Ripped me apart. There was no doubt a sexual element to her attack, I am sure of that. After all I was not guilty of murdering a small child. A lot of other dentists had done the same thing. It was not a fortune. I was going to repay it. And I had always tried to do the best for my patients. For years I had been paid less than I deserved."

He stopped then and we all reflected for a moment on the adversarial savagery of the British legal system. Then to our surprise, and once again reminding us that behind that vulnerable visage there was still a reserve of strength and guile, he suddenly changed direction.

"Actually there was a strange conclusion to the story which I would like to relate."

His voice was lighter as if the moment of confession had released him.

"Six months later I was released. The usual, good behaviour. No longer a danger to society. Could be sent out safely enough. Had a rented room - table, bed, chair, no curtains - all money and worldly goods long gone.

"Then one afternoon. In the supermarket. Filling my basket with packet soup and tuna tins when who do I spy but the prosecuting barrister who had ripped me apart so cruelly. But this time dressed casually in skirt and blouse, perusing the shelves also, though her basket is filled with pasta, olive oil and nuts."

Denis's eyes flashed with anger.

"Then up she looks, our eyes meet, momentary unrecognition, then bingo she has it full tilt, blood rushes to cheeks, eyes flit away to the floor and she gallops up the aisle, one frightened filly, terrified at seeing me also with shopping basket over arm, a human face, no longer a court room bone to devour."

It was then that Echo, suddenly interrupting, ' jumped into' the story. He slapped his thigh and laughed out loud.

"Damn it, Denis," he shouted out. "But you have hit on the inexplicable heart of the whole damn thing! These people, these lawyers, these begowned and bewigged gangsters! They are our models! They are the pillars of our society! They become rich on other people's misfortunes! It is them that we envy and admire!"

Then he stood up from his place by the fire. Echo in full flow was always a sight.

"Well hi ho and here he comes!" His voice echoed out into the night. "And make way, make way for the Prosecuting Barrister and do come to dinner and do marry our daughter!

He stopped and looked around. His eyes were fierce.

"Now play the scene differently. Substitute the usual 'I am a Prosecuting Barrister of whom all Criminals and Poor People are mortally afraid. ' Call him, why not, a Teacher of Children or God forbid a Driver of Tube Trains. Watch how the Good

Lady of the house winces before she says, 'Oh how nice, but please do excuse me, I really must give our new Belgian cook his instructions.'

Echo stopped to draw breath. Poor Denis's story was completely eclipsed now. (While frequently we disagreed with the sentiments Echo expressed we always applauded the lively and enthusiastic way he pronounced them). Then he was continuing:

"And the female of the species! Venezia. I am sorry but how comprehensible is that? A woman spending the day in court torturing Denis and then going home at night to read little Jemima and Florrie a bed time story?"

(If Echo had thought this would endear him to Venezia he was wrong. Venezia turned to Denis when she heard this and said in a soft aside: "I could never marry a man like that. He's not like you Denis. He doesn't know how to treat a woman").

But Echo, unaware of his gaffe, was thundering on regardless.

"Her defence of course is that she is doing her job and that is the way the law works, which as we all know is the cry of the concentration camp guard down through the ages."

He continued on for a while longer but then his motor began to run down and finally he stopped. All that was left then was the silence and the cold stars above us and in the distance below the lights of Logrono.

So when we had finished the last of the wine and with the stories we had heard still rattling about in our brains, we prepared to turn into our tents.

A little while later as he was seeing to his donkeys Jack Phillpotts gave a yawn and pondered Echo's strange intervention. He had always been suspicious of the quick rise of Echo up the business ladder of success. As he turned back toward his tent he wondered if, in that strange and polemical attack on the legal profession, we had not in fact heard the 'echo' of an alternative story being told.

25

We were a dispirited band that set off the next morning.

All that was left for us was to detour miserably on muddy tracks around the southern edge of the city, the hoods of our waterproofs up to protect us from the thin rain which continued to fall.

How we had anticipated our period of rest in Logrono! Good food, good wine, nights slept through. How we missed it now!

Walt calculated we now had more than eighty miles of footslogging drudgery before we arrived at our next stop which was Burgos.

We were enveloped in a dreary and anonymous landscape. The colours around us were wretched browns and drab greens. It was only Roy, bless him, who drove us on, encouraging us with his Scottish wit and humour, making sure that none of us lagged behind. In difficult times he was always our general and our leader.

We had also been discouraged by the story Denis had recounted to us. He was a popular pilgrim and his downfall, even if caused by his own hand, made us sad.

As has been noted before, this camino, this pilgrim route we were on, was in many ways a parallel world. Things that were important in our 'normal' world were unimportant here and vice versa.

A part of our new world were the churches. To begin with we had admired these stately domes that marked our route so clearly but as we walked we began to have a growing feeling of unease. It was Wilson who voiced our concern.

"These places are grotesquely out of proportion," he told us. "They squat on top of the villages like giant insects."

We had a new admiration for Wilson so we listened carefully when he spoke. His free climb up the building and his rescue of the girl had been heroic. And the way he had told his story, which certainly contained something of the ' magic of the camino,' had also entranced us.

We had arrived at the town of Navarrete and the rain had ceased for a moment and the sun had come out so we were able to eat our meagre lunch on a bench opposite the church of Santa Maria de la Asuncion.

When we had finished eating Echo got up and stared at the church in front of us and then advanced forward. Without a word we followed him inside.

From the outside there are a thousand churches like this in Spain. But from the inside we were all astonished by the richness of this particular establishment. The brilliance of the gold and silver ornamentation of the altar and its surrounds, the Spanish refer to it as the retablo, had the dimensions and allure of a robber's cave.

When we re emerged outside the sun had retreated back behind its shelter of clouds and the day had once again turned dreary and grey.

We had all been taken aback by such a horde of glittering riches in such a rough and ready landscape.

It was Echo, who had led us into the church, who finally addressed us. His voice was grave.

"What we saw there was unspeakably beautiful in the way that a sparkling diamond set in a gold ring on the finger of a young bride is unspeakably beautiful. And if you will allow me that is a comparison I will come back to later."

Then he turned to Walt.

"Am I allowed a digression Walt? I want to talk about the Conquistadors."

Walt pulled a face, showing his reluctance.

"If you must Echo, but keep it short. We have to get on. We don't want a history lesson."

Echo looked unhappy at this lack of encouragement but then furrowing his brow, as if in concentration, in a low voice he began his explanation:

"The Conquistadors are leaving Spain for South America on a mission to convert. The hunt is also on for silver and gold. The time is the 16th century. And what a cracking job they are doing! Thousand year old civilisations are being taken apart piece by piece and the silver and gold is being ripped from the ground in awful conditions. The natives are being put to the sword in their thousands, or to elaborate: men, women, children, babies are being cut open and disembowelled and burned. And then in the name of Jesus Christ, Our Lord and Saviour, this priceless treasure is transported back to prop up the empire and decorate the beautiful churches we see before us today!"

Already we wanted Echo to stop. He was pointing toward the church. But we had heard enough. We all knew these stories. Our stomachs were turning. But Echo, as he always did, was taking his argument to the extreme.

(Echo, as has been stated earlier, is a conundrum. He is by far the most intelligent and best read of our pilgrim band but he is also the most eccentric and excitable).

"Pilgrims!" The register and mood had changed. His voice was suddenly booming out. He was like a mad preacher on a soap box.

"Consider this change of nomination for the churches of Spain and the Great Holiness they represent. Give me your suggestions! I propose The Charnel Houses, or The Chambers of Pain or perhaps The Special Centres For The Disembowelling of Small Children!"

Even the unbelievers among us were shocked by this onslaught. We stared at him appalled. The first of the villagers were also appearing in doorways to stare at this strange black orator, spouting his outrageous heresies surrounded by his fellow pilgrims and their donkeys.

A furious Walt put up his hand.

"Echo. For God's sake man," he shouted angrily. "Stop that before there is a riot! You are being an agent provocateur. You will have us run out of town. And it is not fair. Everyone knows these stories. It is nothing new. You are distorting and exaggerating. I will answer your attack at the correct moment, but now is not the time. It is not fair to ambush us like that."

Then he turned on his heel and with Roy by his side and Jack leading our two donkeys he began to march quickly out of town leaving the rest of us no choice but to follow. For the next hour we all walked on in angry silence.

26

In the late afternoon the rain stopped and the sky cleared and we saw to the south of us the outline of the mountain range known as the Sierra de Cebollera. Then in the early evening when we were still a few miles to the East of the town of Najera we crossed over a road to a small wood where we set up our camp for the night.

Echo and Venezia prepared meat balls in a sauce which we ate with bread and red wine. Then after we had complimented them on the quality of their cooking we put aside the topic of religion and the horror of the churches, as described so graphically to us by Echo. Instead we began to discuss the music that Hans Klugman had given us.

"That music has made a great difference to me," Denis said. "It has given me a lot of encouragement."

We all nodded enthusiastically at this. We were glad to be off the topic of the churches.

We all had our favourites among the tunes. Mamani Keita guided us joyously in the morning when we were still light and fresh. The Buena Vista Social Club and the Orchestra Baobab drove us up the hills in the afternoon when our spirits were beginning to flag. Venezia said she could waltz all night to the aria we had been given from Rigoletto and Roy said that he and his wife Mary had always enjoyed dancing to the songs of Charles Trenet.

But it was during this discussion that Oscar unwittingly opened himself up to an attack from Echo. It happened as we were half way through our dinner. Echo had turned to the group and said, in what we took to be rather a self satisfied manner:

"While I appreciate the clever and intricate way the various themes and the different styles of tune have been woven together by our friend Hans Klugman, in my opinion a trick has been missed by not including The Lark Ascending by Ralph Vaughan Williams."

He looked around at us.

"It is well known to be one of the most evocative pieces of music ever composed by an Englishman, with its theme of uplifting pastoral joy. As such I should have thought it qualified as an excellent tune to celebrate our journey."

At this pronouncement Echo stirred himself from the fireside and gave a little cough and a stifled laugh. Wilson laughed as well, recognising the trap into which Oscar had fallen.

Sensing something wrong and fearing ridicule Oscar turned sharply.

"What are you two sniggering at then? What have I said that is funny? What is the joke about Vaughan Williams? You had better tell us."

"Well, you will have to excuse me Oscar." A note of faux embarrassment was now evident in Echo's voice. "But the Lark Ascending is one of the most requested pieces on the BBC's Desert Island Discs programme. It is generally chosen by people without wide musical knowledge."

At this Oscar's face reddened deeply. He had been caught out trying to 'con' the pilgrims. Then he put his plate to one side and stood up.

"Some people may call you the African Autodidact but to me you are still a 'know all' Echo." He looked angrily around at the rest of us. "And I for one have had had enough of it. There is a lot of piss and wind being talked here so I am going to retire to have a shit alongside Thatcher and Blair and I am sure they will be better companions and make more sense. And don't ask because I do not want the rest of my dinner which I have not enjoyed anyway because I know it has come out of a tin."

And with that off he stomped in a high old huff.

Which as it happened was just about the best thing he could have done because a minute later, to our great surprise, a large jeep with Guardia Civil markings on its side turned up the track and stopped in front of us and out stepped three very serious members of that esteemed police force.

"Everyone stay where you are," the senior officer barked out.

With our hearts dropping and sensing with this turn of events that we were in serious trouble we put down our plates and got slowly to our feet.

The police then fanned out, one to either side, the senior officer staying in the middle. We felt like prisoners and none of us dared speak. They held their torches in front of them like pistols as they surveyed us. The headlights of their jeep, which had been parked at an angle, lit up the camp behind us.

"Passports. No one move."

The torches were shone directly in our faces to make sure we understood.

To the shame of the Guardia Civil the officers began with an unpleasant interrogation of Echo, even though, when we considered later, he was the most unlikely of suspects.

His passport was scrutinised intensely and a torch was shone in his face. This attitude of the officers left us feeling pessimistic. We would sure we would be found out.

However providence comes in many forms.

As the senior officer came to Roy Babadouche's passport, and saw that famous name and photograph, he gave a sudden muffled gasp. Then he turned and spoke quickly to one of the other officers. The torch was quickly flashed in Roy's face for confirmation. Then a moment later when the senior officer returned the passport his trembling fingers deliberately brushed the sleeve of Our Magical Football Manager's jacket.

Sensing an easing of the tension Walt stepped forward and addressed the senior officer.

"It would be an honour to help the noble officers of the Guardia Civil if the noble officers of the Guardia Civil would be kind enough to disclose what it is they need help with."

The senior officer, suddenly remembering why he was there, tapped the photo fit he had been holding in his hand.

"This man is suspected of being an accomplice of the notorious bank robber and police killer El Lobo. Following information received we are checking all groups of pilgrims in search of him."

He eyed us one by one but none of us blinked. Oscar told us later that he had seen everything from his hiding point in the bushes.

A search of our tents also revealed nothing - because of course every evening the first thing we did after we pitched camp was to make sure the money was well hidden.

Finally it was Wilson who volunteered to the senior officer:

"We did meet a pilgrim who has a similar visage to the one in your photo fit. But that was several days ago and he was going in the opposite direction."

The senior officer, having received this information, was about to turn away when there was a sudden rustle from the thicket as Oscar, suffering a cramp in his leg, was forced to change his position. All the officers shone their torches in that direction, but luckily for us all they lit up were the rear ends of Thatcher and poor Blair.

At the same time, as a further diversion, Venezia put her hand on the senior officer's arm and said in her most winsome voice:

"Senor, it is my pleasure to tell you that the Guardia Civil of Spain is much admired in my native Canada where my father is a serving officer in the Calgary force."

The senior officer, flattered, returned the compliment.

"Senorita." He gave a half bow. "It is always a pleasure to encounter a beautiful woman who is also a pilgrim."

Then a few moments later with a last admiring glance toward Roy and an unpleasant scowl in the direction of Echo, the three gallant officers of the Guardia Civil got back into their jeep reversed up the track and disappeared.

After that we all exhaled our breath. Then when we estimated the coast was clear we whistled and a dishevelled looking Oscar emerged from the bushes.

Later that night while we were going over the detail of our lucky escape Walt observed:

"While some of you pilgrims may not believe in divine intervention at other times it is so blindingly obvious it is a wonder that you do not all see it straightaway."

Was Walt, in an indirect manner, trying to offer some sort of response to Echo's earlier attack on the church?

27

The following morning, chastened by our experience of the night before, our little band made its way through the town of Najera and then out again across open ground in the direction of Santa Domingo de la Calzada. In the spring, Walt told us, the fields would be full of bright red poppies and green barley would sway in the wind, but today under grey skies everything was barren and brown. This also, it has to be declared, was a reflection of our mood.

"This whole business with El Lobo will end badly," said Jack gloomily.

During the course of the morning we stopped to talk to a shepherd with a large flock of sheep. He reported that a golf course that had opened up nearby was draining off so much water that the level of the water table underneath was starting to drop. This was killing off the vegetation and making it more difficult for his sheep, he told us sadly.

Half an hour later we passed by the golf club in question and observed an obese young man getting out of a car. As we watched he slung a bag of clubs over his shoulder and went into the club house. This was the first obese man we had seen on all our travels in Spain.

An hour later we stopped at a tavern in Santa Domingo de la Calzada to eat our lunch. After the waiter had taken our order Echo went up to the bar and picked up a paper.

As he turned the pages he whistled through his teeth and looked up at Oscar.

"You have not been straight with us Oscar old chum, have you?"

He read a few more lines and then shook his head.

"This is about the robbery in Zaragoza."

Oscar stared back at Echo across the table.

"I don't know what you are talking about Pilgrim Echo."

Oscar was grateful to his companions for protecting him from the Guardia Civil but having to hide in a thicket with the donkeys had been a compromise to his dignity.

Echo put the paper down on the table.

"You never told us that shooters were involved in that robbery."

At this significant and serious development, which we certainly should have been informed about at the beginning, we all turned to stare at Oscar.

Then Echo gave us the detail of the article. El Lobo was wanted for bank robberies all over Spain going back ten years. In previous attacks he had shot dead two policemen and wounded several cashiers. (We were already aware of this). The new information was that during the Zaragoza raid he had threatened a policeman with his gun and then fired a shot which had wounded a female bank cashier in the leg.

Echo picked up the paper again.

"You can rob the bank, but shooting up a cashier that is something different. I am not surprised the Guardia Civil are after us."

"Well I am not going to apologise for that," Oscar replied defiantly. His face was hard. "It was not me who fired any gun. In fact I did not know anything about the shooting."

At the point the food was brought to our table and we dropped the subject though we were all still furious with Oscar. He should have informed us fully of the danger we were in.

It was left to Roy, as he cut into his pork chop, to ease the mood.

"I wouldna worry if I was you Oscar." The rough familiarity of his strange Scottish accent, which had so disturbed us at the beginning, was a pleasure to us now. "These Spanish polis couldna catch a butterfly wi' a net ten foot wide. The polis in Dundee would no have given up so easy, I'll tell yer that."

There was a further defusing of the tension when Echo reached the concluding paragraph of the article.

'The man driving the getaway car was described by eyewitnesses as being young and sleek looking with slicked back hair and wearing dark glasses. After extensive enquiries police have now discounted the theory that he is a pilgrim on his way to Santiago de Compostela. They are now looking for a career criminal, probably a professional driver, who may have worked with El Lobo before.'

This allowed our lunch to finish on a more positive note.

That afternoon as we made our way toward the town of Belorado we had an example of a phenomenon that affects all pilgrims. (It will be discussed in more detail later in the narrative but essentially when pilgrims become tired and discouraged they can become unreasonable and act out of character).

In this instance Walt had suggested to Jack that as the short Autumn day was already beginning to draw in we might consider pitching camp earlier than normal.

But this observation, which had certainly not been intended as controversial, brought an unexpected and furious reaction from Venezia. She stopped abruptly, jerking Thatcher to a halt with her.

"Walt. The hell with you." Her face was pale and her voice cut sharply across us. "I stink like a pole cat. We were supposed to stop in Logrono. If I do not get a decent bed and a wash up in Belorado I am out of it. This pilgrimage is turning to hell. I am on my way home. I don't care about anyone else."

This sudden outburst, so unreasonable and so out of character, took us all by surprise. However Walt, who could have replied in equal strong manner, remained calm. He was wise enough to know when to back down. He turned to Jack.

"Venezia is right. We do need to wash and brush up and get ourselves a decent night's sleep. There's a good little hotel on the edge of Belorado. I've stayed there a couple of times."

This strange incident, which was over as quickly as it had blown up, was an indication of the priorities of our new life. Food, lodgings, the state of the footpath, these were our new concerns. At home our equivalent worries would have been work, finances, family.

(It was also an indication that Walt was an old hand at dealing with the caprices of pilgrims).

What we ate when we were on our pilgrimage was almost as important as where we stayed. When we met other pilgrims on the road we always took advice and swopped recommendations of good places to eat, or conversely of places to avoid.

As we had left Viana we had encountered two women from Croatia, schoolteachers from Dubrovnik. They had told us a story of the meanness of the Italian inhabitants of the Po Valley.

"In a refuge in Bologna at breakfast the cook placed a basket of stale rolls placed next to a colourful notice saying please take one roll and no more."

They were still angry as they told us the story.

"In Reggio and Modena the locals regularly double charged us. And in Parma we were even offered re heated supermarket meals disguised as local cuisine."

By contrast pilgrims we met who had crossed Portugal from the West told us they had been served plates groaning with potatoes and good cod fish.

Readers will also ask why we did not more often, in the tradition of authentic pilgrims, stay in the refuges, especially when the weather was so inhospitable for sleeping out.

Walt answered that question with a grim laugh.

"Aimery Picaud called the refuges the 'Stinking Shithouses' and I can tell you, that for some of them, especially in Galicia, that name is still appropriate today."

Even if we did not stay in as many refuges as other pilgrims we did learn about the various establishments, and their peculiarities, from other pilgrims.

We heard so many stories. In typical pilgrim manner there were embellishments and exaggerations, but a few examples will give the reader an idea:

We heard reports of the horrors of the refuge at St Juan de Ortega, which we would pass by soon. We were told that pilgrims are awakened before dawn by terrible cries from the monks, or is it the nuns, urging them from the beds.

Then there was the refuge at Ruitelan (further to the West) where the hospitalero serves quails eggs for supper and awakens pilgrims in the morning with a recording of the soft tones of a Mozart violin concerto.

We heard conflicting reports of the English hospitaleros who run the refuge at Rabanal. Some pilgrims told us they were mean and forced pilgrims to sleep on hard beds without pillows while others reported the same hospitaleros serving tea in the 'English style' in china cups free of charge. The brand of tea used was said to be the same as that served to the Queen in Buckingham Palace.

But if we return now to that small hotel on the edge of the inconsequential town of Belorado. That evening after we had 'washed and scrubbed up' as Walt put it and eaten a decent dinner and made our way through two bottles of good Rioja wine, Venezia's visage was once again glittering and lively. And once again, to the disappointment of Denis, her arm was proudly linked through Echo's.

Our mood was then sufficiently relaxed that Wilson felt he could ask Venezia the question to which we had all been seeking an answer.

The question was: How had she been given such a name, a name which, though we did not dare to say out loud, we considered perfectly suited to her balletic form and her dark and seductive Latin features?

As we topped up our glasses and pushed aside our dinner plates and lit up our cigarettes Venezia replied:

"Well Wilson you have asked an interesting question. And there is certainly a story behind that name. It is an unusual name and the way I gained it even more so."

After that we all leaned forward to listen. And so she began:

"I was brought up in the Italian district of the dear old port city of Montreal. We were near the Jean-Talon market, which is the area where my mother and father are both still school teachers. Grandparents, both sides, came from Italy. They never fully got to grips with things Canadian."

She looked around and smiled beautifully at her two men, Echo and Denis. Our wine glasses were topped up discreetly by Roy.

"So it is winter. Deep winter. Cold winter. Montreal winter. And my wonderful parents to be, Dorotea and Francesco, my dear Mama and Papa, are about to set off on their honeymoon. They are full of excitement. They are going back to the old country!"

Venezia laughed.

"We are a very fertile family. We have cousins everywhere. Ravenna, Ferrara, Padua. But for us it was always Venice. When we visited our grandparents we always pulled out the photo albums from the shelves and begged to hear the stories."

As we listened we imagined an evening en famille with the young Venezia at her grandmother's knee being instructed in the glories of The Doge's Palace and The Grand Canal.

"Dorotea and Francesco are young." Venezia is continuing with her story. "They are in love, they are just married, they are excited. It is their first trip abroad."

She looked around our little group.

"The first evening will be a candle lit dinner in a restaurant by the water's edge. After that there will be a stroll hand in hand through St Mark's Square and then well..." Venezia looked suddenly embarrassed. "I guess after that it was back to the hotel. Allow me my name. Do the deed. Create me. Conceive me."

She turned to Wilson and laughed.

"For God's sake Wilson you are the writer! Can't you come up with a metaphor that does not make it sound as if I was a project in a school science lab?"

"But the problem was it didn't happen like that." It was Walt speaking softly.

Venezia sighed.

"No Walt, of course, you are right. They are on their way to the airport in Montreal. It's snowing hard. They're probably late. Going too fast. The taxi skids and hits a telephone pole. For Dorotea it's shock and bruises but for Francesco, the papa to be (or not) it's a busted leg and a month in hospital."

"But they could have gone another time." Denis was leaning forward anxiously. "A few months would not have made any difference."

Venezia shook her head.

"Sorry Denis but no. It was a question of momentum. Term started again, time moved on, they had other bills to pay, the moment was lost. Mother explained it to me years later."

Her voice sounded sad but then suddenly she brightened and started to laugh.

"They are out walking one day, there is snow everywhere, it is once again mid winter. They take a turn down a side street and they are almost past the little shop before my father stops in front of a sign in the window.

"There it is, bold as anything. The Venice Furniture Company of Montreal (Venezia Mobili, Montreal). Of course it is impossible to resist. Ten minutes later they come out having ordered themselves a brand new double bed.

"And of course it is upon said brand new double bed," Venezia was looking around at us with a smile on her face, "with the name of the company, Venezia Mobili, Montreal, emblazoned firmly on the head board that, according to family legend, I am conceived."

28

The following morning we rose early to see to our great joy that the dreary sky of yesterday had cleared and everything above us was now clear and blue and warm and sunny. So it was in high good mood that we left our hotel to set off in the direction of the great monastery of St Juan de Ortega. As ever the music that Hans Klugman had given us was our encouragement. We had also enjoyed the story that Venezia had told us.

Jack and Oscar were in the lead with our two donkeys. The path was already beginning to dry out under the warmth of the sun and we were making good progress. Ahead of us we could see that the path would soon begin to rise toward a forested area.

It was then that Venezia, in ' impish' mood following the success of her story decided to confront an old problem that was still a daily concern to her. This was the question of which of her two suitors, Echo or Denis, she should finally choose.

She decided on this occasion to seek the advice, on this delicate question, of Our Great Football Manager.

"My hero." She put her hand lightly on his arm. "My big man eating tiger hunting Scottish hero." She tipped her face up cheekily to him. "Is a mere Canadian woman, a Canuck, a petite Quebecoise even, allowed to ask the great Sir a delicate question?"

"Well," said Roy laughing and colouring slightly at this unexpected form of address and putting his arm around her shoulder. "What's it yer wanna know then lassie?"

"Well, my question is this." Venezia was laughing. "I cannot decide between that great big Congolese layabout, who is attempting to lay siege to my heart, and the more vulnerable and delicate charms of a certain dentist, demi Belge, recently fallen from grace. So tell me My Lord Roy how does a girl choose. How does she know when she has got the right man?"

Then Venezia stopped to look at Roy squarely.

"Every girl in the world wants to throw herself at you and yet you are faithful always to your beautiful wife Mary. How do you do it Uncle Roy? Do tell us mortals. What is the secret of a happy marriage ?"

This was a deliberately provocative interrogation that on another morning could have caused a terrible argument to break out among the pilgrims, especially Denis and Echo, but because the day was so light and clear and our mood so suddenly optimistic and happy, the question was received by our little group in the same light and airy way that it had been posed.

Even Wilson, who in matters of love had the stern morals of a socialist, could not help but smile.

"There is no way out of that Roy. You cannot refuse a request when it is put in that way."

"That's right," said Denis and Echo together. They were laughing as they spoke. "You had better give us some hints, it sounds like we need them."

The track we were walking on was wide and sandy. We had been ascending the last hour through scented pine trees and had now emerged onto a ridge which gave us views down over open country to the West and South.

As we stopped to draw breath Walt looked toward the position of the sun in the sky and then declared that it was time for us to halt and eat our lunch.

All this time Roy was deep in silence as he contemplated a response to the question he had been asked.

Jack supervised the unloading of the donkeys so that they could graze and Echo took out from the panniers the sandwiches that had been prepared for us by the hotel in Belorado and we settled down to eat.

"Well," said Roy finally, turning to Venezia as he finished his sandwich. "Yous asked me a question hen and while I was helping Jack unload the donkeys I was trying to think of ma response."

Ahead of us, lit by the soft afternoon sun, we could see the sandy path descending gently back down into the valley below. We were all listening to Roy now.

"The day I met Mary I'd played centre forward for ma club in the afternoon. But by the evenin' I'm ready to go out. I've a new suit on and there's a dab ah expensive eau de cologne on the Babadouche cheek. After that there's a couple of bevvies to bolster the confidence and then a gang of us sets off up the town to the ballroom."

We looked down at that gentle slope that would lead us back into the pine forest again, imagining at the same time this point when two young lives were about to change for ever.

"Was it love at first sight Roy?"

"Aye, Venezia, as soon as I set eyes on ma Mary that night I knew she would be ma wife. I never had a moment's doubt. The sparkling lights lit up her eyes and the way she danced was as light as air. I married ma Mary a year later and she has been at ma side ever since."

"But what is your secret Roy?" Venezia said impatiently. "I do wish I could meet her. I would ask how she picks her perfect man. There is no way for a woman to choose between these two rascals."

We could all hear the light mocking tone to Venezia's voice and sensed that she was now taking a risk. Roy heard it as well. So he gave her this reply:

"Yous think I'm just a simple football manager hen. But I looked into ma Mary's eyes and I told her I loved her and that I'd always be there for her. She told me the same thing too. There was none of the fancy footwork of yous modern ones, we was being honest with each other. You're asking for our secret, that's it."

This response from Roy and the direct way in which it was delivered was a severe riposte to Venezia. It was a moment we always recalled when we were looking back on our pilgrimage.

Once again we realised how wrong we had been to mock Roy. We recalled with shame that behind his back Oscar had called him Biffo the Dundee Mule and Old Mutton Head. Echo had even described him as our Noble Savage.

When Roy had finished speaking we got to our feet and stretched and loaded up the donkeys. Then we continued our journey, slowly descending the path back into the forest. An hour later the path opened on to a glade. Then on a borne by the side of the path we saw where a pilgrim had abandoned an old worn out pair of boots. After that we continued on until we heard the great bell of the monastery at San Juan de Ortega begin to ring out in the distance and Walt said it was time to find a decent place where we could put up our tents for the night.

29

As has been noted already in this narrative, the mood of our pilgrim group could change quickly. While we had been light and almost a little ' giddy' during the day the mood after we had eaten our meal and while we were drinking our wine became more reflective and serious. We noted in particular that Jack had gone quiet and that his visage looked sombre. Then Walt turned to him.

"There is a certain story that you need to get out Jack. It's time to do it now."

Jack did not reply for a long time, instead just staring into the fire, but eventually, clearing his throat, and in a low voice, he did finally begin.

"I will tell you pilgrims that I was nineteen years of age when I was called up from my home in Plymouth to do my National Service."

He paused here for a moment so that we could see the direction his narrative was taking.

"They gave us our training and then they sent us out to Aden. They call it Yemen now. Give a dog a new name if you want, but it'll still be a basket case."

"Oh that's good Jack." Echo rubbed his hands together in front of the fire and laughed out loud. "I love an end of empire story. You are either going to recount to us how you lost your cherry in a back street Cairo brothel or you are going to give a colourful account of how you bravely lobbed your last grenade to clear a fuzzy wuzzy sniper post."

But Echo, as he had done so many times before, had misjudged the situation. Jack was deadly serious. His reply when it came was in a low voice.

"You shouldn't talk like that Echo. It was bloody awful. People died every day."

There was a pause. Then he stared directly and coldly at Echo and said:

"What we were actually trying to do Echo was to defend civilisation from bastards like you."

There was stifled intake of breath from all the pilgrims at this insult. But Echo, seeing the level of Jack's anger, and realising how badly he had read the moment, retreated in silence.

Walt attempted to fill the gap that followed.

"I had a brother who was a prisoner in the Civil War. When they finally let him go he had aged ten years and was thin as a piece of string."

But Jack was still staring hard at Echo, daring him to advance toward him. Discreetly Roy passed around the bottle of wine and we filled our mugs. Wilson added wood to the fire.

Then Walt sighed and rubbed his hand across his face.

"Governments feed their young men into the infernal machine and they come out changed for ever. No one ever learns the lesson. I shall have more to say about that later, about the way hatred can be whipped up."

He looked around at us carefully.

"But if you will allow me for now pilgrims, as this is a serious moment, I would like to give you this short poem."

And so we sat still and listened.

A sight in camp in the daybreak gray and dim,
As from my tent I emerge so early sleepless,
As slow I walk in the cool fresh air the path near by the
hospital tent,
Three forms I see on stretchers lying, brought out there
untended lying,
Over each the blanket spread, ample brownish woolen
blanket,
Gray and heavy blanket, folding, covering all.
Curious I halt and silent stand,
Then with light fingers I from the face of the nearest the
first just lift the blanket;
Who are you elderly man so gaunt and grim, with well-
gray'd hair, and flesh all sunken about the eyes?
Who are you my dear comrade?
Then to the second I step--and who are you my child and
darling?
Who are you sweet boy with cheeks yet blooming?
Then to the third--a face nor child nor old, very calm,
as of beautiful yellow-white ivory;
Young man I think I know you--I think this face is
the face of the Christ himself,
Dead and divine and brother of all, and here again he lies.

When he had finished we considered the poem for a moment. Then Walt turned to Jack.

"You had a fine singing voice and it was noted by your commanding officer. It led to you entertaining the troops in Aden."

Jack laughed in response but there was a bitter tone to his voice.

"Typical bloody Yank. Exaggerating as always. It was a couple of evenings in the barracks. Some of the other lads did card tricks and a major did imitations."

There was a pause and then Venezia said in a slow voice:

"Well, a singer huh, whoever would have believed that..."

She let her voice trail off deliberately into the evening air.

Jack turned slowly towards Venezia.

"My father God bless him, now long gone, was a well known publican in the city of Plymouth who also sang in amateur productions at the Athenaeum theatre. I was in the audience as a boy when they gave him a standing ovation. There were people who said Reginald Phillpotts could have given Mario Lanza a run for his money."

Jack closed his eyes for a moment. When he opened them again he said:

"We were due to go to the famous concert in Blackpool where Josef Locke evaded the revenue inspectors but it never happened because the night before, dear old Dad, dear old Reggie, who I loved dearly and feared mightily, had a heart attack and upped and died and that was the end of that."

Jack shook his head. He took a breath.

"Didn't let him down though, never did that. Learned to sing decently. Always kept a tidy house, always served a good pint, never any trouble."

He turned to Walt.

"You're right. The CO said I could take up singing professionally if I applied myself."

After that Wilson added wood to the fire and Roy refilled our mugs with wine. Then Jack continued.

"They had no idea. But they weren't all brutes. Not at least when they first come out. But they'd never been abroad before. Some of them could hardly read. The officers showed them Aden on the map and told them why they were fighting but they may as well have been talking to the wall. They shut their eyes or smoked cigarettes. And the terrorists were animals. They put booby traps everywhere so you had to be on alert the whole time. On top of that it was scorching hot."

We were listening carefully to what Jack had to say now. His face was dark and serious.

"We all killed people. I shot a sniper in a doorway but we never got the body because they dragged it away."

He stared over the flickering flames of the fire to where Echo and Wilson sat.

"You can blame whoever you want. But don't say it was the soldier's fault, because it wasn't. Blame the politicians or whoever it was who sent them there. But don't blame the poor bloody soldier. He was too young. Drop him into that mess he's bound to blow up. Anyone would."

The fire was beginning to die down so Wilson got to his feet and added a couple more small logs from the pile of wood he had cut.

"A week after I shot the sniper instead of getting a medal the officers decide I've seen one too many dead bodies and they transfer me out. They send me down to the cell block to help out the MPs and the guards with the prisoners. But that's alright. Most of the day there's nothing to do and there's only a handful of prisoners. We have them out of their cells playing cards and drinking tea. We're counting the days until we can go home."

Jack stopped here for a moment, as if to remember what came next in his story.

"But then they change everything round. An officer comes down the stairs and tells us there's a drive on to get the ringleaders. We've got to get the cells ready because they'll be bringing them in to us. It's none of our business. We know what they've been up to. There's a special cell at the end of the corridor and they take them in there and give them what for and good riddance to them as far as we're concerned."

Jack stopped. The flames of the fire flickered.

"It died down a bit after that. Maybe they had all the information they wanted. I don't know. I was still doing some singing and everyone said I had a future. I just wanted to go home."

Then there was a long silence and for a moment we thought that was the end of the story. Walt's eyes began to close and Venezia rested her arm on Echo's knee. Above us, above the fire, the millions of stars glittered.

"Then it all starts up again." Jack's voice is low and serious. "This time they say they're sure they've got the ring leaders. The officers say they're going to do whatever it takes to get them to talk. To gee us up they show us pictures of soldiers who'd been killed. Mangled arms, bits of legs. Horrible stuff."

We could feel the wind starting to rise and when we looked up at the night sky the stars to the East which had been bright and clear a minute ago were now covered over. Jack was continuing.

"We can smell the fear when they drag them down to the cell at the end of the block. Terrible. They've got them screaming and shouting. But the officers threaten us if we don't go along. They couldn't risk leaving anyone out. Anyone with clean hands could turn them in."

We were all listening carefully now. Jack's voice sounded horrible.

"They've got him flat on his back on the cell floor when I go in. His mouth's open and there's blood everywhere. Then the officer says: 'You've got to sit on his chest to hold him down.' They've already got a squaddie on each of his arms and legs and there's another one behind me next to the generator. Then the officer gives the command and he starts to crank the handle."

The sky was completely covered to the East now. The wind was rising and even with the warmth of the fire we were shivering.

Jack's voice was so low and hoarse we had to lean forward to hear.

"A wild animal doesn't scream like that. They had him twisted round in the end. Voice went up and up. We were ripping him apart. We were punching him as hard as we could. At the same time we were shouting out the names of the soldiers he'd killed. In the end even the officers couldn't stand it. They were yelling at us and trying to pull us off.

When they finally got him out he'd gone all limp and the medics said he was dead."

There was a long pause and we could feel the way the wind was rising. We felt sick to our stomachs with what he'd heard. Then Jack gave us the final line of his story.

"We were mad for it. We were drunk on it. That is what we were all ashamed of afterwards. We'd enjoyed what we were doing. We'd enjoyed making the poor bloody bastard suffer. We'd certainly got our revenge for what he'd done to our lot."

There was a terrible silence then. We noted that the sky had almost completely clouded over and that the wind had risen further. Then Roy got slowly to his feet. Going over to Jack he put a hand under his arm and helped him up. Then he pointed at Echo.

"I'll need yous too."

Jack's face was sickly pale. His voice was weak.

"Been with me all the time. Never leaves me. Shouldn't have let it out. Never sung another note after that. Very weak. Ashamed of myself. First time I've talked about it since."

Roy turned to face the other pilgrims.

"We's going to have a wee walk round with Jack here. Calm him down. Get him sorted out. We'll be a while so the rest of yous away to yer beds."

We watched silently as the two big men, their arms around him, helped our dear Pilgrim Jack into the darkness.

As we made our way to our tents we could see them by the light of the moon at the edge of the clearing. Roy had his arm around Jack's shoulder and Jack appeared to be crying. What was said then, whether there were further confessions, was never disclosed.

30

None of us slept well that night. We were all revolted by the images Jack had given us. The next morning was sharp and cold so we packed up our camp quickly, eating breakfast as we stood. Then we made our way the short distance down to the great monastery at San Juan de Ortega. What a bleak old place that is!

Roy and Walt went inside to see if any information had been received about the whereabouts of El Lobo. We needed to know if he had been spotted in Burgos. Jack sat on a bench outside the monastery with his eyes closed. His face was pale and after a few moments Echo went to sit next to him. The morning sunshine began to warm us and Jack's head slipped onto Echo's shoulder and soon he was asleep.

The exterior of the monastery was dour and unwelcoming. Pilgrims getting ready to set off told us that the dormitories were dirty and cold. One pilgrim said he felt as if he had spent the night in a prison.

Then two French pilgrims who were making their way back from Santiago to their home in Marseille came to talk to us. They had spent some days in Burgos and were able to confirm, to our great joy, that El Lobo had left the town.

"Yes, we saw him go," one of them said. "He was going West toward Leon. He is now a sad looking figure with long hair and a straggly beard."

This information was confirmed by Roy and Walt a few minutes later.

"Returning pilgrims have told the monks he has left Burgos," Walt told us as they emerged from the monastery. "So for the moment we are safe."

So that was how, an hour later, with the day now pleasantly warm, allowing us to take off sweaters and heavy jackets, and with some colour slowly returning to Jack's shattered visage, we set off toward the city of Burgos.

There are two landmarks to guide pilgrims on this section of the route. The first is a tall cross which is at the top of a hill which is called Matagrande. The second is a series of stones laid out in a circular pattern a little further along on the right hand side. Walt also told us that in this region of the Atapuerca mountains there was now a great archaeological site where evidence had been found of man's earliest entry into Western Europe.

Under different circumstances this would have no doubt provoked a lively discussion among our pilgrim band as to our origins and perhaps also as to our future destiny. Certainly both Walt and Echo were well informed about the discoveries. But today we were tired. Grey clouds had now covered the sky once again snuffing out the earlier sunshine and we were anxious to arrive in Burgos.

But before we finally did arrive in that fair city we were troubled by one further incident. This was when Jack called an unexpected stop to our progress.

(We will give our reaction to Jack's confession a little later).

"Halt the caravan!" His shout was clear and sudden. "One of my donkeys has gone lame."

When we were stationery he lifted up poor Blair's offside front foot and shook his head.

"We shall have to find a vet for this poor fellow." He turned to Walt. "He can't carry on. His foot needs attention."

Walt looked pensive.

"If we can continue for half an hour we will arrive at the farm where I had planned to leave the donkeys while we were in Burgos. I am sure that the farmer, who I know well, will be able to fix us up with a vet."

Oddly enough that half hour journey down the hill toward Burgos when we hobbled slowly along, Thatcher complaining bitterly about the extra burden she was having to carry (we had transferred the weight off poor Blair), was beneficial for Jack. He was so concerned about the welfare of his donkeys that the story he had disclosed to us last night was temporarily forgotten. His face lost some of its pained look.

Jack, we would joke, had become so attached to his two donkeys that he put concern for their welfare before his own. There was also a further connection, with both Jack and now poor Blair suffering with their feet.

Jack was aware of all their habits. In the evening after they had been relieved of their packs both the donkeys would find a patch of dusty earth to roll in.

"They are having their bath," Jack would say as he watched them admiringly.

Then he would groom their coats with a special brush and ensure that they drank their fill and had plenty of grass before tethering them for the night.

He also knew when to indulge them and let them graze by the side of the road and when to pull their heads back and force them on their way.

(He was also aware, as we all were, of the idiosyncrasies of our two creatures. If Blair saw an inviting patch of greenery by the roadside there was no stopping him as he lunged for it. And Roy, when he was acting as Jack's ' understrapper' and tightening Thatcher's girth, had to be aware of her tendency to kick out if he tightened the girth too quickly. But on the whole we would say that both our donkeys were good natured).

When we finally arrived at the home of the farmer and his wife and explained our problem to them they said they would certainly transport the donkeys to the far side of Burgos where there was a blacksmith and where we could pick them up.

Our entry into the town, which was as usual through the extensive industrial zone, took us a further three hours so it was not until night had fallen and the street lights had been switched on that we found ourselves in the city centre.

Walt guided us to a hotel where we had to pass through a large oak outer door and climb several flights of stone steps. Our rooms did not have the homely feel of the lodging house in Pamplona. The floors were linoleum and the bed frames were iron. Walt said it was a hotel normally frequented by working men rather than pilgrims.

We were tired so we did not go out to eat. Instead after we had selected our rooms and our beds Echo went out with Oscar returning half an hour later with bottles of wine, fruit, bread and meat and potato pies.

We were almost silent as we ate. Whenever we arrived in a city after days on the road the tiredness which we had accumulated seemed to overwhelm us. This level of our fatigue was illustrated the following morning when both Oscar and Denis admitted that they had fallen asleep fully clothed. They had only woken after several hours to undress and get into bed.

In the end we stayed three days in Burgos. We did all the things that pilgrims do when they have a ' stop over' in a town. We washed our clothes and attempted to make ourselves more civilised and presentable. Oscar went to a barber's shop for a haircut. Venezia and Echo bought supplies for our onward journey. In the evenings we ate at a cheap Chinese restaurant that we had discovered.

There was no heating in the rooms at all and the nights were cold, however there were a series of paraffin heaters in the hallway. So to keep our rooms warm we had to leave our doors open. This led to certain sociability. A group of Portuguese workmen were staying in the rooms next door to us and we became a party to all their comings and goings and arguments and disputes.

Then one evening we had been dining at our Chinese restaurant and were making our way back over the Puente de Santa Maria, the bridge which traverses the Rio Arlanzon.

We had stopped briefly on the bridge, as people do, to look at the twinkling lights on either bank and to look down on the dark of the water when Echo turned to us. His voice was rich and vibrant in the night air.

"Pilgrims, who will be the first among you to name the valuable substance that forms the heart of the story I am going to relate?"

Venezia was the first to make a guess. She slipped her arm through Echo's and looked up at him hopefully.

"Am I allowed to guess, dear heart, that this valuable substance might be the love of a beautiful woman?"

Echo laughed in reply and squeezed her arm.

"Good answer ma petite Quebecoise. But on this occasion sadly not the one I am looking for."

After that we walked on a little further. (Venezia feeling rather snubbed had released his arm). Oscar guessed silver and Jack said gold, but neither was judged correct.

Then we turned into the street where our hotel was situated and approached the great outer oak door. A few minutes later we reached our landing and entered our rooms leaving the doors open so that the heat from the corridors could permeate inside.

Then Roy opened a bottle of wine and mugs were produced and we settled down on our beds (there being no chairs in the rooms) and Echo began his story:

"Pilgrims, the description I gave you of my life as an asylum seeker on the streets of Plymouth was something of an exaggeration. I was not completely destitute. I always had a small amount of money stitched into the lining of my coat in case of emergencies. And my first ambition on arrival was to be a taxi driver. So I knew I had to learn all about this strange old port city and its geography. So I went everywhere on foot until I knew the city of Plymouth as well as I knew Kinshasa or Brazzaville."

He paused for a moment. Then he said:

"I could close my eyes now and take you there."

(Readers will hopefully excuse this little recitation from Echo but it filled us with nostalgia for our dear old home city of Plymouth).

"I could take you along Royal Parade, past Debenhams, past Dingles where they had the terrible fire, past Marks and Spencer on Cornwall Street where one day they will surely erect a statue to their great saviour Sir Stuart Rose. And then we could go up North Hill, university to the left, library to the right, and on to Mutley Plain, Baptist church and Swarthmore to the left, Hyde Park at the end. Then we turn down again, past Charles Church, bombed in the war and left as a ruin in memory, down to Sutton Harbour, past the Thai Coffee House, on to the Barbican, obeisance and homage being paid at the gallery of Robert Lenkiewicz, a stop at Captain Jaspers, a stop at Jack's pub, then up on to the Hoe with all its history. Then drop down to the Civic Centre, past the Theatre Royal and all the betting shops, pubs and restaurants, a detour around the tarts parlours on Union Street, before turning back again to pass, with salute, the former offices of our esteemed morning and evening daily periodicals, the Western Morning News and the Herald, past the cinemas, past the casinos, in and out through the market, buying a Ginsters pasty, taking a pint at the Newmarket, looking in through the window of the Steak and Omelette on Cornwall Street and the Grecian Taverna adjacent to Frankfort Gate, finally stopping to stare at the rows of wonderful shining sparklers that make up the window collection of our well known city jewellers. There are five them principally, none of whom I am willing to name, for fear of becoming involved in a crippling libel action."

Echo paused then to draw breath and Roy topped up our mugs with wine. Those of us who smoked lit cigarettes.

"You have an obsession with the jewellery trade Echo," Oscar said finally. "When we were in Navarrete you had it on a par with the evil activities of the Conquistadors. And that I am sure is the answer to your question. Diamonds are the valuable substance to which you will refer."

"Correct, Pilgrim Oscar." Echo nodded his head solemnly.

But it was Walt, when his mug had been re filled with wine by Roy, who next addressed Echo. He was less accepting than the rest of us of Echo's rather long winded story.

"I have told you before Echo that this is a pilgrimage, we are not here to settle grudges." His voice was stern. "We all know the jewellery trade is crooked. Always has been, always will be. Nothing new in that."

Then he stopped and looked at Echo.

"Of course I know your circumstances." Then he sighed. "Oh get on with it then, but just don't take all night and don't go about getting everybody's blood pressure up like you normally do."

Echo scratched his head and paused.

"Walt is right. The excesses and cruelties of the diamond mining companies are well documented. Everyone knows the market is rigged and that a young buck buying a diamond for his bride is going to be scammed."

He paused as he marshalled his argument. Then he looked toward Walt.

"Walt can I say that in the same way that people should know that the silver and gold ornaments in the Spanish churches are the product of a system of obscene and terrifying cruelty, even if it was hundreds of years ago, so people should know that the diamond on display in the window of a jewellery store, mined in South Africa a generation ago, still bears the blood of the tortured worker who ripped it from the ground."

We listened to this in silence. Jack thought he was exaggerating but the rest of us believed him.

But then Denis asked: "But the owners of the jewellery shops. Are they complicit ? Did they know what was going on?"

Echo laughed bitterly.

"Oh yes," he replied. "They know alright. Don't worry about that Denis. I have the proof."

"The proof?" Jack's voice was hostile. He was always in favour of business and did not like to hear the jewellery trade being trashed.

"It was a look." Echo's reply was sharp.

"A look?" Jack was now staring at Echo contemptuously. "How can a look be proof?"

"Well, I will tell you Jack," Echo replied. He raised the mug containing the wine to his lips and continued his story.

"The winter's evening is cold. There will be snow later so all the citizens coats are buttoned up to their throats. The glistening sparklers are on display in the city centre jewellery store. I am standing on the pavement looking in. Eeny, Meeny, Miney, Moe. Now which of these beauties came from the mine that collapsed on top of Tresor who was married to Madeleine and who was father to Benjamin, now known to the citizens of the fair port city of Plymouth as Echo? Was it the little delicate one, 18 carat, back row to the left? Or maybe the handsome fellow at the front, chunky and square and solid?"

We were all listening carefully to Echo now. His voice was low and serious.

"The emporium owner, tall, stooped, grave, suit three piece, watch fob, the works, is staring back out at me. He knows who I am and I know who he is. Don't worry pilgrims, the research has all been done. He is Chamber of Commerce, Rotary, Church Warden and Parish Council. Straight as a dye. Gives to charity, all taxes paid. But there have been others before me. He knows exactly what I plan to do. He knows that when I put my ear to the glass I will be listening to the sound of a dying man's screams."

Echo looked at Jack.

"The look that he gave me went from comprehension to fear to hate. He knew that I could shout out Murderer,

Torturer, Exploiter, Abuser and that he couldn't touch me for it. I am the mirror to his corruption. I know that his discrete and high class emporium is no better than the whore's house church we saw in Navarrete. And he knows that I would certainly be within my rights to place a sign above his shop door reading Welcome to the House of Horrors, Come and Taste My Blood."

Echo paused here for a moment. We could not imagine making our pilgrimage without him. He was an integral part of our little group. But at the same time there were moments, such as this, when his intensity threatened to overwhelm us. He continued:

"In a minute the emporium owner breaks off eye contact and dips back into his shop and a moment later a rough looking security man emerges to announce - 'Alright Sunny Jim time to move on,' and that brings the show to a close."

While the rest of us were touched by this story Walt (along with Jack) was left unimpressed.

"Well thank you for that Echo. Thank you for informing us that the sun sets in the West in the evening. I had understood actually it was the other half of your story that you were going to tell us."

We all looked at Echo. We had been shocked by the tale he told us. There was a pause while Roy refilled our mugs.

Then Echo told us that following the death of his father Tresor in the mine collapse in South Africa he had returned home to the Congo with his mother Madeleine.

"I have given you a too rosy view of my Congolese homeland," he said, looking around. "The truth is that the mining companies have joined forces with what we call our 'government' to create a gangster administration so bad that evolution is now starting to operate in reverse. Each generation is now poorer and more ignorant of the outside world than the last. Schools are closing, roads are crumbling, the jungle is recovering whole towns."

We could hear the pain in his voice as he recounted these details.

"So I stayed some time in the Congo and then I went on to Sierre Leone." Echo looked serious. "But that was worse. The people who run that beautiful country were chopping off people's hands and gouging out their eyes to gain control of the diamond industry."

Echo stopped for a moment recalling.

"I worked in an open pit mine sieving piles of earth under the hot sun. You could count my ribs. Then one day a diamond big enough to be my ticket out came into my view, glinting at the bottom of the sieve. So I palmed it into my mouth and slipped away into the forest and made my way to the coast where I bought passage on a leaky old boat going to the Canary Islands."

"You were taking a chance there Echo." It was Denis speaking again.

"You are right there Denis. It was like in the films."

Echo raised his voice in keeping with the dramatic events he was narrating.

"We were baling for our lives, women and children being sick, a mad skipper . In short even the bravest and strongest were terrified."

"And when you arrived?"

"Oh Denis, what a lovely image!" Echo slapped his thigh and laughed out loud. "When we arrived! When our boat docked! When we strolled carefree down the gang plank to be greeted by loved ones!"

Denis looked abashed.

"No Denis, our rusty old hull broke up on the beach tossing us into the waves so that we had to crawl ashore in our rags of clothes where we fell into the laps of the astonished holiday makers. North meets south as it were."

"Who were they these holiday makers Echo?"

"They were the Brits."

"And what were they like?"

Echo's eyes filled with tears. He turned to Venezia.

"Venezia my dear, excuse my French, please, but really they were fucking marvellous. Brits always rise to a crisis. There were cups of tea, sandwiches, blankets, offers of places to stay. I thought I had died and gone to heaven."

This information left Jack in a dilemma. He wanted to be critical of people who were refugees but at the same time he was proud of the humanity displayed by his fellow countrymen so he kept his visage neutral. Echo was concluding his story now:

"So we were processed and lived in a camp until one day the Red Cross said I could go to Spain which I did and then someone else said there is a truck with vegetables going North so I booked a place on that and twenty four hours later the driver turned us all out on the hard shoulder near Folkestone. And there I was, or here I am, or which ever way it is you want to view it."

31

For the record, from our start point to the East of Marciac in southern France we had now covered about two hundred and seventy miles and by our calculations had another three hundred and sixty miles to go. We had crossed the Pyrenees, and walked through the valley of the Rio Aragon. But we still had to cross the vast open plain of the Meseta and then at the end climb up into the cool damp hills of Galicia.

***

The writer of this narrative has already admitted that an omission was made when it was not stated clearly enough at the beginning of this account that we shared this route with many other pilgrims, some walking singly, some walking in pairs or in groups.

Though, as has also been previously stated, because of Walt's detailed knowledge of the route we were often able to travel cross country on paths known only to him and so because of that we did encounter fewer pilgrims than might have been expected.

Walt also told us that the number of pilgrims setting off was increasing every year. But then he added that this was simply part of the natural cycle. He called it the constantly changing rhythm of the camino. This was a topic we could come back to later.

But if we were to seek a common denominator for our fellow pilgrims it would be their diversity. We were sure that if we continued on the camino long enough we would meet a representative of every nation under the sun.

However there are certain groups that do stand out.

There are the Brazilians who follow in the footsteps of their 'prophet,' the extraordinary writer Paulo de Coelho - the mention of whose name turned Walt's normally sanguine visage a shade of puce.

"I have no wish to be sued for libel," he told us through gritted teeth, "so I will refrain from giving an opinion on his books, or even on his character, except to record that I consider him to be an unprintable blank."

We also met Americans who, except for groups of youths who regard walking the camino as a sort of race, we thought of as strong and independent.

We discovered a surprising number of Venezia's compatriots, Quebecois, French Canadians. But on the whole they were a disappointment. They insisted on speaking only French and were defensive. They seemed to have their backs turned against the world. Venezia explained that in predominately English speaking Canada they considered themselves a threatened minority.

Obviously there are many Spaniards. But they travel only in groups, never alone, and never for long distances.

There are many French as well. They are always well equipped and on occasions Jack referred to them as ' bloody fussy.' We also heard them called 'maitres de danse' at times. This is because they tend to choose the best seasons, spring and early autumn, the more extreme seasons not agreeing with them.

We did not meet many other English pilgrims. We were given various reasons for this. It was said that they had become 'enfeebled' and had lost the urge to travel, although they do run the refuge at Rabanal in the manner of an English seaside boarding house. There are also some Irish.

To us however the most interesting people were those who had travelled the longest distances and usually alone. When we met a Swede or a Russian or a Serb who had started from

Stockholm or St Petersburg or Belgrade we always stopped to listen knowing they would have an interesting story to tell.

We heard many stories told by these pilgrims as we walked and it is only possible to recount a small number of them here.

For instance we were told a story about a pilgrim from Denmark. He had been walking with his dog but the dog had hurt his leg (so the story went). So the pilgrim had obtained a child's pram and was now pushing the dog in the pram. We also heard a number of stories about well known personalities who were thought to be walking the camino. On several occasions we were told that the actress Meryl Streep had been seen in the town of Burgos.

But there was one story that we heard that touched us. We were lucky. We had travelled together in a group. But there were other pilgrims who had come from afar walking by themselves and they suffered considerably from loneliness.

The story we heard concerned a pilgrim who had begun his walk alone in a distant Northern country. Sometimes we heard it as Latvia or Lithuania, at other times it was Russia or the Ukraine. Sometimes the man was an artist, sometimes a student or a priest. On several occasions we heard he was a professor of linguistics at the University of Uppsala in Sweden and another time an unemployed truck driver. At other times she was even a beautiful red headed woman struggling to get over a divorce.

So, our pilgrim is walking his (or her) lonely road, the sky overhead is heavy and grey, the rain will begin again soon. The pine forest stretches for miles around him. Occasionally a truck laden with timber passes to break the silence. Apart from that all he can hear is the sound of his own breathing. Then he hears a noise and turns to see a cyclist approaching. They stop and talk. The cyclist who is on a journey unspecified tells him that three days previously he had met a pilgrim, rucksack on his back, who was also walking to Santiago.

The cyclist continues, leaving the pilgrim by the side of the road, shivering with excitement, barely able to believe the news. He will have someone to talk to at last. As the rain begins to fall he consults his map. Ahead there is a crossroads with a small village where he can await the arrival of the second pilgrim.

As the daylight fades he pitches his tent by the crossroads. That night he hardly sleeps at all. Every time he hears a sound he is up and out of the tent and staring back down the road in case the pilgrim is approaching. But there is nothing except the continuing rain.

The morning finds him exhausted. He emerges from his tent. The sky is still grey but it has stopped raining. The village is no more than a handful of wooden houses and a poor looking shop. Quickly he crosses the road to the shop to ask if the pilgrim had passed by while he had been sleeping, but no one has heard anything.

The days pass. At first the villagers are suspicious. The woman who runs the shop furrows her brow as she listens to his story. But then the clouds clear and there are days of brilliant blue sky. The pilgrim cooks his food over his small stove and waits contented, enjoying the warm weather. The villagers bring him bottles of beer and tell him stories about their lives. Nothing much happens in the village. Half a dozen trucks laden with timber pass in a day but none of them stop.

But on the fourth day the rain begins again, heavier than ever, forcing the pilgrim to stay in his tent. No one from the village comes to visit. The pilgrim once again feels the pangs of the terrible loneliness that have gripped him for weeks. He get out the map, perhaps the pilgrim has taken another route.

The rain continues for the fifth day. He eats by himself, convinced now that the pilgrim will never come. He feels a deep sadness welling up inside.

Finally on the morning of the sixth day, early, before it is properly light and before anyone from the village has risen, he packs up his tent and sets off again to continue his lonely journey, shaking at his head at his own stupidity, disgusted at himself for wasting so much precious time.

The nearer we came to Santiago the more pilgrims we encountered but this story was a reminder of the great distances some pilgrims had walked and of the loneliness they had felt.

32

There is probably no good point in any novel to begin a discussion on podiatry - but this is actually of crucial importance to anyone contemplating walking the Camino de Santiago. So in brief summary:

A pilgrim should take in his or her pack two pairs of shoes. One should be a pair of lightweight but good quality open sandals. This is the ' default' walking option. To be worn with cotton or wool socks. Specialist waterproof socks, which are also warm, can be added if needed. If the track is muddy or wet change to lightweight waterproof walking shoes or trainers. In the evenings always rub hydrating cream into the feet to keep them supple.

It is to be hoped also that patient readers will allow a small diversion to describe the yellow arrows that guided us West as we walked.

Each arrow, in Spanish 'flecha amarillo' and in French 'fleche jaune', is approximately nine inches long and about an inch wide. It is always hand painted on with a good thick stroke and is straight or curved according to direction intended. The colour when painted on new is rich and bright. After some time the paint becomes faded and worn.

We quickly observed that these arrows were only visible to those who needed to see them.

If we came to a junction on the path our eyes would be drawn to the arrow half hidden on the side of the path. It might be painted discretely on the side of a rock. Certainly it would not have been apparent to a casual observer.

In a town the arrows might be placed on a kerbstone or a pavement or on a wall. Ordinary citizens passing by would not be aware of their significance at all. So they came to feel to us like our secret guide.

(These yellow arrows are only of use to people travelling West toward Santiago. They are of no use to people travelling home in the opposite direction).

Walt also told us the story of how on one occasion he had been bringing a group of pilgrims north from Seville on the Via de la Plata.

"We arrived at a small village called Granja de Moreruela," he told us. "This is where the path splits. One path carries on North to join the Camino Frances at Astorga while the other forks left to carry pilgrims through the hills of Galicia to Santiago via Ourense. However, strangely, the only indication that was available to pilgrims to mark the turning was a faded yellow arrow painted on to the side of a rubbish bin that was on wheels and so movable. Of course I knew the turning but pilgrims missing it would have added several hundred miles to their journey."

33

As we made our way out of Burgos on a fine Autumn morning a few days later we saw the open countryside ahead of us once again and our pace quickened.

Then Jack turned to Roy and said in a tone that was intended to be light:

"I shall certainly be pleased to see that pair of donkeys again. I hope the blacksmith will do a good job of shooing poor Blair."

A number of days had now passed since Jack had made his confession and so there had been time for us to consider our reaction.

It would have been easy for us to have excused Jack for what he had done. We could have said, correctly enough, that he was young, that he was naive, that he was coerced, and that others with a stronger character than he had also succumbed. He had also made a clean breast of everything in his confession to us.

Walt could also have said that in the Civil War in America he had seen atrocities committed by men who were normally law abiding citizens and Echo could have given us descriptions of terrible things done in the Congo, by ordinary people, that would have turned our stomachs.

But however we looked at it we could not deny that Jack had been a member of a group that had tortured a man to death in the most terrible and sadistic of circumstances. He could have disobeyed orders and refused to take part and suffered the consequences.

Certainly if he had been before a court all his protestations that he had not put a foot wrong since leaving the army would not have saved him from a long jail sentence. In fact his admission that he, and the rest of them, had taken some sort of disgusting pleasure in their acts - well, that would have gone badly against him.

But it was not our intention to make Jack an outcast because of this. We simply knew that we had to call his actions by their correct title. He had committed murder and he was a murderer. That was it. No more, no less.

Walt then told us that when he had been writing his poems in New York he had walked the streets and met all sorts - from saints to charlatans and had recognised them all. Then he went further when he told us in a short extract:

What blurt is this about virtue and about vice?
Evil propels me and reform of evil propels me, I stand indifferent,
My gait is no fault-finder's or rejecter's gait,
I moisten the roots of all that has grown.

It also has to be said also that there was an element of self preservation in our reaction. For the short duration of this pilgrimage we were all together in our own small boat on the high seas - all with our own particular secrets we would rather not disclose. Too much grandstanding and we would all have been in the water together.

But there was no thought that Jack had somehow 'got off.' The pain of what he had done was written on his face. Since telling us his story, he had looked pale and ill. He had also lost more weight than the rest of us and even the new clothes he had bought now hung off him, giving him rather the look of a scarecrow.

34

After we had walked for an hour and had passed the village of Villabilla de Burgos we were directed to the premises of the village blacksmith. There we were delighted to find Thatcher and Blair along with the farmer and all our equipment waiting for us.

Jack took a deep breath and shook his head, as if to rid himself of those terrible memories of the past. Then having greeted his two beasts again he explained to the blacksmith:

"I noticed poor Blair was lame the day before we arrived at the monastery at San Juan de Ortega. We transferred as much of the load as we could to the other donkey."

After he had listened to this tale the blacksmith picked up Blair's off side front foot and examined it. Then he glanced over at Thatcher.

"I had better clip that donkey's feet as well," he said after a moment. "If I don't you will have trouble with her later on as well."

As the blacksmith worked we noted that in stature he was short and diminutive, but we could also see that he had a 'way' with animals as neither Blair nor Thatcher flinched as he cut back their hooves. When he was halfway through his wife emerged from the house to join us and we noted with amusement that her build was heavyset and strong, as if their roles had been reversed.

Finally when the operation was completed and both our donkeys were correctly shod and in good condition once again the blacksmith's wife invited us to join them for lunch. We ate sitting at a table in the garden under the shade of a large tree.

"It is a pleasure to see pilgrims still travelling with pack animals and looking after them so well," our blacksmith said as we ate. "Can I ask where you bought them Sir?"

"Certainly," Jack replied. We could see he was pleased to receive this compliment from the blacksmith. "We bought them from a farmer near the town of Oloron Sainte Marie which is in the Vallee d'Aspe on the French side of the Pyrenees."

The blacksmith nodded again gravely. He raised a bottle of beer to his lips.

"In that case Senor I hope you will not be insulted if I ask how much you paid for them?"

When Jack told him the amount, saying we had been informed they were good donkeys in their prime and that they had never caused us a moment's bother, so that we did not begrudge the money paid, the blacksmith whistled through his teeth.

Then he put got up from the table and went over to where our two donkeys were quietly grazing.

We regarded him as he opened their mouths and inspected their teeth. Then he checked behind their ears and we saw him smile as he noted the red and blue dots. After that he walked behind and lifted up their tails. Then he nodded his head before returning to the table and looking at his wife.

"I think I am right there Senor."

Jack looked at him. A worried frown had appeared on his face.

"One of the donkeys, the one with the red spot, you call her Thatcher, she is actually much older than the one you call Blair, the one with the blue spot." He glanced at his wife again.

"It is not impossible Senor," he said finally. "That Thatcher is the mother of Blair."

Jack looked stunned at this information. He turned to the blacksmith.

"But are you sure Senor? Blair is always snuffling up Thatcher's rear end. We are always having to pull him away."

The blacksmith looked grave at this.

"I am certain Senor. My advice is that you reduce the burden you place on the older donkey. The younger donkey is in better condition and more able to take the extra weight."

This revelation caused much mirth among the pilgrims. Roy who despite having risen to a position of great importance because of his football prowess still retained the politics of the place of his birth, the city of Dundee. Sadly the actual words he used to express his views on this occasion are unprintable in a family journal.

We all had our say then, Tory and Labour, the old battles resumed. But it was Venezia, being Quebecois and therefore not party to our domestic disputes, who was the most stylish and original in her commentary.

Jack was supervising the loading up of the donkeys. He was shouting instructions to Roy and Denis to make sure the new weight distributions were correct. Thatcher was in foul mood and Roy had to move quickly to avoid being kicked when she lashed out with a hind leg.

It was then that Venezia disappeared into a nearby field, reappearing moments later with a handful of poppies which she quickly wove into two rough red garlands.

Then as we were ready to set off she stepped forward in front of our two patient beasts. Carefully placing the garlands around their ears she took a pace back and gave a little curtsey before announcing in a faux serious voice:

"Oh wonderful Queens and Kings of the donkey world, I do now pronounce you Mother and Son."

We all laughed at this with the exception of Jack. His visage had turned sour. He hated it when we mocked his donkeys.

35

After that we once again recommenced our journey West and slowly and mysteriously a new landscape began to roll out in front of us.

We had grown tired of our descent through Navarre and Rioja. On reflection it seemed to us that it was a paysage that lacked a character by which it could be defined. We had felt excited and alive when we had crossed the mighty Pyrenees and when we had followed the Rio Aragon we had imagined ourselves as heroic explorers.

But now we felt excited again as ahead of us we could see the beginning of a wide open ancient land with rocky surfaces and flat topped buttes. We took deep breaths and looked at the horizon stretching away ahead of us.

During the course of the afternoon we came to the village of Hornillos where we stopped to drink at the fountain. Here Walt turned to Jack and said that it was time he finally got rid of what he called, 'those damned old army boots' which had caused him so much trouble.

So a few minutes later we found a borne on the edge of the village and Jack removed the boots from the pannier on poor Blair's back and placed them by the stone marker.

As has been mentioned before all pilgrims place stones on the bornes as they pass. It is part of the pilgrim ritual.

But it was not only stones that were left on the bornes. We saw lockets, beads and occasionally scarves. Several times we found a piece of wood inscribed with a name or a blessing. The largest item we saw was a bicycle with a buckled wheel propped up against a borne.

Could the leaving of his old army boots be taken as some sort of act of atonement on the part of Jack? Was it the final discarding of an old life?

As the sun began to drop toward the western horizon we spotted a small stand of trees and sending Denis ahead he was able to report back ten minutes later that there was a stream running through it and that there was also sufficient grass for the donkeys.

As the night fell and we put up our tents and Venezia and Echo worked around the fire. Soon we could see two pans on the fire and smell the sizzling pork chops and the mound of fried potatoes.

It was half an hour later when we were sitting around the fire consuming our delicious dinner that Jack, who was now recovering his authority and composure, turned to Oscar.

"It is time we decided finally what it is was we were going to do with the money from that bloody robbery Oscar."

Oscar's reply to this suggestion, when it came, was quick and sharp.

"Actually Pilgrim Jack it is my money if you remember. So in that case and if you don't mind I am going to decide what we do with it."

This led Jack to reply equally sharply:

"Actually you are wrong there Pilgrim Oscar. It is not your money, you stole it. If we are honest people we should certainly return it to the bank."

At that point in the dispute a dreadful silence descended on the camp and we knew that we had reached an important moment on our pilgrimage. We could hear the sound of the fire crackling and Roy refilled our mugs with wine.

We knew that Oscar would have been within his rights to reply to Jack :

' Well hold on Jack, you have confessed a horrendous and sadistic crime to us. You have admitted torturing a man to death and laughing while you were on the job. Because of that that you have certainly forfeited your right to lecture the rest of us on how to behave…'

But Oscar knew, as we all knew, that if that if we held that sword over Jack's head for the rest of our pilgrimage it would be ruinous for the unity of our little group.

It was Wilson who finally spoke up.

"I would not worry too much about the bank if I were you Jack. The bank is rich and corrupt, the bank can look after itself."

But instead of calming Jack's anger this comment only added fuel to it. Abruptly he put his plate of pork chops and fried potatoes to one side.

"No Wilson. That is the sort of attitude I could never go along with. I have always played fair and never taken a penny that was not mine and I am not going to alter my habits now."

At this Echo gave a contemptuous laugh.

"If a citizen of Kinshasa or Brazzaville is gifted One Million Euro and he turns it down he is regarded as a chump."

Venezia began to collect up the plates as Roy suddenly joined in the argument:

"In ma time in football I've seen terrific changes. Footballers were very poor when I started but now everything's different. There's some players that has got more money than's good for them, but there's others that are very skilful, great entertainers."

He paused for a moment and looked round and then added in his low Scottish patois:

"Ah say we keeps the bloody money, the hell with the bank."

Jack turned to stare at Roy. This was not the sort of response he expected from a man in Roy's position. Then he struggled slowly to his feet.

"I can tell you my fellow pilgrims that I am deeply concerned by what I have heard here tonight."

He looked around at us sternly.

"Have any of you given a thought to the poor woman who was shot in the leg by El Lobo during the raid? And that is not to mention the other staff. They must have been frightened out of their wits by all the carryings on."

Here Venezia who had poured water into a bowl and was starting to wash the dishes alongside Echo called out to Walt:

"You are supposed to be our guide Walt. We're faced with a moral dilemma. You should be helping us."

But Walt was grumpy. The debate did not interest him. His eyes were half closed. Finally he sniffed and replied:

"Don't give a damn. Throw it away for all I care. Far as I'm concerned money never bought anyone any happiness."

Then he sniffed again.

"But now you've got the damn stuff you might as well give it to the poor. They'll have some use for it at least."

Wilson added more wood to the fire to keep us warm and the discussion continued a little longer before Oscar put up his hand and said finally:

"I have received all your views fellow pilgrims and they have been most instructive but now I have decided what it is I am going to do with the money."

So we settled back to hear what he had to say. His voice was clear and direct.

"First taking into account the view of fellow pilgrim Jack Phillpotts I propose that we return a portion of the money to the bank on the strict understanding that it is used to alleviate the suffering of the poor woman who was shot and for the others who were in the bank at the time."

Jack nodded his assent to this.

"I next propose that a further portion of the money be divided up amongst each of the pilgrims to do with as they see fit and after that the main part of the money be given to a worthwhile charitable cause on which we can all decide."

Seeing that he was finished Echo called out from the other side of the fire.

"That is a fair and equitable solution Pilgrim Oscar."

It was only Wilson who raised his hand and said he was going to vote against.

"I have made my position clear before on this matter of principle."

His green eyes glistened behind his thick glasses and we wondered for a moment what had happened to that romantic character who had acted so heroically in rescuing the girl.

"I have told you that I do not believe in giving money to charity. By looking after the poor ourselves we are allowing the state to abandon its responsibilities."

Whatever the intellectual merit of Wilson's argument it certainly lacked heart and nobody else supported it.

But then as the rest of us were about vote in favour Denis cut in:

"I would like to propose an amendment. As we are on the adventure of a lifetime I think we should all spend our part of the money with that spirit of adventure in mind."

We all nodded our agreement to that and the proposition was then passed on a show of hands. After that another bottle of wine was opened and cigarettes lit from the embers of the fire. Then Oscar drafted out a letter on a notepad which we would send to the bank with the money. After several attempts this was the wording on which we agreed:

Dear Sirs,

We hereby return a portion of the money taken from your bank by the notorious bank robber El Lobo on the strict understanding that half of it is given to the poor lady who was shot and that the rest is dispersed among the other staff in compensation for what they have suffered during the raid.

Yours etc

Your Faithful Friends

36

There were many times on our pilgrimage when we were aware that we had broken the normal laws of the scientific world. Oscar sometimes went further accusing our writer of suspending the laws of commonsense.

However as our writer pointed out, Einstein had overturned the laws of physics as outlined by Newton and it was certainly only a ' matter of time' before a ' new kid on the block' took his own wrecking ball to Einstein's theories.

We were beginning to see evidence of this with the presence all around us of the ghosts of pilgrims past. We saw them every night. We were sure about that. They had their fire and their encampments next to ours.

And so while at present it may not scientifically possible to foretell the future there were occasions when we knew, with certainty, as we did that night, that we were about to experience a moment of importance.

As Oscar returned his notebook to his bag it was agreed that we would wait until we arrived in Leon before we posted the letter with the money. Oscar said that if we posted such a package in a small country post office there was the danger of it being recognised and traced.

After that there was a silence. The sky overhead was clear and a half moon hung over us. Then a wind got up and we started to feel the cold. Denis added more wood to the fire and Roy refilled our mugs.

We all looked expectantly at Walt who was still in his somnolent pose. He had the appearance of a large strange bearded Buddha, with mug of wine to hand. Then finally he opened his eyes and gave a half stifled yawn before shaking his head as if waking from a deep sleep. Finally he turned to Jack.

"It has been a long time my friend." He sniffed again. "But sometime you are going to have to open that mouth of yours and give us a song or we will never know."

Jack hesitated. With a certain dread he had been anticipating the request. Venezia put her hand on his shoulder to steady him.

"It was said on occasion I could have passed for the Irish tenor Josef Locke."

He looked around the circle of faces lit up by the fire.

"But that was a long time ago now."

His voice began to quaver.

"I don't know if I could do it again."

Venezia let her hand run down the side of his arm and drop away. Then finally Jack got to his feet.

He went to the edge of the circle of our fire and stood for a moment with his back to us. We could see his shoulders moving as he drew breath in and out to prepare himself. Then he turned around and looking past us into the night opened his mouth and began to sing.

He hesitated at first and at one point he stopped briefly but as he gained confidence his voice grew stronger. Then as he sang the years slid off him and the torment in which he had become engulfed dropped away.

When he had finished quiet returned to the night so that all we could hear was the crackle of sticks on the fire and the sound of the donkeys hooves as they moved.

Then Venezia got up and went over to where he was standing and put her arms around him and hugged him tight and never let on to anyone that she could feel her shoulder wet with his tears.

37

We loved the landscape that was now unfolding in front of us. Hard old rock ridges traversed the landscape in the way a rolling wave crosses an ocean. Even in autumn, when the summer crops are gone, the smell of dust lingers in the air. The path is worn from millions of feet.

There are certain points on the journey that stay in the mind of pilgrims. They are mentioned when they meet, when other places are forgotten. These spots would certainly include the Col du Somport in the Pyrenees and the drop down into Jaca on the Spanish side. And ahead of us was the climb up to the Cruz de Ferro in Galicia and the ascent of O'Cebreiro. To these memorable locations we would certainly add the small town of Castrojeriz.

Up behind the town there are the remains of the old Roman fort where pilgrims can turn three sixty degrees and survey the flat top buttes and the roads coming from the four points of the compass. They can absorb the heat of the brown rock hard country, listen to the tramp of the feet of the old Roman legions, hear the slow movement of millions of pilgrims as they move slowly West. This is an old worn country that still gives comfort to pilgrims as they pass through.

It was as we left Castrojeriz that we found the letter.

It was late in the afternoon and we had climbed up the steep pitch to the summit of the next butte. We could feel the cold wind biting into us as the day began to fade. It was Denis who called out:

"There's a note on that borne."

Venezia who was nearby advanced and picked up the stone on the top of the borne and removed the paper and holding it up to the fading light read out in her Quebecois accent.

Felix, I will meet you in Fromista (day after tomorrow) love you for ever (!) Rachel (Australia).

We looked quickly ahead but the path was empty.

Venezia passed the note to Denis but then Walt called out:

"You can't alter the course of history. Replace it the way it was so it can be found correctly."

We had left Castrojeriz late in the afternoon so there was insufficient time, before darkness fell, to descend into the next valley to find a sheltered location where we could pitch our camp. All we could discover in the end was a small rock outcrop that gave us some poor relief from the elements. Luckily there was a dip in the ground that had accumulated rain water enough for our donkeys. As we set up camp the last of the light faded and the town of Castrojeriz, now behind us, blended into the rough rock of the landscape. By the time night had fallen properly we had the tents up and Wilson and Denis had scrounged enough scrub wood for a small fire. Provided we kept our backs to the wind we could eat our dinner in modest comfort.

As we ate we discussed the note and speculated on who Felix and Rachel might be and marvelled that the stone bornes were now also being used as letterboxes by pilgrims.

"It is well known that you have aspirations to be a writer Wilson," said Walt finally. "So now you have a situation. A mysterious billet doux, left under a stone. I am sure you could turn that into a story."

"You are actually pointing the finger in the wrong direction," Wilson replied after a moment. "It is Venezia who is the one who has the imagination."

He turned to Venezia, who had her arm around Echo and was gazing into the fire.

"The tale you told us about how you received your name. That was very inventive. I am sure there is a continuation to it."

"Well," said Venezia smiling and releasing her arm from around the shoulders of Echo. "You certainly gave us a dramatic story of rescuing a maiden in distress Wilson."

She paused and Roy refilled her mug.

"Give me my jacket Echo dear. It's getting cold here." She glanced up at the clear cold sky with a million stars twinkling in it.

"You certainly chose a good place to camp Walt. We are on top of a ridge exposed to the wind in the middle of nowhere. We will be lucky if we do not freeze to death tonight."

Oscar put a log on the fire and the flames jumped up into the night.

"But I will continue my story if you like." She lit a cigarette that Echo had passed to her and pulled her jacket around her shoulders. Then she began:

"What I am about to recount to you happened three years ago when I was working temporarily, on account of a certain financial insolvency, for a well known insurance company in the heart of downtown Montreal."

She laughed quietly to herself at the memory.

"It is a winter's afternoon. The sky is already dark, and the snow has started to fall. In the office we are getting ready to go home. I have put on my coat and a moment later I am standing outside the building and about to set off. I turn to my left as usual, and then, well, that is when it all begins."

Echo was looking at her.

"When what all begins Venezia?"

"When I was not able to advance in the direction I wanted to go Echo." Venezia paused. "There was something blocking my passage."

"Something?" Echo looked puzzled.

"Well whatever it was," Venezia replied impatiently. "He, she, they, it. It was invisible and transparent. There was no one with a suitcase, no one with a bag of golf clubs. There was nobody there. And before you ask, yes, other pedestrians were able to pass. I was the only one it was blocking."

She looked at us for a moment across the flames of the fire.

"You can think what you want boys but I am telling you. Something was stopping me from turning left down that street and it was pissing me off. I was expected home for Christ's sake. Mother was cooking supper."

As we waited for her to continue we recalled the many facets of Venezia's character. We recalled, as we always did, how Oscar said she took her cue from the Book of Imagination.

"I waited for a gap in the traffic," she was continuing now. "And then I made my way through the snow to the coffee shop over the road."

She paused then and Oscar took the last of our store of wood and placed it on the fire so that it burned up brightly. Then she changed the direction of her story slightly.

"There had been times recently when I had begun to suspect there was someone else in our house."

We all leaned forward to listen.

"There were little darts of colour, blues, yellows, reds, just at the edge of my vision. If I turned my head too quickly they disappeared. There was also the trace of a scent, almonds and lemon."

"Any voices, any sound?" Walt was looking at her anxiously across the fire.

"No." She shook her head. "Nothing like that."

We waited for her to continue.

"It was quite dark in the coffee shop. I got some money out of my purse and went over to the pay phone on the wall and called Mother to say I had met an old friend and that I would not be home for supper."

She paused for a long time here and we watched the flames crackling up off the fire until we thought she was declining to continue until in a low voice she said:

"This time the colours were so faint if I had not been looking out for them I would probably not have noticed them at all."

"And the scent? The perfume? The lemon and the almonds?" It was Denis asking.

"Like the colours Denis. Just the slightest trace."

Roy refilled her mug with good red wine.

"Thank you Roy dear." She turned toward him and smiled. "You are always so attentive."

She took a sip of the wine.

"I was in no hurry now. Mother had been phoned. I had the rest of the evening to myself. At that stage I was still curious."

There was a pause and she leaned over and touched Echo's hand and then looked at the rest of us.

"I was trying to work out what was happening to me, what had blocked me on the pavement outside my office and what the significance was of the scent and the coloured darts of light."

She paused again, as if uncertain. Then she took a deep breath and continued.

"There was only one explanation I could come up with. I have already told you that my conception was planned in Venice - but due to the car crash and all that, the deed was done later on in Montreal."

Echo smiled and touched her arm. For once he spoke gently.

"Are we talking about the emergence of a life unborn, a life that according to the laws of the scientific world should not be possible?"

"Well I suppose so," said Venezia slowly after a minute. "That is the only thing that made any sense."

She looked nervously over to Walt but he did not react. Then she continued quickly on.

"I stayed there for a further ten minutes, finished my coffee, then I got up and went outside and walked to the nearest metro station and took the next train down to Verdun by the river."

She paused for a moment and looked around as if checking the direction the story was taking.

"By the time I got out onto the street it was snowing hard. I was getting nervous. Verdun was not normally a place I visited. But something, whatever it was, had sent me there. I stood there for a moment, trying to get my bearings, looking out at the rows of duplexes and small apartment blocks."

We were all watching Venezia carefully now.

"Then I began walking. I went up and down the streets as the snow fell, observing the front of the houses by the light of the street lamps. Don't ask me how long I walked, maybe an hour, maybe more. I couldn't feel my hands or my feet, I was shivering. I felt horrible. I was sure I was being drawn into something."

"And then you discovered what you had been searching for." It was Walt interrupting quietly. Venezia nodded.

"It was a couple of streets back from the metro station. I was sure I had checked the street already but I must have missed it. It was a three storey apartment building, quite old, painted white. I carefully checked each window, working my way up the floors, stopping where a light was on or where the curtain was of a particular style. It was on the second floor, third window along. The window was not fully closed which was unusual and there was an edge of a curtain flapping outside. There was no light on inside.

"For a long time I had no image, nothing at all. Then a picture came of a woman, about my own age. She was inside the apartment, looking out of the window down on to the street where I was standing. She could see the snow lying on the ground. She was terribly unhappy. There was something wrong with her face. I was sure she had been waiting for me. There was a strong smell of polish, as if she had been waxing a wooden floor."

"What was the time of day?" Walt was looking at her.

"Late afternoon. The light was fading."

"But when you were standing there looking up it was dark?"

"That's right."

Venezia thought for a long time before she spoke again. Her voice was low and sad.

"I don't know how I made it home that night. She needed me. It was awful to have missed her like that."

The fire was dying down now and glowing red. Venezia's face looked tired.

"There is another part to the story," she said finally, "but it is too late now. I am not going to tell you about it tonight."

38

When we woke in the morning we found that the sky was cold and grey and that the water in the little dip and in our water bottles had a thin film of ice on it.

We emerged reluctantly from our tents cursing the cold and whoever it was who had decided to plant our camp on this exposed ridge.

"I am too old for this game," Jack grumbled. He was bundled up in a thick coat. He untethered Thatcher and poor Blair and brought them into camp. "My legs are stiff as hell. I doubt I shall be able to walk five miles today."

The night cold had killed our fire stone dead so Echo and Venezia brewed up our coffee on the gas stove and we drank it quickly, consuming slices of bread and jam as we stood. As we breathed out we could see our breath heavy and frosty.

We all had our tasks and we went to them. Venezia and Echo cleaned and stowed our cooking gear and Roy, Oscar and Denis took down our tents and packed all our possessions into the panniers. Jack fussed over his donkeys, making sure their tackle was correct and in order. He then supervised the loading process, shouting at Roy to put his back into it as he pulled poor Blair's girth tight. As usual Walt took no part in this physical activity. Instead he consulted his map and looked out over our path ahead.

As we breathed in the cold morning air and felt the frost crunching under our boots we became so absorbed in our tasks we failed to notice that already the clouds were beginning to disperse, to make way for the warming sun.

After half an hour when we stopped to allow Jack to make an adjustment to Thatcher's girth we found to our surprise that we were able to strip off our outer coats and feel once again the pleasant warmth on our backs.

After that we continued on our way descending and ascending the hard rock ridges. We noted piles of stones by the side of the path which Walt said had no connection to any of our pilgrim myths. They had been drawn off the fields by the farmers and it was a further pointer to us that this was a rough harsh land. As we followed the dusty path we could see across the brown terrain stretching for miles in all directions.

As the sun warmed us that morning it caused a great sense of contentment to well up inside us. The sadness of Venezia's story was temporarily forgotten. We were barely able to believe the good fortune that allowed us to tramp across this beautiful old landscape.

The songs that Hans Klugman had given us, magically selected we now knew, were our inspiration. They led us in the morning, tripping light and thin as air over the lovely landscape, and in evening guided us slow footed and tired to our night's resting spot.

In the village of Boadilla where we stopped to eat our lunch we met again the two German pilgrims, we now officially named them Hang Dog Heinz and his Charming Wife, whom we had encountered as we had left Pamplona. They had taken our photographs as we posed beside the metallic statues on the Alto Perdon.

As we ate, still effused with the pleasant sensation of contentment, the Charming Wife, who had long flowing hair, explained to us that her poor husband had suffered a form of breakdown due to the way he had been treated by his superiors at the timber firm near Munich where he was employed.

She turned and lovingly touched her husband's arm. His face was downcast and certainly the appellation we had given him at that moment seemed very appropriate.

"We have great hopes that the camino will be a cure for him," the Charming Wife was saying. "The fresh air is always so good."

As we studied him we were not so sure. He was rolling a cigarette and avoiding eye contact. We all felt there was a certain shiftiness about him.

Late in the afternoon, still in good humour, despite hearing of Hang Dog Heinz and his misfortunes, we found ourselves walking by the side of the Canal de Castilla.

"We will be in the town of Fromista soon." Walt looked at Echo. "There is a church there I want to show you. It is the opposite of the church in Navarrete that you disliked so much. It's also time we tried out one of those pilgrim refuges. The one I am thinking of has a good enough reputation."

But an hour later when we had entered the refuge, having unloaded our donkeys and found them pasture on the edge of the town, it was Aimery Picaud's description of refuges as the 'Stinking Shithouses' that was at the forefront of our minds.

We were used to being on our own, either in cheap hotels or in our own encampment. The noise and number of the pilgrims, the shared sleeping accommodation and the crowded kitchen, all destabilised us.

It was Roy, inspecting one of the dormitories filled with a dozen untidy pilgrims, who gave our reaction.

"Yer pal was right Walt. I wouldna' put ma dog in a place like this. They must no have health inspectors in Spain."

But when we were outside again we could see that Walt was laughing hard.

"That was a good introduction for you pilgrims. Believe me that is one of the better refuges. We will stay here tonight and continue with our normal way of life again tomorrow."

Walt then took us to visit the church of St Martin de Tours (Romanesque, 11th Century). He explained that it was known even by its exterior to be one of the most beautiful of all churches on this pilgrim route.

"Its lines have a simplicity and harmony that are a contrast to the ostentation and vulgarity we have seen in some of the other churches." Walt was addressing himself pointedly to Echo.

Walt was right. Inside there was no great ornamentation, no signs of the gold and silver 'overkill' that we had seen in Navarrete and the other churches.

What we saw instead, as we all stood quietly and looked around, was a harmony of line that was geometric in its perfection. Walt let us absorb this perfection in silence.

"As you can imagine Echo," he said finally. "I find this place to be an inspiration. It is here I sense something more than just the hand of man." Then he paused for a moment before adding, "I hope you do too."

Echo did not reply to this. Instead he looked thoughtful. There was no doubt, we were sure, that he would give us the full benefit of his opinion later.

After that we ate simply in a small restaurant before returning to the refuge to to our pleasant surprise that the noise and confusion had evaporated as most pilgrims had now retired to their beds in the dormitories.

We received a second pleasant surprise when we discovered sitting around the kitchen table Hang Dog Heinz and his Charming Wife. They were talking to two Austrian girls who we had also met earlier. Next to them were two other pilgrims, an elderly Frenchman and his younger Dutch walking companion, neither of whom we had encountered before.

Chairs were drawn up and we were invited to join the group and more bottles of wine were opened. The light in the kitchen was dim and there were smoky candles on the table. Faces flickered in the shadows. Our little group that night was an excellent example of the way pilgrims from all over the world come together to tell their odd and unusual stories.

The Frenchman told us that as a young man he had fought with the French Foreign Legion at the battle of Dien Bien Phu. By contrast his Dutch walking companion told us he had been at the last concert Joy Division gave before the singer Ian Curtis hanged himself. The Frenchman said that when he slept he still heard the terrible sound of the artillery barrage as the Vietnamese moved in on the encircled camp. The young Dutchman said if he could have traded places with the singer Ian Curtis he would have done so. We never learned the real names of these two characters but referred to them, when we met them again, as simply Dien and Joy.

After we had heard these stories we looked toward Hang Dog Heinz but he only put his head back and blew cigarette smoke at the ceiling while his Charming Wife gazed at him with worried attention.

Eventually when there was a pause Jack judged that the time was right. He turned to Roy.

"We're all telling our stories Pilgrim Roy. We think it's your turn now if you're ready."

At this request Roy looked around, for a moment undecided. He stared at the other pilgrims in the room who had now turned to face him. The Austrian girls passed around the bottles of wine. Then in this flickering half light and in the quiet of the night he finally spoke.

"I've never breathed a word about this to anybody till now," he said slowly. Then he looked around. "No even to ma lovely wife Mary."

There was a further silence. His voice was low. It seemed to have the consistency of gravel. "I know yous lot have said things about me in the past."

He started straight at Oscar.

"I know yous have referred to me as Old Mutton Head and Biffo the Dundee Mule. And yous."

He turned to Echo.

"And I know yous call me the Noble Savage."

Roy's face began to redden menacingly. Then his gaze swept slowly around the room until it came to rest on the two Austrian girls.

"This includes you two wee lassies as well. Oscar, Echo." He pointed his finger at them. "I'm holding yous personally responsible. I'm no telling this story if it's going to be all over the journals in the morning. I'll have yer head on a pole, the pair of yous."

He swung around to the startled Austrian girls again.

"The BBC's always insultin' me and ma family. Terrible treatment, inexcusable. They're very biased, never give us a break. They've never a good word to say about me or ma team."

He looked hard at the Austrian girls again, leaving us to wonder if at some time he had suffered a bad experience with an Austrian broadcasting service.

There was a silence then Jack said formally:

"I am sure I can speak for our pilgrim band that no word of any story you are about to recount will pass our lips."

Then the two Austrian girls, Hangdog Heinz and his Charming Wife and Dien and Joy also gave similar assents.

The candles flickered in the room as a breeze entered from a half opened window. So finally with a sigh he did begin.

"Well, I've got to start somewhere boys so I'll begin by sayin' I'd spent the day at the dog track. Ma father trained greyhounds in Dundee. Our family's always done it."

He paused and looked around.

"There was even certain people criticisin' me for that. They said I was neglectin' ma duties." He gave a throaty laugh. "They said I was getting in with the wrong crowd and it was doin' me naw good."

Jack nodded thoughtfully.

"Yes we know about them. The Welshmen."

Roy nodded. "Aye, the bampots (trans: idiots) who write for the journals said I was out of ma depth. They said the company of those fellas from the dog track was too rich for a wee boy from Dundee."

"That's right," said Echo thoughtfully. "I do remember it now. They described it as an error of judgement."

Roy turned sharply, and we could see his face suddenly reddening again in the flickering candlelight. We recalled with a shiver of fear the fight between these two Leviathans on the banks of the Rio Aragon. But then he muttered a series of low expletives to himself in his Scottish patois. This had the effect of dissipating his anger and allowing him to continue.

"I canna tell yous the exact time I left the dog track. All I know it was bloody baltic (trans: cold). I had a thick coat on and ma hat on ma jaggy bunnet (trans: head) but I was still bloody freezing. As soon as I was away I switched the heater on in the Bentley full blast.

Walt leaned forward.

"So you have no recollection of turning off the main road?"

"Nothin' at all Walt. One minute I'm away up the motorway to ma home in Godalming, dreaming of ma wife Mary, and the next minute I'm on a wee pokey country road with hedges on either side."

"Were you scared then Roy?" It was Venezia who asked the question.

"Me. Feart?" He looked at Venezia in astonishment. "No hen, I've never been feart in ma life."

He turned back to Walt.

"I thought it was the bloody Sat Nav that was all. It'd been playing up all week."

Luckily for us Echo managed to stifle his laugh and Roy did not notice.

(There was the story we all knew, we learned later that it was almost certainly an Urban Myth, that the garage had been forced to remove the latest Sat Nav from Roy's car because it could not understand his rich Scottish accent).

He was continuing with his story.

"Next thing the road's come to a dead end and in front of me's a set a country gates, the sort a thing yous see on television going up to the big house."

"And did you keep going Roy?" Venezia sounded nervous.

"Aye, I'd no bloody choice Venezia. The Bentley was taking it me where it wanted."

He looked round at us.

"It was black o' night when I finally stepped out of the car. I told yous it was cold when I set off, well it was worse there. Jack Frost covering everything. Then the moon's up lightin' up the ghost house right behind me, like in the horror pictures."

At this juncture we could see that Venezia was not happy with the way the story was going. She felt that Our Great Football Manager was not being truthful about his state of mind. So she leaned across the table. She was the only one who could take such a risk with the Great Man. Her voice was sharp.

"We all know that you are the biggest lion in the jungle Roy and that you beat your chest with a wooden spoon before meals, but if you tell me you weren't scared by what was happening to you I will call you once again a Fausse Couche which as I have told you before is rude Quebecois French to indicate that you are the runt of the litter and therefore a poor specimen for a human being."

We all laughed at this, even Roy, who held up his hand.

"OK. Yous got me there Venezia. Admitted. If I could have got back in ma motor and driven straight home to ma home in Godalming and slipped into bed beside ma beautifully bejewelled wife Mary, I would have done it. Just like that. Trust me."

"So what happened next then Roy?" It was Wilson asking.

Roy rubbed his hand across his face.

"Well Wilson what can ah say? Suddenly I feels like I've drunk a couple a bottles ah Buckie (trans: strong drink). Heid's as light as a hen's feather. Then I'm over the gravel, through the door of the house, up the stairs, light's on in a bedroom, door's open. And get this." He looked around at us in the flickering half light of the candle. "Only ma own bloody pyjamas laid out on the bed! I'm thinking I've either turned into a mincy heid (trans: mad man) or this is the queerest bloody thing that ever happened. Then I've brushed my teeth, done a jimmy riddle and I've got the sheets tucked under my chin like I'm on ma holidays in a five star hotel and I'm dreamin' away and probably snorin' away as well."

We were all alert now. None of us knew where Roy was going to take his story. He looked around.

"Then suddenly I'm awake. Sober as an Edinburgh judge. Heid working well."

"You'd heard a noise?" Echo looked at him.

"No, no. Opposite way round."

We looked at him, not understanding.

"Nothin' at all. Silence. Silence like when y'er buried alive and all ye can hear is yer own breathing."

"And did that scare you Roy dear?" Venezia asked softly.

"It scared the hell out of me Venezia," Roy replied slowly. He turned to face us. "Scared the livin' bloody daylights out ah me. Admitted now in front ah the whole company."

We waited.

"So ah gets slowly out of bed and goes over to the window and puts up ma hand to draw back the curtain."

It was here that Roy showed us that in addition to being a Celebrity Football Manager he had also developed, like Venezia, a good sense of theatrical timing. He deliberately let the story hang in the air for an extra couple of beats - long enough for Echo to be drawn in and shout out excitedly:

"Hold on! Wait! I've got it! When you drew back the curtain you were shown the future of the universe!"

We all looked at him astonished.

Excitedly he turned toward us to explain:

"It's 1929. Edwin Hubble has stunned the scientific community by showing that the universe is expanding, in other words the stars are drawing further apart. So if Roy is being shown the future when he draws back the curtain the night sky is certainly going to be emptier than it is today. That would explain the profundity of the silence."

Following this we turned quickly back to Roy to see if Echo had been right. But once again he used his sense of theatrical timing correctly, pausing a couple of beats before announcing in his rough Scottish voice:

"They call yous the African Autodidact because of yer learning when there's no schools, but if yous ask me they should change that to the African Bampot. Ma players could give a better answer than that and some of them cannae even read or write."

Then he looked round at all of us disdainfully.

Because he had got it so wrong Echo now had to hold his tongue and wait to see, along with the rest of us, what it was that Roy had been shown when he pulled the curtain back.

Finally he lifted the mug of wine to his lips. "I'll tell yous what I saw then."

Then as he spoke we noted that his voice had begun to lose some of its usual roughness.

"I'm like a bird flyin' over a city laid out below me. There's houses, streets, factories wi' great chimneys pouring out smoke. I can see cars, buses, parks, people. The vision's pin sharp. I can read a number plate and make out a baby's face in a pram.

"And this city is?" Echo had regained his confidence and was looking hard at him.

"Well it's naw Dundee. The houses is all wrong for that. And it's naw London. And it's certainly naw Godalming where I stay. Then I have ma clues. I've taken teams up there often enough. Should have recognised it easy. There's the Ship Canal and Trafford Park and then the football ground and I can see ahm looking down at the great city ah Manchester.

"Do we have a date yet Roy?" It was Walt speaking.

"Naw." Roy shook his head. "Although I can see it's back a good few years. The buildings all still reekie (trans: dirty or smokey). They've all been cleaned up since."

"What time of day is it?"

"Afternoon. Light beginnin' to drop away. Cold to freeze yer baws off. Could turn the heid and see to the west there's ah coverin' ah snow lying there on the hills."

Roy paused to clear his throat before continuing. He was trying to give us a picture of what he saw.

"The people of the city's going about their business. Folk doing their shoppin'. Publicans gettin' ready to open for the evening. That sorta thing."

He shakes his head.

"I can see it all. People getting on and off buses. Conductors handin' out tickets. It's that clear I can hear them callin' out the stops. There's unemployed men on street corners, lads kickin' footballs in back alleys. Women taking in their washing. All sorts goin' on."

Roy paused again. We were all looking at him. In the flickering candle light he held us entranced.

"There's a street to the south of where I'm looking. There's a factory gate and a boy cyclin' toward it with the evening papers. He stops gets off his bike and props it up against a wall. Goes through the factory gate. Then he's up to the factory door and he's opening it and shoutin' inside 'Evening News, Late Final.' I told yous I could hear it clear as day. I can see inside the factory. A thin woman comes out from behind a counter and takes the paper. The boy's on his way, the woman looks at the headline on the front page. Then she puts up her hand to her mouth and for a moment she's no movin'. It's like she's frozen wi' the horror ah it."

We were all looking at Roy now. His face was serious and had lost its usual red ruddy image.

Finally Walt said:

"So now we have the date. It's the sixth of February 1958. The Munich air disaster. Eight Manchester United footballers are dead in a terrible plane crash. They have been playing a game in Belgrade and the plane has put down to refuel in Munich. Eight men of Manchester, the beating heart, the pride of a great city."

"Aye, yous right there Walt," said Roy. For a second his Scottish voice faltered. The whole country had been touched by this tragedy. Then he continued.

"There's lines of girls sittin' at sewing machines. When each girl hears the news she stops work and passes it on to the girl behind. Soon all the machines are stopped. All the girls in tears. They're calling out the names over the radio:

Roger Byrne gone. Charlton in the hospital. Matt Busby critical.

"I can see inside the office now where the managers are sittin'. They can hear the machines have stopped. They turn to each other. Then one of them gets up and goes out on to the factory floor. He's askin' one of the girls what's goin' on. She tells him. His hand goes to his mouth. Then someone hands him a copy of the paper. The radio's still calling out the names:

Billy Foulkes alive. Duncan Edwards unconscious. Harry Gregg rescues two from wreckage.

"The manager takes the paper back into the office. The other managers pore over it. They cannae believe it. One of them, a big fella with a 'tash, gets up and goes out on to the factory floor. He's talkin' to the supervisor, 'Tell the girls, no more work today, everyone to go home. Terrible tragedy.' He goes down the lines of silent machines touchin' the girls on the arm offerin' comfort. Then he puts his arm around the supervisor."

Roy has stopped now and is looking around. Then Walt turns to the Austrian girls and to Hangdog Heinz and his Charming Wife and to Dien and Joy and explains:

"That was a different time. Those players were not the pampered pussycats they are today. They were local men, the best the city had to offer. Even today it is still remembered."

After that Roy continued.

"I'm looking at the same thing all over the city. Newsboys takin' the paper into the police station and the copy being passed through to the sergeants and the inspectors. Even the prisoners in the cells are told what's goin' on.

David Pegg, Tommy Taylor, Billy Whelan. All dead. Slush on the runway. Take off failed.

"I could see men sittin' silent in pubs, housewives callin' the news over garden walls."

Roy's voice is soft now.

"Now night's fallin' now over the great city. Lights's appearin'. All made yellow by the smog from a thousand chimneys. Buses and cars crawlin' home through the fog. People walkin', pulling hats low and tightenin' scarves around their throats against the cold. Then the scene's slowly fading. Lights going out one by one. Whole city sinking into a fitful sort of sleep."

Roy looked up suddenly as if he too had wakened from some sort of a dream. His visage was once again fierce - as if to compensate for a temporary lapse into sentimentality.

"Anyway that's what I saw, I'm telling ya."

Venezia touched his arm.

"The day ah got back ah packed in all the nonsense with the Welshmen and the dog racing. Went in to see the owner. Big chap. Irishman. Held ma hand up, said I'd not been doing ma job. Promised him a top four finish and a place in Europe. Straightened everythin' out. Remembered ma responsibilities. That's what it taught me. Went back to managing ma football club."

Then he looked sharply at Echo and pointed a finger directly at him.

"Remember wha' I told yous Echo. Never said a word to anyone about what ah saw. Not even to Mary. Any of that gets out its yer heid on the flagpole Jimmy."

After that we sat for a while in silence. The candles still flickered around us. We were considering the story Roy had told us.

Finally it was Denis who turned to Walt. "What lesson can we draw from that Walt?"

"Same one as always." Walt's voice sounded casual, almost slothful, as if he were already half asleep. "Bit of humbleness, bit of humility. Never does us any harm."

But it was then that Venezia turned to Walt and asked if she might say something. Walt nodded.

"The story that Roy has told us was extremely moving. But I was also reminded somehow of the way you described events in your poems."

"Was you there too Walt?" Roy looked at him sharply.

Walt sighed, suddenly it seemed like the sigh of an old man. Then he shook his head. "Not as close as you Roy. Nothing like. I didn't see it as clearly as you did at all."

39

We left the town of Fromista the following morning and began our approach to the Meseta.

As they walk pilgrims tell terrible stories of the Meseta.

(The Meseta: the great bare high plain of northern Spain).

Pilgrims say that in the depths of winter bodies are discovered frozen in the snow and that in the summer skeletons are picked clean under the burning sun.

"But when Aimery Picaud and I were walking this route years ago the main danger wasn't the weather." Walt had his thick coat buttoned up against the cold as we walked along. "What we were scared of was being rolled in one of the taverns."

He looked round at us to make sure he had our attention.

"Carrion de Los Condes, we will come to it soon, had a terrible reputation. The landlords filled pilgrims full of cheap liquor, then when they were sleeping it off they stripped them down to their underwear and left them out in the cold without a penny to their name."

As we considered all this, we also recalled a well known maxim of the road - that when a pilgrim tells a tale, the tale is generally in two parts, a factual part and an invented or exaggerated part. Both can be valid but it is simply a good idea to know which is which.

However even allowing for exaggerations pilgrims should still be warned that if they are crossing the Meseta in summer they should carry sufficient water and that if they are crossing in winter that the nights can be bitterly cold.

When we camped out on the Meseta we always built our fire higher than usual and slept fully clothed in our tents. It was cold enough even then, but we were fortunate to be spared the bitterest of winter winds that can sweep across this plain, accompanied by heavy snow. Certainly pilgrims sleeping out without proper protection late in the year take a serious risk.

Our traverse of the Meseta took place in the late autumn. Our route took us from Fromista to Carrion de los Condes to Ledigos to Sahagun. This is a town that was at one time considered to be at the heart of the pilgrim road due to its Benedictine monastery which housed one of the first European universities.

After Sahagun we travelled via El Burgo Ranero and Mansilla de las Mulas to arrive finally at the great city of Leon. The total distance travelled between Fromista and Leon was about a hundred miles and it took us five days and four nights. Our compass bearing was always West and when the day was clear we estimated that we could see at least fifty miles to the horizon in all directions.

Our path was as always well indicated by our system of yellow arrows. Occasionally we deviated from the recognised path to follow a particular track that Walt knew. He had a nose and an instinct for the correct direction that we always trusted.

We met French pilgrims who told us that the Meseta reminded them of the flat lands of the Camargue. In other words the landscape is bare, open, devoid largely of people and habitation. In the autumn the fields are a dull brown and stretch as far as the eye can see to the horizon. There are tractors at work turning the soil. In spring and early summer, Walt told us, the land was full of red poppies and green ripening corn.

(Motorists who pass across the Meseta generally do so at great speed, describing the plain as boring, flat and dull. We found the opposite to be true).

40

At midday we stopped our little caravan by the side of the path and after removing the panniers from the backs of Thatcher and Blair and finding them a spot where they could graze we set to on the bread and fruit and ham we had bought in Fromista that morning.

The sky above us was light and limpid blue and a faint breeze touched our cheeks.

After we had finished eating and had drunk the coffee which Venezia and Echo had prepared over our small gas stove and were resting for a moment in the sunshine, Wilson turned to Walt.

"I am beginning to see what our writer is doing. He is composing this narrative as a collection of stories."

"Yes, you are right there," Walt replied. "That is what Aimery did as well. He was always listening to people, always picking up their stories."

He leaned forward to explain himself.

"It's the constant 'fizz and pop' of change. On a crowded street a thousand different stories being recounted. That's what our poor bloody writer, God bless him and keep him, is doing. He's reflecting our journey in the stories we tell."

We considered this for a moment and then Walt got to his feet and stretched and one by one we followed him and once again we were on our way.

The subjects we discussed as we walked were many and diverse. If they were all to be included here they would fill another book of the same size.

Echo kept up his attack on all things Belgian, referring to the citizens of that country as ' our former colonial masters.' At the same time he challenged Denis on the state of NHS dentistry and we went, at some depth, into all the old political feuds, fighting battles long forgotten by most people. On the occasions when we met Dien and Joy we discussed the French Foreign Legion and received an extensive biography and 'discography' of the group Joy Division and its singer Ian Curtis. Roy gave us fascinating detail of life at his London football club and we learned interesting ' snippets' about the players. However this information was disclosed on the understanding that it stayed within the pilgrim circle. Jack told us tales of the Bastard's Baby and we learned about the real state of his marriage to his wife Marjorie. From Walt we had life in the American Civil War and his adventures in New Orleans.

***

Many days on our pilgrimage passed by like this, with talk and stories being told. However there were moments when this conversation would die away. Then as we walked all we could hear was the sound of our footsteps. There were moments when even those were silenced. Then all we were left with was the sound of our own breathing.

We became sensitive to the strength and changes in direction of the wind. We would watch ahead of us a stand of trees bend before a gust and then a few seconds later the same gust would strike us. Then we would watch as the trees across the other side of a Galician valley moved under the pressure of the wind.

The wind of the Meseta was different from the wind of the Galician hills. It was a strong wind and blew directly at us, its voice rougher.

How we loved the wind in our faces as we walked across the wide open Meseta. The ploughed fields, the earth dark waiting for the sowing of the crops. The flat plain stretching ahead, ending only in a ridge of mountains at least three days walk away. The big sky above, so clear and blue. The sun just warm enough in its autumn glow.

The trees, the colours of autumn, the wind shaking the branches so that on coming into a village the leaves golden and yellow fluttered to the floor at our feet, all these things thrilled us.

On our journey West we were also privileged to witness dozens of sunrises and sunsets and these became part of our day.

41

R eaders might have expected after our stay in Fromista that we would have been eager to restart our debate on religion or perhaps to consider further the strange and moving tale that Roy had recounted. The tale had confirmed to us that Roy, as well as being heroic, was also capable of what Echo called a Noble Vision.

Instead it was Oscar who took us off in another direction. The path was wide open in front of us. There were large ploughed fields to either side. He was walking alongside Venezia and leading poor Blair. Then he turned to Venezia and asked:

"Venezia we have heard something of your adventures at home in Quebec, but how is it you arrived in England?"

After a pause and to our surprise it was Echo, and not Venezia, who responded to this question. He addressed himself brightly to Oscar.

"Well the business was starting to step up. So I decided, to kill two birds with one stone, to place a certain advertisement on an internet dating site. As I recall it, the wording was:

'Congolese man, serving up good Chinese grub in Plymouth (UK) takeaway seeks helper, preferably female.' "

We all looked at Venezia. The sun which was slowly beginning to dip toward the West was lighting up her face making it lovelier than ever. Her voice when she spoke was confident.

"I have already told you I had an adventurous spirit. I was ready to set off, Mexico or wherever. There was a co incidence as well. When I was a little girl we had a pet dog, he was a family favourite. But my father said he had a black heart, so we called him Congo, so that seemed like a good omen."

When he heard this Jack, who in matters of family was always conservative, simply stared at our Balletic Beauty. His visage was astonished. He could not believe that someone could leave their home on such a flimsy pretext.

But Venezia was unrepentant. She turned and squeezed Echo's arm lovingly.

"So I was on the good old National Express coach, alighting at the famous Bretonside bus station in Plymouth and wondering as we all do on first contact if I had not been time transported to the German Democratic Republic circa 1950. But then I looked around and saw my dearest Echo for the first time. He was wearing his bright red tee shirt with that comic inscription, The Emperor of Peking Rules Innit? This of course and his conical rice growers hat and he was grinning wildly as well, so I knew of course that I had made the right decision and that it was love at first sight."

With that she turned and gazed lovingly at her man and then leaned forward and put her arms around him and kissed him on the lips. (Leaving Denis once again to avert his eyes in terrible despair).

42

Half an hour after the conclusion of this strange story we did arrive at the small town of Carrion de los Condes. In front of us a tall grain silo stood, clear against the evening sky.

The following day when we met a Canadian pilgrim carrying a large back pack, he said he was from Winnipeg, he gave us this impression of Carrion de los Condes:

"It feels like an old prairie town from back home. I expected to see tumbleweed rolling down Main Street and to hear the mournful sound of a train whistle calling."

But that evening when Walt gave us a choice between staying outside as normal or staying at a refuge in town, we voted unanimously to sleep out. Roy summed up our mood.

"I've no got rid of the bloody stink from the last place yet. We'll take our chances out on the Meseta, Walt."

Walt looked up at the sky which was clear and cold and replied with a shake of his head:

"Well old Jack Frost will be nipping at our fingers and toes but we'll carry on anyway."

In the fading light we stopped briefly in the town to top up our supplies for the night - including on this occasion purchasing a bottle of good Spanish brandy to keep us warm.

Then we sent Denis on ahead as our scout and he was able to locate the wall of a ruined barn which would offer us protection from the cold wind. Walt had warned us it was likely to get up fiercely from the East during the night.

Nearby there was a stand of trees and Jack found at the edge of this stand a small stream where the donkeys could drink.

As we pitched our camp the sky darkened into night and a million stars were soon shining up above us. Oscar and Wilson built a solid fire that warmed us and Venezia and Echo gave us plates of fried potatoes and bacon which also served as an inner protection from the cold of the Meseta night that was beginning to press in on us.

As we were eating Oscar turned to Wilson.

"When we were listening to Roy's story about the air crash in Munich I recalled a visit I made to Germany some years ago."

He took a mouthful of his dinner.

"Were you ever in Stuttgart, Wilson ?"

When Wilson shook his head in the negative Oscar put his plate to one side and explained.

"We had a sales conference there. The company wanted to export into Europe. I was in the hotel with a German colleague when he told me something that had happened in the city that afternoon."

Oscar looked at Wilson to see if this stirred any memories but Wilson's face was impassive. His eyes glistened behind his glasses.

"It was a young man. He'd defied police and the fire brigade to climb the outside face of a municipal building. They called it free climbing. He was going to rescue a girl stranded on a ledge. The story was similar to yours though in that case the young man fell and died."

When we heard this we turned to Wilson.

"So I am not the only one to have tried such an enterprise." His voice was cold. "But if it is an alternative ending to the story you want I can certainly give you that."

Roy then passed around the bottle of brandy and we waited for Wilson to start. We recalled how he had told us his heroic story. After a pause to gather himself he began this new version. He was approaching the end of his climb. His voice was firm as he spoke.

"I had to surmount the metal strut work of the balcony which was directly above me. But I failed and in a moment I was falling back into space. I dropped away from the wall, slowly at first, then quicker and quicker, until I was tumbling over and over in mid air, totally disoriented, brain bursting with terror."

There was a moment's terrible silence then Wilson continued:

"I was approaching the ground ready to impact with the hard concrete and awaiting certain death when the quick thinking crowd, under instruction of police and fire officers, formed their arms into a cat's cradle so that before I struck the concrete they were able to catch me and lower me to the ground so that I suffered only bruising and shock."

"And the girl?" It was Venezia asking. We could hear the disappointment and resentment in her voice.

"Came down ten minutes later. Only a lover's tiff from the night before. Never even bothered to come and see me in hospital to thank me. Everyone said I was well out of it."

"And the climbing?"

"No change there. Nerve gone. A fall like that and you do not want to do it again I can tell you."

When we had finished Venezia said she was going to her tent, leaving Echo to wash up the dishes.

When she was gone we asked Wilson for an explanation for this sudden volte face but he refused point blank. He was a man who could be stubborn and arrogant. All he would say was that he had been asked for an alterative ending and he had given one.

Puzzled by this turn of events we were all glad to retreat to our tents and the warmth of our sleeping bags. During the night we heard the wind howl around us. Jack woke several times concerned about the welfare of his donkeys.

43

When we emerged from our tents in the morning, still troubled over Wilson and his story (although we did press him further in the days that followed he refused all explanation) it was to find that the storm had blown itself out. But instead of a bright clear morning the day was grey and drab and there was a humidity in the air which threatened rain.

There is the phenomenon we all experienced, as described earlier, of unpredictable changes to our mood. We were all ' at risk' it seemed, though Venezia, Walt and Roy were the most vulnerable.

Walt suffered particularly badly affected when he was hungry or tired. On an empty stomach he could become very tart.

But this morning we had a sudden and unpleasant example of how this particular phenomenon could affect Roy.

Venezia, who was almost completely enveloped in an oversized blue jacket, was walking beside Echo.

Roy was behind them. His hands were deep in his jacket pockets and his shoulders were hunched forward to keep out the clammy cold. He had replaced his normal headgear with a red baseball cap. We should have known that this was a Storm Warning, but that morning we failed to register the danger.

Venezia and Echo were in discussion between themselves. The rest of us were walking in silence. We were calculating the distance to the next village where we hoped a warming tavern would provide us lunch.

As we were walking Venezia and Echo began to laugh at a shared joke. This made Roy raise his head sharply. We could see that the blood was beginning to pump around his cheeks. Then in a second, to our horror, he was shouting out in his rough Scottish accent:

"If yous two is mockin' me over ma story about th' air crash I's'll floor the pair of yous."

This sudden and unprovoked attack made Echo and Venezia stop and turn. Venezia then making the mistake of laughing again. This further enraged Roy.

"I dunna know wha' yous laughing at ya wee scarlet hussy." He was shouting loudly now. His head was forward and he was stabbing the air with his finger. "Everybody knows yous been behind the bushes wi' every buck in Canada. And you ya African numpty why dunna ya clear off back where you came from."

After that events moved quickly. With a great cry Echo turned and lunged at Roy, but Roy dodged to one side and then got his hands around Echo's throat. Oscar and Jack then ran up from behind and with their combined force managed to drag Roy off, leaving an astonished Echo flat on his back on the ground.

Walt then called a halt to our progress and Oscar and Jack took Roy firmly by the arm and walked him a little way off to calm him down. Echo then got up and walked off in the opposite direction with Venezia. We could see him taking deep breaths and twisting his neck where Roy had grabbed him.

Our little caravan was halted while this problem was resolved. Finally under Walt's instruction hands were shaken, apologies offered and accepted and so we were able to continue on our way once again.

As we walked we pondered on all the strange things that had happened on our pilgrimage. There were the tales we had heard, the memorable moments we had experienced, both wretched and glorious, and now there were these odd bursts of violence and anger.

In seeking an explanation Denis, with his medical training as a dentist, talked about blood sugar levels and fatigue and irregular sleeping and eating patterns and that was probably as good an explanation as any.

But by the time we had reached our village and were enjoying our lunch Roy had regained his good humour. As we ate he regaled us with tales of the life and characters at his football club.

44

Is this the moment for a brief description of the character of Walt?

He was as complex as any of the other pilgrims and his views, and on occasion his behaviour, were at times odd and eccentric.

For instance our discussion of what we should do with the money from the robbery left him bored. He said money was paper and had never brought anyone happiness.

(When he was not listening Jack made fun of this saying he would like to see him pay for his night's lodgings without one of the pieces of paper he so despised).

But if Walt was bored by money he was alive to everything else.

He might be recounting to us his adventures with Aimery Picaud and then half an hour later we would find him in a cheap tavern listening to a waiter disclosing the detail of his life.

People, sensing his interest, always warmed to him.

For instance if we had eaten a good meal in a restaurant he would go without a second thought into the kitchen to congratulate the chef and to enquire how he had prepared his trout or his lamb or whatever it was we had eaten.

He was also keen to discuss events in Africa with Echo and talk the politics of French Quebec with Venezia. He also knew the names of all the plants and bushes and trees.

On one occasion when we stopped at a tavern in a village the older men invited him to take part in a noisy game of cards. When we looked for him later at first we missed him, so successfully had he blended in with the other card players. But when eventually we did catch his eye he gave a sly wink to signal he knew perfectly well what he was doing.

There were times when Walt was so full of energy and bonhomie. He would be everywhere, chatting to this person and that until Oscar said he was like a dog that had to pee on every lamp post.

But at other times he gave the impression of being lazy and indifferent. By build he was large and fleshy and there were occasions when he would be overcome by a sort of slothfulness. He would constantly yawn and rub his mouth as if he could barely keep awake. We might find him either asleep in his tent, his mouth wide open and snoring, or if we were camping out in open country we might discover him a little way off from the camp lying looking up at the stars. When we would enquire what he was up to he might reply that he was simply studying the night sky or listening out for a particular animal or bird or that he was contemplating a new poem.

Walt was not a practical person. Unless there was good reason he never helped with the donkeys or the erection of our camp, though he was always willing to offer advice.

However he did have an excellent sense of our direction. He could put his nose to the wind or survey a distant crest and say exactly where we were.

There were also times in the evening when he would disappear from the camp for half an hour and then return with his hat full of delicious berries or mushrooms which he would hand silently to the kitchen.

Walt was a good eater and a good drinker and most of the time, as stated, he was in exuberant humour. But there were occasions, especially when he was tired or when he was hungry, that he could become difficult and quarrelsome. (This was part of that same phenomenon that affected us all). The large fleshy face would take on a thin peeved air. When he was like this Wilson would say, "Watch out the Old

Woman is on the war path," and we would all give a quiet snigger.

45

After we had finished our lunch that day we continued our journey once more in the direction of Sahagun.

Echo and Roy, to show they were reconciled after their ' little spat' took the lead with our two donkeys.

It was then the conversation reverted back, as we knew that at some point it inevitably would, to the vexed subject of religion.

Echo had described to us in chilling detail the rape of the Americas by the Spanish Conquistadors in the name of one Jesus Christ. He had also explained to us how the plundered wealth had been used to fund the Catholic church back home in Spain. Such was our shock at learning of the extent of this terror that in the following days when we saw in the distance the spire of yet another enormous church, towering over yet another small village, we shuddered at the cruelty it represented.

But now we had visited the church of St Martin de Tours in Fromista and appreciated its simple beauty. It was Denis turning to Echo who opened the argument.

"Echo, can you name a society that has survived without some form of religion being present? We need a religious outlet. It is a way for us to manifest our innermost feelings."

"I agree," said Walt. He turned to Echo. "You have confounded power with religion. The Conquistadors were using religion as a cover to mask their real purpose which was to control."

Then Venezia piled in saying :

"Answer me this if you can Echo. Why when I go into a church and sit watching the sunlight streaming through the stained glass windows, falling onto the white robes of the choristers and the coloured robes of the priests, and why when I look way up past the fluted columns to the large and ornate ceiling a hundred feet above me, and why when I listen to the lovely voices of the choristers and hear the familiar words of the prayers being intoned, and why when I smell the incense as it drifts through the light, why do I feel for that moment as if I am at the heart of everything?"

"Oh that is easy Venezia," Echo suavely replied. "You have been gulled by a mendacious fraud. All your senses - your eyes, your ears, your nose, all have been deliberately touched. It is all planned, I can assure you. Even the church in Fromista."

"No," Walt said. "You are wrong there Echo. The ritual of the ceremony is vitally important. I will have more to say on that later."

But before he could continue Echo had interrupted.

"I despise the bobbing and the turning and the chanting."

This made Walt smile and he said:

"When I was in the city of Thessalonika in Northern Greece I attended Orthodox services. You talk of bobbing and turning and chanting, well it was all like that. There were dark red lights and priests in coloured robes disappearing in and out through secret doors. There were individual comfortable seats with arms so it was very theatrical. I also noted how broad the seats were - no doubt to accommodate the broad bottoms of the Greek ladies."

This, as Walt had intended, made us laugh and served to defuse the tension of our argument.

That night we pitched our camp five miles to the East of Sahagun. As we ate the sky cleared and once again we were able to see the brilliant tapestry of the stars above us. After we had finished eating and because the temperature was less extreme than it had been the previous night we were able, after we had piled our fire up high, to sit comfortably enough while Walt explained the arrangement of the night sky to us.

It was a pleasure, as always, to listen to Walt's languid American accent. As he talked it seemed to us that he was as familiar with the paths of the stars above our heads as he was with the earthen path that was below our feet.

When he had finished and Roy had passed around the last of the wine Walt looked at the circle of our faces sitting around the fire.

"I thought you pilgrims were softer than the pilgrims of old but I am beginning to change my mind." He laughed. "You wouldn't have caught old Aimery roughing it, not if he had the chance of a nice soft bed indoors and no doubt someone to share it with."

Before we turned in we asked Jack if he would give us a song. Once again there was a moment of hesitation but when he finally began we could see that his confidence was returning.

So has there ever been a stranger scene ?

A group of pilgrims, around a fire in the middle of the Meseta, being entertained by a man who could have passed, both in voice and look, for the great Irish tenor Josef Locke.

46

The following day our path crested a slight rise and we saw ahead of us, about two miles distant over the plain, a line of white houses and behind them a large church which signified that we were approaching the town of Sahagun.

We were contemplating this scene when we heard the loud siren of a police car racing toward the town on a road about a mile to our right.

When it was followed a minute later by a second and then a third police car, in turn followed by an ambulance, all with sirens going and lights flashing, we began to guess at the cause of this commotion.

As the vehicles disappeared into the town it was Oscar who enunciated our thoughts.

"Well there is a drama for you pilgrims. And I will bet you a pound to a penny that it is our old friend El Lobo attempting once again to replenish his coffers."

It seemed that we could not escape the presence of this man. We looked toward the town. If he was cornered and captured our pilgrimage would be safer and easier, but a part of us hoped he would pull it off and escape. He was our outlaw, our rebel, and we did not want him to be captured by the police.

After a brief debate it was decided that Oscar, who could easily be recognised, would stay with the donkeys while the rest of us would advance into Sahagun to discover the outcome of events.

The scene when we arrived was as previewed. The main square was cordoned off with tape and uniformed police were standing guard in front of the bank while detectives went in and out.

We took up a position on the edge of the square with the other onlookers and Echo struck up a conversation with a policeman.

"Que pasa jefe? Looks like plenty of excitement."

The policeman who wore aviator style dark glasses and had a belly that extended over his belt turned to him slowly.

"You suppose those guys are standing outside the bank for the fun of it? Robbery, what do you think ?"

Echo let a second pass.

"I guess it's got to be El Lobo then."

We watched as the policeman licked his lips then his hand touched the holster of his gun.

"Yeah, but this time we going to get him."

He pointed at the bank.

"The detectives they got the video from the CCTV. They're looking at it in the truck. I seen it already."

He turned toward us.

"It's clear as day. He's shouting at the biddy behind the counter your money or your life and she's standing there mouth open like a drowning fish."

He gave a strange gurgle of laughter that seemed to rumble from deep inside his stomach.

"You can see it. He's getting ready to give her a shot, but the fucker, we going to catch him soon, there's a pop not a bang, the gun misfires, and the old biddy behind the counter, these old bats are hard, they're all sinew and bone believe me, I've got one at home, reaches behind the counter and picks up a file and smacks it over his head."

Again there was the strange gurgling laughing from deep inside the belly of the policeman. He continued with his story:

"This sort of battering from the stringy old biddy he can't take so he turns and runs out of the door. That's it. But this time we're going to find him for sure."

With El Lobo's ability to flee a scene and the inefficiency of the Spanish police we doubted this.

"How would you rate his demeanour officer?' Echo asked when the tale had concluded. "Would you say he is still a dangerous man ?"

At this question the policeman swung his large head with the aviator style dark glasses toward Echo.

"I told you. You want an official description?"

His hand brushed over his holster again.

"Who are you guys anyway ?" His gaze travelled slowly around our little group. "Why you wanna know all this sort of stuff ?"

"We are pilgrims," Walt cut in reassuringly. "We are walking to Santiago."

The aviator glasses moved slowly over us. Then he spoke again. This time his voice was official.

"You'd better move along. There's nothing to see here. Nothing here's any of your business."

After that we waited until life in the square had returned to normal. Then Denis went back to get Oscar and the donkeys and we made our way through the town stopping at a tavern on the far side to eat our lunch.

As we sipped our beers and waited for our lunch to appear we discussed the morning's events and the manner in which El Lobo had once again evaded the arms of the law. Then Jack turned to Oscar.

"We know you are an enthusiast for cars because you told us but we do not understand how you could get caught up in a bank robbery with someone like El Lobo. I have been a publican all my life and it is the strangest story I have ever heard."

As he considered his reply Oscar raised his beer glass to his lips and drank.

"Well, I can start by telling you that I have always been lucky," he said finally. The tavern was full of people and noisy so we had to lean forward and listen carefully.

"If there was a draw or a raffle I always won a prize. It was the same at work. Others would be let go but I'd always be kept on. I always got the promotions. They used to call me Lucky Beb. But then they got jealous. They thought I had an in with the bosses."

He stared round at us.

"But then they brought in a new general manager. It was one quarter, my division had done badly. We came to the end of the sales meeting and the new man says, it was supposed to be a joke, 'Go on then Oscar you had better to do a forfeit, you can sing us the company song.' So I stood on a chair and gave some sort of a warble."

He looked at Jack.

"I'm afraid I don't have the gift of your voice Jack."

He drank from his beer glass again.

"When the meeting was over the new manager called me into his office and he swore at me. In the old days we never swore. Then he called me Bebbington. Just like that, even though he was twenty years my junior. 'Well,' he said. I can see his bloated little mouth now. 'Your lot have been sitting on your arses this month.' That got my blood up. So I replied, 'It's surprising we sell anything at all with the product you are providing us with nowadays.' "

Oscar stopped as the waiter brought our plates to the table. He cut up a piece of the fish and put it into his mouth.

"That was the moment I turned against the company. I began to hate everything about it. I could see it had gutted our souls, devoured us up, eaten us alive. And what had we got out of it? Nothing. We had our small houses and our small lives while the rich men who owned the company had all the good things."

He looked round at us and we could hear the anger in his voice.

"I began to dream of getting my own back. I thought about putting on a mask and robbing head office or assassinating the chairman. But then I got the call to come out here. You have guessed it of course. A Saturday morning. I came down the stairs and there it was lying on the mat. The same package as Wilson got. Hand delivered, all that. Same instructions and so on."

He looked around at us. His face was animated now.

"Wilson gave us his story about his ascent of the building to save the girl. He took the chance when it presented itself. That's how I felt when El Lobo asked me to drive the getaway car. It was an instant decision. Later when I thought about it I assumed a Spanish bank would treat their staff in the same way we were treated. I was sure they would be the same style of operation."

There was a pause here. We pushed our plates to one side and Walt asked the waiter to bring coffee.

Then Roy leaned across the table.

"But did you no think of what yer was doin' with a gun Oscar?"

"I don't know what you are talking about Pilgrim Roy." There was a sharp tone to Oscar's voice now. "I never handled a gun."

Wilson leaned across the table to interrupt this exchange.

"Whenever I do a free climb I am always full of tension. I am on the edge. It's the best feeling."

"You are right there Wilson," Oscar replied. "Driving the getaway car was the best moment of my life. I don't suppose I shall ever feel so alive again."

"No Oscar, I dunnae agree," Roy cut in firmly. "Yous canna go round shootin' up bank workers and just say it was some sorta prank like getting yer end away on a Saturday night. Oh no, dearie me no."

The conversation continued on until we had finished our coffee and paid our bill. Then with our donkeys loaded up again we continued on our way across the wide open Meseta.

In an hour we could look back and see behind us, as we had seen earlier that day in front of us, a thin line of white buildings and the outline of the church. This was our last view of the town of Sahagun.

As we walked our conversation turned back to El Lobo. We had begun to realise that, thanks to Oscar, we knew as much about El Lobo as the police and the journalists.

But it was Echo who asked Oscar the question to which we had all been seeking an answer.

"Pilgrim Oscar. El Lobo is an accomplished bank robber with nerves of steel. He has killed two police officers and wounded three bank cashiers and has managed to evade the arms of the law for ten years. So why, pray, would such an experienced criminal unmask himself to one Oscar Bebbington, an Englishman, a recently retired vendor of soft drinks with, so we are told, no previous experience of bank robbing?"

Oscar was about to reply to this provocative interrogation when Walt interjected :

"It is the amount that El Lobo planned to steal from the bank in Zaragoza that should be concerning us."

"That is correct Walt," said Oscar, nodding his head affirmatively. "Normally El Lobo steals only enough to keep him going until the next robbery. But this time he is going for the big prize, the payoff that will take him comfortably into retirement. The One Million Euro."

We are all listening carefully to Oscar now.

"El Lobo's nerves are shot. He is downing double Scotches in the hotel bar and his hands are shaking. He has a big job coming up and he hasn't arranged a get away driver. And suddenly there I am. The best driver in the area and even better, a foreigner, an outsider, unknown to the police. He must have thought he had died and gone to heaven."

"What do you think destroyed his nerve ?" Jack asked Oscar.

Before Oscar could reply Roy interrupted.

"Pressure over time. It's the same wi' footballers. They get injured, they lose a yard in pace, they cannae find the net and their confidence goes. I've see it a hundred times."

"And now of course," said Venezia, "Thanks to Oscar, the poor man is driven completely mad."

Wilson laughed.

"He leans over the seat, picks up the wrong bag and suddenly that's it, retirement fund gone. Last chance disappeared. No wonder he is after our blood."

That observation from Wilson, which concluded our debate on El Lobo, confirmed our fears that we had made a dangerous enemy in the notorious Spanish bank robber and that we should have to show extreme care during the remainder of our pilgrimage to avoid being attacked again.

47

Walt had a wonderful phrase. He used to tell us: "The camino changes its coat with the seasons."

That afternoon he expanded on that when he said: "In the early summer the land is dry and full of light. Many pilgrims report that it is then they feel the soles of their boots and the souls of their hearts starting to mould to the earth beneath them. But in the autumn the terrain is brown, the rain falls, and the path is muddy and sloppy underfoot."

But that evening we discovered that the camino also 'changes its coat' when it is travelled by night.

In the city of Leon, which we reached some days later, we heard of a young Frenchman and his wife who were walking the road only by the light of the stars. It was said that their appearance was now ghostly pale and that they were both very thin, but it was also said that they were still full of enthusiasm for their project.

That evening we had our own brief experience of walking at night.

Because we had now slept out in the cold for two nights we had planned to stay that evening at the refuge in El Burgo Ranero. (Walt said it was small and that because it was not a regular stop over point for pilgrims we would probably have it to ourselves). However due to the delay we had experienced in Sahagun and because we had taken longer over lunch than normal, we were forced to complete the last stretch into El Burgo Ranero in the dark.

As we walked, with the sky clear and the stars bright and the temperature dropping so that we could feel the cold creeping in on us, we found ourselves on a path bordered by heavy leafed trees.

Spiders webs hung down from the branches and mysteriously brushed our faces. Our world, normally flooded with bright colour, was now reduced to shades of black and grey. Pools of dark water turned silver under the moon so that the path resembled a photographic negative. We found ourselves completely absorbed by this strange inversion of the light. Soon we discovered our night vision and found we could make our way easily.

(Of course what we were doing was nothing new. We were only walking at by the light of the moon, but for some reason that night we were much touched by it).

Pilgrims arriving at El Burgo Ranero as we did later that night should be aware that if they stay in the refuge there (which is clean and adequate) they may be obliged in the morning to sing good Christian hymns and say good Christian prayers if they want any breakfast in their bellies before they set off.

48

The path now turns in a direction to the North of West as it passes through Mansilla de las Mulas and then on toward the great city of Leon. The paysage is beginning to change once more. Patches of cultivation and verdure start to appear and the pilgrim is made aware that the end of this portion of the Meseta is being reached.

We came to Mansilla de las Mulas about midday. Walt who had been talking quietly to Oscar stopped to look at the houses ahead. We could see his nose was up, he was like a dog sensing the air. Then he nodded to Oscar and turned to us.

"You pilgrims wait here. Oscar and I are going to advance into the town. We have some business to conduct there."

We all had questions to ask about this surprising move but before we could compose them the pair had set off.

"I am sure I don't know what is going on here," said Jack in a puzzled tone.

We had unloaded Thatcher and Blair and after lounging around for a while we were getting bored.

"My stomach is telling me that it is time for lunch," Jack said finally. "I propose that we set to and prepare a lunch as best we can from the provisions we have. We can then hope that the smell of good honest cooking will lure those two rascals back here by their noses from whatever it is they are doing."

So Echo and Venezia searched through our provisions and found packets of soups and added spices and slices of dried ham so that we soon had a delicious pot of thick broth bubbling on our stove.

"I knew that would do it," said Jack as a short time later we spied Walt and Oscar coming toward us. Walt was carrying a large cardboard box in front of him while Oscar was transporting two full carrier bags, one in either hand.

"Eat first," said Venezia eyeing the box and the carrier bags which Oscar and Walt had dumped on the ground. "You can explain what you have been up to afterwards."

When we had filled up our stomachs with bowls of Venezia's delicious soup and finished off with bread and cheese Oscar said:

"We have cleaned out the local clothes shops of shirts, trousers, sweaters and socks."

Venezia who along with Echo was clearing up the dishes and preparing coffee looked puzzled.

"Why in the heck would you want to do that Oscar?"

"We are going to send them to the leper colony that Hans Klugman's wife Lottie told us about," Walt replied. "We have the address."

"Yes, that is what we have decided." Then Oscar added with a smile. "But with a little additional surprise."

As Oscar was speaking Walt was taking all the pairs of socks out of the box and the carrier bags.

"What we are going to do," Oscar continued, "is pack the bundles of new money into the socks. Then we will hide the socks among the clothes that we are going to dispatch to the poor unfortunates in the leper colony. That way the money will not attract the attention of police or customs officers but will give the residents of the leper colony a nice surprise when they put on their new pairs of socks."

Roy raised his blue baseball hat and scratched his head in puzzlement when he heard this.

"But are yous sure lepers wear socks Oscar?" A little smile appeared at the corner of his lips. "It's very warm in the Congo. And if they're no ones for wearing socks because they no have proper feet they'll be wondering what's going on."

We looked at Echo, with his knowledge of the Congo, to see if he had an answer to this query. He put down the pot he was in the process of cleaning and replied to Roy's provocative interrogation:

"The lepers of my country will be overwhelmed by the generosity of this group of pilgrims. As to whether they wear socks with their sandals everyday, or instead reserve them for high days and holidays and trips to the beach, perhaps in respectful imitation of Scottish holidaymakers in the Spanish town of Benidorm, that I cannot tell."

Before Roy could reply to this Oscar opened the flap of the bag in which he kept the money. We watched carefully as he drew out the packets containing the new notes and handed them to Walt. Then he looked around at the rest of us.

"It is what we decided. Half for the lepers, a portion to be returned to the bank, that will go in the post from Leon, and the rest for us to spend."

Once again we nodded our assent to this. (Our only dissenter was Wilson. He told us that his principle of not giving to charity because it let the state renege on its responsibilities still stood). After the money had been placed into the socks and the socks had been mixed up with the shirts and trousers we packed up the box and secured it with heavy sticky tape. Then Oscar wrote on the outside of the box, next to the address of the leper colony:

'A gift of clothes from a band of pilgrims on their way to Santiago de Compostela."

Then the two of them, Walt and Oscar, returned to the town to the post office.

***

After we had disposed of the socks and the money, sending them on their way to the lepers in the old Belgian Congo, we spent one more night out on the Meseta before we arrived in Leon.

It has been stated before in this narrative that on our pilgrim route we felt as if we had moved into a parallel world. There were so many things that we saw and experienced that did not feature in our normal lives.

For instance we became used to the nightly presence of the 'other' pilgrims.

We would be sitting around our fire, as we were that night, and a short distance away we would be able to see the camp fires of the pilgrims of old. The clothes they wore were different to ours and they were thinner and poorer looking than us. But the way they talked among themselves, the way their cooking pots hung over the fire, the way flagons of drink were being passed around and stories were being told, the soft murmur of their voices, all this showed that actually they were no different from us.

Then one of us might get up, perhaps Jack Phillpotts would want to check on his donkeys, and he would approach a little too close and the images would shimmer and fade.

There were also times when we woke in the middle of the night and felt their presence very near to us.

49

We spent three days in the city of Leon, Walt finding us rooms on the Calle de Martin Sarmiento. During the course of our visit we once again met up with Hang Dog Heinz and his Charming Wife and with Dien and

Joy. Oscar also surprised us when he revealed how he had spent his portion of the money from the bank robbery.

The writer of this narrative could fill a separate book with the accounts given to us by pilgrims of memorable places they passed through on their journey.

A French lady of ' a certain age' told us that a particular bar in Seville is run by three brothers who all have peculiar faces, "rough hewn and square as if struck from granite." She said every time she saw a stone gargoyle on a Cathedral exterior she was reminded of those spectacular visages.

Another French pilgrim told us that as he traversed the raised levees of the Vendee in western France he had the impression that he was walking on the water itself. He said that at one point he had briefly lost the distinction between water and sky and had become strangely disoriented.

We also heard in detail how the sun set on the Golden Horn in Istanbul. Then a young Italian pilgrim told us that when he descended down the Taro Valley in northern Italy in the autumn season and saw the colour of the leaves as they turned and felt the way the sun warmed his back he was sure he was as near to heaven as he was likely to get on this earth.

We heard of the marvels of the Roman ruins in Merida and the magnificence of the Plaza Mayor in Salamanca.

Our vision of the city of Leon itself was influenced by our pleasure at being off the dull and dreary Meseta. We also noted the ' confidence' of this city of Leon. The local citizens on their evening paseo seemed to us to be as solid and prosperous as the streets of the city through which they walked.

Oddly enough the Cathedral, which was only a few minutes walk from our hotel, gave us the opposite impression. When we stood on the Plaza Regla and looked up at the great building we were astonished by how light and delicate it appeared.

In fact it was Echo himself, who had been such a stern critic of all things religious, who summed up our view.

"You do have to wonder," he said as we stood in front of the cathedral, "how those masons of old could have constructed such a giant edifice and yet given it such a light and ethereal countenance."

He made us smile when he added:

"You know I really do believe that if they tied balloons to each of its corners the damn thing would simply sail up into the sky and float away."

When we entered inside we were also moved by the way the light shone through the stained glass windows. There were reds and blues and greens and shades of aquamarine and turquoise that were so rich and fine and delicate and fragile that they took away our breath.

Then during an evening we spent in a tapas bar off the Calle Ancha with our other pilgrims friends, including Hang Dog Heinz and his Charming Wife, a consensus began to build that Walt should tell us something about his life in America.

He considered this request for a moment and then replied :

"There are so many things I could tell you pilgrims but the period of my life which I will never forget is the time I spent during the Civil War when I visited the hospitals and tried to offer some comfort to the wounded. The point I would like to make is that these were innocent boys. I have already given you a poem on that."

He turned to Jack.

"They were the same as you when you went out to Aden. The politicians got them all into a lather and then they were marching them away. Some of them did terrible things to people who in normal times they would call their neighbour."

He looked round at us. It was still early in the evening and the bar was quiet.

"I will lay you a small wager pilgrims that I could whip you all up into a sweat and have you marching as well. It is not a difficult operation for a government. You have to be a strong person to resist that call."

(We were to recall this comment by Walt later in our journey).

But for now he paused and looked around.

"What else can I tell you ? I saw President Lincoln regularly when I was in Washington. He rode past me on his horse and he always greeted me. He was a man I loved dearly. I could tell you also that I was a newspaper editor in both New York and New Orleans. Prior to that I had been a school teacher and a printer."

We fell silent then. We were waiting for Walt to continue. But it was at this moment that Hang Dog Heinz made his interruption.

Ignoring Walt, as if he was not there, he sat up straight and declared out loud in a high thin voice:

"My life will be over soon because I am sure my wife no longer loves me."

This caused us all to turn sharply away from Walt and toward him. At the same time the Charming Wife (with whom we were all secretly a little in love) gave a gasp and put her arm around him.

"No, no Heinz this is not true." Her voice was breaking. "You know I will always love you. Your life is not over at all."

But Hang Dog, who knew how to manipulate his wife's emotions, simply sighed and shook his head.

Then a moment later, as this small domestic drama unfolded, he reached down to a small bag by his feet and drew out a battered hard back book. Then he placed it slowly on the table in front of him.

Then he looked around before finally catching Walt's eye.

(Walt we learned later had been irritated by this scene. He had been a planning to tell us more about his life and his adventures in New York but the wind had been taken out of his sails).

"What I have here is a volume of Napoleon's memoirs," Hang Dog's voice was thin and sharp. "His time on Saint Helena. A translation into German. He is a man to admire also."

When he said this he nodded in the direction of Walt as if making a connection between the two men.

Then he opened up the book, at random it seemed to us, and read half a page silently to himself. Then he stopped and looked up at his wife as if noticing her for the first time.

We waited for him to continue. We expected that he would read out loud some important passage to us, but he didn't. Instead he simply closed up the book and placed it back on the table in front of him and sat silently staring into space.

He repeated this little scene several times during the evening, occasionally rolling a cigarette and taking deep draws before leaning back and expelling the smoke up toward the ceiling. We never did discover why this narrative of the life of Napoleon was so important to him.

This was only a little tableau, an aside, but it was an indication of some of the strange things we experienced on our journey.

The following evening we dined by ourselves in an excellent Chinese restaurant. We had finished our meal and had ordered coffee and glasses of brandy. Our mood was relaxed. Roy had been invited by Jack and Echo to describe certain tactics he favoured with his team and was using the salt and pepper pots to illustrate his moves. Denis and Venezia were talking amongst themselves and Walt was recounting to Wilson a story from the American Civil War.

It was then that Oscar, who disliked football and who was bored by the other conversations, raised his head and announced suddenly:

"Well Pilgrims, here is a surprise for you all. I have brought a car and we are all going for a ride in it tomorrow."

At this Roy put down the salt and pepper pots and we all looked at Oscar in surprise. At the same time the waiter arrived with our coffees and brandies.

"But this is a pilgrimage Oscar." The tone of Venezia's voice was surprised. "We are going on foot. We can't travel in a car."

In reply to this Oscar, pleased at having gained all our attention, leaned forward across the table.

"We all agreed before. We would return a portion of the money back to the bank, give a portion to the lepers and keep a portion for ourselves. Well that is what I have done. I have bought a car with my share."

Echo, who was the most perceptive of our pilgrims, sensed the direction of Oscar's argument.

"I am guessing Pilgrim Oscar that you have bought a car that is a little bit special."

Oscar beamed at him.

"You are right there Echo old chum. What I have bought is a Derby Bentley."

Echo, being an African Autodidact, understood the significance of that and whistled through his teeth appreciatively.

"What year ?"

"1938. Four and a half litre engine. Convertible."

"Ouch!" Echo looked impressed. "That is a very rare motor indeed."

Oscar looked around the table.

"I have made a decision. When this pilgrimage is over I will stay in Spain and open a dealership offering classic cars for sale. Because as you know cars are my passion and for the moment for various reasons it is not suitable for me to return to England. This Derby Bentley will be the first car in my collection. The car will stay in Leon but I will pick it up later. But tomorrow as a treat for everyone I have arranged that we can use it for a day trip out."

So that is how the following morning found us in our rooms on the Calle de Martin Sarmiento washed and ' scrubbed up' and changed into our best clothes as we awaited the arrival of Oscar and the car.

Venezia, as if in rehearsal for a future role, had this morning decided to mother and boss us. Denis had his hair wetted down and Echo was told to change his shirt a second time. Finally she turned on Roy when she saw him place his bright blue baseball cap, with its football club logo, on his head.

"No Roy," she told him bluntly. "You cannot go out in Oscar's new car in that terrible ratty old thing."

Roy, startled, took off the hat and looked at it.

(We had already learned of the importance of hats to Roy on this journey. The last time he had worn the red hat we had ignored the Storm Warning and we had paid the price for it).

"Denis," Venezia called out. "There is a shop that sells hats opposite the Cathedral. I saw it yesterday. There is still time. You had better go and buy a decent hat for Roy to wear."

So that was how a quarter of an hour later Roy was standing in front of the mirror adjusting a smart checked trilby hat with a brown feather poking out of the back. But our gestures of admiration, which we would have willingly given, were forestalled by the roar of a powerful motor as Oscar turned into the Calle de Martin Sarmiento in his open topped car, pursued by a gang of small boys.

"Oh my God !" Echo shouted out as we descended down into the street. "It's Mr Toad himself !"

We could see that the Derby Bentley needed restoration. Some of the leather work was ripped and there was evidence that chickens had been roosting on the back seat, leading us to assume it had been kept in a farmer's barn.

"That will certainly have reduced the price," Oscar said as he walked round the car examining it. "But it is still a noble machine."

Roy was also full of admiration. He adjusted the hat on his head. "Ah drives ma own Bentley around The West End ah London but I'd gladly swap it for a machine like that."

Even those of us who knew nothing about cars could appreciate that it was a work of art, a beast from a bygone age. It stood before us its great motor throbbing.

Then Oscar opened the doors and we got inside. Walt went in the front and the rest of us squeezed in the back. Then Oscar put on his aviator goggles, engaged the motor and soon we were making our way out of the city. Shortly after that we were bowling along the open road in exhilarated mood.

"I feel as if I'm flying," Venezia yelled out above the roar of the engine and the wind.

"My feet are loving it," Jack yelled back. "They are not having to do the work for once."

In the excitement, as Echo leaned his head out of the side to feel the wind on his face, Denis took the opportunity to squeeze Venezia's hand. This was a move, again in the excitement of the moment, that was eagerly reciprocated.

Eventually we entered a small town and stopped. The feeling of being stationery once again after such a burst of speed left us temporarily disoriented.

Finally, when we had regained our senses, we looked around to see on our right hand side a large circular stone stadium.

"Naw Oscar you's surely no takin' us to a local Spanish footbaw game?" Roy's Scottish accent rang out as he replaced his trilby hat on his head. "I can watch that stuff back home anytime ah wants."

"No, don't worry Roy," Oscar replied. "For once, thank God, this has nothing to do with football."

He removed his driving goggles and turned back from his driving seat to face us.

"Courtesy of Oscar Bebbington and his deep and generous pocket what you are going to witness today Pilgrims is the glory and the bravery of the Spanish Bullfight!"

After that we got out and looked around and Oscar organised a couple of boys to stand guard over the car. Then as were about to enter the stadium we saw that Walt was looking around nervously, holding the brim of his slouch hat.

"You look as if you are expecting someone," Denis commented.

"Yes well I am actually," Walt replied.

A few moments later a slight looking man, wearing a dark old fashioned suit with collar and tie came toward us. He had a sallow complexion and we noticed he had a slight limp. When he spoke Walt clasped his hand and they spoke together quickly in Spanish so that none of us could understand what was being said.

Then Walt turned to us.

"An old friend of mine. The poet Federico Garcia Lorca. He will be our guide through the bull fight. I have also asked him to join us this evening for dinner if that is acceptable to pilgrims."

We all shook hands.

"Yes. But..."

"A minor point Wilson."

"The Spanish Civil War. A bullet to the back of the head, a crude execution, 1936..."

Walt sighed.

"Yes I know. For most of us such a thing would certainly be fatal. But for a select few it is really no more than a minor inconvenience, I can assure you."

It was here that Oscar interrupted this conversation.

"I thought we had agreed. We would not introduce any more characters into the narrative. We are getting bunged up as it is. It will get too confusing for the reader."

Walt sighed again.

"Yes, I'm sorry, but I could not resist it. He is such a character and he will be an excellent guide this afternoon."

It was then that Echo looked at Walt with a sceptical eye.

"Oh no Walt. That is not the reason. You invited him because he flattered you. He wrote a poem in praise of you."

"Oh you are well read Echo," Walt was blushing slightly, embarrassed at being caught out. "The time you spent gaining an education in the libraries of Kinshasa was certainly not wasted."

In the end after a short debate it was agreed that Lorca would accompany us to the bullfight but thereafter he would leave the story.

It is not the intention of the writer of this narrative to enter into a dispute over the the rights and wrongs of bullfighting.

Suffice it to say that there were some aspects of the spectacle (for which the poet Lorca was our knowledgeable and voluble commentator) that we found disturbing. We did not like the way the Picador seated on his horse drove his lance into the side of the poor bull. But at the same time we admired the courage and the balletic skills of the Matadors.

However there was one incident during the course of this Corrida which stood out above others.

A young matador from Cordoba, Lorca told us it was only his second fight, was acquitting himself well against a heavy bull.

Nearing the end of the phase which is known as the Tercio de Muerte the bull was standing panting and exhausted. The Matador had raised above his head the sharp killing sword called the Estoque. At an exact moment he would plunge this Estoque down into the neck of the bull. This was a blow, that if correctly executed, would kill the bull instantly and would earn him the applause of the crowd.

But on this occasion, as he made the downward thrust, the bull reared up its head and the Estoque, caught by the bull's horn, was thrown high up into the air.

We all watched gasping as it flew up and then reaching the zenith of its journey began its descent, blade glittering in the sunlight, coming directly toward us.

We all screamed and Lorca pushed us all forward so that the Estoque instead struck a man sitting behind us. It caught him on the wrist leaving his arm cut open and covered in blood.

Immediately, as the poor man was led away to be patched up, Lorca began a jabbering commentary on the incident, saying that he was bound to construct a new poem or a play around it.

We saw the man again as we were leaving the stadium. He was at the centre of a group, his heavily bandaged arm in a sling. He was obviously enjoying the fame of the moment as he retold the tale.

On the way home that evening Jack Phillpotts called Lorca a "yappy little dog" because he never stopped talking.

But as he were dining that evening Walt said that Lorca was a great poet and playwright. Then he offered us these famous lines from his poem Lament for the Death of a Bullfighter.

> Like a river of lions
> His marvellous strength
> And like a marble torso
> His outstanding wisdom.
> An air of Andalucian Rome
> Makes his head appear golden,
> And his laugh was a spikenard
> Of wit and intelligence.
> How great a fighter of bulls!
> How good a mountaineer!
> How gentle with the corn
> And how hard the spurs!
> How tender with the dew!
> How dazzling in the fair!
> How tremendous with the last
> Banderillas of darkness!

When he had finished we were silent for a moment and we all regretted acting hastily in not asking a man who could write such noble thoughts to spend a little more time with us.

50

The exit from Leon via an extended industrial zone is lengthy. Pilgrims who have delayed their start may still find themselves passing through this strange wilderness of garages and tyre plants and cheap hotels as darkness falls.

(Those walking the camino in the winter season should remember that the short days, when darkness falls early, curtail walking time).

These entrances and exits to cities, via the industrial and commercial zones, are always a point of dispute between pilgrims.

Many pilgrims told us that breathing in what they called the 'rotten carcinogenic fumes' of the regular highways, by the side of which on occasion the modern camino does pass, left them revolted.

They added also that they found those lines of small factories and tyre depots and refuse dumps at the edge of towns a 'disgusting turn off.'

Some pilgrims told us they thought they had been sold what they called a ' bill of goods.'

What they had imagined, they told us, was a pilgrimage where they would breathe only clear mountain and forest air and drink only from fast flowing brooks.

After a while we became tired of hearing this argument.

Walt especially, with his encyclopaedic knowledge of every aspect of this pilgrim route, was short with these people, who it has to be said were largely young and American.

"If you had passed this way in the Middle Ages," he told them, "you would have risked being rolled by bandits or dying from a dozen diseases which are easily curable today.

And if you were to pass this way in the future there will certainly be other obstacles to surmount."

It was the day following our exit from Leon that we encountered a silver haired pilgrim, a retired doctor, who read us this short extract from his diary about the exit from Leon:

'It was almost evening when the last of the zone was reached, the sky was ragged and dirty with streaks of red and there were trucks going by. I felt I was leaving Chicago rather than a majestic Spanish city. However this did not worry me, because for me the smell of the road is as much tarmac and diesel as open country.'

(Pilgrims staying in the main refuge in the middle of Leon should be advised that it is run by nuns, who expect attendance at evening service. You will also find yourself, courtesy of these same nuns, leaving the refuge before daybreak, when the stars are still shining bright in the night sky).

But as we negotiated our way out of the city that grey and windy morning, (we were to meet our donkeys at a pre arranged point outside the city as usual) our coats were buttoned up tight against the cold.

Jack and Roy were walking together.

"I have a mind," Jack was saying, " to put my portion of the bank robbery money toward purchasing a share in a bar here in Spain. But it will all depend," and here he looked at Roy gravely, "whether I can persuade Marjorie to release me from my obligations at the Bastard's Baby."

Roy nodded sympathetically at this dilemma.

"Aye well, I wish yous luck with that Jack. It's always a problem to know wha' to do for the best with the lassies."

He buttoned his coat a little tighter as the cold wind swirled around them. Then he began again.

"Take ma Mary. I have to admit she's been on ma conscience too."

He turned to Jack.

"I'm away from our home in Godalming with ma team an awful lot so she's had to bring up our girls and it's no been easy for her. I always bring her something back o' course, but its no the same."

He stopped for a moment as a truck went by us.

"And the reporters from the journals have harassed us somethin' terrible. The things they've written about me and ma family. You wouldna believe it Jack.

"Sometimes it's been that bad she's been in tears, the poor wee lass. I've had to come home and take the paper away from her."

Venezia had quickened her pace slightly and was now walking alongside them to listen to this interesting conversation. Roy turned to her.

"I was tellin' Jack I'd like to spend ma share of the money getting something for ma Mary. But the problem is hen, I dunna know wha' to get her. The wee lassie's got everythin' she needs in the house. Yous could feed a Highland regiment with all the stuff she's stacked up in the kitchen. And the rest of the house. Oh ma God! She's had it done over a dozen times in the last five years. There's times when I come home from a trip and I go through the front door and I dunnae recognise the place."

We all smiled at this.

"What can I get for ma Mary then Venezia?" There was a plaintiff note in Roy's voice. "I love her very much and she is the rock of ma life."

We were all watching Venezia now to see how she would deal with this request.

We had noted the softening of Roy's manner. This was an indication, we were sure, of his great love for his wife Mary.

"Before I can answer that question Roy dear," Venezia replied after reflecting, "We need to know a little more about your wife Mary."

She paused to think.

"For instance does Mary appreciate football? Or is it a subject of conversation that is banned in your household?"

Roy looked serious at being asked that question.

"Well," he said finally. "Ma Mary does not always enjoy the game but she always like to see ma team winning."

"But what happens when your team doesn't win?"

"If they dunna win?"

Roy looked round at her quickly and his visage, even on that cold and windy morning as we exited via the industrial zone of Leon, started to change.

"Naw, naw. I'm no happy with that line ah questioning at all Venezia."

We could see the blood beginning to pump into his cheeks giving him a sulphurous air. Then he moved closer to Venezia and began that familiar stabbing movement with his finger.

"You's been listenin' to all the rumour and gossip and scuttlebutt goin' around. Yous no better than the rest ah them. You'd sell your own granny for ten shillings and a pint ah Guinness to get a story about me and ma family. And I'll tell yous another thing."

He looked around angrily at the rest of us.

"If any of yous write anythin' about me and ma family imputin' any domestic disharmony when I return to the house where I stay after losin' a match there'll be no more co operation from me or ma club and ma lawyers will be on to yous. Yous can trust me on that."

After that outburst we walked on in shocked silence for the next few moments. Roy had pulled on an old ratty red baseball cap and was striding ahead of us, hands deep in his pockets.

"We'll shortly be at the point where we can divert off this God awful highway and get back into the country," Walt said finally. "We can meet the farmer and pick up our donkeys again and that will please Jack."

After that he dropped back and leaning in toward Venezia added quietly:

"Do not worry about that little outburst. You should know by now that Roy is a man of great pride and sensitivity. You must learn how to handle him discreetly."

When we had been reunited with our donkeys once again and Jack had pronounced them fit and healthy we set out once more on the road that would take us to the village of Villadangos del Paramo where it was intended we would camp that night. The following day we planned to follow a route that would take us through to the town of Astorga.

Soon after that, with the sun beginning to break through the grey clouds, Venezia advanced to the head of our party and came alongside Roy. She was the only one of us who could confront The Great Man directly when he was ' in a mood.'

She pitched her voice so that it was deliberately sweet and light.

"Roy you are a Grumpy Old Bear. And I have been told off for tweaking your tale."

She slipped her hand through his arm.

"But you asked me a question and I was only trying to answer it, so you should not take offence. You don't know what to buy as a present for your wonderful wife Mary. Well if I am going to help you there you are going to have to give me a tweeny weeny bit of information about what it is that your wonderful wife Mary actually likes."

Roy, seduced by Venezia's charm removed his cap and we were able to see by the colour of his cheeks that his fiery mood had subsided. Then he turned to Venezia. His eyes were now bright and cheerful and clear once more. He began to address her, forgetting that this was the second time he had told the story.

"I'll tell yous now Venezia I'll no forget the evenin' I first set on eyes on ma Mary. I'd a new shirt ironed and a suit that showed me off well. I was a vain wee shite in those days ya know, always checking ma self in front of the mirror. And the final thing was always a drop of special after shave on the Babadouche cheek. Never failed. After that a couple of bevvies with the lads and then we were all up to the dance hall, a gang of us. I tell you, hen, I was fit that night. I was top o' the world. I could ah had anyone I wanted."

Venezia was listening carefully.

"And so you did, bless you Roy, so you did."

A far away look entered Roy's eye as he recounted that first meeting.

"When I first set eyes on ma Mary in the dance hall in Dundee I knew straight off she was the one for me. In ma eyes the wee hen glistened like a diamond. We were married twelve months later in the register office and she's been at ma side ever since."

Then he looked around quickly as if to challenge anyone who might query this sequence of events.

"And afterwards you went straight off to play football," Venezia added in the same sweet voice.

"Fer Christ's sake Venezia, there was a match, it was important."

Venezia sighed. She was now walking next to Blair and ran her hand down his back.

"It is certainly a puzzle to think of what you can give Mary that will convince her of your undying love."

"Aye yer right," Roy responded in an equally puzzled tone and we all fell into silence as we considered.

Then Venezia lifted her hand suddenly from Blair's back.

"Hold on I know!"

She turned to Roy with a smile on her face.

"Where did you finally go for your honeymoon Roy?"

"We didn'a have one hen," Roy replied. "It was mid season. I've told yer. There were matches to play."

"Alright then," Venezia said patiently. "Where would Mary have like to have gone?"

Roy looked blank for a moment and then his face slowly brightened until a broad grin split his lopsided face.

"Aye, I've got it Venezia. We was courting in ma first car, the Ford Consul. I said where do you want to go on yer honeymoon hen if you could go anywhere you want and she says Roy pet, I've always wanted to go on a touring holiday in the Western Isles!"

"Well there you are Roy," Venezia cried excitedly, grasping him by the arm. "That is the solution. Now you can do it. That is how you can spend your share of the money. Give your wonderful wife Mary the honeymoon for which she has waited all these years!"

Roy looked suddenly doubtful but the rest of us were bowled over by the proposition.

Oscar who was walking next to Thatcher chipped in confidently:

"I could certainly arrange the purchase of a Ford Consul from a classic car dealer I know."

"To get there you will have to go by the bridge to Skye," Echo added confidently. "After that it's over to Tarbert on Harris by the Caledonian MacBrayne ferry. There are daily services in the summer although people are complaining that the fares have become expensive."

Venezia was laughing and clapping her hands as she imagined the trip.

"Yes, and you can tour the Western Isles staying at B&Bs as you would have done all those years ago!"

We watched as Roy thought carefully through this proposition.

Then slowly a smile emerged on to his face and a moment later he slapped his thigh and gave a roar of delight.

"Oh, you're right there ma boyos! That's what I'll do, that's how I'll spend ma share ah the money. And it'll make ma Mary happy too!"

After that we discussed the detail of the itinerary and Echo once again showed why he was called the African Autodidact with his off the top of his head selection of sites and places that the happy couple could visit.

Then Wilson said we had to consider the music to accompany such a happy event. Hans Klugman had given us the songs of Charles Trenet and we thought they would be suitable.

We then added further popular numbers to which the happy couple would certainly have danced all those years ago at the dance hall in Dundee.

Wilson was about to enlarge on this further by saying he could imagine the newly weds on the beach at sunset, arm in arm, gliding across the warm sand in the manner of figures in a Jack Vettriano painting when Walt, ascertaining his intention, signalled him to stop and so a further potential crisis was averted.

51

We slept out uneventfully overnight near Villadangos del Paramo. Early the next day we were packing up our encampment ready to move on. None of us realised that we were shortly to experience an incident that would severely strain relations between pilgrims.

The sky was clear and a warm day was promised. We were well away from the Meseta by this time and the paysage around us was rough and green. Oscar with the help of Denis had struck our tents and was now watching as Jack led our two donkeys into the camp preparatory to loading up.

There was a pause in our activities as we waited for Venezia and Echo to finish packing up the last of our kitchen utensils so that along with the tents they could be placed in the panniers and the whole ensemble loaded on to the backs of our donkeys.

It was as we waited that Jack and Oscar found themselves in a casual 'bantering' conversation (as between men in the absence of women) which led to Jack asserting in a louder voice than he had intended:

"I don't call myself religious but I certainly find it very feminine to see a woman on bended knee before an altar."

It was unfortunate for Jack that Venezia, in poor humour as she struggled to get all our kitchen equipment into its allocated bags, overheard this comment. She was quickly on her feet. Her voice was sharp.

"I am not at all surprised that your wife has ejected you Jack Phillpotts if that is how you think. If it was me I would have done the same thing only I would have done it ten years earlier."

Jack looked astonished at this unprovoked attack. Oscar in turn tried to defend him.

"It was only boys talk Venezia. Nothing was meant by it. It was not intended for public consumption."

However this had the opposite effect from that which had been intended with Venezia picking up a kitchen knife that was lying on the ground and pointing it directly at Oscar.

"I don't know why you are getting involved in this argument Oscar."

Her voice was tense.

"It is nothing to do with you. And in any case you are worse than Jack as we think you may have interred your poor wife Sheila in a shallow grave in the back garden of your house."

This further attack left poor Oscar horrified and speechless. Venezia then turned her attention to the hapless Roy who had moved quietly behind one of the donkeys hoping to avoid attention.

"And you are a poor specimen too. You didn't even take your poor wife Mary on a honeymoon until we shamed you into it thirty years later!"

After that and before any of the men could reply to the charges she threw the knife to the ground and stormed off to find Walt who was returning to our encampment cupping in his hat a quantity of berries. Ambushing him as he entered the camp she demanded angrily:

"How do you expect women to read this book that is being written when almost all the characters are men?"

Walt advanced into the camp and placed his hat with the berries on the ground. Then he looked around at the rest of the pilgrims as he assessed the situation.

"And look at the way the writer has treated women in the story." There was nothing stopping Venezia now. "How do you expect us to react to that? Do you have an explanation?"

Walt sighed. He had been hoping to avoid this attack but knew in his heart that it had to come.

"There was a slip up with the organisation." He tried to sound conciliatory. "On previous occasions we have always had more women and they have given the party a balance."

"Well then what happened?" Venezia was standing face on to Walt.

Walt sighed again.

"We had contracted with a certain well known actress to be our celebrity guest pilgrim. I am legally bound not to name her but she had to pull out at the last minute for personal reasons. That is why we have Roy. He is a personality of equal stature who was available straightaway."

"But unfortunately he is the wrong sex." Venezia's voice was still angry.

"Yes," Walt agreed. "That is certainly unfortunate."

There was a silence here while we all considered the situation. Oscar and Jack were starting to move about again to get our donkeys loaded. Echo had picked up the knife Venezia had discarded and placed it among the other kitchen utensils.

Then suddenly (how many times had we seen this sudden change with pilgrims?) Venezia's mood altered and her face brightened.

"Hold on. I have had an idea! Why doesn't Roy invite Mary to come out and join us? There is no doubt she would be a great asset to our little group!"

Walt looked thoughtful at this and so all our eyes settled on Roy. But when he heard the suggestion he considered for a moment and then to our great sadness began to shake his Great Scottish Head. His voice was low.

"Yer a great wee lassie Venezia and I admire yer spirit but that one is no going to run. I was on ma mobile phone half the night tryin' to persuade Mary to go on honeymoon to the Western Isles in an old Ford Consul. So ah can tell ya straight off she wouldna come out here. A hiking trip? Oh dearie me no. I'd have better luck if I suggested a coffee morning in the centre of Godalming. No, no. These days ma Mary prefers the comforts of our lovely home."

When we heard this news, and the sad voice in which Roy delivered it, we understood the situation and the question of Lady Mary Babadouche joining us on pilgrimage was not raised again.

52

When we stopped for our midday break at Hospital de Orbigo, with its fine old bridge crossing the Rio Orbigo, we all began to consider how we might spend our share of the robbery money. We had been impressed by Oscar's acquisition of his classic car in Leon. But Denis's suggestion that he might use his share to retrain and re equip and return better informed to the world of dentistry was rejected on the grounds that it contravened his own condition, that we should spend our money adventurously.

In the end it was Echo who gave us our most novel proposition, disclosing it in a reply to this subtly planted question from Venezia.

"How will you spend your share of the money Echo dear?" We were eating as she asked. "Will you spend it on yourself or will you consider someone else?"

"Well what I am waiting for," he replied carefully, "is that special person, that someone who will tell me a story that will pull at the strings of my heart."

This raised Venezia's hopes greatly. But they were straightaway dashed when Echo explained:

"When I was young I was very poor. So I know how poor people dream. They dream that one day on the street they will find a penny, or a centime, or a rupee and with it they buy a winning ticket on the lottery. And so suddenly their lives are transformed and they can do all the things they want."

At this Venezia got up abruptly from the table.

"Well, you are a dreamer too." She sounded bad tempered. "You are like all other men you only think of yourself. You will certainly never find a deserving case like that here in Spain."

After that, with Venezia refusing further discussion on the subject, we drank up our coffee, paid our bill and got back on the road.

We dipped down into a wood two miles before the town of Astorga just as the sun was setting. We stopped for a moment to watch as the last red rays of day filtered through the branches.

Aside from a visit to the Episcopal Palace designed by the architect Antoni Gaudi there is little to detain pilgrims in the town of Astorga. However, that being stated, it is a town well known by pilgrims. This is because it is the junction point where the path coming up from the South, the Via de la Plata, joins in with the Camino Frances.

Walt said for that reason (and others) he would not put us in the refuge.

"It will be full of pilgrims talking about their adventures in towns such as Seville and Salamanca. We can stay at a small hotel I know which is quiet."

An hour later when Jack had made suitable arrangements for his donkeys and when we had washed and changed and the sleeping arrangements in the rooms had been sorted out, we descended down into the street again and found a small bar that was quiet enough and that would serve us a meal.

Normally, as has been stated before, pilgrims retire to their beds soon after supper. This is the consequence of an early start and a day spent out in the open. However that night in Astorga was the exception to the rule.

It began when Echo looked at his watch and with a yawn announced:

"It is still early enough and there is a bar across the street where I can hear music playing. We could certainly take a beer there to while away an hour."

So with everyone in agreement we crossed the road and entered into the establishment where we had heard the music to discover, after we had been directed downstairs, that it was not a bar but a night club.

The music was loud and there were already a good number of people dancing and soon we were enveloped, along with the others, in a swirl of cigar smoke and scent and music.

And that was how for one evening we forgot that we were a band of humble pilgrims making our way to Santiago de

Compostela on foot for reasons religious and unspecified and instead became unlikely night club revellers.

But we were not ashamed of this. If Walt was trying to teach us that we could not live properly without nourishing our souls, we could make a reasonable argument that from time to time we also needed to nourish other parts of ourselves - with in this case cigars, whiskey and music.

Of all our number it was Roy who was soon most at home in this night club atmosphere. He was seated on a rich velvet banquette and his arm was firmly around the waist of a plump young girl. On the low table in front of him was a glass of whiskey and a good fat cigar and his face was red with drink and laughter as he recounted to his young companion tales of life ' on the pitch' at his football club.

Opposite him was the great poet Walt Whitman, his hair and beard dishevelled, his shirt open. He was looking around him smiling, surveying everything with a splendid eye. In a minute he was joined by two long haired Spanish poets.

Wilson and Oscar had found girls to dance with and Jack and Echo were at the bar also drinking whiskey.

Only Venezia, who was sitting next to Denis was unhappy. She was still considering the manner in which Echo had slighted her that afternoon. She sipped a small glass of wine and ran her hand distractedly through Denis's hair.

"I know you have suffered terribly Denis dear." She leaned in toward him. "And I can see that as a result you have developed a soul as sensitive as any painter or writer."

She was about to develop this theme further (with the full encouragement of Denis) when she saw to her horror that Echo's attention had diverted from Jack, and the story he was telling, to a Beautiful Leggy Blonde who had positioned herself next to him at the bar.

Venezia detached herself from Denis and stood up quickly. But a glance around showed the impossibility of rounding up all the pilgrims and returning them to the hotel. Roy was entertaining his plump companion and Walt was holding court to his two long haired Spanish poets.

Quickly she turned to Denis.

"Denis dear, I'm exhausted." She tried to keep her voice calm. She could see the Beautiful Leggy Blonde advancing on Echo. "It's been a long day. Do tell Echo I've gone back to the hotel."

However her exit did not go un noticed. Oscar, who had also observed Echo at the bar with the Beautiful Leggy Blonde, leaned towards Wilson to say:

"It looks as if Echo may have found his deserving case."

With or without Venezia the rest of us enjoyed the evening. It was only when the lights finally came up, and the plump girl and the long haired Spanish poets had made their excuses and left, that we emerged once again into the street.

Made hungry by our exertions we went for a late supper to a nearby restaurant. We were the number we always were, except that on this occasion Venezia's place had been taken, memorably, by the Beautiful Leggy Blonde.

As we ate we listened to an account of her plans to become an actress.

"I am sure I will go to Hollywood one day." Her voice was high and slightly unsteady.

"But first," she lowered her voice an octave and placed her hand over Echo's. "I must attend drama school in Madrid which is terribly expensive."

Here the evening hung in the balance. Echo could have sympathised and wished her well and that would have been that.

But instead we watched in horror as he reached into his pocket and took out his share of the money and in full view of the rest of the pilgrim band handed it over to the Grateful Future Star Of Hollywood.

53

The next morning we were the same group, minus one, in the simple dining room of our hotel. The Beautiful Leggy Blonde had mysteriously melted away with the dawn light. Venezia had stayed in her room pleading ill health.

All our eyes were on Echo who was sitting with his head in his hands, taking only coffee and refusing all food.

It was Roy who spoke first:

"Yer a wee bloody gobshite Echo. Even the rawest ah ma players wouldna had made a fool ah himself like that. What's wrong with yer man, could ya na see the way the wee hussy was waggling her tail feathers at ya? They call you the African Autodidact, wha'ever that is. From now on I'm going to change yer name to the African Bampot."

There was no mercy from other quarters either. Jack ploughed in after Roy:

"In all my time in the pub trade, man and boy thirty years, and my father before me, I've never seen such an exhibition."

Oscar, in turn, added with a wry smile:

"You were well and truly skinned there old chum."

Echo tried a feeble defence which had us all looking at the stairs hoping that Venezia would not come down to hear it.

"She is genuine." He was holding his head and groaning. "I am sure of it. You could see the way she looked. In a few years I am sure she will be a great actress. There is no doubt we will see her on the silver screen in Hollywood."

None of us had the heart to respond to that and the breakfast continued on in silence. We also reflected as we ate, with some measure of satisfaction, that even someone as clever and well informed as Echo was capable of making a total idiot of himself.

54

It was not until mid afternoon that we finally left Astorga. Venezia ignored Echo, choosing instead to walk alongside Denis. This was despite both Oscar and Jack pleading his cause.

"Nothing happened," Jack informed Venezia. "Echo's actress slipped away when the meal was over. She had an early audition in the morning."

But Venezia did not reply to this. Instead she continued to stride ahead purposefully, her faithful Denis by her side.

The distance from Astorga to Rabanal (which is our approach to Galicia) is no more than dozen miles but there is a change of landscape which is striking, the dry southern terrain giving way to rough tussocky grass and heather, reminiscent of the Highlands of Scotland.

When we stopped for a break Echo declared, in an attempt to be cheerful:

"If we were passing through in the early morning it would not surprise to me see a great twelve point stag appear out of the mist."

Roy was sour in his response to this.

"Ah dunna know how yous are expected to know what the Highlands of Scotland look like comin' from where you do Echo. I reckon you must have seen some pictures in one of yer books."

Venezia then added to this unpleasant mood.

"You had better keep away from me for ever Echo." She glared directly at him. "There is no doubt that you are unclean and have the pox because of the people you have been consorting with. And if you are so taken with this scenery we are walking through perhaps you would like to go and live in the Highlands of Scotland where you can spend the rest of your life chasing the deer if that is what you want."

After that we carried on pretty much in silence.

As we had been preparing to leave Astorga we had encountered both Dien and Joy as well as Hang Dog Heinz and his Charming Wife and we hoped to see them that night in Rabanal.

We had heard so many reports of the English refuge in Rabanal that we were eagerly looking forward to experiencing it for ourselves. Some pilgrims had told us that it was the 'best of British' with tea served in the kitchen and a roaring fire where boots and damp clothes could be dried, but other described it as having the atmosphere of an English boarding house of the ' worst sort.'

When we did finally arrive in Rabanal it was dark. Walt went to enquire at the refuge but he was told that because we had arrived late there was no place for us. He was advised to try the municipal refuge instead.

"That is a disappointment," he said. "And I do not want to put you in that municipal refuge. However there is a small hotel which I am sure can accommodate us."

Our spirits were improved when we found that Hang Dog Heinz and his Charming Wife were lodged there. Dien and Joy had gone to the municipal refuge having also been turned away from the English establishment.

Walt then took us the small chapel across the street where Vespers was being celebrated. It was cold and we had to huddle in our coats but the simple chanting of the two priests filled us with joy and we returned to our small hotel to eat dinner in calmer and easier mood. We also noted as we exited the chapel that Venezia had slipped her arm discreetly into Echo's signalling, we hoped, that the episode was coming to an end.

Hang Dog Heinz and his Charming Wife and Dien and Joy joined us for dinner and as we talked, largely of inconsequential things, we were glad to put our ' Astorga crisis' behind us. As we ate we noted that Hang Dog seemed more relaxed than normal. After the meal was over and we were sitting around the fire Venezia turned to him.

"I have never seen you laughing and smiling before as you did at dinner tonight Heinz. You must be feeling better."

At this Hang Dog, confirming all our suspicions, quickly changed his humour. Going suddenly silent he glanced down at the bag at his feet and for a moment we thought we were going to have a repetition of his previous strange performance with the book.

Instead he shocked us all once again by suddenly declaring in his thin Germanic voice, the tone sharp and unpleasant:

"I am convinced now that my wife does not love me and that she has never loved me in all the time of our marriage."

At this the Charming Wife put her hand to her mouth.

"Oh, Heinz how could you say such a terrible thing!" Her voice sounded desperate. "You know I love you more than anything and that I have always done so!"

But Hang Dog, satisfied with the damage that he had done now retired to his corner, rolling a cigarette and blowing smoke at the ceiling and declining to talk further. This left the Charming Wife to try and carry on our conversation as if nothing had happened.

When we went up to our rooms a little later we were of one mind. We felt that the Charming Wife was being put upon and abused by her difficult husband and that if she wanted to have any sort of life she needed to take a firm hand with him.

But then as we prepared to sleep our thoughts turned to the morning when we would ascend a first ridge of hills to enter into the province of Galicia. Walt told us that it was an important moment on our journey as we would be passing by the Cruz de Ferro, the giant cross which is an indication to pilgrims that they were now beginning the final leg of their long journey.

55

We left the hotel early in the morning. Walt led us out. Night stars still shone in the sky and the world around us was mysterious, silent and cold. Occasionally we caught sight of other pilgrims as they walked beside us but the only sound we heard was the tink of our donkeys' feet as they struck the tarmac of the road.

After an hour we had ascended sufficiently so that we could look down on the lights of the houses in the village of Rabanal. If we looked further into the distance we were also able to see the faint glow of the lights from the town of Astorga in the distance. Then above us we could see that clouds were beginning to cover over the stars.

Shortly after that, with the first grey light of dawn starting to appear, we arrived at a significant point on our journey. This is the stone monolith that is decorated by the blazons of Galicia and the heavy red cross, in the form of a sword, that is the symbol of Santiago Matamoros or Saint James the Moor Slayer. (According to legend Saint James led the Christian armies as they drove the Moors from northern Spain). This great stone monolith also marked our entry into the Magical Kingdom of Galicia.

"If you wait here a moment Pilgrims," Walt said as we drew breath, the climb up had been steep. "I will show you something."

Roy took water bottles from the panniers and handed them round. Then Jack released his two donkeys for a moment so that they could graze on the rough ground.

After that we turned and looked down the valley and saw a thin line of light on the dark horizon indicating that the sun was preparing to rise.

Then the clouds parted suddenly and we were taken by surprise as the whole of the Eastern sky was flooded an astonishing blood red. For a moment we were paralysed by this spectacle. If we had been generations of before we would certainly have gone down on our knees. Instead we stared silently. Then the round edge of the sun, appearing like a sharp curved knife, also revealed itself. This effect lingered for several minutes before it was swallowed up once more by the clouds.

During this moment of theatre Walt had removed his hat. Then when the spectacle had finished he ran his hand through hair before turning to us.

"That is what I have been trying to say to you pilgrims." His voice was solid and firm. "That is why we are here. I show it to all my groups of pilgrims. It is the Glory of it that is important."

Then he replaced his hat on his head and paused for a moment as if he was going to say something else. But then he changed his mind and said abruptly:

"Enough for the moment. We have other things to consider now. We are going to divert off the road now to get up to the Cruz de Ferro and we will have to watch the donkeys because it is steep enough and it will also be slippy."

Walt was correct in that assertion. Ten minutes later, all thoughts of the glory of the sunrise were forgotten because we were well and truly stuck on the steep muddy path. Our donkeys could not move. The mist swirled coldly around us.

When poor Blair had slipped back for a third time Jack, his stout frame now trembling with anger, shouted out furiously:

"Halt this damn business right now. If you keep going you are going to damage my donkeys."

He turned to Walt.

"I knew we should have gone by the road." His face was red with indignation. "Never mind watching the dawn, you don't know what you are doing. These donkeys are not mountain goats."

He stared back down the steep slope to the road below us. We could see his breath coming hard.

"You have got us stuck now because I am not going to risk them going down again either."

Walt had no reply to this attack so it was left to Roy to shout out the solution - which in truth should been obvious to all.

"What ya wanna do is unload the donkeys and carry the bags up the hill till there's flatter ground. That'll sort ya problem out."

So that is what we did. We complained and cursed as we unloaded our panniers and distributed the load among ourselves. Then as the mist still swirled around us we continued our slow ascent, now burdened down by all our equipment.

Then after twenty minutes we heard Denis, who had gone on ahead, suddenly yell out :

"Pilgrims I tell you ! Raise your eyes ! Look up ahead !"

As we did so, slowly out of the mist we saw emerge the tall spindle thin cross, the Cruz de Ferro, known to all pilgrims to mark the entry point into Galicia. It was an indication also that we were now on the last leg of our long journey. Even unbelievers such as Echo and Wilson were moved.

Finally as we stood before the cross, bedraggled and muddy, our equipment and donkeys beside us, we thought, with great emotion, of the millions of pilgrims who had made the journey before us and of the millions who would follow us in the future.

We saw that the foot of the Cruz de Ferro was encircled by a giant pile of stones that reached six feet tall at the centre. Walt had told us before that many pilgrims brought stones from home, or picked up stones from special spots en route, to place there.

Jack was the first our of our pilgrim group to step forward. He added to the pile a stone he had slipped into his pocket after he had placed his old boots on the borne outside Burgos. Venezia then added a stone she had collected as she got out of Oscar's car at the bullfight.

The rest of us followed with stones we found lying around us in the mist.

We stayed at the top of the pass looking around until the cold began to enter our bones. We noted the way other pilgrims had ascended the pile of stones to attach messages and photographs and even feathers and pieces of coloured cloth to the upright of the cross.

We also puzzled over the formation of stones that had been laid out on the ground surrounding the cross. Some of them were neat geometric designs while others were more anarchic in form. Some of the stones had been laid out to make the shape of arrows pointing ever West. We recalled the bornes we had seen in the wood at Puente la Reine de Jaca and the circular stone patterns we had seen on the Matagrande just before our entry into Burgos.

The only conclusion we could reach after we had examined everything was that this strange and beautiful place, with its feathers and brightly coloured pieces of cloth and its patterns of stones, was about something more primitive than the Christian path we now followed.

As the mist swirled around us it was left to Echo to revert to theatrical type.

"It's Primitive Art for the twenty first century !" He cried out loudly, abruptly breaking our reflective silence. "Bravo and Hurrah! It's back to the future we go on the Camino de Santiago !"

Then as the cold and the clamminess started to make us shiver we loaded up our donkeys. Then we turned our back on the Cruz de Ferro and everything that had gone before it.

56

Within ten minutes we were looking down in bright sunlight to our first Galician valley, which to our eyes was green and welcoming.

Below us was Ponferrada, a city of seventy thousand inhabitants and a ruined castle. It was our last city before Santiago. To the right of the city we could see the giant cooling towers of an electricity generating station.

We watched as wisps of white vapour escaped from the cooling towers. To our left was the faint outline of a rainbow.

Some readers of this narrative, anticipating the Camino de Santiago as wholly pastoral and peaceful and always full of spiritual meaning, will be disappointed by the way we were guided by these industrial landmarks.

But the cooling towers cannot be ignored, in the same way that the Volkswagen car plant situated to the south of Pamplona on the Camino Aragones cannot be ignored.

So we began the descent that took us first through the small village of El Acebo and then on to Molinaseca. We planned to camp near there before going on to Ponferrada the following day.

As we descended Echo was still laughing.

"I can tell you Pilgrims," he said in his strong African voice. "In the Congolese jungle I have encountered poles and shrines identical to the ones we have just passed."

It was Venezia who gave our response to all this.

"Most of the people we have met do consider themselves on pilgrimage. It's a question of whether you can call it a Christian pilgrimage."

As we continued to descend and still with the image of the Cruz de Ferro in our mind, we considered the many different types of people there are walking this road.

Some come for historical reasons, to examine churches and monuments. Some come for specifically religious reasons. Others come for athletic and sporting purposes. Some want to challenge themselves. Others are here to mark a turning point in their life.

Then as we paused to look down the valley and to rest our legs for a moment Venezia said:

"Do you know I think the whole of the human race is represented here."

Walt smiled at this.

That evening we clattered across the cobbles of the old Roman bridge into Molinaseca. Then we stopped to allow Echo and Venezia to buy our provisions.

While we waited Denis went on ahead, reporting back in half an hour that he had found a site where we could cut wood for our fire and where there was good grass and a stream for our two donkeys.

As we were unloading our donkeys and setting up our camp we received a surprise when we noted a group of four other pilgrims coming down the track toward us. As they drew nearer we saw they were the two Austrian girls and Dien and Joy.

"We spotted your encampment," Joy said. "We have been walking together as a small group and like you we also prefer to pitch our tents outside to sleep if we can."

Once we had got over our surprise, it was the first time on our pilgrimage that we had been joined by other people camping out, we welcomed our guests unreservedly and with pleasure.

It was agreed after discussion that we would pool our provisions for the night. Venezia and Echo were elected our cooks, the two Austrian girls went to help Wilson chop wood and Roy was, as usual, put in charge of the distribution of the wine.

Echo and Venezia made up a stew with meat and vegetables and as we ate we exchanged information, as pilgrims do, of who we had met on the road and so on.

We told the two Austrian girls of the strange behaviour of Hang Dog Heinz in the hotel at Rabanal. They nodded gravely and said they had walked with that couple for several days and had found sensible communication with Hang Dog impossible, even though a common language was shared.

The two Austrian girls then turned to Roy and said that his story of the Munich air crash had moved them to tears, but as instructed they had not told anyone else about it.

Then Joy began a story about a romance that he had heard was flourishing between two Australians. The boy was called Felix and the girl was called Rachel. It was said that after several false starts they were now walking together every day and there was talk of a marriage back in Australia sometime the following year.

As this information was disclosed Denis suddenly shouted out:

"Well hold on! But that was us! We found the note under the stone outside Castrojeriz!"

He put down his plate and turned to Walt.

"Walt. You remember. You told us to replace the note so as not to alter the course of history."

After we had congratulated ourselves on our actions the two Austrian girls helped Venezia and Echo clear up our dinner. Then Wilson added more wood to our fire. Finally it was Echo who said:

"Walt you were beginning a discourse this morning, when we saw the sun rise. Perhaps you could continue it now, especially as we have guests."

Walt who liked nothing better than an audience fell for this ruse straightaway and so after Roy had refilled our wine mugs he stood up.

"What I have been trying to impress on my people." He was addressing himself to Dien and Joy and the two Austrian girls. "Is that if they do not attend to the important things in life and I will give them the names of Glory, Magic, Myth and Ritual they will curl up and die from the inside as surely as they would if they did not have food in their bellies."

He stopped and looked around.

"That was what I was trying to show them this morning. To open their eyes to the Glory that is all around them. Even to the way the path bends round the side of a hill, and to their relations with each other, even to the grass under their feet."

After that he stopped, puzzled, as if once again he had forgotten something. Then, realising that he had said all he wanted to say, he placed his hat back on his head and sat down. We watched his pleasant visage dancing in the fire light and thought, as we had so many times before, that we were privileged to be here with him.

We had settled by the fire once again when Venezia put her hand on Jack's shoulder.

"We have a very important man here," she said slowly, addressing our guests. "If his life had pursued a different course he would have been known as one of the finest singers of his day."

We could see Jack looking embarrassed at this introduction. Venezia turned to him.

"Jack, you've got your audience tonight, are you going to sing for them?"

At first Jack demurred but his objections were overcome and so he finally stood up and after a nervous introduction gave us a fine selection of songs in a voice as rich and powerful as Josef Locke or Mario Lanza.

As we listened Venezia slipped her arm through Walt's and whispered in his ear:

"Look around. The size of the audience is increasing. They are enjoying the concert as well."

Walt peered out into the night at the pale images.

"Oh yes." He smiled. "They are always there. I wonder if Aimery is with them. He liked a good song the same as the rest of us."

57

The following morning we rose early and made our way the short distance into the town of Ponferrada.

Because we had now lived so closely together for so long we were able to predict accurately what one of our number might do or say next.

So that evening, having spent the day doing our normal chores, we were not at all surprised to hear Walt declare:

"We will feed well tonight my fellow pilgrims, you don't have to worry about that."

We also guessed, again correctly, that this would mean a discreet restaurant down a narrow side street where the proprietor would greet us warmly before offering us a good table and an equally good repast.

(As has been stated before food is of great importance to pilgrims. When we were having difficulty recalling a location that we had passed through weeks before, our memories were always jogged by remembering the meals we had eaten there).

But what we did not forecast that evening was the expression of horror that would register on Echo's visage as we saw titled above the doorway of the restaurant the words The Queen of Antwerp.

"What have you done Walt !" he shouted out suddenly. "But this is basically a Belgian restaurant !"

When we had been seated and had identified, by their girth and complexion (although they looked jovial and content as they ate) the nationality of the other diners, Echo turned angrily on Walt.

"I am going to have to demand an explanation here Walt. You are well aware of my feelings about our former colonial masters and all things Belgian."

But Walt had turned his back and was in deep (and deliberate) discussion with our buxom waitress.

(It is at this point of course that we should recall Walt's comment to us in Leon - that he could easily whip us into a lather against any innocent third party. That is the way wars are begun, he had told us).

Echo picked up the menu and read it through before throwing it down angrily on the table. Then he addressed himself to Jack.

"It is well known that aside from England, Belgium has the worst food in Europe."

After that he turned quickly to Walt, as if seeking confirmation of this prejudice, but Walt was still engaged in discussions with our waitress. So he addressed the pilgrims in general.

"It is a cuisine certainly not acceptable to middle class diners in Kinshasa."

Echo was looking around. We sensed we were in for one of his theatrical outbursts. He was starting to attract the attention of the other diners. Then he raised his voice deliberately.

"And the name! The Queen of Antwerp! That is the real insult. Everyone knows that Antwerp is at the heart of the diamond industry that has left my people ravaged."

Behind us two Belgian couples looked discomforted at hearing this extreme discourse.

"And of course I recognise the types here." Echo was staring hard now at individual diners in the restaurant. "I am sure they are all descendents of the colonists who so disfigured my nation."

Then he leaned forward across the table. Walt had finished talking to the waitress and had turned back toward us.

"Listen," Echo said. His voice had developed a peculiar intensity. "There are things you should know about our former colonial masters that will change your view. And I am going to give you five of them."

Then, his voice loud enough to carry to nearby tables, he numbered off this eccentric list:

"1. Our Kleptomaniac and Murderous King Leopold. A very ugly man, there are still statues to him in Brussels. Reduced my fellow countrymen to animal status. Arms chopped off.

Best estimates that ten million people, half the population of the time, are brutally slaughtered.

2. Georges Simenon, the writer. You all so admire him but actually he is rather pathetic. Certainly only a second rate author. He is also a serial seducer of poverty stricken women.

3. Our charming Eddy Merckx. Our national hero in Belgium. Wins the Tour de France on five occasions but tests positive for drugs three times. (All impropriety denied).

4. Our rotten country itself. So divided between the revolting Flemish and the disgusting Walloons that actually it does not work as a country at all. So divide it up! Simply abandon it!

5. And finally our wonderful Marc Dutroux ! Now there is a man. I would make him our national symbol. Put a statue up to him alright. He is our paedophile de jour, our serial killer, our abuser of young girls. Wonderful cover up in that chap's case. Magistrates menaced. Everyone knows he is protected by people high up in government."

Echo concluded his bizarre indictment with a scowl and fierce regard around the dining chamber. At the same time Oscar and Jack observed that the four stout Belgians behind us had risen to their feet and thrown their napkins down and were angrily signally the buxom waitress to bring them the bill.

When we had entered the Queen of Antwerp half an hour before we had seen only a chamberful of diners laughing and joking. But now looking round again, and noting the way the four stout Belgians were brushing rudely past us, we did feel the bile starting to stir in our stomachs. For a moment we did see the other side of this happy group - its legacy of sadistic colonial oppression and its deep well of sordid sexual dysfunctionality.

However (thank goodness) we were able to put these dark prejudices to one side as our buxom smiling waitress unloaded great pots of wheat beer. When we had quaffed we had to declare that it was some of the best beer we had ever tasted.

Soon after that a further brick was removed from Echo's anti Belgian wall when our patron Leonard, in physique as

Belgian as the rest of his customers, with wide girth and long hair and marvellous thick moustaches, came over to our table.

"My oldest friend." He clapped his arms around Walt's shoulders. " My best and most valued customer."

"Leonard, my favourite chef," Walt responded equally happily. "The reputation of The Queen of Antwerp is now assured across all of Spain."

Walt then introduced our little group, coming at last to Echo.

"Leonard. It is my pleasure to introduce one of the cleverest men in the Congo. We are proud to have him in our pilgrim band."

Leonard gave Echo a little bow and clicked his heels together.

"Monsieur, enchante. It is always a pleasure to greet a distinguished gentleman from such a distinguished country."

After that he fell into deep discussion with Walt over our menu. Echo, still angry, made a final half hearted attempt to recruit Denis to his position, on the grounds of his Belgian ancestry, but when this failed (as it always did) he fell temporarily silent, contenting himself with malign glowers at any unfortunate diner who caught his eye.

Our attention was diverted further from this argument when in a far corner we saw Hang Dog Heinz and his Charming Wife. They were dining with a young man we established as the French student we had met at the beginning of our journey. He had sold Roy his tartan combinations. We didn't recognise him at first as he had shaved off his long dark locks and his head was now close cropped. But we could see that the three of them were in deep discussion.

When we had identified the young man Roy turned to glare at him. Then he said sharply:

"I's goin' to have a word with that fella. The colours in ma combinations has run when I washed 'em in Leon. I'll bet ya a pint a Guinness that wee stoat's still at the same game sellin' his tat."

And with that, and before we could stop him, he had risen from our table and was striding over toward the unsuspecting trio, his Great Scottish Football Manager's Head erect and purposeful. Again we could see that the other diners were watching us.

We had anticipated a fierce dispute over the combinations, with the possibility also of an exhibition of his terrible temper. Instead when he returned to our table a few moments later he was grinning that familiar lop sided grin.

He chuckled as he seated himself. "Told me I was using the wrong temperature when I was washin' them. Says he's got a line in tartan caps which ah'd go well with ma tartan knickers and vest but I said to him if he tried peddling tat like that in Dundee city centre he'd be head first off the Tay Bridge and nobody would bother fishin' him out."

We all looked at Roy for a moment and then to change the direction of the conversation as we waited for our meal, and to forestall Echo who was intent on re opening the vexed subject of Belgian colonialism, Jack turned to Wilson. His voice had an air of concern.

"Are you sure you are alright Wilson ?"

We looked first at Wilson and then at Jack.

"I noted you coming out of the hotel this morning. You had quite a limp on you. You were like an old soldier nursing a war wound."

Surprised, never having suspected that Wilson might be unwell, we turned back to him.

"Well," he said after a moment and with a slow smile on his face. "That is observant of you Jack and I can certainly give you an explanation."

Here Venezia, suddenly suspecting what was coming, leaned over the table.

"Well hold on a minute there buddy." Her voice was sharp. " If you are going to give us a another version of that climbing story it will be the third !"

We looked back at Wilson.

"Well this will be the last version I can promise you that." We noted that his voice had a slight mocking tone to it.

Wilson had gained great authority in our pilgrim group after he had recounted his heroic story of saving the girl but we had been perturbed by the way he had changed the conclusion.

However the start of this story was delayed when the first dishes of our meal were brought to the table and we tucked in.

For the record, and it was excellent, among the many dishes we ate that night was a dish of eels in a green sorrel sauce known in Flemish, according to the menu, as 'Paling in 't groen.' The good quality of this repast was a further riposte to Echo and his evaluation of all things Belgian.

We were well into our meal and Roy had topped up our glasses of wine when we returned to Wilson and invited him to tell us his story.

This new version of the story began, as the other had, as he was approaching the end of his climb.

As he spoke Wilson's voice was direct and clear.

"I had to surmount the metal strut work of the balcony which was directly above me. But I failed and in a moment I was falling back into space. I dropped away from the wall, slowly at first, then quicker and quicker, until I was tumbling over and over in mid air, totally disoriented, brain bursting with terror."

We stared at him. We had this part of the story before. He went on:

"So I was approaching the ground ready to impact with the hard concrete and awaiting certain death when the quick thinking crowd, under instruction of police and fire officers, formed their arms into a cat's cradle but this failed and all they could do was slow down my rate of descent as I crashed through to the ground below."

Wilson took a sip of his wine and looked around to see how this new version of his story was being received. Then he continued.

"When I opened my eyes the doctors were already there and they soon had me in the ambulance. They kept me in the hospital for three months suffering from smashed this and smashed that. They said I was lucky to be alive."

Venezia put down her fork and looked at him sceptically.

"And the rest of the story ?"

"No change. As before."

He turned to Jack.

"So that's what you saw. The hip is a bugger in damp weather. It takes me a few moments to get going."

We were silent for a moment as we considered this new conclusion to Wilson's story. The hubbub of the dining chamber still surrounded us.

The Echo said in a low voice :

"I have got you now mate. Dr Zhivago, the film. Tom Courtenay plays the part. You are Strelnikov, the political agitator. The romantic who turns into the fanatic, the inadequate who finds his role as the political commissar."

Wilson was considering this provocation and how to respond when Oscar, pushing his plate to one side, joined in.

"You are a queer fish Wilson and no mistake. Rescuing damsels and falling off buildings and I don't know what else."

Then Echo took up the attack again.

"Pilgrims, I have worked out this art business that obsesses our friend here. It is the romantic in him that enjoys Robert Lenkiewicz. And of course he detests the modern artists because he is a communist and communists hate all things abstract. As to Jack Vettriano, his paintings are capitalist trinkets - cheap beer and football for the middle class masses. They keep them happy and stop them revolting. Am I right Wilson?"

But before he could respond Jack was speaking.

"You card carriers are all the same. A check on your bedroom wall will certainly find pictures of the ladies, but they will be of the Bulgarian variety and lifting their weights."

We were once again interrupted here as the waitress removed our plates and served us cheese and fresh bottles of wine.

As we were eating Roy turned to Wilson :

"Have yer never been in love then? Apart from the lassie who took the tumble from the building we nae heard mention ah any other girls."

Wilson took a moment before he replied to this question, Finally he said, his voice cold :

"Two years ago I did consider proposing marriage to a waitress who worked in a Kurdish fish bar on Union Street in

Plymouth but when I returned to pop the question the owner said that it was too late that she had been taken away by the immigration service in a van with blacked out windows and a chimney on top and that was the end of that."

Venezia closed her eyes and shook her head in disbelief at this story.

Then Oscar was speaking.

"They say the best way to find out what a man is thinking is ask him to list his prejudices."

Echo turned to Wilson. His voice was grim. "Well Pilgrim Wilson can you do that for us ?"

"Of course," Wilson replied. "But I will start with my likes rather than dislikes if that is alright."

So he took a sip of his wine and in that strange Belgian restaurant this is what he came out with:

"Buccaneers, mountaineers, people with the nerve to stay on the street when the tanks are on the rumble, writers who tell the truth, egalitarians, Plymouth Argyle Football Club and of course Robert Lenkiewicz."

"OK," said Echo, unconvinced. " And now the dislikes."

Wilson laughed.

"Those are easy. Journalists who mock the poor in speeches and articles and entrepreneurs who abuse their workers - I would hang them all up by their testicles from the lamp posts in the public squares. Along side them you can also suspend those fraudulent and talentless modern painters who spend their days hawking their backsides around the galleries tricking innocent citizens out of their savings."

This list, despite its predictability (Echo said later that it was ' a bit leaden') did (finally) make Venezia laugh. She turned to Wilson, some of her confidence restored.

"I want to say that in a previous life you were a pirate on the Spanish Main with a mouthful of glittering gold teeth."

But Echo shook his head.

"A more likely scenario would see him hanged as a revolutionary agitator in some cold Northern climate."

At this finally Wilson called a halt.

"Now you are going too far," he said gruffly. "You are searching for meanings that are not there. You know I am just an out of work article writer with a smashed up hip."

Then he turned to address himself to Jack and Oscar.

"You can call me a socialist if you like and I will not deny the label. And yes I do believe in fare shares for all and if you can tell me what is wrong with that I would like to hear it!"

After that the conversation rather fizzled out and we were contemplating our next move, our excellent dinner having finally put an end to Echo's attack on all things Belgian. Then Leonard sent over glasses of digestives from the bar and a few moments later he came over to join us again.

We offered our appreciation of the meal he had served. Then he leaned forward and said in a conspiratorial whisper:

"The camino is full of rumour my friends. Only yesterday I heard a story that the pilgrim who drove the getaway car in the Zaragoza bank robbery leaned out of the window and shot out the tyres of a pursuing police car in the style of a Chicago gangster."

He looked around our table and touched his moustaches.

"I have it on good authority pilgrims. There is a man in the police who lets me know. They say that El Lobo has been seen in town and that he will never give up."

He looked around the now half empty dining chamber and lowered his voice even further.

"They say he is planning to lay an ambush for the pilgrims who stole his money."

After that he was called to another table and we paid our bill and left. As we made our way back to our hotel we reflected on a strange evening. We had eaten an excellent meal, heard a new version of Wilson's story and been offered a re interpretation of the small country of Belgium. But as we went to our beds all that was overshadowed by the news that El Lobo was still chasing after us.

58

We were now on the forty sixth day of our journey and our direction by the compass was for the moment to the North West. The day was cold and blustery but the path was firm under our feet and the countryside around us was verdant.

However our mood was sombre due to the warning we had received the previous evening from Leonard, our patron at The Queen of Antwerp restaurant.

In the distance ahead of us (still two days walk away) rose the line of hills that we would have to cross, via the steep climb up O'Cebreiro, to gain entry proper into the mountainous Kingdom of Galicia.

As we walked we noted that the overbearing churches which had so disturbed us before, Wilson had said they squatted over the towns and villages like insects, were giving way to smaller stone chapels.

Some of these chapels are similar in appearance to chapels in Wales. This is an indication for pilgrims that they are entering Celtic territory.

(Galicia is part of the Celtic arc that takes in Brittany, Cornwall and the west of Wales, Ireland and Scotland).

There is a word of warning that should be issued to pilgrims when they do finally hike up O'Cebreiro to cross that line of hills - anticipate the rain. And when the rain stops, well, anticipate more rain.

An examination of an atlas will show why. Galicia butts out into the Atlantic and in the winter months attracts the rain in torrents as well as buckets. Shepherds when out tending their flocks always carry a strong framed umbrella. Pilgrims should also be warned that on occasion these heavy rains can turn foot paths into water courses.

We also noted, once we were into Galicia proper, a change in the appearance of the villages. They are poorer and are built low to the terrain. The houses are constructed from ancient square granite blocks. The way these ancient dwellings lean in toward each other across the narrow streets tends also to mirror the state of the elderly and equally stooped inhabitants.

In some of these hill villages the inhabitants still wear raised wooden clogs to keep their feet up out of the wet - and on occasion also out of the cow shit that flows down the steep streets. Venezia, using her camera, also took photographs of dwellings where villagers were still living directly above their animals.

But the narrator has got a little ahead of the tale here. This was all a couple of days walk away yet. This morning we set off from Ponferrada, the paysage still green and rolling in front of us.

Roy Babadouche had taken to wearing the check trilby hat with the feather in it that had been bought for him in Leon. When it was atop his Great Football Manager's Head it was an indication that his disposition was sunny.

But to our alarm we saw that it had been replaced this morning by the notorious red baseball cap. We never did discover why this particular Storm Warning had been raised, although there was speculation that he had received certain (unspecified) information from home via his mobile phone. But his wishes were respected and he was left alone.

Oscar was wearing the quilted jacket that his wife Sheila had created for him, but this morning with the darker side, with its greens and browns, exposed to the exterior.

It was only when we were well out into open country, and as the sun broke through the grey clouds, that we felt we had escaped the attentions of El Lobo.

Then poor Blair, spying a patch of lush green vegetation by the side of the path, pulled sharply at his rein and we paused for a moment to let the pair of them graze. The sun was now pleasantly warm on our backs and we were able to take off our jackets. In a minute Venezia placed a straw hat on her head to shade the sun.

Jack and Roy were at the front of our little group with our two donkeys. Roy, we noted to our relief, had now removed his red baseball cap replacing it with his check trilby.

Jack was barely recognisable from the stout publican with whom we had begun our journey. In our hotel in Ponferrada the previous night Oscar had looked at him and shaken his head.

"When we finally get you back to the Bastard's Baby your dear wife Marjorie is not going to recognise you. She will think we have substituted you for another."

We had all laughed at this, hoping at the same time that Marjorie would be content to receive back this slimmed down and less choleric version of her husband. We reflected on the confession he had made to us and the way it had allowed him to sing again.

But as we walked that morning it was Roy who finally broke our silence. He turned to Venezia.

"Yous was telling us that story about yer sister." His voice was strangely hesitant. Like the rest of us he was troubled by the abstract nature of Venetia's ' sister.'

We all now turned to Venezia.

"Well Roy, actually there is a conclusion to the story," she said finally after a long pause.

We paused for a moment as Jack halted our caravan to adjust a pannier.

"So yer went back to the house again?" Roy asked when we were moving once more.

"Yes Roy. Twice. Once during the day and once in the evening. I got out at the same metro station and followed the same route, but every time I thought I recognised a street or a building it turned out to be wrong. It was like being in a maze, the streets weren't joining up in the way they should. Eventually I had to give up. I had other things to do, I couldn't spend all my time there."

A brief silence followed after that, but then Venezia said suddenly:

"But we did meet in the end."

We turned quickly back to face her. For a moment the delicate Latin features, which we all knew and loved, looked older.

"There's a clearing. It's mid winter and the snow is lying thick on the ground. We're deep in the forest. In front of us is a large wooden house. The colours and shapes are vivid and intense. There is also a deep stillness which I find disturbing."

Venezia paused for a moment recalling the images.

"Then we're all in the house getting ready. Lots of people, all chattering and happy. Now there's a car standing in front of the house. We've all spilled out to look. It's vintage, with a low slung running board. I can see the exhaust fumes hanging in the frosty air."

We were all watching Venezia carefully now.

"Then it jumps a bit. The next scene is my sister holding up her wedding skirts and stepping forward into the car. In the back seat there's an older man, stern looking, dressed in a morning coat. Then a moment later the car moves off. We're all waving. Then she, my sister, turns and looks out of the rear view window and for a second our eyes meet."

Venezia shivered as she recalled the image.

"It was horrible. There was nothing in the eyes at all. They were dark, blank, blind. They were crow pecked hollow orbs."

We were all shocked as we listened to this story. We could feel the terrible sadness pulling at Venezia.

"But she did give me one last scene." Venezia was looking round at us. "The snow is falling again. The car is moving away slowly down the track. Then it turns out of the clearing and is gone from view, leaving lying unabsorbed on the snow several heavy pools of dark red blood shaped in the form of an artist's palette."

Venezia exhaled deeply. Then she was rushing on quickly to get the rest of the story out.

"That was what came to me on three consecutive nights. They were the most vivid dreams I have ever experienced. There were slight variations. On one night the man in the back seat was not there and on another the blood was explained to me as good news, a symbol of fertility, but then on the third night they said it could also have been the result of a serious knife wound."

Venezia looked straight ahead as she finished. She had concluded her story abruptly. We could see that her visage, normally buoyant was now sad and downcast.

After that we walked on for a long time in silence, all deep in our thoughts.

59

We ate our lunch that day in the village of Cacabelos. After that we set off early in the afternoon for Villafranco del Bierzo where we planned to plant our camp that night. Venezia was still upset by the conclusion of the story she had narrated.

Then as we walked she turned to Walt and asked:

"How she would live then Walt ? What should we do?"

Walt considered for a long moment until we thought he was not going to answer at all. Finally he did respond.

"The pilgrimage you are making." He circled his hand round our little band as we walked. "The donkeys, the tents, the fire what can I say, look at you."

Denis turned toward him.

"How will they regard us in the future Walt?"

Walt replied quickly to that question.

"They will be astonished by your historical ignorance and your lack of understanding, both of yourselves and of the world around you, but they will be impressed by your fragility and your humanity."

We could see that Venezia was becoming frustrated by these roundabout answers. She pressed her original point.

"But what is it that is important Walt?"

Again there was a long pause before Walt replied slowly.

"Richness in texture and colour, houses made of darkened wood. Fire, flowing wine and talk. Food, song, and a day's work done by a craftsman. Friendship, community, family. The list is not exhaustive, but you know what I mean."

"Do you have you any other advice for us?" Echo asked.

"Yes," Walt replied. "Don't be careless with other people's lives. You don't have the right to do that."

We all stopped to consider that for a moment.

Then Denis asked: "Will we be remembered? You have told us before that every generation needs a myth."

Walt smiled at this.

"Unlikely, but not impossible. You will be considered but I cannot guarantee more than that. The competition is intense and, as you know with evolution, there is always the element of chance."

As we walked on that afternoon, the sun still warm on our backs, the line of hills that would lead us further into Galicia drew nearer.

Walt was leading one of the donkeys.

"When I was a boy," he said, "I asked my mother, 'Why do they build the churches so tall.' She replied that they built them tall to make man feel small. That was an old joke even then. But I would like to say now that I think they build churches big enough to fit a man's soul."

After that we walked on a little further, feeling the soft earth under our feet. Then we heard Denis say in an odd sort of a voice, as if he was talking to himself :

"There is height but no glory in a shopping centre."

We were taken by this, even if it had not been intended for general consumption, and it allowed us a brief diversion into a topic to which we had returned on occasion during our journey, namely what title we would give eventually to this narrative.

Echo had favoured Break Open The Kalashnikovs! while Roy said that Do Lepers Wear Socks? might catch the reader's eye. Jack and Oscar had gone for the more conservative Field of Stars. But now thanks to Denis we had a new candidate, The Height and the Glory.

Then Walt was speaking again.

"Pilgrims, examine the way you have changed. When Jack looks at the sky and estimates there is an hour of day light left that it is now an important calculation. When he says the weather front that is moving toward us is carrying rain we have to act."

He looked at us severely before continuing.

"I consider that our main purpose, that We Go on Pilgrimage To Regain Our Humanity, still stands. But after some weeks we can add a second benefit - Going on Pilgrimage Teaches You to Open Your Eyes."

These musings on things philosophical were brought to a halt by Jack who expressed concern about his donkeys.

"We will have to stop for a moment to let out their girths. They have been eating too much grass by the side of the path, especially poor Blair. Their stomachs have become swollen and they are uncomfortable."

60

An hour later we approached the town of Villafranca del Bierzo.

As we did so the sun disappeared behind a bank of cloud and the wind began to rise.

Jack was anxious that we should get our camp up as soon as possible. It was Walt who stopped him.

"No Jack. The weather's going to get rougher than you imagine tonight. We don't want to be sleeping out. On previous occasions I've found the refuge here satisfactory, better than the other places."

So with that, and in the company of Echo, Walt set off to the town to make enquiries. When they returned Walt had a smile on his face.

"There are no other pilgrims and the hospitalero doesn't stay on site. He has given me the key so we've got the run of the place."

So that is how, a short time after, with the wind getting up strongly we approached the old wooden building on the edge of town that was the Villafranca de Bierzo refuge.

"This place looks more like a barn than a refuge," Oscar commented grimly as we unloaded the donkeys by the door and looked around. There was a rumble of thunder in the distance.

Jack took his animals around to the field at the back while the rest of us entered inside. The floor boards creaked and the doors banged in the wind.

Half an hour later Jack, having quartered his donkeys for the night, was upstairs looking out of the window. He noted that the black clouds now covered most of the sky, shutting out the evening light.

"That was a good decision you made," he called out to Walt. "We'd have got a real soaking if we had stayed out."

As he spoke a gust of wind from the impending storm struck the wooden building hard making the walls bend.

Downstairs Venezia and Echo examined the kitchen and pronounced it workable. Then they said, in a spirit of optimism, that they could prepare us a ' good feed' that would give the Queen of Antwerp a 'run for its money.' So after that the two of them, taking jackets and hats and waterproofs with them, descended down into the village to buy provisions.

After they had gone Jack, suddenly anxious about his donkeys, went outside in the gloom to check that the stable door was propped open so that his donkeys could get inside when the rain hit.

When our two cooks finally returned the wind had risen further and they battened the front door closed behind them. The rain was already coming down hard.

Denis laid a table and Roy opened bottles of wine and we were distracted briefly from the events outside by the delicious scents of cooking coming from the kitchen. As we waited we sampled a selection of tapas that Echo had bought from the village.

The disaster began to unfold from the moment Venezia approached the table with steaming pots of spaghetti topped with a sauce made from her mother's special recipe.

We had taken several mouthfuls and Walt had warmly complimented Venezia saying, "This is as good as anything I sampled on all my voyages through Italy."

Then just as he raised another forkful to his mouth Echo opened up what he later called his ' rationalist counter attack.'

"We do not understand Walt." He spoke slowly and carefully. "How, in an age of Scientific Explanation, when our existence can be understood without reference to God, you can take this camino trail and all it represents, so seriously."

As has been stated before a good meal is the highlight of a pilgrim's day and is looked forward to eagerly. Echo should have known better than to interrupt it, especially with such a contentious proposition.

When Walt gave his reply he did so slowly and with an elaborate patience, the spaghetti with its special sauce temporarily put to one side.

"I have told you before, Echo. If you neglect your outer life, the need to make your way in a modern world, you will likely end up bankrupt, but at the same time if you neglect your inner life, which we manifest through what we loosely call religion or in some cases spirituality, because we have no other way of expressing it, you will experience another but similar form of bankruptcy. That is why you will find a computer expert prostrating himself before a sacred icon and why I am, God bless us and save us, taking you on this damned trip."

After that he raised another forkful of spaghetti to his mouth and began chewing it angrily as if the strength of his mastication would add weight to his arguments.

But it was then that Oscar, blind as to the danger he was in, took over the attack.

"No, we are not going to accept that Walt." His tone was sharp. "You are trying to fob us off with the simple idea of an inner life, we can all grasp that, we are not children."

Once again Walt put down his fork. Then he pushed his plate to one side altogether and picked up and drank heavily from his wine mug. He lowered his head. The thunder drew closer.

It was at this point that Oscar's attack tipped over from the daring to the reckless.

"Actually Walt some of us have come to the conclusion that the story does not stand up at all." His tone was overconfident. "We think it is a nonsense. We think it is built on shifting sand."

He looked around the table at our little pilgrim band, searching for an example to buttress his argument. Finally he pointed at Roy.

"I mean, for God's sake Walt. Roy is a Protestant. He played football for Dundee. He would rather catch AIDS in a Chinese brothel than go on a holy Catholic pilgrimage."

As he spoke, and we ingested the bizarre nature of this simile, the force of the wind suddenly increased until it was ripping into the side of the house. Oscar was staring at Walt. All caution was gone now.

"If we continue on like this we are in danger of making fools of ourselves. It is a narrative riddled with flaws. You must ask the writer to go back and reconsider."

Walt, whose eyes were half closed, as if he had lost interest in the debate, took another deep draught from his wine mug and then signalled to Roy to refill it. He seemed unperturbed by the story. His reply when it came was off hand.

"You place too much emphasis on names and labels. Mary Babadouche is a Dundee Catholic so the marriage is mixed. Rather undermines your point."

He raised his mug to his lips again.

"You will be worrying about which way to eat an egg next. I have told you before it is a broad church. You are too concerned about detail."

But this reply, which he took to be flippant, only enraged Oscar further. He leant forward and replied:

"All this stuff you are giving us. Glory, Magic, Ritual, Myth. None of us has the slightest idea what you mean."

He smacked his tin mug down suddenly on to the table.

"Look. This mug."

He had raised his voice now. We were all looking at him.

"It contains wine. Nothing else."

He stared hard at Walt.

"Wine is wine. Things are as they are. This is not some fantastic illusion, some crazy game we are all involved in. Things are as we see them. That's all there is to it."

Walt lifted his mug to his lips and drank deeply before responding.

"It was a close call as to whether you would be invited to join us on this journey Pilgrim Oscar," he said finally. His manner had changed now, he was coming awake, his visage was stern. "We were warned you were a trouble maker and there were others who were desperate to come."

At that point a bolt of lightning struck close to the house making us all jump. Then a peel of thunder crashed directly over us and the clumsy wooden door frames shuddered. The lights flickered but then resumed.

Then Walt's head dipped down and he began to sway slightly. He was like an old boxer getting ready to punch.

"The question you all want answered." His voice was down to a rough growl barely audible above the noise of the storm. "You finally breathe your last. So are you going to be greeted upstairs by previous generations of your revolting and parasitic families? Or is it the other way round? Heave him over the side and sail on me hearties, because there is no heaven, no hell, no other life."

Another flash of lightning lights up the sky. Then Walt gets slowly to his feet, large, demonic almost. He is changing direction. He is raising his voice to compete against the elements.

Suddenly he is roaring, our angry prophet, messianic in his fury. "Oscar Bebbington! I accuse you of robbing banks, ruining the teeth of a generation of children and leaving your wife Sheila in a shallow grave with axe wounds to face and neck!"

He stares at Oscar out of his great bearded fleshy face. The thunder strikes again. Roy refills his mug with wine. We realise that for the moment he is completely mad.

"And how do you plead then Pilgrim Oscar?" From his new standing position Walt stares at him hard. A flash of lightning illuminates his face. "Speak up. We can't hear. Guilty as charged? Good. Officer, hang him by the neck."

Oscar, his position completely demolished, looks horrified at this performance. He opens his mouth to protest but Walt in his craziness is already moving on.

"The rest of you are much worse."

Another flash of lightning illuminates the room brilliantly. The lights flicker dangerously again. He stabs a finger at Wilson.

"People like you bring only death and destruction. I will expose you soon as a great liar."

The thunder crashes again. The wind screams. Walt roars:

"Leave people alone. That is what they want. They don't need you - or the other side, the rich lot. "

He takes a deep draught from his mug of wine and then swaying slightly looks around our battered group. We are horrified by this sudden mad performance we are witnessing. Then he singles out Venezia. He shouts at her:

"And you Madam, learn to watch your bloody tongue. It's getting sharp enough to cut your bloody mouth. And the way you play those two boys off it's shameful."

He is laughing out loud now. Then there is another crack of thunder overhead and a lightning strike suddenly illuminates the frightened face of Jack.

Walt lowers his voice and starts to laugh.

"Diddums da da ... Still hear the echoes of the screams do we Jack ? In the middle of the night. Can't sleep. Tink, tink. Hello there. It's your past calling."

He stares into Jack's face.

"Conscience troubling you old boy?"

He laughs again, a mocking unpleasant laugh.

Roy leans forward and refills his wine mug and he takes a deep draught. The wind and the rain are making the wooden walls creak and sway madly. He swivels around toward Echo. His voice is violent.

"And you! Of course ! How could we forget ! Echo ! Our African Autodidact ! Our ace Restaurant Owner ! Even our African Bampot ! The soubriquets ! The garlands !

Then he stops and looks at Echo contemptuously.

"No, not so fast my friend. I long ago lost count of the number of precious heads you trampled on as you climbed up the brutal ladder to prosperity."

Then he turns away and surveys the rest of us.

"Only two of you any good. This man here." He points to Roy. "Cut above the rest of you. Give him a blank sheet of paper and tell him to write down strengths and weaknesses he gets it right every time."

He turns toward Roy and enunciates slowly.

"Good points: Athleticism, High Intelligence, Great Determination. Bad points: Lust, Avarice and a Great Ability to Deceive."

He stops and sniffs.

"The rest of you blind as day old puppies ... "

His voice tails off as if he has for a moment lost his train of thought. Then he looks around again. The lightning flashes once more. His voice is softer.

"Poor Denis. Only one I've got any time for. Put through the wringer. They tried to crack him, but he's here with us now. Learned his lesson. Only one of you knows his frailties, knows who he is."

The thunder is moving away now rumbling in the distance as it turns around the valley.

"Brings me back to the question you all want answer to." He leans forward. His voice is low and rumbling. "Actually a fly crawling over a piece of shit understands as much as you do."

He wrinkles his nose imagining the disgusting spectacle. Then he leans back and this time we hear him say clearly and precisely :

"In answer to your interrogation I can guarantee you pilgrims that there is more to this world than you can either see or imagine."

There is a pause while we digest this explosive information.

Then we watch as he sways unsteadily on his feet. He clears his throat and Roy hands him his wine mug. Then he is off again but this time in a tuneless sing song mocking voice:

"Time, time, that is the devil. Goes all over and won't keep the hour. Die before you live, live before you die, do it all together, watch it fall apart. All possible, all possible. Living proof, that's me. (He sways unsteadily as he speaks). The whole meal laid out on the restaurant table and all you can see is the bill coming. Pity really. Smoke a cigarette and watch the stub end grow. Roll up, roll up, it's a magical circus and you is the flea. Trying to tell you boys and girls you cut me I bleed. Is there more? Oh boy is there more! (Waves away Roy who is offering more wine). There are golden lights and railway carriages, and magical machines that fly in the air. There are day trips to Mars and excursions to the past and masks made of silver that lie at the bottom of the sea. It is a great adventure! Everything is before you!"

Then suddenly he stops as the thunder returns one more time to crash overhead and rattle the sides of our building. When it's finished he shakes his head as if he's trying to remember something else.

But he's all dried up now. All words gone. A minute later he bows his head solemnly and then turns and makes his way slowly and unsteadily up the stairs. Shortly after that we hear the sound of deep snoring coming from his room.

61

The following day was the worst of our pilgrimage.

A storm such as we had experienced the night before should have cleared the air and left a morning that was fresh and clear, but the opposite was the case.

The clouds were low and grey, a light drizzle fell and the air was humid. There was no wind and flies buzzed around our faces. If we walked with the hoods of our capes up we were hot and uncomfortable but if we walked bareheaded the rain ran down our faces.

Walt had said not a word. He had avoided breakfast. We could see his face was white and his lips were pursed and shut tight.

The mood of the other pilgrims at breakfast had been mutinous. Venezia had slammed a plate with bread and jam down on the table and announced:

"If there is no explanation for last night I am getting out of this whole damn mess at the next stop."

She had looked hard at Echo.

"You can stay if you want, but I know when I have had enough."

She was backed up by Oscar and Jack who said that if things did not improve they would take the train out when we arrived at Sarria.

Even the donkeys shared our perverse mood, protesting loudly as they were loaded up by Jack and Roy.

As we exited Villa Franca del Bierzo and the rain started to come down more heavily Walt indicated silently that we should leave the road and take a path to our right. We soon discovered that this turned into a steep ascent.

We struggled slowly upward until on a particularly steep section, where the rain had reduced the path to a mud slide, poor Blair finally lost his footing and slipped and fell and became lodged on his side in the disgusting mud, the weight of the panniers leaving him well and truly stuck and unable to get up.

For a moment we stood and observed this bizarre spectacle, the rain coming down heavily on top of us. The mood among us was so mutinous that with one wrong word we would have abandoned the expedition there and then and walked back down the side of the hill, leaving donkeys and panniers and all the rest of it behind.

It was Roy, as ever in time of crisis our leader, who drove us on.

"If yous damn Pilgrims dunna get yourselves movin'," he shouted, "I'll kick yous all the way from Greenock to Aberdeen."

His face was red, his trousers were muddy. He was bareheaded and the rain was streaming down his cheeks.

He shouted over to Jack.

"Fer Christ's sake. Donkey man. Dunna just stand there. Pull at the wee bugger's head."

"And you." He stabbed a finger at Denis. " Grab a hold ah the panniers. See if we can push the wee bugger up from this side."

Then he turned to the others.

"Oscar, Echo. Grab hold o' the straps your side. Pull when I shout. Venezia. Get round the arse end and give him a heave from there."

At first we could make no progress. Poor Blair was firmly stuck and beginning to bellow loudly. His stalemate gazed on concernedly, but alas was unable to help.

But finally in that miserable mud and rain, with Roy bellowing loud enough to equal the vocal efforts of poor Blair, the donkey began to work himself loose and finally we were able to restore him to his feet and proceed slowly on to the top. What we saw there enraged us even further.

This was because if we walked ten yards to our left we could look down and see the road below us curving gently round to the village of Trabadelo which was our next destination. Walt had deliberately taken us over the top, through all the mud and the havoc, when we could as easily have gone by the road.

But before we could demand an explanation Walt, with Roy beside him, had started down the other side of the hill leaving Oscar and Jack to lead Thatcher and poor Blair.

Fortunately the path here was in part gravelled so that we were able to retain our footing, but still a descent that should have taken us no more than an hour took in the end twice that.

In the village of Trabadelo where we had hoped to clean up and eat our lunch we were refused entry to the hotel on the grounds of the state of our clothes, and no doubt also due to the villainous look on our faces, and were directed instead to a barn at the rear where there were bales of hay on which we could sit and a tap from which we could drink.

For a long time we did not speak. We just sat exhausted on the bales of hay. Then Denis got up and went into the hotel returning with drinks and plates of sandwiches.

Before we ate we washed our hands and faces under the tap and cleaned the worst of the mud off our boots and our clothes. Then at last we began our meal.

It was left to Echo to turn to Walt and say quietly:

"Walt, my friend, I think we are owed an explanation."

Walt did not speak for a long time but then finally he gave a deep sigh.

"Sometimes the expectation is too much. The pressure is too great. I get hungry and over tired, I am not as young as I was. I have a drink, and well I go off like some sort of a missile. It's unfortunate. A weakness, I lose control. I'm sorry."

He looked around.

"Don't let this ruin our pilgrimage. Please, let's stay together until we reach Santiago. It's important."

Again we did not respond to that, sitting there with our eyes closed until some of us had even drifted off into a light sleep.

It was Venezia who got up first and going over to Walt touched him lightly on the hand. She then went outside coming back a few minutes later to report:

"The sun is out and there is a wind up which is freshening the air."

With that we all emerged from the barn and shook ourselves, as if we had woken from a particularly nasty dream. Jack and Roy busied themselves with the panniers. Roy dipped under Blair's belly to pull the girth tight. (As ever with Thatcher he had to be mindful. If the girth was pulled tight too quickly she had a tendency to kick out).

When we finally set off we had a light breeze on our faces and the sun on our backs and the world which had looked a dark and fearful place in the morning now took on a brighter aspect.

As an explanation for this incident readers should recall passages written by the writer of this narrative before, about the speed which the humours of those walking the camino can change according to levels of fatigue and so on.

When we arrived that evening at the refuge in Ruitelan, which is at the foot of O'Cebrerio, we were pleased to be received by the hospitalero for whom the appellation 'gentleman' can properly be given.

It is rare on the Camino de Santiago for reality to equal rumour. We had heard that in this refuge we would be served quails eggs for supper and that we would sleep on comfortable beds and that in the morning we would be gently woken by a recording of a Mozart violin concerto.

But that, dear readers, is what did happen. Our only regret is that we do not have the name or further information about this hospitalero so that we can record our thanks more fully.

But that evening, after we had finished supper, and before we went to our beds Walt talked to us quietly. Once again we heard that soft and languid American tone that we had learned to love so well.

"A people without roots are a lost people," he told us slowly. "Their families are dispersed, their jobs mean nothing. What I am trying to do, in my own poor way, is to give you back your sense of wonder, your sense of taste, so once again you can savour life."

Then he pointed outside.

"That is your heritage now. A footpath walked by a million people before you and a million people who will come after you."

Then his voice trailed off and we saw the face of a tired old man. For a moment the fight seemed to have gone out of him.

"I can only ask your pardon for last night and this morning and the business with the donkey in the mud. I have made a fool of myself and I feel ashamed. But if you will excuse me I must go to bed now, otherwise I am going to fall asleep at this table."

After that he got up and gently touching Echo and Venezia on the shoulder went along the corridor to his bed.

62

There are pilgrims, generally those who have not walked the great distances, who talk of the ascent of O'Cebreiro as if it were an attempt to climb Everest. The truth is we found it easy enough. Part of the climb up is via an old cobbled path and as ever we were accompanied and encouraged by the wonderful music that Hans Klugman had given us. In particular the mournful and haunting tunes of the Galician folk group Luar na Lubre and their vocalist Paula Rey were an inspiration to us. It was only when we had reached the top, the day was still clear and we could look miles to our West over the gentle hills of Galicia, that we realised how far we had ascended. After that we began our long descent down.

Then we arrived at a certain small village. (To save the locals embarrassment we will not give out its name). Darkness had already fallen and the good Galician rain was pouring heavily down. This meant that once again we were forced to seek shelter in a refuge.

As soon as we entered inside we realised our mistake.

We immediately distinguished the putrid and particular smell coming from the ablutions area. There was also no heating and it was cold and damp. We had found a place that exactly fitted Aimery Picaud's 'Stinking Shithouses' definition.

Three other pilgrims sat in gloomy silence around the kitchen table. They were two women from Australia and a man from Bulgaria. They looked morose and greeted us monosyllabically.

When our donkeys had been accommodated in a barn at the rear we went upstairs and laid out our wet clothes, but with no hope that they would dry. When we came down again the three pilgrims were still sitting silently round the table.

"There is no hot water," the taller of the two Australian women told us. Her face was sour. "The stove doesn't work either and there's a broken window in the room you're sleeping in so you're going to be cold. Don't ask how we are going to eat."

It was Echo who was able to resolve this problem. Noting a card pinned to the wall next to the payphone, with the address and telephone number of a bar ten miles away, he ordered sandwiches and bottles of beer to be brought out.

After we had eaten our simple meal in this gloomy place we began to exchange information and we soon discovered that our Bulgarian pilgrim was also a dentist.

When Denis said he was of the same profession the pair of them were soon chatting happily together, comparing different methods and ways of working, complaining about the behaviour of patients and even discussing levels of remuneration and conditions of work.

As they talked Denis was unaware that he was opening himself up to criticism of those actions which had led to him being sent to prison. This was something he had avoided up until this point.

The attack, from our two ' businessmen pilgrims,' when it came was brutal. There was a pause in the discussion and Jack started in first.

"I have worked all my life, man and boy, for myself and for my father before me, and some people say I keep a good pub. I have always paid my taxes and never taken a penny that was not mine. I can tell you Denis that at the Bastard's Baby we have names for people who take more than they are entitled to, we call them chisellers, cheats, frauds and thieves."

Oscar nodded in agreement.

"Yes Jack you are right. Like you I do not like the way that Denis is trying to capture our hearts and make us sympathetic toward him. You only have to consider what he has done. I worked for my company for thirty years giving good service. I never had a complaint against me and never took any more than I should."

Our sympathies, which might have wavered a little before, now came down firmly on the side of Denis after we heard this hypocritical and dishonest nonsense from Jack and Oscar.

It was Echo, bless him, who led the counter attack. His voice when he stood up to address us (he was our Theatrical Pilgrim) was strong and clear.

"Fellow pilgrims, in the time that I have run my Chinese takeaway, the Emperor of Peking, on Ebrington Street in Plymouth, I have been visited on many occasions by health inspectors and planning officers and officers from the police and officers from the immigration all of whom have sat at my table and drunk my beer and eaten my food and all of whom have told me a singular tale. And the tale is that a businessman exists, sometimes he is reported as being from the Midlands, occasionally from London or the North West, sometimes he is tall and fair haired, at other times he is small and round and dark, but his defining feature is that he is completely honest. He pays his taxes on time, correctly to the penny, never shirks implementing a regulation, European or otherwise, and pays his staff exactly their due desert."

Echo stopped and sniffed.

"Personally I would rather believe in the existence of the unicorn, but there it is, it is the sworn testimony of many men I know to be above reproach."

We all smiled at Echo's little tale and Jack and Echo looked discomforted, which was as he intended.

Then he quickly changed the direction of his argument.

"My fishermen friends down on the Barbican in Plymouth tell me a fish always stinks from the head."

He began to laugh.

"There is one in Plymouth. He is a lad, he really is. He can't be named for fear of a libel action, but he did long service in the Royal Navy, the Queen's Fleet, and now sits deservedly on all the public boards in the County of Devon. Onshore, offshore he has a hand in every pocket, a finger in every till - and so it is said a girl, or is it a boy, in every port. Providing his health holds out, his girth expands by the year, it is reported he will soon receive a great honour from Our Sovereign. And Lord bless us and save us I am sure he will deserve it."

This discourse was greeted with a wry smile by Wilson. He nodded his head in appreciation. However the irony of the tale was lost on the two Australians and their Bulgarian.

63

As we prepared to go to bed we thought this refuge was the gloomiest place we had ever seen. The lights in the dormitory were dim and Echo was forced to place a blanket over the cracked window to stop the wind getting in. The revolting smell from the drains we were forced to inhale every time the door was opened.

Then in the early hours a series of sharp and piercing screams suddenly awakened us.

Echo, who was in the bed by the door, jumped up and snapped on the light. Our first alarmed thought as we looked hurriedly around was that El Lobo had got in among us and was wreaking his havoc.

But then we saw that the cries were originating from Denis. He was in the grip of a terrible nightmare, writhing about on his bed as if he was fitting, his sleeping bag half opened, his covering blanket on the floor.

The first reaction to this event came from Roy and it was typical and unthinking and unkind.

"Shut it, ye daft wee bugger." His voice was rough. Then he unzipped his sleeping bag and sat up, briefly exposing his tartan undergarments so that we could see where the colours had all run together. "Some ah us ah got ta get up in the morning. Yous yelling the house down."

But before he could continue and before the rest of us could add anything Venezia was up and by Denis's bed. Using her hand she shielded his eyes from the light.

"Denis. It's me Venezia." Her voice was soft. "It's alright. You're safe. You're here with us. We're your friends."

Slowly this approach worked and soon Denis's plaintive cries eased, his writhing slowly stopped and his breathing which had been frantic and alarmed began to calm. After a few moments when she was confident he was once again sleeping Venezia indicated to Echo to turn out the light and we returned to our beds.

But it was a long time before any of us went back to sleep. As we lay in our beds we cursed ourselves for not being aware of the depth of the despair to which Denis had sunk and for allowing Oscar and Jack to mount their absurd attack which had obviously been so distressing for him.

Some hours later, when we opened our eyes to see that it was another cold and grey morning, we were still restless and uneasy. It was Roy who reacted first to what had happened.

"The wee bugger's up and gone," he shouted. " Denis has done a runner."

Then Echo went quickly over to Denis's empty bed and felt the blanket and sleeping bag.

"He hasn't gone far. The bed is still warm."

Jack then descended quickly downstairs and putting on his boots went outside into the half light where a mist was still down, checking even the donkeys in the barn, but again there was no sight of him.

After that, the pits of our stomachs full of fear for our poor fellow pilgrim who we now knew had been so cruelly and unjustly abused, we ate a hurried breakfast of bread and jam in the kitchen and drank cold water from the tap while Walt spread a map on the table and explained to Venezia and Echo our route ahead for the day and several rendezvous points where we could meet up.

After that they set off quickly in the hope of catching Denis up, while Wilson was sent back to retrace our path from yesterday in case he had decided to go that way.

The rest of us packed up our belongings and then Jack brought the donkeys around to the front of the refuge and our loading up process began. Jack supervised while Oscar and Walt, pressed into unwilling service, lifted the panniers and Roy pulled the girths tight underneath the bellies of our two donkeys.

Normally we found early mornings in Galicia to be a mysterious delight. In the half light and the mist we would steal through the old stone villages, smelling the turf smoke from early morning fires, feeling like adventurers from centuries past.

But that dismal morning we were not a happy company. We were full of anxiety for our friend Denis.

Whenever we met a villager out early we asked if they had seen a pilgrim passing by on his own but always they shook their heads silently and looked at us strangely hearing the fear and worry in our voices.

Even the music of Hans Klugman which normally accompanied us, buoying up our spirits, deserted us that morning. Everything was grey and quiet and ringing with damp as we walked on through the half light, waiting for the day to fully break.

Meanwhile Venezia and Echo had advanced quickly on, following the path through a wooded area full of strange shapes and shadows.

Suddenly Venezia cried out:

"Oh my God. Echo. Look. Over there."

Echo followed Venezia's gaze and, as she had done, saw swinging from a branch in the wind what appeared to be a body. The pair of them raced forward until they were standing sick and shivering before a branch that had half fallen and was now moving loosely in the wind.

After that they continued on in sober mood emerging an hour later out of the wood to find the day fully broken and opposite them over the other side of the valley, climbing up the bare hillside by the road, a small figure who they immediately identified with the greatest joy as our lost pilgrim.

They raced down the other side of the hill, crossed the valley floor to rejoin the road and went quickly up the other side in pursuit of him. They finally caught him up as he emerged on to the road at the top where a cold wind was whipping sharply across.

Venezia shouted out as they ran up to join him.

"Denis ! Denis !"

Denis slowed and then stopped and turned round puzzled to hear his name being called out.

"Venezia, Echo. What on earth are you doing here ?"

Before any reply could be given Venezia had run up and flung her arms around his neck .

They reported later that Denis's eyes had a puzzled vacant look, as if he had been sleep walking - which in a way he had been, because as he told us later, he had no memory of leaving the refuge.

A hundred yards up the road to the right was a tavern outside which various trucks and cars were parked. The three of them proceeded toward it, walking through the slush, there had been a light snowfall on the pass overnight, relieved to have all found each other again.

Inside, they got Denis out of his damp coat and drew up chairs in front of the fire that was burning in the chimney corner. Echo then went and ordered breakfast for three people which they all ate heartily as they warmed.

By the time they were joined an hour later by the rest of the group, and shortly after that by Wilson who had moved quickly to cover his ground, Denis had closed his eyes and put back his head so that he was resting against the wall.

When he awoke an hour later it was to shake his head with puzzlement.

"I certainly recall the nightmare but I don't know how I ended up here." He looked around at us. "I was in a darkened cinema. We were watching a film, it was in Italian. Then suddenly a man sitting beside me began to push a sharp knife into my side. The pain of it was sickening."

He turned to Venezia.

"That was why I was shouting. I know you helped me back to sleep but I woke up again later. I felt like a leper. I should have been wearing a bell round my neck to warn people. But that was about it, I don't remember much else until I came up from the valley to the road here and heard you shouting after me."

After we had heard this account of what had happened, and Jack and Oscar had muttered that they felt 'partly responsible' following their brutal and unnecessary attack, Walt said:

"We have plenty of time. We can stay here for today and recover our equilibrium."

But Denis rejected this offer replying :

"No Walt give me an hour and I will be fine. I have disrupted everyone enough today I do not want to do it any more."

So after that we sat quietly in silence drinking coffee and gazing into the fire until Venezia went over to Denis and put her arm around him and hugged him and whispered some further words of encouragement into his ear. When he had heard what she had to say he brushed away a tear away from his eye and hugged Venezia back and said he felt much better now.

After that we ordered our lunch. One of the advantages of being pilgrims is that gaps between meal times can easily be contracted so that, if circumstances allow, lunch can immediately follow on from breakfast without comment.

As the food was brought to the table it was left to Venezia to say to Denis:

"I think you have been more affected by your fall from grace and your time in prison than you have told us."

We looked at him. He nodded slowly in agreement. Then he said:

"The people who run those places. Who chooses to work in a place like that?"

He looked at Echo as if expecting he could give him an answer.

"Who chooses it?"

His voice was sharp now.

"Who chooses to govern a prison, set the rules, turn the keys, order the punishments, measure out the tortures?"

But none of us could give him an answer except to reflect that it was probably the same sort of person who became a public hang man or a Lord Chief Justice, someone who liked to poke his nose into other people's business and control things.

But a moment later Echo, to ease the tension of the debate, raised a finger.

"Denis," he said. "I am going to date your recovery from the day you started work for me."

Suddenly Denis's face lightened.

"Oh no Echo. You are not going to ask me to tell me that story."

"I certainly am," Echo replied firmly. " And if you do not tell it, I will tell it for you."

"Yes, come on," said Venezia, joining in with this attempt to lift Denis's mood. "Even if it is going to be a tale of some disgraceful adventure then I am going to be pleased to hear it because it will be a pleasant alternative to all this misery."

"Alright then," said Denis. His face had coloured slightly. He put his fork down.

"I am on my second night working for Echo delivering takeaways and he has given me an order to take out to an address. I arrive on the Vespa and a woman comes to the door. She's in a tight blouse and a short skirt and not a lot else and when I say, looking down at the delivery docket, 'Are you

Elsie then,' she begins to laugh and says you can call me what you like darling."

"OK, OK." Venezia put out a hand to interrupt. "I get the picture now. Boomtitty boomtitty boom. Boys games. I can even finish the goddamn story for you Denis you goddamn idiot."

We were all laughing now.

"Half an hour later you're out, buttoning up your flies, a stupid swagger in your walk. Then you drive off on your bike yelling Geronimo and ever since then you have been hunky dory and on top of the world."

Denis was about to respond to this but then he saw we were all laughing he joined in as well. And so that was how the atmosphere was finally lightened and how shortly after we were able to continue on our way toward the town of Sarria.

64

Several hours later, having passed through the town of Triacastela, we descended toward Sarria. The short day was already beginning to fade as Walt stopped our little caravan and turned to Jack.

"We should find a place to pitch camp now before it is dark. There is a refuge in Sarria but it is so awful I would not put a dog in it."

With that information to mind we sent Denis on ahead to find a site but he reported back with a shake of his head a few minutes later that the first houses of the town were just ahead of us and that there was nowhere he could see where we could put up our tents and light a fire and find water and grazing for our donkeys.

"In that case we will have to proceed into the town," Walt replied with a shake of his head. "But I've never stayed in a hotel there before so we'll have to take our chances."

But luck as it turned out was on our side. This is because as we entered the town, the darkness had now settled and street lights had been switched on and there was a dankness and dampness in the air which made us wrap our jackets tight around us, we came quickly on our right hand side to a modest looking hotel. Walt went inside to make enquiries and came out a few minutes later.

"We are in luck pilgrims. The patron is accommodating and has rooms free and he says also there is a barn and small field one street over at the back of the hotel where we can leave our two donkeys."

So that is how we entered the hotel and took all our kit upstairs to the rooms. Jack then took our beasts round to the rear, reporting back a little while later that while it was not perfect, he had been forced to leave water from a tap in a bucket and the grass in the field was not of the best quality, it would do for the night, especially as we had no other alternative.

So after that we descended down into the dining room. At the bar we ordered beers and made brief acquaintance with a group of locals who were also at the bar discussing the affairs of the town, as locals do.

In the dining room there was only other person eating, an elderly man in a brown suit who gave the impression of being a regular diner and who did not acknowledge our presence.

A few minutes later the waiter who wore thick glasses and was slightly stooped and who had also been serving behind the bar came over to take our orders. He read out our choices, it seemed to us with some difficulty, from a roughly written sheet he held in his hand.

At the same time Roy took the precaution of ordering a couple of bottles of red wine which were brought to the table shortly afterwards.

After that we were a content group as we settled down to wait for our dinner to be brought. We felt we had overcome many obstacles and that whatever else awaited us before we arrived at our destination of the great city of Santiago de Compostela, we were firmly together as never before.

We were attentive to Denis, aware of the wrong we had done him. We also looked at Walt with a new eye. In a way his stature had been increased because as we understood his greatness, we also now understood his frailties, which made him seem to us so human.

It was half an hour later, we were enjoying the pork chops that had been laid before us and were easily making our way through the second bottle of wine, when our waiter approached our table with a certain hesitancy. He then announced to our surprise:

"Senors please. But there is a lady outside waiting."

We put down our eating implements and looked at him. For a terrible moment we thought we might have been tracked down by the actress to whom Echo had so foolishly given his share of the robbery money in Astorga.

The waiter looked down at the paper in his hand.

"She is asking for a Senor Roy."

"Aw no," Roy looked up at the waiter and then turned away sharply. "No way Jimmy. It'll be a fan wantin' an autograph. Tell her I'm eating ma dinner. I never do autographs when I'm eatin' ."

But the poor waiter glanced down nervously again at the piece of paper in his hand.

"The lady says she knows you."

He hesitated for a moment and then glanced at Roy again.

"The lady speaks with the same Scottish accent as you Senor."

Roy's head swivelled back round at this information.

"Eh ? What d'ye say Jimmy ?"

The poor waiter was plainly unhappy with his mission.

"She does not look happy Senor. She has a suitcase with her as well."

It was then to our alarm that we saw the colour drain from Roy's cheeks. The face which was normally so ruddy and red and positive had suddenly turned a ghostly and terrible white.

"Ma God," he muttered softly. "I dunna believe it. It's ma Mary. She's come ta check up on me."

He stared blankly around the room and there followed a terrible silence. Then we watched as he rose from the table. Then he made his way slowly toward the door, his Great Scottish Head bent forward as he went.

How long did we sit there shocked into silence by this astonishing turn of events ?

When we looked back later we realised it could not have been more than a few seconds, although at the time it seemed much longer.

It was Jack, with his publican's nose for things afoot, who first noticed that the drinkers at the bar had all disappeared, as had our hunched over waiter. Even our fellow diner in the brown suit had vacated his table, his coffee undrunk.

"It's a trick !" he shouted out suddenly. His voice was full of alarm. "Quick. Outside. Roy has been ambushed!"

He led us at a run out of the dining room and through the front door of the hotel. There we saw, to our horror, Roy lying on his back in the street with El Lobo on top of him. His arm was raised and a knife blade was flashing as it was readied for its cruel descent onto Roy's exposed chest.

Without hesitation and showing great bravery Oscar launched himself forward and smashed his leg into El Lobo's hand so that the knife was sent spinning out into the deserted street. After that Echo and Jack were on top of El Lobo dragging the shouting and deranged man away.

But then in the confusion of the moment El Lobo slipped through their arms and was back on to his feet and scampering for the safety of a side street. Denis and Wilson gave preliminary chase but Jack called them back.

"No boys. He gave us the slip in Pamplona and there is no doubt he will also know the back streets of Sarria so any chase is a waste of time."

So instead we knelt to tend to Roy who was now sitting up and shaking his head. A quick examination showed only bruising and shock and no broken bones.

A few moments later when we had got Roy to his feet and upstairs to our rooms, where we locked the doors and sat down on the beds, we realised how lucky our escape had been. If Jack had not been alert it could have turned out very badly indeed.

But with the help of a bottle of brandy which we kept secreted away for emergencies we recovered our spirits and soon Roy, propped up on one of the beds, a pillow behind his neck which he said he had ricked as he went down, was chuckling over the incident.

"Dearie me. Oh dear. I'm supposed to ha' seen it all and I'm caught out by an old trick like that. I'm getting past it. It's time ah packed it and retired to ma home and to ma pipe and ma slippers."

He looked around.

"The wee stoat nearly had me. He was goin' for his revenge for what I did to him before. I was only just out o' the door and looking round for ma Mary when he jumped on ma back and rolled me over. Oh dearie me. The old Roy Babadouche would never ha' fallen for a trick like that. Oh no. I'm getting old, that's ma problem."

He shook his head again and continued to chuckle.

A few minutes later Jack and Oscar, accompanied by Echo, went downstairs to confront the waiter to demand an explanation but they found the dining area and the bar locked up and in darkness and returned upstairs to our rooms.

In case of further attack during the night we mounted watches. We then left at first light, recovering our donkeys and forsaking breakfast until we were well clear of that damned town.

65

The last leg of our journey, which we entered on now, was five days and four nights and covered a distance of about eighty miles. Readers of this narrative may query the slow nature of our progress. The argument will be that having walked this far we should be fit as fiddles and in the manner of Roman Legionnaires have the ability to stride out all day. The response to that is we had our rhythm and that, with the exception of Jack, we had suffered few problems with our legs and feet. By contrast other pilgrims who pushed on at a quicker speed encountered severe difficulties, some having to abandon their pilgrimage altogether. We also had to be considerate of our donkeys. They had performed heroic efforts on our behalf and they also had their limits.

When we left Sarria that morning we were still shocked by the events of the previous night. Even though we were quickly out in open country we were still nervous and watchful. We thought now that a new ambush could come from any direction. There was also a feeling among us, such had been the narrowness of our escape, that the sooner we reached Santiago and finished our pilgrimage the better.

"I'm afraid the gilt has gone off the gingerbread for me pilgrims," Jack said as we walked along. I shall be glad to get done now and get on home."

We continued on in this same unhappy mood for another hour. Our sense of equilibrium and well being was only restored by an incident that befell us as we passed through a small hamlet.

Our stomachs empty, we had missed out on our breakfast in Sarria, we had been disappointed to find that this hamlet was too small to boast either bar or shop. However our position was rescued when we noted a small group of villagers standing beside a dark coloured van. This turned out to be a mobile shop.

Waiting our turn we conversed with the villagers. We told them of our journey, recounting how we had started in France and that by our calculation we had now been on the road for forty nine days. They in turn wished us well.

After we had made our purchases, we took fruit and packets of biscuits, the shopkeeper, a small elderly man, leaned across and slipped Denis a one Euro piece. Then he looked him in the eye and said in a low voice:

"Pilgrim, say a prayer for me in Santiago." (Which when we arrived there we did).

This little encounter, along with the daily arrival of the warming sun, snapped us out of our pessimistic mood and made us remember why we were here, that we were pilgrims on pilgrimage.

Also for the first time that morning we were able to gaze around and observe the changes to the paysage that were once again creeping up on us.

The change was gradual but over the next days our camino did slowly become a series of narrow sunken woodland paths.

These paths twist and turn, mysterious and magical, ascending and descending. They are bordered by stone walls, moss covered from age. Sometimes they open onto a glade before plunging back into the trees, many of which are eucalyptus. In autumn these paths squelch under foot. In summer they are dry, shaded and cool.

(Gone, as if they had never existed before, as if they were part of some other life, were the open tracks of the wide Meseta. Our rough descent, weeks before now, down to Jaca in the foothills of the Pyrenees, was only a vague and distant memory).

In the late afternoon of that day we arrived at the Rio Mino and looked over to the strange town of Portomarin on the opposite bank.

Walt explained that the river valley had been dammed and flooded and that the old town had been abandoned and rebuilt on the other bank where we could see it now.

We advanced to the edge of the river and looked down to where we could pick out the outline of the abandoned houses lying under the water.

"In the old days I stayed there many times." Walt looked down and shook his head sadly. "They have rebuilt the town stone by stone at the new site."

But as we made out the traces of the old village under the water we became uneasy. We felt as if were staring at a graveyard or the scene of a disaster.

Soon after that we turned our backs on that mournful site and made our camp for the night in a clearing in the wood behind us.

As we set about erecting our tents and building our fire we noted that Wilson had a distant air about him. Normally he collected his wood for the fire, his communal duty, with a sense of purpose and determination. He was a strong lean man and could drag big branches into camp with ease.

But that night he was distracted. Jack noted that at one point he put down the hatchet he was using for cutting firewood and stared away from the camp for an age. It was as if he were listening to a sound or a voice that the rest of us could not hear.

After dinner, when Venezia and Echo had cleared away the plates and Roy had opened a new bottle of wine and cigarettes had been lit, we all fell silent waiting for Wilson to begin. The night had an uncomfortable dampness about it and despite the warmth from the fire we had all put on our thick coats.

Eventually Wilson gave a sigh and without any sort of a preamble or introduction and in a low voice that was almost a monotone, so that we had to lean forward to hear, all except for Walt, who of course knew what was coming, he began his story:

"The day is blustery, cold, the wind too strong for going up scaffolding. So my uncle, I work for my uncle, it's a family business, gives us the day off. He says there's no point in hanging round here today."

He looked around the fire gauging the reaction to this opening.

"So I come into town, I am going to post an article and some photographs to a climbing magazine."

He stopped and sniffed again. We all felt the damp of that cold evening pressing in around us.

"We're branching out. We've done a climb in the Swiss Alps, we're thinking next year of trying the Himalayas."

We watched his shadow dance over our camp fire. Then he sighed as if he has recited the story a hundred times before and now it bored him.

"When I come round the corner on to Royal Parade I see a crowd has gathered round one of the buildings by the Civic Centre."

"What was it you saw then?" Venezia asked. She was trying to keep the tone of her voice neutral.

"A girl high up on a ledge," Wilson replied. "Long flowing hair, threatening to jump. Police and fire brigade with ladders. A crowd gathered below."

We waited for Wilson to continue but he simply stopped for a long time. Wilson held his 'progressive' views with a stubborn certainty which on occasion infuriated us. But now his tall frame seemed to have shrunk and he was bowed forward. He had gathered his thick coat around him and for a long moment he said nothing. He stared into the fire.

"I'm standing at the edge of the crowd, at the back," he began again finally. "We're all staring up at the ledge. The firemen have put up a ladder but she's shouted down if they do it again she'll jump. So then a policeman turns to the crowd and calls out: 'If there's anyone here who's a climber who could get up underneath the ledge, there might be a chance.' "

"OK. So what stopped you?" Venezia's voice was cold and unfriendly.

Again there was a long silence. We could hear the fire crackling and the donkeys moving at the edge of our camp. Then Wilson turned to Venezia. His eyes behind his glasses, which normally sparkled with certainty, were now dull and unhappy.

"I have asked myself that question a thousand times Venezia. There was a chance I could have rescued her. You could say my nerve went or that I lacked courage. When I explain it to myself I use another formulation. I tell myself that I lacked the confidence. That is what it was. It would have been a difficult climb. She might have seen me. I might have made the situation worse. I didn't want to do that."

"Well did anyone else try?" It was Echo taking up the interrogation. His voice was also harsh and unfriendly.

"There's a man next to me who says he'll give it a go." Wilson moved his position by the fire. "He strips off and gets up over the first block but then he gets stuck and has to come down. He looks sick with fear."

"What happened in the end Wilson?" It was Oscar leaning forward to ask.

"What happened was that she jumped," Wilson replied. His voice was a low monotone. "She gave a scream and jumped right out, tumbled over, skirts flying everywhere landed head first, hell of a crack, not six feet from where I was standing."

We were all watching Wilson anxiously. His face was awful. His voice was low.

"I thought I knew her, I thought I recognised the long hair, but when they turned her over she was a stranger. Never seen her before. They all said later that it was no one's fault. Everyone did what they could, but when a person makes up their mind to jump they jump, it's as simple as that."

There was a terrible silence in our small encampment after Wilson had finished. He had misled us right from the beginning. To us this was more shocking even than Jack's confession. We had understood Jack, he had been straightforward with us. It had also been a long time ago, the circumstances were terrible and we could see that he had suffered. But Wilson had tried to persuade us that he was a hero. Even now, in his admission, he had tried to make an excuse. He had been unable to get out the word 'coward,' which we considered was the term he should have used.

We sat for a long time considering all this. We looked for a comment from Roy but his lips were shut tight and his face was grim. This was a terrible moment on our pilgrimage.

It was left in the end to Walt to offer an explanation for Wilson's behaviour.

"There is not one of you here who has not lied and cheated and dissembled," he told us slowly. "Wilson is right. The girl had decided to jump. There was no way anyone could have climbed up. The handholds were too shallow and the wind was too high. If Wilson is guilty of a crime it is the crime of vanity. And we can all admit our guilt to that."

This plea from Walt softened our mood. Eventually Venezia went over and kneeled by Wilson. She put her arm briefly around him. Then she said quietly:

"Thank you for telling us Wilson."

"I'm sorry I deceived you," was his low voiced reply.

After that she got up and went quickly to her tent. Jack was next to his feet, going over to his donkeys to check that they had sufficient grass for the night. Soon after that we were all in our tents. However it was a long time before any of us fell asleep. In the end after we had considered what Walt had said by way of defense and after we had also gone through in our minds all the strange things that had happened on our pilgrimage, we became calmer. It was only Denis, who had such a clear vision of seeing and hearing Wilson's extraordinary climb being feted on the local television stations in Plymouth, who was left puzzled. But in the end our camp fell silent and we slept.

66

The following day we made the fifteen miles from Portomarin to Palas de Rey. We were now only a couple of days a way from our destination, the great city of Santiago de Compostela.

That was a day, after the conclusion to Wilson's story and as we neared the end of our pilgrimage, that we began to reflect on many of the things that had happened to us.

It is not possible to over emphasise the importance of the music that Hans Klugman gave us. Those musicians, those voices, they all knew the right time to come in and lift our mood and drive us on.

Mamani Keita was for the mornings. Her voice, light as a bird, enticed us forward. When we were at ' full march' we liked to be accompanied by snappy songs such as Happy Days are Here Again and Sing Hosanna. Driss El Maloumi reflected a more serious mood. When we were tired and needed to be driven up the final hill there was always the 'swing' from the Orchestra Baobab. Then the old men of the Buena Vista Social Club would give us a final push. The wonderful haunting tunes of Luar na Lubre, led by their vocalist Paula Rey, are the signature tune of all pilgrims. And of course for romance, for smooch (for Echo and Venezia) there was always dear old Charles Trenet.

But when the ' going got tough' and when we were tired and dispirited and there were still miles to go and the rain was coming down and the path was muddy and the ascent seemed just too steep there was always one person we could rely on. And that, of course, was Sir Roy Babadouche, our Great Scottish Football Manager.

Walt had a lovely term for him. When we were irritated or frustrated by something he had said or done and had gone to Walt to complain, he would shake his head ruefully and respond with, "I know Pilgrim Roy is a bit salty," as if somehow that explained everything.

But if toward the end of the day we were climbing a last rise and Jack's legs were beginning to give, it was always Roy who dropped back to offer a word of encouragement. Then he would advance forward again, giving Thatcher a slap on the rump as he passed, to retake his place at the head of our little column.

Another time he might drop back to help Walt. He would engage him in conversation and then slowly lengthen his stride so drawing him forward until they reached the top of the next rise.

That night we camped out near Palas de Rey and the following day made the eighteen miles on to Arzua.

During the morning we passed through the village of Furelos and were signalled into a small church by the plump parish priest. After we had been given a brief tour of the interior, in truth there was not a lot to see, we were invited to make a donation into a wooden box that had three precise openings cut into it. The first was the exact size of a one Euro piece, the second the exact size of a two Euro piece and the third was for notes. The plump priest then positioned himself behind us to watch as we fumbled for change in our pockets.

As Walt said afterward: "That is a fellow who never misses a trick."

We next arrived in the town of Melide where Walt insisted that for our midday break we sample in a small restaurant the Galician speciality of pulpo or octopus.

The octopus is cooked in a large copper pot before being chopped up and served piping hot on a wooden platter. Our reaction to this dish was mixed. Walt wolfed it down and called loudly for more.

"I have been dreaming of this place ever since we left Leon," he said with a grin as a second platter was placed in front of him.

Oscar, on the other hand, pushed his offering to one side after only a few mouthfuls.

"It is like eating cooked rubber," he said eyeing the plate distastefully.

That afternoon Walt took us on one of the sunken paths through a forest. At one point the trees closed in over us blocking out the light. But when we stopped briefly in a clearing, to re arrange a pannier on Thatcher's back that had begun to slip, we saw coming up behind us two other pilgrims.

They introduced themselves as Tilly and Martin from Utrecht, and both being of a certain age and feeling their feet, they were glad to stop for a moment.

When they had taken a drink from their water bottles and looked around they asked if we had 'heard the news.'

"So what's that then," Jack said looking up from the donkey he was tending. "What's been happening that we have missed?"

(Oh how pilgrims love their gossip! There was also a concern among our little group, it has to be said, that the 'news' might relate to El Lobo and his continuing search for us).

But instead Tilly who had her hair cut short and who we could see, to our amusement, had legs that were more muscled than her husband's, informed us:

"Well, there was a fight between two pilgrims in a bar in Melide last night and actually we witnessed it."

"It was most surprising," said Martin, taking up the story. "There seemed no cause for provocation at all. In fact you may have heard of the man. He is tall, thin, German."

"Oh yes," Oscar answered. We had all gathered around the Dutch couple by this time. "Did he stand like this?" Then he imitated the way Hang Dog Heinz let his head drop forward.

"Certainly," said the Dutch couple, this time in unison. "In that case you know him?"

"Oh we know him well enough," replied Jack with a smile. "He is Hang Dog Heinz from Munich. Was the other man badly hurt?"

"Well Heinz, if that is his name, certainly had the man down on the ground. He had his hands around his neck and was banging his head against the wooden boards," Tilly replied.

"Who was this other pilgrim ?" It was Echo asking. "Do we know him too? What was the fight all about?"

It was Tilly who responded to this question. "People in the bar told us that this pilgrim, he was a Frenchman, had been trying to sell your German friend something."

She turned to her husband.

"What did they say Martin dear?"

"They said that the Frenchman had been showing your friend a selection of tee shirts, but your friend took exception to whatever was written on the front of the shirts."

This brought a shout and a quick reaction from Roy.

"Oh aye that wee bugger. I'm no surprised he's had his heed stoved in. Very shoddy workmanship. He sold me a pair ah tartan combinations but the colours ran when I tried to wash 'em. Couldna' take them home to ma wife in that state. Wee stoat got all he deserved."

Tilly and Martin looked at Roy. Like all Dutch people they prided themselves on speaking good English, but Roy's rich Scottish patois, delivered at such a sharp and arrhythmic pace, had overwhelmed them.

"The police came of course," Tilly continued after a moment, addressing herself to Jack now. "The poor man was taken away in tears. And his poor wife she was also terribly upset. She went away with the police also. I don't know what will happen to them. I am sure the police will not allow them to continue their pilgrimage."

"That does not surprise me at all," said Jack as he tugged on Thatcher's lead and we got ready to move on. "That fellow has been ready to blow for some time."

67

The night before we finally entered the great city of Santiago de Compostela we pitched our tents for the last time near the small village of Rua O Pino and then in the morning we made our way to the home of a farmer just outside Lavacolla.

This was a difficult moment for Jack who was especially attached to our donkeys and who was not happy to let them go.

"It is going to be a wrench chums, I can tell you that," he said sadly. He turned to address himself to Walt.

"I hope you know this family Walt. I do not want to leave them with someone who does not understand donkeys."

"You need not be concerned Jack," Walt replied. Then he placed his arm around Jack's shoulder. "I have passed this way on many occasions in the past."

Our faith in Walt's judgement was confirmed when as we approached the farm we saw that it was in good repair. Jack was also delighted to see there were other donkeys in a field by the side of the house. We watched as he went over and carried out an inspection of the beasts.

"Well that puts me more at my ease," he said as he rejoined us. "They are in good condition and there is plenty of grass and there is a good supply of water. Donkeys are sociable animals so Thatcher and Blair will enjoy the company."

After that we removed our hats and went inside to be greeted by the farmer's wife who was a small jolly women, and by her husband who was tall and thin. But they both had open and honest looking faces. This gave us further confidence that we were leaving Thatcher and Blair in good hands.

Over strong coffee and good cakes we explained to the farmer and his wife the peculiarities of our two donkeys.

"On the whole they are good natured and calm," Jack said. "But Blair has to be watched as he likes to stray from the path if he spots a clump of good green grass. Thatcher is sensible although she will kick out if her girth is tightened too suddenly. Blair should be given the heavier of the two loads as he is the younger of the donkeys."

(Jack did not add the information that Blair might be Thatcher's son, as told to us by the blacksmith outside Burgos, because he still could not believe that it was possible).

However he did look suddenly worried when the farmer informed us that he had been contacted by a Spanish couple with two children who were planning to walk part of the camino, but in the reverse direction toward France. He said that if these two donkeys were as calm and good natured as we had indicated, they would be an ideal pair.

"Well hold on," Jack looked anxiously at the farmer and his wife. "We have walked the best part of six hundred and fifty miles with these two. They will need a rest before they set off again."

The farmer was able to reassure him on that point saying that it was not the intention of the family to set off for several weeks yet.

So then, with all points agreed, we began a brief negotiation for the transfer of our two faithful beasts, plus all their equipment. This was swiftly concluded to everyone's satisfaction.

So after that we told the farmer and his wife of our adventures (excluding details of our involvement with El Lobo and the bank robbery) and they were nodding their heads and laughing until we heard a car draw up outside. Then a moment later we were introduced to the young Spanish couple and their two children who would become the new masters of our two donkeys.

While introductions were being made Walt disappeared into the kitchen to say that we were all invited to eat.

"So clear away those maps and everything else off the table." His face was full of laughter. "We always eat well in this house."

During the course of the meal, which was a happy affair and during which we once again recounted our adventures to the young Spanish couple, the husband eventually turned to Jack.

"So what names have you called these donkeys then? Shall we continue with the same names?"

"Well," Jack replied. "It is a long standing joke though personally I did not hand the names out."

He looked over to Echo and Wilson.

"I am afraid that it is a poor attempt at humour but we have called them Thatcher and Blair."

Our Spanish hosts were initially puzzled by these strange appellations but then slowly the husband began to smile.

"Oh yes. Of course now I understand your reasoning," He looked at Jack. "So I will ask you the obvious question. How do you tell the two of them apart?"

It was at this point that Wilson, who had devised the system, took over from Jack to explain.

"Our system of identification is simple. Behind Thatcher's right ear we have placed a red dot and behind Blair's left ear we have placed a blue dot. In that way we never get confused."

This information was then disclosed and explained to the whole group and a lively discussion then followed, in which we did not take part, before the husband turned to Wilson.

"We have decided. We will certainly continue with the system you have used. We will call the older donkey Aznar and the younger donkey Zapatero and we will use the correct colour markers in the same way that you have done to denote their political affiliations."

After this we all laughed. The new appellations for our two donkeys were then toasted in good Spanish brandy and we prepared to make our departure, confident that we were leaving our two faithful friends in the best possible hands.

After that came the moment to depart. With a tear in his eye Jack went out into the field and put his arm around the pair of them and told them to behave themselves with their new owners. Then we thanked the farmer and his wife for their hospitality and set off, not daring to look back until we had turned the corner so that we could no longer see the farmhouse. Then we continued on our way into the city on foot with our packs on our backs.

68

So much has been written about the glories of the great city of Santiago de Compostela and its Cathedral, not least by Aimery Picaud himself in the Codex Calixtinus, that this narrative will not add greatly to that detail.

However there is an observation that should be made. There are certain cities that are ' hidden gems.' Ones that come to mind and readers of this narrative will no doubt be able to add to the list, are Galway on the West coast of Ireland and Seattle on the West coast of the United States. Cut off from the centre, by geography or climate, they have developed their own specific personalities.

So any visitor arriving in Santiago de Compostela in this remote North West corner of Spain will be struck by the liveliness of this hidden city and its young people. (Although obviously this feeling of 'freshness' is also due in part to the great heat of the Iberian peninsular being regularly cooled by the driving gusts of rain coming in from the Atlantic!)

Pilgrims as they near the end of their journey are always 'hurrying on.' Back packs are now loaded up quickly in the morning and joyous re unions are made with pilgrims last seen weeks ago. Tales are told of adventures befallen and plans are made for the future. Then as the city approaches - 'we are nearly there now lads' - the stride is lengthened.

We were now indistinguishable from the other groups of pilgrims making our way into the city. (In the summer there is a great flood of them. The off season is easier). We were without our two beloved donkeys and Echo had removed his conical rice growers hat. But we still had the music Hans Klugman had given us and this morning it drove us on at a good speed.

We were all looking out for Jack as we knew that he had doted on his two donkeys. However we were pleased to see that he was quickly recovering from this loss.

"I am confident we have left those two donkeys in good hands," he told us as we walked. "They will be well looked after."

"Aye, it's naw worries for yous Jack," Roy encouraged him. "Those Spanish boys'll look after them alright. You've naw worries there."

At this point all pilgrims are heading toward the landmark of Monte do Gozo from where it is possible to see the spires of the cathedral.

An important marker for us had also been the city airport, which we passed by during the morning. As has been recounted we had become keen watchers of the planes as they flew above us. We had speculated as to their path and had contrasted their speed to our snail like progress. That morning as we watched the planes descending into land Denis recalled a moment earlier in our journey.

"I remember passing by the airport in Pau. How long ago that seems now. The planes taking off over our heads. They looked like penguins struggling to fly!"

"And now they are like us," Venezia replied as a jet roared down on its approach. "Touching back to earth again."

After that we hurried on until we did reach Monte do Gozo, where there are certain large statues erected. We shaded our eyes to see the city ahead of us and then it was Denis again who suddenly shouted out.

"I can see them! Look there pilgrims. Ahead of you. The spires of the cathedral!"

Like desperate mariners in the crow's nest we followed Denis's arm, searching the distant city skyline, finally making out the three thin smudges over the red roofs of distant buildings.

We were all impatient to move on now but Venezia insisted that we line up in front of the statues for a last photograph.

"We shall end up sleeping the night here if she does not get a move on," Jack grumbled to Oscar as Venezia organised us.

As ever Walt and Roy were at our centre. The rest of us radiated out either side of them. A young pilgrim from Brazil who was passing was persuaded into shouting 'cheese' as she pressed the button for us.

(If these pictures are ever unearthed and looked at in the future will they show how happy and excited we were that day? Looking carefully an observant viewer should also be able to decode something about who we were. Roy and Echo are both tall and dominant and handsome but at the same time Denis has sneaked in to stand next to Venezia. Jack and Oscar are grinning like two schoolboys and Walt is caught leaning back and with his mouth slightly open as if he is either about to sneeze or share a joke with us).

Then as we passed through the new town, Walt told us:

"I've got a damned good surprise for all of us this evening."

This we took to mean that we would be eating and drinking well to celebrate the end of our journey.

As soon as we set foot in the old city we fell in love with it. We felt a history, a tradition and a continuity in those dark old streets that touched us greatly.

Then finally we descended through the Plaza de la Inmaculada, went through a short passage and then turned to our left into the great and glorious and immense square, the Plaza del Obradoiro.

"Well there you are pilgrims." Walt said proudly as he finally halted us in front of the cathedral. "I always think she looks like a bloody old medieval sky rocket."

There are photographs and images of great buildings, views and paysages that when seen in the flesh disappoint, not having the grandeur previewed. But there are other monuments and spectacles that surpass a thousand times their depiction on canvas or in photo frame or by their description, written or oral.

Walt had given us the example of the Statue of Liberty.

"When immigrants and visitors pass it on the ships going into New York they fall suddenly silent, humbled by what it represents, aware of it's stature and it's significance."

That is how we were that Autumn afternoon. We put down our packs and gazed up at the terrible edifice in front of us, our words temporarily gone from our mouths.

(Some statistics: Using Roy's always reliable comparative measurement system we reckoned the square had the dimensions of about two football pitches. Three of its sides are bounded by rich and historic buildings. On the Western side stands the Palacio de Rajoy which is now the seat of the Junta de Galicia, the regional government. On the Northern side stands the Hostal dos Reis Catolicos which in turn has become a Parador hotel. The Cathedral, which takes up the Eastern side was begun in 1075 and finished in 1122 and is in the Romanesque style. The two towers at the front were added, in a heavy Baroque style, in the sixteenth century).

But the dimensions that floored us were the width and the height of the damn thing.

(Pilgrims actually stand below the cathedral looking up at it. There are some fifty steps up to reach the principle entrance. This alteration of the vertical perspective again increases the impression of height).

To the top of the spires from the ground we estimated at least two hundred and fifty feet and it is also broad across. This sense of width is further exaggerated because the Cathedral is actually part of a complex of religious buildings that stretches for most of the Eastern side of the square.

Of course everything we were seeing and feeling now was deeply coloured by the manner of our journey and our arrival. It was now fifty four days since we had set off and we had covered a distance of some six hundred and fifty miles.

(To test our theory we asked other ' regular' tourists for their impressions. One lady, a silver haired grandma from Kansas City told us the city was, ' a mid level sort of place. Worth an afternoon, no more').

It was Venezia who broke our silence.

"I hadn't expected anything so big." Her voice was low. "It's overwhelming. It's frightening almost, I feel it's alive. I'm waiting to hear a voice. I guess after the stories we have told it's going to tell us we are all for the burning pot."

We all smiled at this but then Echo added: "Venezia you could have used the words dominant and arrogant as well. The masons who built this place were certain they had all the answers. There is no room for doubt here."

We looked at Echo then, remembering his previous harsh criticisms of the church. Would this heavy Baroque spectacle that was in front of us now change his attitude?

When we had gorged ourselves on this view and looked around the square, noting the small groups of other pilgrims also staring up, it was left to Walt to finally declare:

"Enough. Time is moving on pilgrims. We have many things to do. We will enter the Cathedral tomorrow but now we have to find ourselves some decent lodgings. And then tonight we celebrate!"

This celebration turned out to be a lot more than the good meal we had been anticipating.

When we had found lodgings and 'scrubbed up and washed up,' as Walt put it, and attired ourselves in what passed for our best clothes and descended again into the street, we heard the sound of music as well as the footfalls of the citizens as they made their way down to the square.

The first thing that we saw as we entered the square, this time from the southern side, was that a large stage had been erected in front of the Parador.

On the stage musicians were setting up and tuning their instruments. Our senses were then assailed by the brightly coloured lights from the stage and by the anticipatory excited buzz from the crowd that was growing in size around us.

When we turned to our right we saw that the great Cathedral, which had so dominated our vision in the afternoon, had now moved into deep shadow, giving way, for this evening at least, to the entertainment that was being prepared.

As we waited for this entertainment to begin we gratefully accepted the delicious hot pies and glasses of wine that Wilson and Echo had purchased from vendors circulating among the crowd.

The first group to appear on stage was Luar Na Lubre. Their wistful mournful songs evoked so strongly the magical paysage of the Galicia through which we had travelled.

We were also privileged that their vocalist, the charming and talented Paula Rey, who was educated at the University of Santiago de Compostela, had agreed to compere the concert.

It should be remembered also that one of Luar Na Lubre's best known songs Chove en Santiago (trans: It's Raining in Santiago) is from a poem by the poet Lorca whom we had met at the bullfight.

But we were all laughing and joshing that evening. We were 'demob happy.' It was our last night, the end of term, the end of the run. We could finally raise a glass to a successful conclusion of a great adventure.

All that can be said to the reader, by way of explanation for the events that followed, is that was simply the way they happened.

All the old and familiar faces, all the pilgrims we had met, were there. We embraced Hans and Lottie Klugman as they made their way through the crowd to greet us. They were both beaming with happiness.

"My little concert." Hans pointed up at the stage. "Been working on it. Hoping you are going to enjoy. Did my best."

Shortly after that we fell in with Hang Dog Heinz, the Charming Wife and the French Student. Hang Dog was laughing and telling a story about life in Bavaria while the Charming Wife was organising an exchange of addresses so that contacts could be maintained.

Then the French Student took Roy to one side and lowering his voice informed him how disappointed he was that the colours on his tartan combinations had run.

"My dear Roy." He looked at him seriously. "As soon as I return to France I will certainly order a replacement pair for you."

But Roy that evening was at his magnanimous best.

"Away wi' ya Frenchman," he replied fiercely. "Nay bother wi' that. What ah like is a fella wi' baws. It's no many people offer Roy Babadouche tartan knickers and vest and reckon to live another day. Yous my guest in the directors box of ma football club anytime you want."

Everywhere we looked we saw people we had met on our journey. And at the edges of the square (but this may have been our vivid imaginations aided by the wine we were drinking) we were sure we could see the faint images of pilgrims past as they also enjoyed the spectacle.

Luar na Lubre concluded their first set and Paula Rey stepped up to the microphone to announce in her beautiful clear voice that the first of our 'invitados especiales' (trans: special guests) would now sing for us.

When Mamani Keita from Mali came on to the stage we applauded like mad. We all recalled how her delicate bird like voice had risen above us and led us joyfully onward. In front of us now and dressed in a long pink dress she seemed as delicate as porcelain and we delighted in her singing.

After that we were entertained by the solid (but not unjoyful) figure of Driss El Maloumi from the Lebanon. We listened quietly as the rich and deep reflective notes from his oud echoed round the square. He had been a special favourite of Denis as we walked.

Then suddenly with the appearance of the wonderful Orchestra Baobab from Senegal the mood changed and we were all swaying and dancing. We moved with this band of African showmen as they blew into their trumpets and saxophones. As with all the songs that Hans Klugman had given us, their sensual and rhythmic music had driven us forward.

It was when they had finished (the crowd stamped their feet and shouted encore) that once again a smiling Paula Rey approached the microphone.

"A concert in the square is a special occasion." Her voice echoed around us. "And so of course we are happy to welcome singers from far and wide."

(It was at this point that a glance along the line where we stood showed that one of our number had ' gone missing').

Paula was continuing.

"So it is my special pleasure this evening to welcome a certain tenor who has come from afar to entertain us. Ladies and gentlemen, pilgrims and travellers, I give you, all the way from green and wonderful Ireland, Mr Josef Locke!"

He came down the staircase from the back and on to the stage. He had a scarf around his neck and a trilby hat atop his head but of course we knew who he was instantly.

The songs soared above us and even such toughened campaigners as Roy and Echo were forced to rub a tear from their eyes as they listened.

He did three numbers and the crowd cheered him as they had cheered the Orchestra Baobab. Then he was embraced warmly by Paula Rey before ascending back up the steps at the rear of the stage to appear a moment later beside us, grinning ear to ear.

"Always wanted to that!" We all congratulated him. Venezia put her arms around him and kissed him on the cheek. "Should have done it a long time ago. Forget about the other nonsense. Feel bloody marvellous."

It was then, while there was a brief pause in the music, that Lottie Klugman, detaching herself from Hans who was receiving congratulations from people in the crowd for the quality of the entertainment he had put on, took Echo discreetly to one side.

"Echo my dear, I have received a letter from a certain leper colony in the Congo. There is acknowledgement of a mysterious consignment of clothing."

Then she raised herself up on tip toes to whisper into his ear.

"They asked me to say that they were especially pleased with the socks."

And for the second time that evening a small tear formed at the corner of Echo's eye.

We saw many of the 'old hands' from our pilgrimage. During a long conversation with Ivana from Macedonia, Venezia was informed that due to the intervention of Saint James there had been a ' complete reconciliation' with her husband. Though as Venezia noted to Echo later:

"There was no mention of the pocket knife and the sum of money that went missing."

Wilson said he was sure he had glimpsed Robert Lenkiewicz, but only from a distance, and Walt told us that the poet Lorca had been over on the far side of the square but that he had not been able to get through the crowd to talk to him.

We met and talked directly to Dien and Joy, the two Austrian girls, Martin and Tilly and many of the other people we had met - too many to name here.

However our greatest pleasure and our greatest surprise, even Walt knew nothing about it, was when we saw Venezia in conversation with a good looking young couple. None of us could recall who they were. Even Walt was puzzled. It was only after a second that Echo tapped the side of his head with his finger.

"Oh yes." He was laughing as he spoke. "I have the answer to that one."

"Well they just came up to me," Venezia said as she introduced them.

"They are Rachel and Felix. We found their note under the stone outside Castrojeriz. Walt, you told us to replace it in case we altered the course of history."

"Good job you told them to put the note back Mr Whitman," Felix shook Walt firmly by the hand. His broad accent was obviously Australian.

"That's right," said Rachel patting her tummy. "Because now there's a little one on the way."

We were so full of excellent pies and good Spanish red wine and so full of joy at meeting all our old friends once again that it would have been easy to forget that it was just a few days earlier that we had suffered a near fatal attack from El Lobo. He could have been in the crowd in disguise, but during the course of the evening we saw nothing. And when we questioned other pilgrims they also said that the grape vine had gone silent.

But before the music began again after the interval we noted that Venezia was looking around expectantly.

Echo put his arm around her.

"What is it Venezia dear? Someone not accounted for."

"I don't know." She looked up at Echo's face. "It's Oscar. I was sure we would discover his wife Sheila here. That it would be alright. That she would have come out to meet him at the end of our adventure."

Echo sighed at this and the two of them discreetly surveyed the crowd but no middle aged English housewife ever came forward. This led us to conclude sadly that the suspicions that the police had harboured over her disappearance may after all have had some validity.

A few minutes later Venezia, trying to overcome this disappointment, asked Walt if we could expect to see Aimery Picaud.

Walt laughed at this. "What I would give to see that old rascal again! If he's here he'll be scribbling it all down. If anyone can make a story out of all this it will be him."

The second half of the concert, introduced again by the beautiful Paula Rey, found us once more swaying and dancing to the music. The difficulties of our voyage, all our worries and fears were slipping away. The Orchestra Baobab were followed by the grand old men of the Buena Vista Social Club.

Hans Klugman had arranged the concert with great attention to detail. We listened to Sing Hosanna (how we had marched along to that tune) and then we were entertained by Ben Silvin and his Crooners. They gave us Happy Days are Here Again and once more we were on top of the world dancing the Charleston with FDR and the New Dealers. There was even projected on to the back of the stage an image of FDR himself telling us - The Only Thing We Have to Fear Is Fear Itself.

When this choreographed finale had reached its conclusion Paula Rey stepped up to the microphone and following Walt's lead our little group made its way somewhat nervously to the rear of the stage.

Of course the whole thing was monstrous and absurd and over the top - some pilgrims even said we were so full of vanity we were a bubble waiting to burst - but what the hell, an event like this only happens once in a life time so you take it, enjoy it and if others are jealous and say petty things, well what can you do?

This was how the Santiago correspondent of La Voz de Galicia described it in his account the following morning.

(The opening line shows he was of a 'certain age').

'The events last evening in the square in Santiago were reminiscent of an old time Busby Berkeley musical.

'Indeed the good old square has not seen an event like this for many a year.

'Miss Paula Rey, the vocalist with Luar na Lubre, introduced the concert which was arranged by Mr Hans Klugman, the well known composer and arranger from Bremen in Germany.

'Among the artistes who appeared in front of the packed crowd made up of pilgrims and visitors to our town, as well of course as the citizens of Santiago itself, were the celebrated singer from Mali in Africa, Miss Mamani Keita. She was followed by Mr Driss El Maloumi from the Lebanon.

'However the show was stolen by the Orchestra Baobab who with their rhythmic combination of African and Cuban music had the crowd up and dancing.

'It was even reported, though your correspondent has not been able to confirm this rumour, that the Archbishop himself was in attendance.

'One eyewitness told me: "When the Archbishop danced he raised his legs so high he tore his clerical hem."

'But the highlight of the evening was when a certain group of pilgrims were introduced to the audience.'

At the back of the stage we could hear Paula outlining our adventures to the crowd. Then we heard our names being called out.

Jack, Wilson and Oscar descended the staircase first and bowed low to the audience who whistled and shouted and stamped their feet and clapped heartily.

They were then followed by Denis, Venezia and Echo and the clapping and shouting and whistling went up a good few decibels. Garlands of colourful flowers were thrown up at the stage.

Then Paula Rey was asking for a big hand for a "certain American poet who goes by the name of Walt Whitman" and Walt, the old showman, came dancing down the staircase before removing his hat and giving a low and elaborate bow.

Then a few moments later when we had all slipped back into the audience again there was a burst of excited music from the orchestra pit, and Paula announced in her strong clear voice:

"And now Ladies and Gentleman I give you the stars of our show this evening! All the way from Dundee, Scotland! An inspiration to us all! That wonderful couple! Sir Roy and Lady Mary Babadouche!"

If there had been a roof over the great square surely it would have been raised by the roar of the crowd that evening.

In turn we gasped at the transformation that lay before our eyes. Roy was resplendent in white tie and tails and on his arm was the beautifully bejewelled Mary. To our eyes she looked properly regal in her own right. This magnificent couple paused at the top of the stairway to wave at us all before they slowly descended to a crescendo of music and a further great roar from the crowd. Paula Rey greeted and embraced them. This was no time for making speeches, though we knew that Roy could make as good a speech as anyone.

A pathway was soon made and they were able to descend from the stage. As they did so we could see that Charles Trenet had appeared on the stage behind them. As the first notes from La Mer, that seductively romantic ballad reached us, Roy led Mary off in an impeccable foxtrot. As the sound of Trenet's melodic voice drifted over the crowd, the two dancers moved marvellously in front of us.

It was only with the approach of the dawn that the music finally slowed and stopped. Luar Na Lubre played a last haunting tune over the square. Then the images of the pilgrims of old faded into the morning light, an army of street sweepers descended to clear away the debris and in the side streets we smelt the delicious aromas of hot coffee and churros.

69

When we opened our eyes it was to see that the sun was shining in through the windows of our rooms and that the morning was well advanced. It is only in exceptional circumstances, such as these, that pilgrims oversleep.

In the shower we let the hot water run on our faces to get rid of the thickness of our heads from the night before. Then we all selected the best clothes we had from our small supply.

"It is the Cathedral lads," Walt shouted out. "We have to look our best."

Oscar wore around his neck, in the form of a cravat, the red spotted handkerchief that the Frenchman had sold him. Venezia had on her long turquoise skirt and Echo had been persuaded to abandon his red tee shirt and his conical rice grower's hat for a more modest outfit. Then we all slicked our hair into place and made our way down into the street. There Walt steered us into a small café where we ordered breakfast.

As we ate Walt read us this description, written by Aimery Picaud, all those centuries ago, of the inside of the Cathedral:

In this church, in truth, one cannot find a single crack or defect: it is admirably built, large, spacious, illuminous, of becoming dimensions, well proportioned in width, length and height, of incredibly marvellous worksmanship and even built on two levels as a royal palace.

He who walks through the aisles of the triforium (trans: upper gallery), if he ascended in a sad mood having seen the superior beauty of this temple, will leave happy and contented.'

When we had heard this we were put in the mood to hear Walt give us a last short excerpt from his work Leaves of Grass. He read with great tenderness.

The spotted hawk swoops by and accuses me, he complains of my gab and my loitering.
I too am not a bit tamed, I too am untranslatable,
I sound my barbaric yawp over the roofs of the world.
The last scud of the day holds back for me,
It flings my likeness after the rest and true as any on the shadow'd wilds,
It coaxes me to the vapor and the dusk.
I depart as air, I shake my white locks at the runaway sun,
I effuse my flesh in eddies, and drift it in lacy jags.
I bequeath myself to the dirt to grow from the grass I love,
If you want me again look for me under your boot-soles.
You will hardly know who I am or what I mean,
But I shall be good health to you nevertheless,
And filter and fibre for your blood.
Failing to fetch me at first keep encouraged,
Missing me one place search another,
I stop somewhere waiting for you.

When Walt had concluded his poem we ate the rest of our breakfast in contemplative silence. All of us realised that the words he had given us were his adieu.

Then, our mood rather sombre, we descended once again into the square, the scene of the strange events of the night before. We noted that the giant stage had been dismantled and that everything was now cleared away and returned to normal. After a brief look round we climbed the steps up to the Cathedral.

(There is a ritual to entering the city of Santiago which all pilgrims follow. In the evening they go to Pilgrims Office on Rúa do Vilar where they present the credencial they have had stamped at each point along the route. The pilgrimage is then registered and a certificate issued. The following day at midday is the Pilgrims Mass, at which the numbers and nationalities of pilgrims who arrived the day before is read out. This was the Mass to which we were now going).

The entrance to the Cathedral is through the Portico da Gloria. In front of the pilgrims as they enter is the marble column known as the Tree of Jesse. Here as tradition dictated we placed the fingers of our right hand into an indentation in the column and said a prayer of thanksgiving for our safe arrival.

In the same way that the size and grandeur of the square had surprised us the previous afternoon, we were now confounded by the compactness of the interior of the Cathedral. We sensed a strength and solidity, a muscularity almost, that reassured us.

(This sense of compactness is certainly an illusion. Aimery Picaud himself records the length as being fifty three times a man's stature in length and thirty nine times in width. Modern dimensions are given as three hundred and twenty feet in length and seventy feet in height).

Walt led us down the aisle and we noted how cool the interior of the cathedral felt. Then we descended down the steps behind the altar coming at last to the crypt where lies the silver box that is said to hold the bones of Saint James. The reader will by this time be aware of all our thoughts as we studied this box.

Then we made our way back into the body of the church, now filling up with other pilgrims (how weather beaten and healthy and happy they looked) and took our places in one of the long pews.

Venezia was at the centre of our party with Echo on one side and Denis on the other. The rest of us fanned out from there, with Walt taking up the near end of our pew and Roy the far end.

This Pilgrims Mass is an important and emotional moment and a lot of pilgrims say they will remember it for the rest of their lives.

If a voice could be a colour the voice of the religieuse who sang during the Mass would be a rich ruby red. The notes echoed all around us. Then when it was our turn to sing, pilgrims, visitors, citizens of Santiago, we all filled the old building with our sound. The moment when the Archbishop read out the nationalities of those who had arrived and registered their pilgrimage the night before also moved us.

There was also a fitting conclusion to our story.

We had entered the Cathedral through the main West door, the Portico da Gloria. But there are two other doors, to the North and to the South. We first knew there was something wrong when we saw the Archbishop glance quickly to his left, toward the Southern door.

Then immediately after that we heard a shout - and then a figure, all dressed in white, was rushing up to the altar. He pushed the poor Archbishop sharply to one side, so that he stumbled and almost fell, and then he was standing in front of us all.

Of course we recognised him straightaway as El Lobo. His hair was long and straggly, his beard had lengthened and his teeth were ugly and protruding.

In truth it all happened very quickly, a matter of seconds probably, but as is the way with these things, because of its unexpectedness and its intensity, time seemed to stretch out.

We all watched as El Lobo opened out his arms wide. We could see that in his right hand he had a sort of bag or a sack. Then he yelled out in a coarse rough voice:

"Quiero que me devuelvan mi dinero!" (trans: I want my money back).

It was at that moment that in rushed four burly policemen and El Lobo was wrestled to the ground and taken out. And that was the last we saw of him - but it is safe to assume that his immediate future will include a long and well deserved spell in jail.

After El Lobo had been removed the Archbishop, having dusted himself down, continued rather hesitantly with his service. We sang, we said our prayers and those of us who believed went up and took communion.

And then it was all over and people were standing up and there was a buzz of conversation as we all discussed the incident we had just witnessed.

Then as we filed slowly out, we noted, as we thought might happen, that we were two short. Sometime during the service, Walt Whitman and Roy Babadouche, our two guides, our two stalwarts, their job done, had taken their leave.

After that we walked out of the cathedral onto the steps that looked down over the square to see that a few light drops of rain had begun to fall. Then we descended slowly into the square wondering what the future held for us all.

- THE END -

EPILOGUE

Walt Whitman (1819 -1892)

Leaves of Grass, First Edition. Song of Myself. Verse 46.

*I know I have the best of time and space, and was never
measured and never will be measured.*

*I tramp a perpetual journey, (come listen all!)
My signs are a rain-proof coat, good shoes, and a staff cut
from the woods,*

*No friend of mine takes his ease in my chair,
I have no chair, no church, no philosophy,
I lead no man to a dinner-table, library, exchange,
But each man and each woman of you I lead upon a knoll,
My left hand hooking you round the waist,
My right hand pointing to landscapes of continents and the
public road.*

*Not I, not any one else can travel that road for you,
You must travel it for yourself.
It is not far, it is within reach,
Perhaps you have been on it since you were born and
did not know,
Perhaps it is everywhere on water and on land.*

*Shoulder your duds dear son, and I will mine, and let us
hasten forth,
Wonderful cities and free nations we shall fetch as we go.
If you tire, give me both burdens, and rest the chuff
of your hand on my hip,
And in due time you shall repay the same service to me,
For after we start we never lie by again.*

*This day before dawn I ascended a hill and look'd at
the crowded heaven,
And I said to my spirit
When we become the enfolders of those orbs, and the
pleasure and knowledge of every thing in them, shall we be
fill'd and satisfied then?
And my spirit said No, we but level that lift to pass and
continue beyond.
You are also asking me questions and I hear you,*

I answer that I cannot answer, you must find out for yourself.
Sit a while dear son,
Here are biscuits to eat and here is milk to drink,
But as soon as you sleep and renew yourself in sweet clothes,
I kiss you with a good-by kiss and open the gate for your egress hence.
Long enough have you dream'd contemptible dreams,
Now I wash the gum from your eyes,
You must habit yourself to the dazzle of the light and of every moment of your life.
Long have you timidly waded holding a plank by the shore,
Now I will you to be a bold swimmer,
To jump off in the midst of the sea, rise again, nod to me, shout, and laughingly dash with your hair.